QUEEN OF CHAOS

AMELIA HUTCHINS

Queen of Chaos

Legacy of the Nine Realms

Book Five

Wallstreet Journal Bestselling Author, Amelia Hutchins

Copyright ©October2023 Amelia Hutchins

ISBN: 978-1-952712-17-3

Authored By: Amelia Hutchins

Cover Art Design: Eerily Book Designs

Copy edited by: AW Editing

Edited by: AW Editing

Published by: Amelia Hutchins

Published in (United States of America)
10 9 8 7 6 5 4 3 2 1

A huge thank you to the girls who helped get this book out. Truly helping until the very last minute. Lauren, Erica, Kelly, Michelle, and Mandy, my muffins. Thank you for helping me get this finished and ensuring the right ending of this one was perfect.

For Miranda, the daughter I raised, even though you weren't mine. I'm so sorry that life was painfully hard at the end. I wish I could have saved you. You deserved a happy ending and were so brave at the end. Don't worry about the boy, he's safe with me. I love you more than I ever expected to, and know you're up there holding the light for us.

This one is for those who never back down. The unicorns still standing tall in a world breaking you down. To the ones wishing they were braver, you're braver than you know. To those we've lost this year, and those we'll lose.

Erin, I'm so sorry you lost your ever more, but he'll always be with you. Even if only in your heart. Tyber was lucky to have such a beautiful soul to look down on from his lofty perch. Heaven only takes the good ones early.

BOOKS BY AMELIA HUTCHINS ALONG WITH READING ORDER FOR SERIES

LEGACY OF THE NINE REALMS

Flames of Chaos

Ashes of Chaos

Ruins of Chaos

Crown of Chaos

Queen of Chaos

King of Chaos

Reign of Chaos

THE FAE CHRONICLES

Fighting Destiny

Taunting Destiny

Escaping Destiny

Seducing Destiny

Unraveling Destiny

Embracing Destiny

Crowning Destiny

Finished Series

THE ELITE GUARDS

A Demon's Dark Embrace

Claiming the Dragon King

The Winter Court

A Demon's Plaything

A Touch of Fae coming soon

Wickedly Fae coming soon

A GUARDIAN'S DIARY

Darkest Before Dawn

Death before Dawn

Midnight Rising -TBA

MONSTERS SERIES

Playing with Monsters

Sleeping with Monsters

Becoming his Monster

Revealing the Monster

Finished Series

WICKED KNIGHTS

Oh, Holy Knight

If She's Wicked

If He's Wicked TBA

MIDNIGHT COVEN BOOKS

Forever Immortal

Immortal Hexes

Midnight Coven

Finished Series

BULLETPROOF DAMSEL SERIES

Bulletproof Damsel

Coming Soon

Silverproof Damsel

Fireproof Damsel

Alpha's Claim Standalone

Within the Darkness

Moon-Kissed

Night-Kissed TBA

THE DARKEST FAE: KING OF THE SHADOW FAE

Coming Soon

King of the Night Fae

Queen of the Stars

RED FLAGS

The Devil of London

Fate Series

Whispers of Fate (Intro to Kahleena's book)

If you're following the Fae Chronicles, Elite Guards, and Monsters series, the reading order is as follows.

Fighting Destiny

Taunting Destiny

Escaping Destiny

Seducing Destiny

A Demon's Dark Embrace

Playing with Monsters

Unraveling Destiny

Sleeping with Monsters

Claiming the Dragon King

Oh, Holy Knight

Becoming his Monster

A Demon's Plaything

The Winter Court

If She's Wicked

Embracing Destiny

Crowning Destiny

Revealing the Monster

Whispers of Fate

WARNING!

This book is **dark**. It's **sexy**, **hot**, and **intense**. The author is human, as you are. Is the book perfect? It's as perfect as I could make it. Are there mistakes? Probably, then again, even **New York Times top published books** have minimal mistakes because, like me, they have **human editors.** There are words in this book that are not in the standard dictionary because they were created to set the stage for a paranormal-urban fantasy world. Words in this novel are common in paranormal books and give better descriptions to the action in the story than other words found in standard dictionaries. They are intentional and not mistakes.

About the hero: chances are you may not fall instantly in love with him, that's because **I don't write men you instantly love;** you grow to love them. I don't believe in **instant love.** I write flawed, raw, caveman-like **assholes** that eventually let you see their redeeming qualities. They are aggressive assholes, one step above a caveman when we meet them. You may not even like him by the time you finish this book, but I promise you will love him by the end of this series.

About the heroine: There is a chance you might think she's a bit naïve or weak, but then again, who starts out as a badass? Badass women are a product of growth, and I am going to put her through **hell,** and you get to watch **her** come up **swinging** every time I knock her on her ass. That's just how I do things. How she reacts to the set of circumstances she is put through may not be how you as the reader, or I, as the author would react to that same situation. Everyone reacts differently to circumstances and how she responds to her challenges, is how I see her as a character and as a person.

I don't write love stories: I write fast-paced, knock you on your ass, *make you sit on the edge of your seat wondering what is going to happen next* in the books. If you're looking for cookie-cutter romance, this isn't for you. If you can't handle the ride, *unbuckle your seatbelt and get out of the roller-coaster car now*. **If not, you've been warned.** If nothing outlined above bothers you, carry on and enjoy the ride!

FYI, this is not a romance novel. They're going to **kick** the shit out of each other, and **if** they end up together, well, that's **their** choice. If you are going into this blind, and you complain about abuse between two creatures that are NOT human, well, that's on you. I have done my job and given warning. No babies that occur or are created because of this work of fiction are the author's responsibility. Blame the penis mojo that you rode like a bronco for it, not me.

The Nine Realms

Drach

Dragonaries Ocean

Siren Cove

Nymphs

CHAPTER 1
ARIA

Once upon a time, I'd desired nothing more than to walk within the Nine Realms. To stand on the imposing cliffs that had acted as sentries for the far-reaching Dragonaries Ocean. An ocean which epitomized the color of Knox's eyes, perfectly. I wanted to climb a giant tree in the Carnivora Forest before exploring the remaining Kingdom of Fire. I'd been in love with the history of the realms, seeking the knowledge they held. It had been an addiction to learn everything about the deadly, unforgiving, merciless lands that had once called to me inside the Tenth Realm.

The girl who'd once gobbled up every morsel of information on the Nine Realms, had died. The sweet, naïve, gullible girl had succumbed to the betrayal of those she had idiotically followed, those who had beaten and broken her down. That Aria hadn't known she was born to die. She hadn't known the woman she'd doted on, the woman who she'd believed saved her from the monsters, was actually her mother. Nor had she known that those she'd called sisters, who weren't even her sisters after all.

I no longer trusted people blindly. Instead, I looked for the motives behind why they'd want me close at hand. My loyalty was no longer freely given. It had to be earned because, since I'd come to the Nine Realms, those I'd once considered my closest allies had put me through hell. They couldn't seem to comprehend that I didn't crave power as they did, nor did I covet crowns. I'd watched and read enough *Game of Thrones* to understand I wasn't up for that role. The poor child who'd been tossed from a window had become the king, and the guy who pushed him had betrayed the badass with dragons. Moral of the story? Nothing but calamity came with being a ruler. Hard pass.

Knox had changed, too. He no longer hunted me—for the most part. Nevertheless, he had allowed me to escape from Aurora, who'd entered the chamber to come here, to the Kingdom of Fire. A place that shouldn't exist. I'd wager that the library had learned what happened by forging another realm, when Griffon had constructed this one.

The Kingdom of Fire was vibrant with life flourishing inside the township. The reality was a replica of my dream. I didn't know what I'd expected, but it hadn't been this. As the crowd's excitement grew, I turned my attention to the spectators, who were watching me closely. The path was crowded with people in vibrant attire as we walked toward the palace. I smelled freshly baked goods mixed with earthy scents from nearby shops. Griffon chuckled at a small boy who followed us through town.

The sound of wailing forced my eyes toward the cliffs, where smaller dragons were flying over the edge. My head tilted to follow the smallest dragon's flight down the face of the sheer cliff, until he vanished. Parting my lips in amazement, I watched the waterfalls sloshing over the edges of the high cliffs that surrounded the palace. Several waterfalls lined the edge of the towering cliff before shooting over it. The water dropped hundreds of feet to the river it created below, causing a mist to form at the base, before joining the flow that surrounded the village and palace. It also passed through them. Inside the canal through the village, ferries loaded full of denizens passed beneath the small bridge as we walked across.

Wooden bridges crisscrossed along the edge of town, but they all led to various entrances of the palace. That structure was a sight to behold, and when my gaze eventually tracked to the glowing archway in front of me, my breath faltered. Stones glowing with a welcoming pulse beckoned me closer, drowning out the chatter of those we walked by as the hum grew louder.

Lofty, wide perches hung over the edge of the cliff, as if created for the dragons and phoenixes to observe the township and palace below them. Behind a curtain of water created by a soothing waterfall, light flickered from torches. Beyond the torches, an intricate web of pathways leading to various entrances were visible. Lights flickered from the openings throughout the extensive network of passageways within. At least that's what I assumed the light came from behind the sheet of the translucent screen of water.

I'd never expected to see the Kingdom of Fire. Logically, I knew this wasn't the original kingdom. The recreated Kingdom of Fire brought to life one question: had Hecate truly decimated it and she falsely manufactured the stories. Using it as a warning to others who might rise up against her? What it had once been was now lost in history books written by the victor, which of course were never correct. Of course, it had been by design, not that I'd known it then.

"My mother, Scylla, named it the Palace of Fire for the shimmering rainbow prisms that are cast around the valley when the sun hit the towers," Griffon stated, which meant I'd been staring at the palace long enough to draw his attention. "My mother's people built it soon after the land hardened enough to build on it. The outside walls of the courtyard are translucent quartz, and buried beneath them is selenite to charge their power throughout the monthly cycle until the full moon can charge them again."

"It is so cool," I whispered with nervousness, crawling up my chest to strangle my words. The castle itself was unreal, but outside of those crystal gates that Griffon spoke of were lofty, malicious-looking wrought-iron gates with spikes dissuading anyone from seeking to climb over them.

"Cool?" he parroted.

"It means it's magnificent," Eva supplied. The girl's side-eye was strong when it slid toward me.

"I fear I'm not adept in the colloquialisms of your land, Aria." My lips jerked up at his admission of not knowing something. I wasn't sure what I'd expected him to be like, since I hadn't allowed myself to think much about him. Sure, I held hope of him being a good guy, and that he'd accept me as I was, but hope was often a worthless emotion within the realms. "I'm sure you know that what I showed you in the dreamscape I brought you to, was real."

"I figured it was at least similar," I admitted. "The thing I don't quite understand about that is *how* you could construct a dreamscape? They taught me that crafting a dreamscape, or entering one, was something achievable only by witches."

"Druidry, mana, witchcraft, and siphoning are various types of magic existing throughout the Nine Realms. Of those, druids, mana users, and witches are the ones who can construct a dreamscape. Hecate merely altered the history to make others think only witchcraft remained inside of the realms. I constructed what I did by using mana. Mana comes from the land and nature. It is weaker than what Hecate uses, as it can only be comparable to white magic. But what I showed you, that was my home before Hecate invaded, leaving a once beautiful, fiery realm nothing more than a cemetery."

"I wish I could've seen it before she'd left it in ruins," I muttered, shame heating my cheeks. The very fact that I had her blood in my veins used to be something I was proud of, but not anymore.

"If I could make your wish a reality, I'd do so. Our kingdom's the oldest of all the realms." The wonderment in his tone forced a twist of jealousy. I'd have given anything to see it in all its fiery beauty.

"I want to understand how you crafted a dreamscape. They taught me that only witches wielded enough power to create one and bring another's slumbering mind and awareness into it."

"Magic doesn't solely belong to witches, daughter. You know that already. But then, you are living proof of that, aren't you? Hecate uses reserves of power, but you use the magic fed to you by the realms."

I contemplated his words, nodding slowly. What he said made sense. Even if I didn't know precisely how I was connected to the Nine Realms or why it gave me its power, I knew it did.

"Why is it the realm fuels the magic or mana inside of me?" I asked, to see if he'd give me the answer without seeking shackles to hold me here. Turbulent, blue eyes clashed with mine before his lip twitched. A vice clenched around my heart as my hope of Griffon wanting me for me, diminished. I'd always wanted to know how I'd been able to yank magic to me from the realms. I hadn't cast like the other girls.

"Mana, daughter. The land chooses those worthy of wielding its mana. As it has chosen to give you an endless supply to wield against your enemies. Those shields you raise? They're something only a few witches can actually craft, but something you do effortlessly. You also use alchemy, sorcery, enchantments and incantations, along with witchcraft. A balance of power is inside every universe, and it is that balance that strictly forbids the ability of one entity from wielding both mana and witchcraft. No one else has ever held the ability to house two sources of magic." A frown tugged at my lips and pinched the skin between my eyes until it creased. "At least, until you were born. Eva disclosed that she felt you wielding both a few times." His explanation cleared the confusion.

"And if I were to tell you that, I've witnessed the use of a magic-wielder also channeling mana?" Because Knox had siphoned mine. He'd carried it out without effort, which had been terrifying the first few times he'd done so.

"First, I'd say it's a new world, with new creatures appearing." Griffin hesitated, then exhaled slowly before asking the next question he'd struggled with. "Aden tells me you've mated your dragon king?" Unhappiness seeped into Griffon's tone. When I failed to respond one way or the other, he continued. "Second, I'd tell you that mates sometimes are able to access the mana stored in the well existing in their significant other, but mostly through the connection shared. Though, none had ever held their own magic before they'd accomplished such a feat."

"You're saying that since I mated Knox, the land now sees him as a part of me?"

Griffon's eyes sparkled with pride at my deduction. "Indeed. Tirsynth, my father, was not blessed with magic, but he was able to draw mana, which was stored inside his mate. It's likely why King Karnavious forced you to the altar, ensuring it trapped you in marriage." My lips parted to argue his statement, but he held up his palms in mock surrender. "Those were his objectives, Aria. Regardless of how they may have changed, King Karnavious bound you to his side for the power you house."

I couldn't argue it, not when what Griffon had stated was fact. Facts didn't care about feelings, and if I were going to keep an open mind about his role in my life, I needed to leave my feelings out of it for now.

"How is it he allowed the council that he, himself, had elected to annul your marriage vows?" He was fishing for information, but why? I made them promise that we would not be coerced into anything without our consent. Knox had warned me of how naïve it sounded, but I'd be damned if anyone forced me to do anything.

"If you want to know something, Griffon, ask the question. My time is entirely too short to spend it skirting around what you'd like to know about me." The truth was harsh but undeniable. I didn't have time to waste on dancing around indirectly asked questions.

"Eva and Aden both warned me of your bluntness. I must admit, it's rather refreshing. Not only do you look like my mother, but you also have her curt response to bullshit." I hadn't expected his reply, which left me wondering what she had looked like and what her true nature was. "Do you love your dragon?"

'Unequivocally' was what my response should've been. It wasn't a straightforward answer, though. Knox and I had made strides in our relationship, but I didn't know if he loved me. Love wasn't something he'd readily relinquish of himself, not after what he'd been through, but maybe he'd get there one day. As for me, that information was exactly none of Griffon's business.

"Love can be fleeting and often gets destroyed or becomes a casualty during war. Considering we're preparing to engage in a war, Griffon, I didn't demand a vow of undying love from him. If what you really wish to know is if I'd consider mating another, the answer is no. I don't want, nor do I need another mate. Love is also an emotion, which is conflicting and draining most days." The crooked smile that sliced across his lips told me he knew I was full of shit. "Why would it matter?"

"Because one day you will be a queen, Aria. You need no throne nor crown to be one. The moment you drew air into your lungs and the land fed you its power, was the moment it chose you to lead its revolution as one. The land chose my mother, Scylla Prometheus, to rule the Nine Realms. Like she once did, you'll control the power of the land."

"What if I'm already a queen?" I asked, wondering if he'd allow me to hold the title still. Obviously, I could take it, but that would be another battle, which I didn't want.

"Of Norvalla?" His eyes slid to mine, even as we continued forward. An uneasy tension clung heavily in the surrounding air, as if it were loaded with upheaval at my words.

"Maybe, I've not decided if I intend to fully forgive him yet, or not. It depends on why he'd want the marriage. If it were merely for political gain, or to otherwise use me, then I wouldn't. Knox needs to ask me, and he'd have to want me and nothing else."

"King Karnavious forced you to wed him, he knew what you'd become. He'd seen you using your magic against a keep, which foretold just how powerful you'd eventually become. He may not have known you held the same power as my mother held, but he had to have suspected it was close to what she wielded. Did he not? Maybe not in its entirety, but he had to have known whose blood ran through your veins. He married you, then allowed his private council, hand-selected by none other than himself, to be guided by your mother. A woman who had no right to you, or the throne she seeks to implant her tiresome ass into."

"Knox wasn't aware of how powerful I was, or would become when he married me. Sure, he knew I was the most powerful of the sisters, which he'd chased back into the realms. Beyond that, Knox was as surprised as I was over the true symbol on my forehead. It is true that he assumed I'd be the likely one to ascend the Hecate throne, but that was squashed when she returned and reclaimed it. He didn't leave me then, even knowing I'd bring him no potential gain. Instead, I left him so he could think about his reasoning for ... *certain* things."

Once again, Griffon hadn't been incorrect, though maybe a little misguided. Anyone could see that I possessed the bloodline of Prometheus—or, at least some of it in my genes. The silver hair mixed with the large, cat-shaped turquoise eyes and lighter complexion was hard to ignore. Sure, I'd seen others with similar coloring outside of the hidden Kingdom of Fire, but very few. Not enough that the striking complexion hadn't drawn my attention.

"You're positive he didn't already know?" he asked, which made the line in my forehead crease. "My daughter left a king so that he could think about his behavior toward her?" His head tipped back as laughter burst from his lips. "Aria, you're a breath of fresh air. I'm pleased you came to meet me and see what this side of your family is like." Griffon's laughter was contagious, forcing a smile over my lips.

"I am too, Griffon." After a moment of considering his question, I replied. "Maybe, but he seemed genuinely shocked when the sun appeared in the center of my forehead. Then there's also the fact that when I recited the prophecy, he called it a nursery rhyme." My brows pushed together, seeing the irony of me reciting a prophecy about myself. "I've also seen others outside of this kingdom with a likeness to our people. Sure, some have different eye colors or hair, and vice versa. If I'd not seen the people here, I'd never have assumed who or which people I belonged to," I stated cautiously.

After a moment of walking in silence, I spoke carefully. "Besides, Scylla's coloring wasn't from the Prometheus line at all. It's my understanding that the coloring came from the Vanir, the first inhabitants of the Nine Realms." Of course, the books only ever noted their striking, blue eyes and light skin tone, so mine was an educated assumption based on what few indications there were.

A smile spread over his mouth as he scratched his silvery head. "It pleases me that you are well-apprised of our history, let alone what our people looked like. Few people ever realize that the first people weren't of the realms themselves. I guess it is rather far-fetched that another race entered the Nine Realms when it had yet to form land masses. Probably why they merely assume the Greek gods were among the first, instead of the Vanir." Griffon halted his speech momentarily as we stopped outside the wrought-iron gates, waiting for the guards on the other side to step forward and open them so we could pass.

Power rippled within the space between the iron gates and the crystals lining the entrance into the palace. Goosebumps pebbled my skin as the congregation flooded through the gates behind us. Where there should have been apprehension or a lingering fear of attack, there was nothing but this overwhelming sense of returning home. I didn't feel the need to be alert or on guard about an attack from those around me.

"The Vanir were, of course, the first people. They're the ones who inhabited this world, using mana and other means to create a land sustainable for life."

"And they're from Norse Cosmology?" I asked as my focus shifted to the waterways weaving throughout the courtyard we'd entered.

Birds zipped from one verdant bush to the other. Children placed paper boats into the streams, racing them as cheering echoed through the grand gardens. Large, emerald-green bushes had been trimmed to appear as maze-like passages. Flowers stretched throughout the bushes, covering the edges of passageways and statues of firebirds, dragons and knights with names etched on the bases of each pedestal. A covered vault—or something similar—peeked over the top of the hedges toward the center of the maze, seeming to beckon me forward.

"You're much smarter than Aden forewarned me you'd be, daughter. Indeed, my great-grandfather is Prometheus. My father visited the realms, then left a parting gift, you could say, when he did so. His mother was one of Freyja's Valkyries."

Esme, who I'd assumed was silent because she'd been listening to the conversation, stood beside me. I followed her line of sight to warriors who were swinging deadly blades at one another. The warriors held the same silvery-colored hair as those who'd accompanied us inside the gates. Even from where we stood some distance away, I could see their eyes were a similar shade of blue as mine. One warrior bested another, and when he spun, as if intending to land a killing blow, he turned toward us, pausing in place.

Warmth flooded through me without warning, and a loud, buzzing vibration flooded through my head, bouncing from ear to ear in a looping echo. The sensation of falling filled me as the man took a step forward, pausing only when Aden stepped in front of me, cutting off my view of the warrior.

"This is the part of the story where the great Scylla Fafnir comes in," Aden informed as his hand cupped my cheek, irritably. "I share both bloodlines with you, Little One."

"She's not little," Esme stated, as her eyes narrowed and the skin around them crinkled. Aden gave her a tight smile in response before aiming his attention at Griffon.

"How very *Game of Thrones* that sounds, Aden," I returned in a saccharine tone. "I hear it's done to keep the blood pure?" It took effort to prevent the grimace those words caused from leaving my lips. Not that he'd understand the reference.

"Of course, which is why a union between us would be favorable for the kingdom." Aden's words sent nausea swirling through my belly. It took effort to not point out how it was considered inbreeding, but to each their own. I wouldn't be screwing him, so it was a rather moot point.

"Let's not get ahead of ourselves, Aden." Griffon's jaw clenched as Aden stared at him for a moment, then snorted loudly. It caused my head to tilt, wondering what Aden assumed would happen while I was here. "Aria has just arrived and is in need of respite."

Aden's gaze searched my face, then turned toward Griffon, dismissing me. "They've already locked the gates behind us for the night. We'll retire to the dining hall, where I've already requested a meal be served for those wishing to indulge in one. I suspect my little queen is famished after the trek here and the trials she and her friend faced." At Aden's flourish of flattery, Esme made a gagging sound, which caused all present to peer toward her. Except me. I was too busy frowning at the empty courtyard and wondering where the warriors had gone.

"Thank you. I'm certain Aria greatly appreciates the attentiveness to her needs, Aden," Griffon offered a bit tightly. *Interesting.* Aden reached for my hand once more, and I stepped backward, preventing him from reaching it. Or me, for that matter.

"Aria, are you well?" Aden asked, which caused a hush to fall over the people nearest enough to overhear his worried words.

"I'm *very* well, Aden. Thank you for asking, though." My tone came out more clipped than I'd intended it to, but my point was crystal clear. Before he could conceal it, malice flashed in his cobalt-blue eyes. As fast as it appeared, it vanished behind a veneer of polished politeness. Unease slid through me as he bowed low to Griffon, then took his leave.

"He means well, Aria. Aden has waited a long time for you to return to us. He's one of my fiercest warriors and is devoted to restoring our people to power."

"Aden might mean well, Griffon, but I don't intend to entertain a courtship with him. That isn't why I came. I came because I want to know you, and what the people are like here."

"As I said, I'm very happy you came. But I wonder if you'd be more open to Aden if you hadn't been wed to King

Karnavious?" His question caused a flurry of emotions. If I was being honest, then it was partly that.

"Honestly, no. I didn't come here to be mated, nor wed to anyone. Even if I did not have an attachment, I wouldn't be interested." And definitely wouldn't be interested in Aden's pushy, related ass.

"Admittedly, Aden was upset that you chose another. As I've practically raised him from a babe, I do prefer him over King Karnavious for you. But I also understand that you're not a child, and I've not been in your life. That places me in a precarious position. I only want whatever makes you the happiest, Aria. If I'd raised you, I'd raise a much bigger argument about the choice. However, I did promise Aden I'd at least put in a good word for him. Honestly, I'll be fine either way. So long as you're treated with the respect that you are owed for the position you hold. After all, you are the granddaughter of Scylla and Tirsynth Prometheus. I've also made it clear to everyone that you and Esme are not to be harmed, or touched in any manner unless you invite them to do so."

"Thank you, Griffon." Not that I'd abide by him trying, or anyone seeking to force me to do shit here. I didn't need anyone to save me.

Knox would honor my wishes and wait for me to emerge. But not if I stayed past the time he'd allotted me, he'd break his promise not to retrieve me. The precarious position of them being enemies was bothersome. It made me wonder if at the end of this war, we'd be able to gather without bloodshed.

Knox was the crowned king of Norvalla. But my father, *my people*, were *his* sworn enemy. I couldn't promise him they wouldn't try to capture him, or worse. And if that happened, if they tried, Knox would cut them all down. I'd lose any chance at discovering who I was the second Knox took Griffon's head.

"Where was I? Ah, yes. The Vanir were fleeing from those who sought to persecute them for their differences. Freyja, who is your great-grandmother, was one of them. They used magic to turn the realms of fire to a land that could sustain life through the bond and connection to nature as well as everything connected to it as well."

"You're saying that *we're* from *Freyja's* bloodline? Freyja the Valkyrie?" I questioned in confusion. Not entirely certain that I'd understood what he was trying to tell me.

"My mother, Scylla, is the daughter of Freyja, and Freyja helped form the lands to mirror the Nine Realms of Norse Cosmology. Freyja made each land equal to the next, ensuring no race was above another, and all the Vanir lands were connected. Each was ruled by a lord or lady who'd vowed to uphold the founding ideals of equality and prosperity. Back then, there were no kings or queens, only lords and ladies who helped maintain peace and prosperity throughout every realm. But then they began to change, as everything does. Power corrupts and greed leads to wars for land superiority."

"They're beautiful," I announced, taking in the power that radiated from each. Clear quartz crystals drew energy directly from nature, but these were humming with power unlike any I'd encountered before. "What is feeding them power?" I probed cautiously, edging forward, allured by the energy they held.

"As far as our scholars can discern, they seem to pull

from whatever power source is nearest to them. Though it must be incredibly powerful to fuel them without draining the source. They, like the land, never pull more than the supplier can safely give. So, to answer your question, right now, you are the source they're drawing from, daughter. They're recharged throughout the day by selenite, but right now? They're pulling directly from you," Griffon admitted softly.

Spinning on my heel, I stared at him with confusion tightening my face, but his mouth tugged into a boyish smile. "How can *I* be feeding them power?"

"According to my mother, only the females from our lineage who've been blessed by Freyja to rule, have a special connection with the land. They're linked in such a way that they share power with each other. Freyja's domain included the natural world, and similarly, you feel a connection to the land that reciprocates. That's the soul of it, crying out to you, which only a few have ever truly felt." A quick glance at my face made his eyes sparkle with mirth before he continued his explanation. "As it comes from the land, the crystals are also a part of the world. However, the largest, hollowed cylinders are connected to the Queen of Witches."

"Hecate is the Queen of Witches," I emphasized. Griffon's silvery head tilted as if he were awaiting me to figure something out. When I offered nothing more, he spoke with patience.

When I offered nothing more, he spoke with patience. "She is, but so is Freyja. They condemned Freyja for being the Queen of Witches. Hecate was the Goddess of Magic. One Greek, the other Norse. One helped forge the Nine

Realms into a world while the other is a parasite exiled here for crimes committed against vengeful gods. The power you feel from these cylinders is the same magic that your grandmother and great-grandmother carried. I believe your birth was a true blessing." For a moment, we watched a group of children playing before he continued.

"I'd like to believe it brightened this blighted land. If you decided to do so, I think you'd be able to change the world for the better. Even with your hands bound behind your back, blindfolded if you chose to, Aria. Some people are born to brighten it, while those like you are born to set it ablaze from the fire burning within. I didn't know why my mother desired for me to couple with Aurora, or sent me to the ruins where I found her the day of your conception. I thought she was going mad from seeing too much war, or aging. But I still went and I'm glad I did. Not as a father, who's biased about you, but as a king, I'd still choose you to save us all."

"No pressure, right?" Esme's chuckled response was faint, her bluish-purple eyes lingered on a group of men, then roamed around us with curiosity.

"Go big or go home, right?" I asked before lifting my hand to the large, hollowed-out cylinder.

"Aria, I wouldn't—" My hand touched the crystal, and a sense of falling rippled through me. Then pain tore through my abdomen, legs, and arms until it felt as if my skull was being cleaved in half. Spots dotted my vision. Then everything went dark.

CHAPTER 2
ARIA

Pain forced my hands to my forehead, where I applied pressure. The groan that burst from my lips had my eyelids lifting. Bright, staggering light forced my hand lower, to shield my eyes. What the hell had happened? I felt like someone had beaten me up, stomped on me, and left me on the side of the road to be eaten by scavengers. Forcing my limbs to work, I struggled into a seated position. I'd either fallen through the cylinder or I'd just become Alice, and stepped out of reality, into the fantasy that was Wonderland.

I'd done a lot of stupid shit in my brief life, but I'd never thought I'd add falling through a quartz cylinder to my list.

The marble floor I'd awoken on was *moving*, and sparkling silver orbs were sliding across it. Shifting my hand, I captured some of the sediment material. It sent a burst of pain into my palm, and a yelp of surprise escaped, echoing down the length of the moss-covered hallway as the silverish material sent pain into the fleshy part of it.

"What in the Alice-fell-into-an-acid-trip shit is this?" Rising to my feet, while avoiding touching the strange orbs, I squinted at the hallway as it slowly widened until I could see light at the far end. "I better get a Cheshire Cat. That's all I'm saying," I muttered crossly.

The moment I stepped forward, the silver that covered the marble floor merged, forming several mirrors. By the time the orbs had finished, they lined both sides of the hallway with the reflective surfaces. Then I looked into one, and instead of my face reflecting back at me, a scene was unfolding.

A couple was dancing gently, his arms were covered in dark, inky tendrils wrapped around a woman, with platinum hair past her hips. Stepping closer, I paused as amber eyes drifted to me. Thinning, they drifted down my frame before the purple-blue eyes of his companion slid toward me as well.

The moment she did, he spoke. "That doesn't look like Destiny." His raspy timbre had my head tipping to the side, sliding my eyes over his massive build.

"I have no idea who she is. Definitely not her though, Fairy."

Fairy? Not sure what she'd meant by it, but I dismissed them to look into the next glass. A woman was within it, her body covered in a strange meat suit. My face scrunched up as she opened a fridge, shoving lush, red curls over her shoulder.

"I'm back early, Fred." Was she speaking to the freezer? Cerulean eyes landed on me, even as mine turned as round as saucers at seeing what was *inside* the freezer.

"Pity, I had prayed they'd successfully skewered you

with a blade." The talking head said from inside her freezer.

"Hello," the woman called, even as she moved toward the mirror. The blood drained from my face as I realized she was wearing flesh like a sweatshirt, the head still attached, like a hoodie.

Horror rocked through me as I darted forward, glancing through the silvers lining the hallway. In one, a man with huge, ink-colored wings slammed into a woman, who was bent over a desk. His angry thrust caused her whimpers to reach my ears. Turning at the sound of my gasp, sapphire eyes locked with mine, glowing. Dark, thin tattoos slithered over both arms, then down his torso. Lowering my gaze the moment he moved, I watched a massive cock pulling from the woman he'd been railing. Shooting forward, I shivered as the sound of people's hushed voices slipped from multiple portals.

In another, a redhead was placing what looked like steel into a press. The entire room around her looked like an armory. Frowning as her ample belly was exposed, I began moving forward once more. The next had a dark-haired male, who was holding a tiny baby with horns poking from his head. Smiling at the cute little demon, I flicked my eyes to who I assumed was his father.

"Hello, lovely. Are you lost?" he asked, his darkening eyes filling with curiosity.

"He's adorable," I whispered, not sure he'd hear me.

"As was his mother," he returned before the mirror shifted, returning to silver. As I regarded the silver, it swirled like a vortex, then solidified once more. When it returned, a man with dark hair and vibrant, blue eyes held a little girl. Beside him, a woman with a rounded belly, and a toddler, who was resting his head on her shoulder. The male moved toward the mirror, forcing me to rush forward. He hadn't looked the least bit friendly.

A woman's whispered moan forced my eyes to drift to the one on the other side. In it, a man had his head leaned back on a small couch, his arms extended over the back of it. The woman was on her knees, pleasuring him. "Either get in here and join her on your knees, or move along, pretty kitty." His head raised, even as the woman choked, lifting from an impressive cock lined with a Jacob's ladder. My eyes grew owl shaped as a whispered breath explosively expelled from my dry throat. Snaking my tongue out, I wetted my suddenly dry lips. "Here kitty-kitty. Does the pretty pussy want some cream? Or are you the type who needs to be caught in the spider's web?"

"Do I look like a cat?"

"Trust me, kitty. You'll be purring so prettily for me if you let me play with the fire burning in those lovely eyes."

"Hard pass, but thanks for the offer?" I hastened my movement. Fucking hell. Maybe it was some sort of hostel or a sex club? Did they have sex clubs here? Where the hell was I? Who the hell were they?

I took another step, eyeing the next. A meadow covered in delicate violet-colored flowers swept out as far as I could see. The adjacent one was awash in darkness, yet tiny, gold specks pirouetted against the velvety-black canvas. Several more held similar scenes, like the first few, which appeared to be portals into other worlds. At least, I assumed they were since some creatures didn't look like ones we had here. Maybe I'd been supposed to choose one? How would

I choose? There had to be a reason they were within the same hallway I'd been pulled into, right? But how would I know which one took me back to where I'd been, before I'd ended up in Wonderland?

"A little help would be nice right about now. Not from those people, either," I grumbled. "Alice had a guide. He might have been batshit bonkers, but I enjoy riddles." My words reverberated through the seemingly endless hallway.

Abandoning the portals, I allowed myself to be led toward a dark doorway. It appeared to be the end of the long, winding corridor I'd traveled down. Grabbing the knob, I twisted and pushed it open, peering into a darkened forest. If I entered it and ended up lost . . . what then?

If I got lost, I had a feeling that it wouldn't matter if I never moved another muscle again, no one would come looking for me here. Esme was probably threatening my father and all present by now, which meant I had to get back to her. We'd promised to stay together, but it wasn't as if I'd intended to fall down the rabbit hole, per se. I inhaled deeply and stepped through the shimmering surface of the mirror, gasping as the sensation of falling began anew.

The moment I'd exited the hall of mirrors, I was dropping swiftly toward the ground. A moment before I could crash against the boulders rushing up to meet my face, something grabbed me and tossed me into the sky. A scream of horror ripped from my lips as I landed on a slippery rock face, teetering on the side of a cliff.

"What the actual fuck? I should've gone in the stained-glass window, but no. Not me. No, I have to run toward the one drawing me in, as if I ever choose anything correctly? Nope. Not me. I'm the idiot who refuses to take the simple path forward. Why? Because I'm that bitch." I groaned as I softly beat my head against the rock. It was then that I noticed what, exactly, I was kneeling on, and I flinched. "You've got to be kidding me."

I didn't wait around to plummet to my death. Instead, I began scouting a forward escape from the slate I knew was treacherous and deadly. Knox wasn't here to save me this time, which meant if I were careless with my life, it'd be game over. I wasn't a damsel. I carefully inched over the precarious pathway, needing no one to save me because I could save myself—or, at least, that was what I told myself.

The sound of cracking slate sent ice trickling down my spine. Instead of rushing forward, I continued creeping toward the portion of rock that moved toward the top of the cliff. The chill of the hard surface against my back was sinking into my weary bones with each slide closer to the edge of the next tier of slate. A prickling sensation of being watched grew as I turned toward the cliff and then hoisted myself up to the next.

A tedious amount of time passed before I finally made it to solid ground. Laying on my back on the damp, chilly ground, I gazed up at the startling, blue skies above. As my face scrunched up, I felt my eyebrows pushing together in confusion. Rising to my knees, I braced myself on the edge, peering down the slate-covered side of the towering cliff.

Darkness shadowed the cliff behind me, while daylight filled the wooden terrain before me. Inching back from the edge, I surveyed the thick, silent forest. It took effort to get up this time, as if I'd pressed myself past the point of exhaustion. I had rested little since leaving Norvalla, which was swiftly exhausting my reserved energy. I'd expected some rest before being tossed into the next challenge.

The moment I entered the forest, strange, haunting noises began thrumming through the trees. The light streaming through the treetops above kept me from blindly stumbling over fallen debris, yet every step I took had the sense of foreboding in my stomach growing stronger and stronger. I still felt eyes boring into my spine, but every time I peered back over my shoulder, nothing was there.

"I'd really appreciate that mad little pussy cat right about now," I grumbled beneath my breath. Then a twig snapped somewhere behind me and I spun toward the sound. "Come on, creeper, don't keep a girl waiting. Show yourself!" Sweat trickled down the back of the skin-tight black tunic Aden had provided for us to endure the trials in.

A breeze wafted against my neck, which reminded me of the rather atrocious braid Esme had done in my hair. She'd returned the favor after I'd braided hers, but with nothing to tie the end, it had been a lost cause. The girl had fuck-all knowledge of anything pertaining to girly shit. Closing my fingers against the palms of my hands, I searched through the trees for anything hunting me.

The sound of a branch snapping underfoot forced my head to turn toward the sound. As my eyes narrowed in the vicinity, the sound had come from, a flash of violet captured my attention. Dramatically shaded, heart-shaped petals clung to a lush, navy-colored flower bud. The flower was pretty, but it wasn't why I'd noticed it. The fact that it was attached to something that was rising, is what had caught my eye. It persisted in its ascent until the bushes no longer obscured it, unveiling a sizable, pale stag that fixated its stare on me.

"Holy shit." I swallowed the fear clawing up my throat and threatening to come out in the way of an opera singer's highest note. Its head tilted, as though it were trying to ascertain whether I was a threat. The massive stag stepped closer, which forced me to bolt back toward the road, running blindly. I'd seen enough nature shows to know, not to mess with anything with antlers attached to it.

My heart pounded against my ribcage as fear and adrenaline clashed in my system. It deafened me to any other sound within the forest. I forced myself to keep running through the pain that tore at my side, unwilling to stop even though my body said to do so. It wasn't until the flashes of brilliantly-colored flowers caught my eye, forcing it to a large meadow that allowed the advantage of being able to see around me, that I allowed myself a moment to rest.

Blowing the air from my lungs, I inhaled the crisp, clean mountain air. Gripping my side, I winced as sharp pain persisted from the insane mad dash through the countryside I'd not had on my bingo card for this year. I really hadn't had 'running from an unrealistic stag that looked like something from a fantasy painting' on my card. In front of me, I could see the honey-colored flowers, mixed in with fiery ginger and scarlet hues, peeking from beyond the greenery.

The soft scratch of antlers against bark drew my focus back to the creature hunting me. I shifted just enough to see around the tree, observing as it honed its flower-laden antlers on the thick trunk. Confusion pinched my brows because that stag either wasn't the same as the first one I'd seen or it had stopped to pick up new flowers. This stag had miniature sunflowers connected to a length of lime-colored stems, and someone had artfully wrapped floral vines around its massive rack of horns.

Hesitation morphed into curiosity, which slowly turned into awe because the longer I watched the creature, the clearer I could see the untold power pulsing off it. Its raw, pulsating mana brushed against my flesh, forcing gooseflesh to spread over my naked arms.

"You're beautiful. Aren't you, big boy?" I whispered, my voice too low to be discernible to my own ears. The stag's head lifted and then turned toward me. Eyes the color of midnight peered at me, ancient knowledge promised in their depths. "Hello."

"Hello, Aria," a softly whispered voice replied. "We've been waiting for you to come home."

My mouth opened and my jaw threatened to join my feet on the forest floor. Had it just spoken to me? Either it had or I was hallucinating from dehydration and exhaustion. After taking a slow step forward, I paused, watching as the stag did the same. The moment its hoof touched the ground, my feet anchored in place, threatening to grow roots where I stood. As if it feared spooking me. Licking my dry lips, I considered if I should say something or pretend it hadn't spoken at all.

"Did you just talk?" I called to the stag, uncertain if I'd

29

just made a huge mistake and was losing the weak grip I had on my sanity.

"Aria Primrose, your mind isn't fractured. It's actually sharp for someone so young," the voice said succinctly, though the stag's mouth never moved. "Welcome home, Queen of Sunfire." The stag bowed its head until its velvet, flora-covered horns bushed the carpeted forest floor.

"I'm sorry, but I'm not a queen of anything," I returned carefully, uncertain as to what it had meant by the title. "I am Aria Primrose Prometheus, Queen of Nothing."

"You're not?" it asked, even as it continued toward me at a leisurely gait. "I feel you as surely as you feel me, child. The power rushing through your veins is the same power living in mine. From the first breath you took, I've felt your presence. I am the power which pulses inside you, fueling your endless pool of mana. Don't fear me, for I know your strengths, weaknesses and dreams. You are a part of me as surely as I am a part of you."

"Who are you?" I asked as fear and wonder collided, both threatening to engulf me fully.

"You know who I am," it stated with pride pooling in the navy-colored depths. "I brought you here to me. Do not fear me, girl. I've always been with you. Breathe before you pass out, Queen of Sunfire."

The air filled my lungs and then steadily left them as I lifted my hand, touching the glorious creature's rune-covered fur. The moment my hand connected, the world tilted, and everything inside me eased to calmness I'd never felt before that moment.

"I feel you everywhere," I murmured breathlessly. "Holy shit. You are the power within me. Aren't you?"

"There's more to it than that, though. Several things create a realm, each one a complex combination of those the realm not only chooses to give to, but also to take from. You're correct in your deduction that I am the land. The same land that chose you to become queen and undo the damage by those seeking to take what is not theirs. Aria, your light will drive out the darkness devouring the Nine Realms," he explained. "I wasn't the only one who chose you to lead our people. There's another within this window, one who pushed for your creation before she'd ever birthed the male who'd sire an heir of sun."

Goosebumps erupted over my flesh as a chill raced down my spine. "Who?"

"Follow the path forward. All shall be revealed in time. If your intentions are true, and your heart is free of malice, then you'll find the spring water from the fjord of Vanaheimr awaiting your rebirth."

The stag reared back on its hind legs and then crashed forward with a deafening *crunch* against the forest floor. At the same moment, the sun vanished, leaving me blinded by the darkness enveloping me. Warmth drifted against my face before the brush of fur against my arm had a sad smile playing over my mouth.

"Blessed are those who see beyond the darkness, Aria Prometheus. Follow your soul to the Well of Transformation and be reborn, Queen of Sunfire."

CHAPTER 3
ARIA

The darkness seemed as endless as the night. As I walked through it, I imagined brightness within my mind that triggered a flood of colorful sunflower images. Various types became the sun while others shifted to flowering meadows as their tart, earthy scent tickled my nose.

Giant Sungold sunflowers with fluffy, golden petals that resembled pom poms came first. The land was as soft and as pliant as the petals of the giant flower. Suntastic Yellow sunflowers with striking, yellow petals stretching from the black center came next. As if they were the wheat in the fields, they stretched farther than the eye could track. Little Becka's, with their burnt-orange centers that faded into deep, startling red-and-orange-tipped petals became the trees, flourishing in the high and low lands. Earthwalker's earthy tones of oranges, reds, mahogany, and browns became the soul of the world I built inside my mind, flourishing those who trusted it to nourish and protect them. In the center of them all were the Lemon

Queens. They may have had smaller petals, but they were brighter yellow than any of the others. The queen fed and pollinated everything else, sustaining life through the soul it housed.

Ahead of me, a minuscule light flickered, and I angled my steps toward it, wanting to know what it was. I wasn't sure how far I'd traveled before I again hesitated. The light was suddenly moving toward me, startlingly rapidly. It whizzed through the velvety darkness until it slammed into me, sending us both clattering to the ground in a crash of limb and . . . *fluff*?

The creature purred softly as I took in what appeared to be an arctic fox with wings. Glowing dust seemed to sprinkle from it, without it having to move from where it remained on top of me. The foxlike animal had giant ears, much like those of a fennec fox. A large, puffy cat-like tail flicked from side to side behind it, sending glittering dust shimmering behind the thing.

It rudely stated, "You stink."

"You don't smell like roses either, buddy," I grumbled right back.

"Don't you have wings?"

"I'm a person." Why did he sound so offended by my lack of wings? Shouldn't I be the one to find the lack of them offensive? "Humans don't have wings."

"Pity," it complained before crawling from my chest to sit beside me and loudly lick its paw.

"What are you?" I'd seen nothing like it before.

"Fennix's a Foxtyre, and I'm a Catteris. My name's Fennia," a singsong voice said beside me. I turned to find another creature beside me, having no idea how or when it had gotten there. It also had wings, which fluttered just enough to keep it off the ground for a moment before it dropped down beside Foxtyre. "She's so cute, Fennix! Can we keep her? Can-we-can-we-can-we-please?"

"She stinks," he grouched before changing paws. "I doubt it's den-broken, either. I say we eat her and cut our losses."

Den-broken? Sitting up, I glanced back and forth between the winged creatures, smiling like an idiot. The irony of this shit wasn't lost on me. I empathized with Fennix's concern for his floors, having taken in enough strays to recognize the dangers. Hell, I couldn't even argue that I didn't stink, since I hadn't showered since right before heading to meet Aden at the start of the trials. Once they'd showed us our rooms, I'd intended to request a shower, but I got sidetracked.

"But, Fennix! You said we could get a pet, and I love this one! She's pretty, and her hair matches yours!" Fennix and I glanced at Fennia, offended by her comparison. "What? It's the same silvery color!"

"His is white, and mine is silver. It is *not* the same color," I pointed out crossly, while Fennix made a displeased sound in agreement. "I'm also not a pet. Pretty certain my inner beast wouldn't enjoy being treated like a sweet, fluffy house cat."

"If Fennia wants you as a pet, then a pet you shall be, creature."

At Fennix's sudden sharp tone, I forced myself to stand so I could glower down at the ankle biter. Both stared up at me, as if just noticing I wasn't tiny, like them. When I felt

35

my point was properly made, I knelt and smiled at Fennix, who stepped back.

"You're both cute, but I'll skip asking if you are house-broken and all that jazz." Laughing at the haughty look on Fennix's face, if a Foxtyre could actually look haughty. I may have been projecting. "I don't suppose either of you know the way to the Muffin Man?"

"Muffin Man?" Fennia asked.

"The Muffin Man?" Fennix parroted back, tilting his small head. The slight jostle sent his large, fluffy ears cattywampus, which caused my lips to twitch. "I've never heard of someone named something so preposterous."

"The Muffin Man!" I held the snicker in—barely. "It is indeed a preposterous name, but one must never tell the Muffin Man such a thing," I said in a saccharine tone, rising once again. "It was lovely meeting both of you, but I'm a Walkabout and my time is short. I'm certain Esmeralda probably lost her shit and is raising hell or sitting in a dungeon in chains from doing so."

I started past them, but then I paused because, at some point during our banter, something had changed. In the darkness, it looked as if someone had hung thousands of strands of fairy lights from leafless tree branches. The rock-covered path was lit up by the same silver orbs I'd seen all over the floor of the room I'd landed in. Only, instead of rolling around slowly, they acted like leaves caught in the breeze.

"Did she not see how cute we are?" Fennia asked in a wounded tone from her spot behind me.

A soft puff of air, which I assumed belonged to Fennix,

followed. "She was a heathen, darling. Pay her no mind. We can find another pet. I promise."

"I want her! She's so pretty, Fenny. Please?" she begged, which caused my shoulders to shake.

The way they argued made me wonder if Knox and I would ever reach that point in a relationship. Hell, if we even had one by the time I left here. Would he wait for me? Or would he change his mind as he'd done before? There were entirely too many questions where he was concerned. I could lie to myself all I wanted, but Knox and I wouldn't work with everything between us. Not without us working on it without the world intervening. Despite my sole desire for him, the weight of his experiences made it unlikely for him to forget. I refused to live with his ghosts, which were many. Even without Lilianna, he'd lost so many people because of those who had the same blood as I did, running through my veins. I was also the enemy on more than one front. Now, the secondary line that flowed through my veins was unmistakable. Prometheus and Hecate, both enemies to Karnavious.

"Creature!"

Fennix's cry of alarm forced me from my internal musing, and when I spun to see what was happening, I saw the snake-like creature trying to wring the life out of Fennia. I rushed back to them and instantly began digging my taloned nails into the snake until it released her and slithered off.

"Oh my God! I touched a snake!" I cried as the slimy skin remained on my nails. "Gross!" I made a beeline to the grassy knoll beside us and began wiping my hands off on it.

"See, she is perfect for us! That meanie Slithering Snock won't hurt us with her as our pet."

"Listen," I said as I turned toward the duo, "I have enough on my plate right now. It's heaping with other people who I am helping. I can't be your pet, Fennia. Fennix is right. I'd be a horrible pet. I'm moody and have one hell of an alternate personality who enjoys short walks after bathing in blood. She's also known to, on rare occasions, eat a penis as she skips along here or there."

"She's a little strange, darling."

"I love her." Fennia purred thunderously while rubbing against my foot. "She's perfect!"

"Great," both I and Fennix muttered.

I determinedly stepped back onto the glowing pathway and began again. The longer we walked, the quieter they got, and not once did they offer an opinion on which way we should go when the pathway forked. Despite that, figuring out the right direction to go was easy. I felt it as surely as I felt my nose on my face.

I allowed my soul to lead me down each pathway that brightened as we got farther down each one. It wasn't until the fifth or sixth split in the trail that we began walking over multi-colored flowers. At the end of the flower-covered path, we passed through what appeared to be a doorway. On the other side, I glanced back in time to see the portal vanish, leaving us in a field carpeted in crimson flowers. The meadow ended with an atrium ablaze with light from within.

"How do we get back home?" Fennix asked with tangible fear in his tone.

"Fenny, I'm not going back without her. I owe her a life debt."

I should've asked Fennia what she meant, but I couldn't. My sole focus was on the atrium, which was pulling me to it with invisible strings. As if something beckoned me forth with an invitation I couldn't ignore. The moment I reached the rounded glass atrium, the door opened, revealing a woman who could've been my mirror image. My lips parted in a perfect *O* as she smiled, scrutinizing my face.

"Hello, granddaughter. I've been waiting for you," she welcomed in a pleasant, comforting tone.

"Scylla?" I whispered in shock. How? Scylla Prometheus was dead and buried before my parents had ever thought of me.

"I am your grandmother, Aria Primrose. The dead don't die, they merely go on to the next, or stick around to watch over those they've created. Death's a journey everyone makes alone, even royalty. You're absolutely stunning, and even more beautiful than I thought you'd be. You have my mother's eyes. I understand why you'd be overwhelmed, but I promise, you're right where you're supposed to be."

"Holy shit," I muttered as chills shot down my spine.

"I've waited a very long time to meet you. You've surpassed every expectation I have held for you. Your choice in men could be better, but that's not what you're here for today. Today, you'll bathe in the spring to allow the land to bond with you. In order to accept the full intensity of the land's powers, you must be reborn." I opened my mouth to dispute her claim about rebirth, but her eyes narrowed with warning.

"Calm down, my darling. Rebirth is only the transformation you choose to allow to alter both soul and mind. Tonight's merely for us to discuss what is about to unravel now that your home. There are many questions I wish to ask you, and I can see many more burning in your Vanir-colored stare. Come, my ladies have heated the stones for the spring water. There's much we must do before Esmeralda throws too much of a fit."

CHAPTER 4
ARIA

My heart thundered in my ears as Scylla, my freaking dead grandmother, who was currently leading me through her house. Or what I assumed was her house. From the outside, it had looked like any other atrium, but the deeper we moved through it, the more it altered, changing to mirror a lighted oasis. The further we moved, the more it evolved into being another dimension, one created to mirror the fjords of Norway.

Scylla remained silent, but turned every once in a while, to smile back at me. I fretted over my lip while taking in a large, vibrant swath of glowing, iridescent colors. The moon bathed a massive mountain range in the aurora borealis.

The darkened sky shifted coloring as meteors sailed through the skies above. A lofty mountain sat in the distance, vibrant against the velvet backdrop as the light bathed it in shimmering prisms. As I stood in silent amazement, Scylla chuckled.

"It's beautiful, isn't it?" she asked tenderly.

"I've seen nothing as beautiful as this before. I can feel it beckoning me," I admitted as amazement slid over my face. "This isn't real, is it?"

"It is very real, Aria. This is the Kingdom of Fire that I created through my bond with the land. It reflects the beauty of your soul, or that's what my mother told me. It will change now that it has chosen you to rule in place of me." Her words snapped the spell the realm held over me. "Do try not to look so disappointed."

"It's not that," I returned. "I didn't intend to claim anything." The statement was truthful. I hadn't chosen to rule a kingdom. Technically, I'd denied wanting to be a queen, but I also didn't want Hecate to win this war, either. If I had to claim my birthright in order to drive the bitch out, I'd do whatever it took. "It's just a lot. You know?"

"I can imagine, especially since I ensured that you would not grow up with the mentality of a queen. Any woman can be a queen. A true queen is able to look beyond her own desires or mind, and do what is needed for the kingdom." Scylla exhaled a shaky breath before starting down the staircase, as if she'd walked them a thousand times before.

"And what did it need?"

"I knew the perfect savior couldn't be raised with luxury or affection. She needed to go through much pain to be able to comprehend the Nine Realms. She'd need to endure much pain to understand what those within the Nine Realm have endured. Of course, she'd need a king beside her. Offspring doesn't appear by itself now, does it? But I didn't choose that for you. Instead, I thought you should be the one to pick your ideal mate. I just never imagined Draghana Karnavious' grandson would find you or be the ideal mate you chose. But he's persistent, if nothing else. I knew you'd survive everything the Hecate sisters did to you. Aria, you are my granddaughter and no one can break you. The blood of kings and queens throughout the ages runs through your veins."

"So, you knowingly set me up for a lifetime of traumatic events? I mean, I went through hell at the hands of both Freya and Aurora. You didn't think I should have any kindness in my life? I get the whole 'need of a savior' crap, but they tortured me."

"But you survived it, all the same. It molded you into what you needed to be in order to rule the kingdom." Scylla released a heavy exhale. "If I came to you and told you that everyone you've ever loved or cared about would die if you do nothing, what would you do to stop it from happening? What would you give to stop that from happening?"

"Anything," I answered without hesitation. Esme, Knox, Lore, Greer, Soraya, Avyanna, and so many other faces flashed through my mind as the words slipped from my lips. "I'd do whatever I could do to stop it from happening."

"When the son of the first people finds life through a Hecate witch's womb, the world will turn to chaos and the goddess will be in ruins. When the son rises and reaches for his birthright, the battle will settle upon us, and the world shall rattle with might. For when the beast is unleashed, and the son discovers his truth, he will aim his fire at the goddess and send her back to her tomb." Scylla tilted her head, intently watching for my reaction.

"I don't know if you've noticed, but I don't have testicles." Her mirroring, blue eyes grew rounded before she released a clap of laughter. "It says a son. Sons have certain parts, which I lack."

"I'm very aware of what you lack. Did you think I wanted you found before you were strong enough to stand and fight? Please, I wouldn't have allowed you to be killed before you were born, let alone directly after. I merely changed a few things to ensure you wouldn't be discovered before you were old enough to defend yourself."

Scylla paused as we came to a large portal. Power hummed through it, drifting over my flesh until it pebbled with the sheer amount it offered. "Age before beauty," Scylla stated with a genuine smile pulling at the corners of her full, heart-shaped lips.

The moment she stepped through the portal, everything around me altered once more. Not waiting around to see what happened, I followed her into the unknown. Was I really going to allow the spirit of my dead grandmother to lead me through portals? Apparently, but this shit hadn't been on my bingo card, either.

I stepped out on the other side and found myself in what looked to be a large bathing chamber. Several women stood ready to assist us as Scylla ambled toward an altar placed at the head of the room. The women within the chamber didn't make me pause, and the air around me pulsed with an unsettling amount of power. Thick energy saturated the air and began slithering into my soul.

"Don't worry, darling. They don't bite, at least, not often." Scylla snorted when I refused to find the humor in her sentiment. "Light the torches, Adair, please. They're not servants if that is what you assume."

"I assumed nothing, actually." Scanning the chamber, I felt the skin on my arms pebbling. The women offered encouragement with gentle nods, even as they moved to do as they'd been bid to.

"Good." She came to a stop at the altar, where she picked up one incense and gently blew on it, sending eddies of smoke out in a wave. The glass statue of Freyja sucked in the opaque essence, which sent glowing, blue veins down the altar, stretching out and branching in various directions along the marble flooring.

"It's an antechamber?" My question was answered as the room began to hum and then expanded as the hallway had done. It expanded into a slow-moving waterway, with a pool of water leading into a large, white mosaic building. They had cut wide doors into the face of the temple, and above each side sat a fiery, blue phoenix. "Wow," I whispered over the sound of rushing water, which fell within the temple.

Above the temple, there was a soaring statue with what looked to be billowing smoke encased inside it. The statue was of a woman, who I assumed was Freyja, all things considered. Her hands were open, palms facing the sky, and unlike the smaller version, this one was painted. Silverish curls brushed her narrow hips and lower back. A pewter, circular necklace held up the white goddess gown she wore. Chrome armlets adorned both biceps and there were several more bracelets at her wrists. The sheer dress she wore hugged her full breasts, slid to the center of her abdomen and swept out at her hips. It exposed both legs at the thigh, as if to allow easier movement. Its beauty took my breath away, revealing the origin of Scylla's hair and turquoise eyes.

"Where was I?" Scylla asked as we drifted toward the temple.

"You didn't feed me to the wolf, and altered facts?"

She awarded me a pointed look.

"So, you were listening? I'm impressed. Few would heed the word of a deceased grandmother. Most would assume they'd gone insane."

"I never claimed to be sane, did I? Honestly, on a scale from one to ten? This isn't a five for me in the what-the-fuck-chuck basket I'm crafting. I mean, did you notice the Foxtyre and Catteris? I'd consider that a little higher in the bucket. Well, all things considered."

"I'm going to hold you to that in a few moments." Pausing in front of the large temple, I swallowed past the fear tightening in my throat. I could feel the thrumming of the land inside the structure. "You'll be going through the center of this door. It's the first step of you reaching for your birthright." When I didn't immediately step forward, worry etched into the lines around her eyes. "I'll explain more once you've entered Freyja's Temple, Aria."

Straightening my spine, I inhaled a calming breath before walking beneath the waterfall of mana. The sheer force of it as it hit me, seemed to rip me apart as it passed through my flesh, dissecting me and discovering all my secrets. In return, it offered knowledge and taught me things no amount of studying could ever teach me. By the time I felt a tug on my hand, I was struggling for air.

"Welcome to the heart of the Nine Realms, Aria Primrose Prometheus, Heir to the Kingdom of Fire. Since you didn't die, I'm guessing the land approves of you. Of course, why wouldn't it? You're my granddaughter." Scylla blinked with feigned innocence, as if she hadn't just had me walk through hellfire.

"That fucking hurt," I snapped.

"Did you think rebirth would be painless? Or maybe you thought I'd give you a massage?" Her face twitched, as if she were suppressing laughter.

My lips parted, then closed as I considered my reply. "I don't know what I expected, actually. There're no books or classes to prepare you for a day out with your dead grandmother." It was direct and truthful. My attention diverted to the pool before me, which had steam rolling up from the water.

"I guess there wouldn't be," Scylla agreed, then pointed toward the pool. "They filled this pool with the water from my mother's homeland. The spring for the fjords is the purest within any land. It also holds the very essence of the Vanir people. Those wishing to be claimed by the land, or blessed to ascend to the throne, must bathe here first. We can save time by performing a single blessing for both undertakings."

"Did Griffon bathe here?" What I preferred to know was if Griffon realized I'd be dethroning him.

"No," she admitted. "Griffon is king by proxy, but only in this false land. The true Kingdom of Fire wouldn't recognize him or his brother, Hagen. Tirsynth even bred an army of bastard born princes to seek the approval of my land. Then Hecate laid waste to it, and Griffon crafted this false realm. You felt the weakness of this realm when you entered it, didn't you?" When I nodded in reply, she chuckled. "I know you've felt the call of the true Kingdom of Fire as well."

"I have felt the call to both Norvalla and the Kingdom of Fire. I wasn't sure why I didn't feel this place," I admitted as I considered what she'd disclosed. "Does that mean this land will continually devolve until it ceases to exist?" I'd known something wasn't right the moment we'd entered. This place held no attraction other than wonder for me, yet I felt a strong connection to the Kingdom of Fire.

"Indeed, but my son was aware of what you'd become. Of course, I only meant Griffon to hold the crown until you discovered your truths. Then he created this realm with the help of others, and concealed our people so that they could recover from what Hecate had done to them."

"And what are my truths?" I questioned cautiously, savoring the repartee we participated in.

"There was never a son in the prophecy. The heir of the land inherits the Sunfire, which is what we need to drive Hecate back into her tomb." Scylla systematically began lighting the torches around the pool of water. "My mother ensured no man could take from us, Aria. Freyja lived in a time where women held no worth other than their inheritance, which only a man could spend, or her womb."

"Yet, she forced me to be made in order to remove Hecate?"

"She did nothing of the sort, child." I wasn't enjoying being called a child, but seeing as Scylla was older than dirt, I was letting it slide. "How magnanimous of you, truly." My jaw dropped as she read my thoughts. "Of course, I can read them. You could as well if you'd ever cared to try. Both my mother and I see and alter the future as needed, influencing change when and where it is necessary. How do you think I predicted what you'd become? I've spent half my lifetime running scenarios inside my mind's eye to find one in which Hecate was overthrown. One out of a million, one successfully sent her back into her tomb, which isn't the death you wish for her, but it's the best we can do."

"Fire is a weakness of Hecate's, and I've trapped her inside her true form. If I can wield enough fire, she'll die."

"And so would you, Aria. She isn't worth your life. It's difficult to kill a phoenix, but if someone extinguishes its fire, it dies forever." Her statement had my shoulders dropping as the realization struck me hard. "You cannot kill her. No one can. Not with her magic now a part of the Nine Realms. Without her, there is no land. You weakened her greatly, but your path wasn't ever to kill her. It's sending her to her tomb, which for her is worse than death."

"I don't like this anymore," I pouted with defeat, crushing me.

"You knew it was impossible to kill her. Wanting her dead is normal after what she's done to you. As well as those you care about. It isn't wrong to wish her dead, but it is unrealistic. We cannot kill Hecate without disastrous repercussions."

"You're saying that if we kill her, it will alter the land?"

"Who would be the 'we' you speak of, Aria?"

"King Karnavious, along with the rest of those she's continually tortured throughout the time your people have been here hiding. Outside of this realm, there's a fight going on and we're losing," I informed with emotion heavy in my tone.

"Her magic is a part of the realms now. Which means you could no sooner eradicate it, then you could remove ours. I understand Hecate has not been easy on King Karnavious. He might not be able to change due to his brokenness. Sometimes, it isn't worth the trouble of trying to glue something back together. You're so young, Aria. I was once young too, and I had to let the man I love go. I had to do so in order to wed Tirsynth. It was who blessed me with your father, which I did for the betterment of our world."

"Knox and I are both broken. He understands me better than anyone else could ever hope to. His edges cut hard, and they're very sharp. However, when he forgets that we're sworn enemies, feeling his walls crumble, if even for a moment, it's worth the pain I've endured."

"You love him?" She spoke softly, but she didn't need me to answer the question. "He's not for you, Aria. He will not survive Hecate's obsession with him. I've seen the future, and he's not in it with you." Her eyes showed genuine sympathy, yet it failed to sway my decision.

"Then I don't want to save the world."

CHAPTER 5
ARIA

The chamber grew thick with tension at my outburst, but I refused to back down. I didn't want anyone else. Knox deserved a future, even if that future wasn't with me. He endured unimaginable hardships to safeguard the Nine Realms, so if there was even a slight possibility of his demise, I would battle to avert it. I'd burn down the realms to save him from that fate.

"You'd throw everything away for his future? A future that might not even include you? He may very well turn against you, Aria. Have you considered that?"

"No, because Knox is loyal to those that he considers family."

"Does he consider you such? Or are you merely something he wishes to own?" she asked carefully.

Her question had me backpedaling, but I wouldn't concede. "I honestly don't know what he considers me, but it doesn't matter to me if he does or doesn't. He's my mate, and if you're asking me to disregard that bond and to allow

Hecate to claim his life, you're going to end up disappointed."

"I understand. Karnavious blood is very addictive, but then, who doesn't relish catching the heart of a dragon? Did you know his bloodline's the only one able to actually shift into dragon form? Like our bloodline, the world fuels their shift, and they're cursed because of the fire in their veins."

"I was told as much," I admitted as I let my guard down a sliver. "The future can be altered by a single deed, Scylla. One choice can change everything."

"It can. That much is true. But could you watch the world burn to save him?" she countered with a calculated look burning in her aqua-colored depths. Reading my mind, she exhaled heavily. "A phoenix doesn't always have a singular mate. Sometimes, we have many." When I opened my mouth to argue, she lifted her hand up for me to allow her to speak. "We don't mate purely for love. Love isn't something our breed desires from another. Sometimes we merely mate to create young, if our previous mate isn't producing young. Others mate for protection, be it their own or for their young. Hell, we've even been known to mate merely for companionship. Our breed does what is needed to ensure new phoenixes are born as often as possible and are protected as well afterward. That you are in love with your dragon is most puzzling to me."

"Maybe we're wrong. Maybe I'm not a phoenix?" I offered in explanation.

Her head dropped back as a clap of laughter escaped her lips. "Your fire burns too brightly inside of you for you to be anything but. I've also seen your flames and know your chaos by heart. I should know, after all, I held that same chaos long before you did. Long before you were ever born, it was mine. I sacrificed my life to kindle those flames into the inferno you now hold inside of you. I knew when I made the sacrifice, that it would eventually bring your soul into existence. I've spent all this time here, waiting for you, my darling."

When my jaw dropped open, she reached over, pressed two fingers to my chin, and closed it.

"I didn't know," I whispered, with regret coating my words.

"In order to bring forth the one prophesied to save the world, they demanded a sacrifice. I traded my life for yours, Aria. I was told what would be required of me, and then shown a path to take. The Fates demand a hefty price for altering the future, which is what I have done. They offered me insight into your life. I was shown your desires, tragedies, and the life you'd live. In order to secure your future, I needed to put aside my desire for vengeance against my enemies. I was told who to mate with, who had to fall so you could rise, and then told I'd be given five trials to pass, which cost me dearly. I've never questioned my choices, nor do I know. Seidr magic isn't without cost, and oftentimes the price is hefty."

Goosebumps spread over my flesh. Had she actually sacrificed her life in order to create mine? Sacrifices were rumored to be made for acquiring souls, but it was unprecedented. In fact, it was forbidden to meddle in the crafting of another's soul. Swallowing past the lump forming in my throat, I struggled to put what she was saying together to see the larger picture.

"It isn't something you'll be able to discern or understand fully, Aria," she stated before nodding toward the serene pool. "Please undress and enter the pool. The land waits for no maiden."

I stripped out of the black, skin-tight outfit, and the moment my feet were submerged in the pool, a tranquility flitted through my entire being. At my soft gasp of shock, Scylla chuckled.

"I felt that inner peace the moment I surrendered to the land, too," she explained before lighting the burners of oil around the pool. "When the Fates tell you what to do, you don't question them. Once you're set on a path with them leading, you follow. Each test they handed me, I did without question. However, some left holes in my soul, as I'd known they would. Some forced me to lie to those I loved most, others forced me into uneasy alliances."

"I don't know if I'm worth all of that," I admitted, hating that anyone had sacrificed anything for me. Even so, I refused to be forced into a corner for something I had never asked for.

"I shall be the judge of that. I had to trust an ancient enemy in order to secure your future. The Karnavious Dragons didn't start out as our enemies. The Fafnir bloodline, at one time, were dragons along with the Karnavious line. Draghana was the last to hold the ability to shift. Her grandmother was Hela, who was rumored to be the sister of both Fenrir the wolf and Jörmungandr, the World Serpent. As you know, she was also the queen of the afterlife realm of Hel."

"Holy shit."

"You say that a lot."

"What do you expect when you're dropping some pretty heavy shit on me?" My eyebrows pushed together as I waited for her reply. Her silvery hair swished around her as she nodded, a sly smile played on her lips.

"As I was saying. Draghana held the ability to shift, which my bloodline lacked. We made up for the short-coming with mana. It created a balance, but balance is a fickle thing. A single misstep can shift it, and Draghana did so by creating life with a mortal man. Dracarius Karnavious wasn't like us, nor did he belong in our world. When he appeared in the Nine Realms, he brought others with him. It ruined the balance as Dracarius and Draghana fought one another over land each desired to be theirs." One handmaiden held a basket out for Scylla, who took it with a genuine smile burning in her turquoise eyes.

"What is that?" I questioned with uncertainty clinging to each word.

"It's the flower petals the land chose for you. The land provides us with what is needed to tether our souls to it. Sunflower petals for your burning soul." She pinched a few and dropped them into the pool of water. "Holy basil for endurance. Sage for cognitive-enhancement and brain function. Lavender to ease the fear growing within you. And last but not least, lemongrass oil. You enjoyed its lemony scent when you were an infant."

"Oh," I whispered as the water became a mixing pot of oils, herbs, and flower petals. "It actually smells fantastic," I admitted as the soothing scents calmed the anxious energy growing in my emotions.

"The land wouldn't cause you discomfort, child. It seeks to engage your soul and forge a deeper connection."

Once she was happy with the amount of herbs and petals she'd sprinkled in, she sat at the edge of the pool, soaking her feet in the soothing water.

"I don't have a choice here. Do I?" My question caused her face to tighten as she considered her reply.

"No. Not unless you don't wish to reach for your birthright. If that's the case, then Hecate will continue to rule the land in your stead. But you can walk away from it and bury your head in the sand if you so choose," she explained bluntly.

"Don't hold back on me now," I muttered before sinking beneath the watery surface. When I opened my eyes and looked up through the swirls of petals, there were several skeletal figures around the pool that weren't there before. I emerged, already swimming back and away from the edge as an ear-splitting scream turned my throat raw.

"Aria!" Scylla shouted before flicking her skeletal hand to send a spray of water in my face. "There's no reason to lose your shit, child."

Her tone held humor, which shouldn't have freaked me out, but it did. What the fuck? One minute, she'd looked like me, then she was freaking Skeleton Barbie! A glance around the pool showed everyone in it was dead, other than me. At least, I fucking hoped I wasn't. Backing up, I held my hands in front of me.

"What the fuck?" The whisper barely registered before I screamed it, louder. "What the fuck?"

"I'm dead. What were you expecting? You're literally inside my tomb, Aria. It's a part of the Kingdom of Fire, which cannot be reached other than on the spiritual plane." She shrugged her shoulders, which freaking crackled.

"You didn't think to warn me! I mean, you're a freaking skeleton, for fuck's sake."

"Would it have made you feel better if we had?" Her tone held humor, as if she'd enjoyed my hysterics.

"Maybe?" Her brows pushed up to her silvery hairline. "It would've fit perfectly on the fuck-it-bucket conversation we just had." Crossing my arms over my naked breasts, I scowled at her and the handmaidens, who snickered. Slowly, as I continued to glare at the lot of them, the anger dissipated.

"Don't be cross with my ladies, Aria. They followed me into the afterlife out of loyalty, which isn't something most have chosen to do."

"That's about the only thing that makes sense at the moment," I uttered beneath my breath. "What do I do to let the land know I'm willing to meld with it?"

"You remember how it felt to merge with the land?" Nodding, I felt my face tightening with pain. I remembered merging with each elemental. I also recalled not surviving a few of them. "It will be a lot like that, then the peace shall come."

"How do the elements work? Because they taught me, they belonged to Hecate, but I know they don't. Much of what I was taught was altered, or rewritten to change everything to fit her views."

Scylla smiled, nodding her head subtly. "You're correct. The elements belong to the Nine Realms and are mana. They're not magic. Witches cannot harness, nor house mana. Therefore, when Aurora asked you to retrieve it, she knew you would be the only one who could take it as well as hold it. Though, I did find watching her attempt to hold the sliver you'd handed her, humorous. Of course, the land took it back rather violently from her." Her tone conveyed disapproval, which was understandable. "You mustn't trust her, Aria. She is of the same cloth that her mother was cut from."

"I know that now," I admitted.

"This will hurt for a while."

"I'm not afraid of pain." I wasn't. Pain was an old bedfellow. In fact, I couldn't remember a time before I'd felt some source of pain churning through my system. "Can you tell me what it will feel like?"

"I could, but I won't. Besides, what I endured won't be the same as what you'll soon feel. Everyone's experience is unique. I can tell you I won't abandon you, though." I found comfort in the knowledge that at least I wouldn't be going through this alone. "First, the pool will bless you for your rebirth. The altar will begin your transformation. It isn't something that happens overnight. Gradually, over time, you'll begin to evolve. Normally, you'd have been blessed in the pool at birth, but distance was an issue. Also, it's hard for the dead to speak to the living. It takes me months to consume enough mana to return from the afterlife."

She climbed from the pool, then knelt beside it, placing her hands on her knees. As she spoke in an ancient language, the water began to spin around me. Lines of bright, glittering, golden hues slid up my arms, then twirled around them. Peering down, I frowned at the runes painting my breasts, marring the unkindness beneath them on my sternum. Below it, the circular design I'd placed on myself to ensure only Knox could father my children refused to allow any of the amber runes to even get near it, which forced a smile on my lips.

The water continually churned, glowing brighter until it hurt to continue staring at it. Using my forearm to shield my eyes, I frowned as a humming noise began inside the chamber. The ladies who'd followed her into death were using singing bowls to send soft vibrations throughout the room. It continued growing louder until I felt the compulsion to cover my ears from the humming. A moment before I would have, the water stopped as quickly as it had begun.

"Climb out of the pool so that you can lie on the altar. It is blessed by Freyja, who promised to hold her daughters during their darkest hours. I was born on the same altar. It's also where I honored the arrangement, which we'd brokered to secure the future in the Nine Realms."

The altar was ivory, with delicate runes carved into the base. Antlers littered the surrounding ground, and their tips glowed with small, swaying flames. In the trees around the altar, swords had been forcefully driven through the trunks and sap flooded the earthen floor. A skull with antlers wrapped in startlingly green vines with flowers adorning them sat at the head of the smooth, ivory slab. At the foot of the slab, there was a burner for the incense, which was filling the air with bergamot and sage.

My heartbeat was erratic as I walked, utterly naked, toward where the altar waited. The sound of it thundering in my ears was deafening as the handmaidens chanted, honoring my sacrifice. I'd like to say I didn't want to tuck tail and run like a bitch, but that would be a lie. I feared what was about to unfold. Not for the reasons a sane person would, of course. I knew I had to reach for my birthright in order to face Hecate. I had come here for that very reason.

I couldn't escape the prophecy I'd been born to bring about. Hecate was a poison upon the land, one which needed to be eradicated. I think I'd always known this was my destiny, even when I'd refused to acknowledge the signs or sensations flowing through me.

I'd been a child back then. The land had warned me of what would become of it should I fail to reach for the power it offered. Back then, I had reached for it, but it had been terrifying. As I'd gotten older, I'd allowed myself to feel the raw, unfiltered power slithering through my veins, but I'd never spoken of it to anyone—ever. I'd known it wasn't normal to pull from a land I'd never been in before. Even without the original families in Haven Falls opening the portal, I felt the call of the realms beckoning me home.

Once, Aurora had spoken of sensing a great, untapped power source in front of me, and the land had recoiled from her as if her presence offended it. I'd returned to hiding in the corners, listening to the magic as it told me of the land I'd been forged from. As if they had cut me from the rocks and sculpted me to life by the essence of the world. I'd felt the rocky shores of Norvalla with my fingertips. Danced through the barren land of the Kingdom of Fire, uncaring that the skeletal remains swayed with me. On the highest peak of the Dark Mountains, I'd felt the wind beating against my cheeks as I soared through the breeze, sailing over the great white oak trees.

"Aria," Scylla whispered.

I lifted watery eyes to hers as I realized I'd never been alone. It wasn't the land who'd been beside me, though.

"It was you," I cried as tears broke free, rolling down my cheeks. "You were with me."

"Of course, I was with you. I've always been with you, Aria Primrose. As Aurora and Freya tried to end your life, I kept your soul protected. They may have taken away your life briefly, but you were reborn as something else. Something stronger than what I returned as upon my death, even. Every morning after they'd attempted to extinguish your flame, the sun bathed your cold, lifeless body on that altar, and that spark rekindled stronger than before. You were so beautiful. Neither Aurora nor Freya noticed the speckles of gold shimmering in your pretty turquoise eyes. Lost in their need for power, they failed to see the phoenix peering back at them. The land allowed me to remain with you until you entered the Nine Realms, and your journey to heal it began."

"You could've stopped the pain they forced me to endure." I hated that she'd been privy to every sick and twisted thing they'd put me through. "You could've told me Aurora was my mother and allowed the torture to continue."

"What would it have changed?"

"I don't know. I might have understood why I had to endure hell at the hands of those I loved? Maybe then I wouldn't have felt so much betrayal when it happened." Chewing my lip, I released it with a popping sound. "I could have tried to get back here sooner. Instead, I'd endured hell as I walked alone down a dark, dreary path of isolation."

"A path you had to walk alone down to see the unjustness of what Hecate was doing. Without feeling the pain, you wouldn't be so willing to fight against it, Aria. We are so much of what we live through, or endure. Those scars you hide, they're what crafted you into the fierce, just woman you've become. Besides, if I'd told you what she was, you wouldn't have been with the others at the House of Magic when Knox Karnavious forced the others back here. I am the one who ensured he'd be the one to bring you into the Nine Realms. My guard personally handed the message to the council residing over the Nine Realms at a specific time and date, which ensured he couldn't murder you. My guard carried that letter with him until the exact moment it was needed, then delivered it to them. In it, I shared one detail ensuring they feared repercussions of what would unfold if they failed to hold Knox Karnavious' blade from your neck. I've planned everything right down to who brought you through the portal. I forced you to see the evil within the realms, to discover the rot seeping from the core of those drunk-on power and authority to murder others weaker than themselves." Her eyes swam with unshed tears. The familiarness of her made sense now, which helped me feel safe in her presence.

"I know it wasn't the life you deserved, but too many have paid the price for your existence. I couldn't allow their sacrifices to be in vain. For that, I am eternally sorry."

The moment her speech ended, pain frayed through my entire frame as I twisted and jackknifed on the altar. The scream that escaped pierced my ears as fire burned over my flesh, scorching it as tears ran unchecked down my cheeks. Scylla's hand slid into mine and then held it through the agony, tearing my innards apart. My spine lifted as electric pulses flooded me from foot to head. Water filled my lungs until it gurgled in my throat, exploding out of my lips. Wind slammed into my mind, then whipped against my flesh until it cut it from my bones. Earth rocked through me like a great earthquake, forcing my teeth to chatter through the agonizing torture.

It felt like hours before the pain finally lessened. The only constant thing throughout it was the pressure of Scylla's palm against my own. Torment forced through me at the behest of the land, but in exchange for the torture I'd endured, power rushed through me. An endless well of it churned inside my soul. Where I'd felt misplaced before, I now felt a strange sensation of coming home.

"Welcome home, Aria Primrose, heir to the throne of fire, and true queen of the Nine Realms. We've waited a long time for you," she whispered. "My time here is almost up, so let's do something about your nakedness. I can't have you returning to greet our people in nothing but your birthday suit. What kind of grandmother would I be if I sent you back there without the air of a true queen?"

"Will I ever see you again?" I whispered, past the swelling of my tongue.

"I am always with you, child. I am the air beneath your sails, and the wind when it ruffles through your silvery hair. But to answer your question? I will be there when you prepare to ascend to your throne. I wouldn't miss you reaching for your birthright, for anything."

"What about Fennia and Fennix?" I questioned with worry as I sensed them watching from the shrubbery.

"Once they chose you as their master, it sealed their fate to be yours. I wouldn't worry too much about the critters. They're very resourceful."

CHAPTER 6
KNOX

Aria had been gone much longer than we'd agreed upon. The shit I'd discovered since she'd slipped from my bedchamber was terrifying. If we were correct, the new realm wasn't the same as our own. Many things about it varied, but what those things were hadn't been laid out in the large book. The books we'd requested of the library had us pouring through volume after volume of texts. Nothing explained how to reach the realm, or where she'd be spit out once she'd concluded her business there.

The fire crackled from the fireplace, which was the only other sound within the library. I used to love the silence of it, but Aria had ruined it with her sweet sounds. Now, I craved the chaos she'd created in my space. I both hated and adored the little imp who'd ruined my place and upended my world.

A knock at the door forced my mind from the woman who consumed it wholly. Killian and Brander both entered, their faces both strained with tension.

"I take it you don't come barring good news?"

Killian's snort forced my stomach to churn as he tossed down a bloodied doll. Picking up the small doll crafted from animal hide, I turned it over in my hand.

"They butchered the entire village. The witches spared no one, not even the babes." Killian's words caused my stomach to flip before bile burned against the back of my throat.

"Claddagha?" I asked, praying he hadn't discovered the same at the village on our borderlands. A quick nod of his head forced anger to roil through me. "Everyone?"

Brander sat in the chair across from me, tossing a soiled banner onto the table between us. "Claddagha was worse than the three villages before it, brother." His heavy sigh filled the room with a tinge of despair before he braced his elbows on his knees, peering over the table. "After removing the heart from the body, they then string them up to display the corpse. They pile up the hearts at the entrance of the town after removing them. Whether it's displayed as a warning to those thinking to disavow the new high queen, or a gift to her, is unclear." Nausea churned through me at Brander's words.

Glancing at the map pinned to the wall, I studied the path they'd taken through the Beltane Circle, where I'd forced Aria to marry me. They hadn't stopped there, though. Instead, they'd continued on to Vraegary and entered the forest lining the rocky terrain of the mountains situated farther west of them.

Anyone who opposed the self-appointed, newly crowned high queen was left dead on the path they had trailed through the realms. Aria hadn't been gone days before cries to dethrone me went out far and wide. Shortly after, they'd occupied the capital, taking control of it from me. I didn't care about titles or the politics that went into being the high king. That wasn't what had left the sour taste in my mouth. It was the inhabitants of the realm who were being needlessly slaughtered by the new ruler with no remorse.

The high queen didn't consider anyone who didn't share a bloodline with her worthy of living. Kings and queens often became monsters from the small taste of having a realm bow before them. But those who held dominion over every realm as one? They were corrupted the most by the desire for the world to bow before them, uncaring if it meant slaughtering those who refused to bend the knee.

I had constructed the counsel exclusively for that reason. One entity should never hold all the power or influence. They'd kept the balance of power even throughout the land, which forced me to abide by their laws. Not because I feared being rebuked or overshadowed by their laws. It kept me in check because I allowed it. Well, I had until they'd become Aurora's mouthpiece. Now, they were being hunted down like prey by order of the queen who they'd chosen to crown in my place.

Did I care they were feeling the same travesty they'd forced Aria to feel when they'd allowed others to hunt her down? Not necessarily. Should I have fought to keep the high throne? Maybe, maybe I could've pretended I cared a little about the title. But I didn't. I couldn't even drum up enough to give a fuck to bother myself with it right now.

Aria's absence, and the hole she'd left within me had

distracted me. A hole so deep and vacant without her here to fill it that I'd walked away from Laveran and hadn't looked back. Not even once. Not until news of the witches overthrowing the council, then declaring one of their own as the newly appointed high queen reached Dorcha. That was something I couldn't ignore, even though I was doing just that.

My stare slid from Laveran to the Dark Mountains, and my stomach plummeted. If the witches continued forward, they'd reach the mountain passes, which was the last place Aria was inside of the Nine Realms. If they marched through the edge of the forest, then veered northeast, they'd be at the kingdom where Aria's people remained, hidden and protected by magic both she and I had placed to prevent their discovery.

"They're making their way toward Vraegary, which means they're now marching to the pass within the Dark Mountains." I pondered as my mind was fueled by worry. "If they've been scrying for Aria's location, that's where it would take them. It would hit on the last place she was within the Nine Realms. They're hunting my girl."

"That's a fucking problem," Killian muttered, before scrubbing his palm over his face.

Nodding my head, I agreed with his sentiment on the matter. Turning toward the crackling flame, I studied the delicate features of the woman dominating my mind. So much had happened since the night that she'd walked right into the engagement party, terrified I'd turn against her. As if I'd ever chance losing her again? Not fucking likely.

Aria had changed me so profoundly, that I no longer

cared to think of a world where she didn't exist. She'd healed the wounds I'd allowed to control my direction, shifting the course until it aligned our paths together as one.

"That's a huge fucking problem." Sitting up, I slid my regard between both men, even as the crease in my forehead deepened. "If the realm spits her out where she went in, Aria will end up falling right into their laps."

"I can dispatch men to the passes to defend it from them accessing it, or being there when Aria returns," Brander offered.

"We can't afford to be spread that thin."

As it stood, I had deployed men to guard the castle where Aria's people were hiding. Unfortunately, I couldn't afford to be spread thin with Hecate making waves with her needless murdering sprees. Not without Aria being here to access her power to deflect the attacks occurring frequently throughout the realms.

"Hecate and Aurora are both making moves to prevent Aria from rising to power. Aurora is afraid of what Griffon will do once he's aware of his daughter's existence. I don't share her fear. I think he knew about her long before anyone else did. In fact, I think he knew what she'd become, but also knew the part she'd play in preventing Hecate from total domination of the realms."

"Lore said you'd discovered a book written in the first language?" Brander inquired as he leaned back, placing his booted foot on the table. My gaze lowered to it, even as he removed it from my table.

"I did," I admitted after a moment of silence passed between the room. "I think Scylla Prometheus died when she used the magic of seidr to manipulate the future. It spoke of a savior, one born in the darkest hour, to deliver salvation to the Nine Realms. At one time, Scylla was friends with Draghana Karnavious, or as close as two warring queens could be. In the tome I found, it claimed that in order to change the fate of the realms, each queen was forced to sacrifice something deemed worthy in the eyes of the Fates to forge two parts of one prophecy."

Killian whistled before standing and moving to the decanter of whiskey. "You're saying that both queens agreed in order to forge Aria?" Returning with glasses, he placed them on the table before pouring two fingers of brandy into them. "How would that even be possible? They couldn't have known she would ever exist. Both died long before she was ever born."

"Seidr magic is used to sway outcomes, or the future. It was widely known that Scylla could use it to wage battle. I think she used it to save her people. If I'm right, Scylla forged an alliance with our lines, one which forced both of our people to unite. The only time our people have been at peace with the Kingdom of Fire, was right before the beginning of the Last War of Fire. Scylla Prometheus died in a skirmish according to the tome. Though, they blamed us even though we'd been at peace with them."

"You're saying Scylla forced the Fates to create a savior, which is Aria?"

"Seidr doesn't offer a timeline for when something unfolds." I rubbed my temples. "It gives the user a price which must be paid, then throughout time, it weaves the fibers until the perfect solution is brought into existence."

"That's a fucking lot of weaving."

Leaning forward, I accepted the glass he offered, then continued explaining what I'd stumbled upon. "No, Aria is merely one aspect of the prophecy and it doesn't mention her defeating Hecate alone. She is one piece on a board, which has many other pieces already set into motion. The book stated that in order to find a savior, Scylla and a person from the Kingdom of Fire had to make sacrifices. A son born of the first people through a Hecate witch's womb. We know without a doubt that Aria's the one Scylla forged through the means of seidr magic. The question is, who was the second being forged through Draghana's sacrifice?"

"You're saying Aria isn't the only one prophesied to end Hecate?" Brander pondered out loud, his finger causing his glass to whistle as he slowly rubbed it over the rim.

"If the book is correct, then Aria's merely one half of the power needed to end the goddess." Heat rushed through me as the image of Aria fucking me sliced through my mind. The girl was mine, period. I didn't give a fuck what preordained bullshit our ancestors had put into work. I wouldn't be sharing my girl with anyone else. Fate be damned. "It forced Draghana to sacrifice something for what she molded into existence through seidr magic—"

"I know we all assumed it was Hecate's doing, with us not being able to take dragon form. But what if Draghana's sacrifice was our ability to take our feral forms?" Brander questioned as he cut me off. "If she was the last to take dragon form, maybe she gave up it to protect her people."

"It is possible," I agreed with his perceptive reasoning. "But we need to consider Dracarius as well. After all, he held the ability to foretell the future and shapeshifted into a dragon in order to breed with Draghana. I think they prevented us from shifting, but it's weakening. It is possible that it wasn't what she sacrificed. In fact, I don't think she would remove our ability to protect ourselves or that of future generations. Whatever she did, she did it after Hecate was within the Nine Realms. I don't believe she'd leave us defenseless against the goddess demanding we concede to her reign of terror throughout the land. I think Dracarius bound our ability to shift in order to protect us from ourselves. Whatever Draghana sacrificed is irrelevant right now. It's who she sacrificed it for, that is."

"You're saying both women sacrificed something in order to create one weapon?" Killian asked with a perplexed look tightening over his face. "You?"

"I don't think so," I admitted. "I can wield her magic. That isn't a question, but it takes a lot of effort for me to manage siphoning enough to do serious damage. It doesn't come freely to me, which it should if Draghana sacrificed to create the second half of the weapon designed to force the goddess back to her tomb." It was irrefutable. Acting as a conduit for Aria's magic was difficult. If they'd used seidr magic to forge me, it wouldn't be so.

"You think the one prophesied to be the conductor of Aria's magic is within the new realm?" Brander questioned as a soft rap of knuckles sounded from outside the library. He waited until Lore and Greer both entered the spacious room before continuing.

"It's possible, but in order for her to be what they prophesied, she had to reach for the crown. Once she reaches for her throne, it will set everything else into motion. Once Aria reaches for her crown, whatever the old gods promised Draghana will come to pass in all the realms. Her going there was inevitable. If it wasn't, I'd have prevented her from leaving us." Greer's eyes met mine briefly before he sat down beside me.

"It's rather amusing that you think you could prevent her from going, Knox. I assure you of this, that girl's chaos in motion. Aria Prometheus is the chaos effect. What Scylla and Draghana did, it's the butterfly effect. A small action that produced something larger. Aria is small, but her impact within the Nine Realms won't be. Scylla wasn't selfless. She was a great queen skilled in both warfare and seidr magic," he said with a sly look in his eyes.

"That much I'll agree with," I uttered.

"After all, Scylla knew what she was doing when she set forth the prophecy pertaining to the child born of the first people. Scylla was among the first people within the Nine Realms. They're mirrored after the nine worlds in Norse mythology. Her blood houses the gift of fertility through it, which is how she could influence and design the matter of Aria's birth. Scylla didn't blindly select Aria as a champion. Instead, she molded her from magic and carefully built her into what would be needed to end the suffering of her people. Everything Aria is, or will be, isn't by chance. It's by design."

"How do you know that?" I queried as Lore picked up the volume I'd been reading earlier and began tossing the ancient tome into the air. "Lore, that's older than you are. Put it down." Greer glanced across the room at Lore, smirking as he begrudgingly placed the heavy tome back on the table.

"You're not the only one who has access to the

library, Knox. Do you think I waste away pining for you when you go out to safeguard against attacks? I pity you if you truly thought I did so. I enjoy history, but I love learning about the little queen driving you up the wall. Your pretty peasant is a mystery to even those of us who know it all." Dusting an invisible speck of lint from his tunic, he returned his attention to me. "If you'd have been paying attention instead of fantasizing about Aria, you'd have read the part where Scylla didn't merely call upon the old gods. She called on the Norns. The beings who shaped the course of destinies from two beings into that of one."

"What does that mean for Aria?" I demanded, as emotion shot through me. Fear of losing her after I'd finally learned to see more than my anger. I'd never craved to be bound to anyone. Definitely not as badly as I wanted Aria to be tethered to me.

"It means, you dolt, that she's destined to discover who she is and then, once she has, whoever is connected to her will grasp onto the thread. Once they do, it will either intertwine their destinies and souls together, or create inner turmoil until both rip it from their souls to free themselves of the connection. The Norns were both malevolent and benevolent maidens. Which one answered Scylla's call remains unknown."

"Are you telling me Scylla was unaware of *which* type of Norn answered her fucking plea before she sacrificed god only knows what in order to create Aria?" If that were true, it meant Aria could be malevolent, as well. If what Greer said was factual, it meant she might turn into the monster the Nine Realms feared she'd become. Which would leave us with a new, stronger, more calculated monster running rampant through the world.

"It's impossible to know which type answered her call. I can tell you that the malevolent Norns enjoyed causing tragic events, while the benevolent Norns were both kind and protective. If you're asking if either taints Aria, then the answer is no. She's neither. That girl is the monster you and others created. They couldn't influence her any more than I could. Who and what they are isn't the issue at hand. It's who they twined the thread of fate to, which should worry you the most. If the latter of the two held the thread, then Aria would know much more tragedy before she unravels it, severing the thread. Aria will have to decide whether she wants to intertwine her fate with someone else or cut the thread that connects them together. But if Aria breaks the thread, she may lose her own life."

The blood humming through my veins stilled, then began thundering in my head. I wouldn't allow her to cut shit if it ended her life. Nothing was worth that happening, even if it meant abandoning her. I wanted her with every fiber of my being. I knew I didn't deserve her after the shit I'd done to her, but I planned to do whatever it took to ensure she remained mine. Unless the cost was her life.

Without that girl, the world held no value to me. I'd rather watch it burn to ashes than live without her light burning within the realms. If given the choice between her life, and saving this world? I'd choose her. If I couldn't have her, so be it, then. I'd walk away to ensure she survived at all costs, even my happiness. I had been raised to become a king since I came into this world. But it had also forced me to sacrifice what I wanted for most of my life. It was ruled by a fundamental element, all pertaining to my reign. As king, my wishes and wants came dead last to the entire kingdoms. They had taught me that since my father had told me what would be expected of me. She'd be another thing I'd sacrificed for the greater good.

"Stop that," Greer growled, forcing me out of my mind. "You haven't lost her yet. I doubt you can easily sway her to give you up. The difference here is, you're both fighting for one another. Aria didn't leave you for another, Knox. She left to discover who she was and where she came from. Don't you give up on her merely because you're uncertain if she'll end up tethered to another? I doubt she'd ever allow anyone other than herself to choose her path, let alone a preordained destiny not of her own making. That thread? It doesn't attach to her pussy, either. It's merely a connection, one she'll decide how deeply embedded into her soul she'll allow it to touch or link with."

Greer stood, then sauntered to the whiskey where he poured himself two fingers of bourbon. Swirling it in his glass, he sniffed the amber liquid before pegging me with an arrogant stare.

"The issue at hand is this: Time isn't the same between their realm and ours. There's no telling exactly how much time has passed there. I'd also advise you to worry about her brothers. Not all will be so willing to step aside and let the youngest *daughter* of the Prometheus bloodline sit upon their throne."

His words forced tension to fill the space we occupied within the library. A quick glance at both Killian and Brander told me they'd felt the same fear churning within them as I did. Lore, on the other hand, was Lore. His eyes lifted as they met mine, then slid to Greer, who frowned as Lore's brows shot up and a smirk pulled up the corners of his lips. Then he broke the silence with the question churning through all our minds.

"So, how do we go get my girl back? Daddy needs to be sure his future baby momma is safe. Can't have her having all the fun, either. I mean, I get she needed to do this, even if it was a stupid idea. But think about this, gents. If Daddy Lore rides in on a stallion to save the pretty princess? Shit, Aria may saddle up and ride me like a cowgirl in reverse while milking my balls," Lore stated as he turned his head to peer at a picture of the magazine he held. "I don't know who this Marilyn Monroe is, but baby girl is on fire! Bet she'd be fun between the sheets. Think she's still single? Because I'm going to be honest here, I wouldn't mind rolling around with her. Hell, I don't even care if it's in the grass or mud."

My palm scrubbed over my face at his inability to stay on one subject. Lore was much younger than the rest of us, but his brain had its own thought process, which bordered on chaos and strategic planning. Unfortunately, the former was normally holding the reins. The others chortled before tossing back their whiskey while buying time to find a polite way to break Lore's heart.

"If by sheets you mean a body bag? I'm certain Norma Jean's currently turning in hers after hearing your crudeness, Lore." Greer's rebuttal had Brander and Killian chuckling as Lore's frown deepened.

"Who the hell is Norma Jean?" Lore asked with confusion stamped over his face.

"Marilyn Monroe was a stage name. Norma Jean was her actual name," Greer explained with the patience of a saint. "I swear, you and peasant have more in common than she and the king do. For the record, she's off-limits. I'll not have you tarnishing her image with your . . . juices. Find someone other than the Blonde Bombshell's image to deface."

"Is there a way into the new realm?" I interjected during a moment of silence between them. Both missed Aria and her sass. Greer missed her litany of slander, while Lore missed her down-to-earth attitude and rattles.

"If there is, well, you'd find the answer you seek here. This library houses information pertaining to every land within its cosmos, but also every magical being living in them as well. If it were my girl who'd gone traipsing off to a strange place, I'd be devouring every book pertaining to the creation of it. Then I'd tear it apart until I knew how to enter it as well. But that's just me," Greer stated.

"I've searched every annex in this place. There's no mention of the new realm, not that I've discovered." Did he think I wasn't scouring the entire library for any hint on how to reach her? From the second I'd felt her leaving this place, I'd become obsessed with forcing her back here, to me.

Greer shrugged indifferently before finishing the two fingers of bourbon in a single drink. "Then you're not looking hard enough, King Karnavious. If you want her? Fight for her. That girl's worth fighting to keep. If you want her, then fight. If you don't, then you'll only have yourself to blame when your prideful ass is alone with no one but your miserable, ill-tempered disposition for company."

"Damn, Greer," Brander muttered. "At least use some lube before you fuck his heart that hard. He intends to fight for Aria. It's Knox. The poor bastard is infatuated with her. Shit, we all are. Knox knows that if he doesn't fight for her, we'll all be willing to take his place. He isn't about to lose her, not after we forced him to face what we've all known."

"And what is that?" I demanded as his words caused Lennox to rear his head, preparing to rattle until they bowed before him.

"That Aria is your queen. She's your other half, asshole. That girl was born to bring you to your knees. But she's also the one who's helped heal your wounds." Brander's eyes slipped to obsidian as Lennox released a soft rattle, as if he respected my brother's overall opinion of Aria.

"He's not wrong, Knox," Killian agreed with his eyes downcast from Lennox, who sat beneath the surface of the veneer I wore. "As someone who was against her to start with? You know I hate admitting to ever being incorrect. But I was about Aria. She makes you a better king. That girl makes us all see beyond the hate we held against witches. Fuck, you know I tried to hate her. It was impossible to hate her, though. She sings to babies and carries them as if they're her own. She's the queen, to your king, and there's not another I'd approve of sitting beside you on the throne of Norvalla." Killian shoved his fingers through his messy hair and smiled. "So, where do we look for the answers to gain entrance into the new realm? Because I sure as fuck don't intend to watch you sulk until she returns. Besides, my guess is this within that realm? There are other women who rattle and purr. I'm glad you got one, but that doesn't mean I'm not jealous that you did." The other men snorted their agreement as I rose, smiling.

"Then we best get to it, assholes. If Greer is correct. Which, we know, he normally is, Aria's walking into a hostile environment. She assumed they'd welcomed her with open arms. But that might not be the case."

"Have you met Aria?" Lore asked with one eyebrow pushed up to his hairline. "Because that little momma isn't about the 'fuck around life lifestyle'. My future woman is more about the 'find out what happens when you do.' We should pray for them. They'll underestimate her. Aria's dainty like a flower, but that is a gross miscalculation. Nah, Aria's the nuclear option. And when she chooses violence?" He shivered, as if imagining what she'd do. "Let's just say if they force her to that point, we won't need a doorway into their realm. They'll be rushing out of there in hordes, which'll be a hard thing to miss for anyone watching for her to return to the realms."

CHAPTER 7
ARIA

Scylla's handmaidens had given me a flowing white gown with gold thread sewn within the waistline and bust. Matching suns pinned a flowing cape to my shoulders, and my unbound hair cascaded to my hips. I had felt the heat of the armlets that Scylla had placed on me to symbolize her approval of my claim to the throne.

Still, the entire outfit looked like something stolen from the *Game of Thrones* wardrobe.

The moment I reappeared, I found myself surrounded by hedges. After a moment of uncertainty, my feet began moving toward the palace discernable in the distance. I rounded a corner and then crashed into a solid, unmovable frame.

The hands that shot out to steady me sent a shock rushing through me, forcing me to jerk away from the unfamiliar touch. A warrior studied my face with interest simmering in turquoise eyes. His silver hair was cut shorter than most men wore it here. There was a braid, which held midnight strands woven behind his ear. He almost resembled Henry Cavill in his role of the Witcher, only with more pronounced features and far colder eyes.

"Your father is looking for you, Your Highness," he said in a deep, gravelly tone. The moment he stepped back to allow me to pass, I realized he was the same warrior I'd locked eyes with in the courtyard.

"I . . ." What was I supposed to say had happened? That I fell down a rabbit hole and had a chat with my dead-by-not-really dead grandmother? Fennix and Fennia chose that moment to appear and rub against the warrior's boots. A soft smile played on my lips. A bubble of laughter escaped before I could prevent it, which caused a soft grunt to expel from the man. "I'm afraid I got lost down a rabbit hole."

"A rabbit hole, Your Majesty?" he questioned with a look of confusion tugging on his handsome features.

"My name is Aria," I offered, dodging his question.

The warrior didn't offer a name, which left me awkwardly standing before him. Instead of waiting to see if he scoffed at me, I started down the path without a backward glance at him.

"I'm afraid you're going the wrong way," he called to my back. Spinning around, I felt heat scorching my cheeks. "If you'll follow me, I will take you to your father."

"Please," I muttered with annoyance, lathering the word.

"If we hurry, maybe we can stop your colorful friend from threatening the king's life for the thirteenth time tonight."

"I'm honestly shocked she's only threatened him a

dozen times. I expected the count to be much higher," I returned with exhaustion sinking into my bones.

"You're not fearful of her overstepping and threatening a king's life? Or losing her head for doing so?"

"It isn't me who should be worried. We came here under a white flag for the duration of time we're here. I fail to see what one girl screaming obscenities could harm. Not if they don't want a problem, anyway."

"Are you normally such a brat?"

"Are you normally such an ass?" I shot back with ire rising in my veins as I stomped forward. "I've endured the trials to reach the kingdom. It took days to do so. During that time, I didn't sleep or eat. Then I was sucked into a crystal and taken to God only knows where. Excuse me if I'm a little short-fused after having the land shock, burn, shake, and whip the ever-loving shit out of me."

"That isn't a reason to be rude to someone offering to assist you, Your Highness." The asshole folded his arms over his wide chest, daring me to argue further.

My stomach growled loudly, which caused those sinfully turquoise-colored eyes to drop to the sweeping V-line of the gown. He seemed to dissect every inch of exposed flesh while I cursed Scylla's choice of attire. Returning the favor, I slid my regard over the expanse of his powerful chest until it landed on a round medallion. On it, twin phoenixes were perched opposite of one another. Both were grasping at the sun, which resembled a sunflower.

"Follow. Let us feed you so that you may retire for the night, Your Majesty." At his low bow, I stifled a smile. His thinned lips told me he wasn't impressed with me wandering alone after dark. Either he didn't like me or he didn't trust me, but no matter which, neither was my problem.

No sooner had we rounded the next corner, than a flash of silver shot toward my face. Another one moved toward the first as the thundering sound of steel clashing steel tore through the gardens. An arm caged me against the powerful body of the warrior behind me.

"Unhand me this instant!" I demanded as emotion churned through me. I'd felt the asshole to the very marrow of my being as if an invisible thread connected us somehow. The first man didn't remove his arm, but the warrior who'd struck at me grappled for words at the sharp end of the warrior's sword.

"You dare strike against the princess?" he growled, threat flooding his every word.

The soldier on the ground was evidently at a loss for words, sputtering them out. "No, I thought it was merely you, Zyion! I was catching you off guard to win the earlier game we'd played. You have to believe that I did not know you'd located the princess. I swear it on my oath to the king!" The warrior dropped to his knees and awkwardly began kissing the hemline of my dress as he pleaded for mercy.

"It was a mistake. No harm was done," I offered, much to the disagreement of the warrior at my back. "Release me, now," I hissed through clenched teeth. The hand clasping me firmly loosened and started to fall away, but as it lowered to my hip, a thumb trailed over the exposed skin. Then he stepped away, offering me much-needed distance. "Please, get up. It was merely an accident."

"Return to the barracks, Rayson. Report to the sergeant for being out past curfew and mention your slight against the princess. Tomorrow, you'll tend the stables."

"That's unnecessary," I argued, but the younger warrior rose to his feet, and then vanished from sight.

"Do not intervene between me and the recruits, Your Majesty. It is not your place to do so. You're not the king, unless I am mistaken about what lies beneath the thin bodice of your gown?"

"They're called boobs, block head," I muttered before starting toward the path. "I'll find my father myself. You're dismissed, or whatever they say." Holding my hand up, I waved at him like an adolescent child throwing a fit. His chuckle trailed me as I wove through the maze of shrubs lining the pathway. I stopped at the fountain in the center of the garden as the sound of Aden's raised voice pulled me toward the entrance.

"Find her, now! She cannot have vanished. I'll not have my future pet out here lost, or worse, rutting with the trash. We need her on our side if we're ever to return home again. Plus, I cannot ascend the throne without her. Once I've ascended, she can be punished for such things." The bottom dropped out of my stomach as repulsion tightened my throat. That slimy little fucker was about to find out I wasn't *that* bitch.

"Good thing the princess isn't hard on the eyes since you'll also need to bed the bitch," a masculine voice joined the others.

"The princess is a means to an end. Griffon may be blinded by his daughter and willing to look beyond her blatant disregard for our people, but I am not," Aden snapped coldly. "Aria Hecate is not loyal to this kingdom, nor can she be allowed to lead our people. Aria willingly traveled with the enemy, which proved she's a dragon's whore. I may wed her, but she'll never hold authority over the Kingdom of Fire. I won't allow it, ever. Once we're wed, her power becomes mine to wield."

"Eavesdropping is beneath you, princess," the guard I'd dismissed whispered against my ear as his hand clamped over my lips. I jerked back and let out a startled scream against his palm. "Stop struggling against me and be silent. Don't make me skewer the prince tonight. Not only would it be tediously messy, but would also not look good for either of us if your intended fiancé ended up dead by my blade." After he put some distance between us and Aden and his men, he removed his hand from my mouth.

"Care to explain what he meant when he said he intended to *wed* me?" I hissed through clenched teeth. To his credit, the poor guy looked uncomfortable, but answered, anyway.

"Aden is your father's choice for your hand. Shouldn't you be rejoicing that he chose the most loyal, eligible bachelor for his only daughter."

"Fuck that shit," I growled as I touched my fingertips to my lips. "I'd rather marry a pineapple and ride it into battle like a steed." His eyes sparkled at my vehemently hissed words.

"You are a lot like your grandmother. A pretty face did not sway her either. A word of warning, if I may." I nodded. "No one will accept your claim without you earning it first because you're an outsider here. It won't matter that you're supposed to be our savior, everyone is aware that you're sleeping with the enemy. That won't win over your people."

"And I should listen to you, why? I don't know you, nor do I trust you. So, who do I have the privilege of speaking to?" I asked, exhausted by the insanity of whiplash this place was handing out. Wasn't enduring that torture enough?

"I'm the head of your guard and the one man who swore to protect you from harm. I am Zyion, Head of the Queen's Guard, and Crown Prince of the Vanir. I was your grandmother's guard, protector, and confidant for her entire life. Griffon isn't against you, but his brothers won't step aside for an outsider to steal the throne from beneath them. They'll band together against you and easily win the vote of the people. I hope you didn't plan to claim it merely by strolling in, Aria."

"I didn't assume it would be easy, no. I also never intended to claim the throne. Scylla told me I didn't have a choice. According to her, if I don't claim my birthright, which is the throne, Hecate won't be forced from the land until I do so."

"Then it seems as if you need me after all," he stated.

"I didn't say that. In fact, I don't need your help at all, Zyion of the Blah-blah-blah," I muttered crossly. If the prick expected me to remember his titles at the sheer level of exhaustion I'd hit, he was mistaken. "Good night, sir." I dodged his hand as it shot out to catch my arm, but then we both paused at the sound of footsteps. A second later, Aden rounded the bend and chuckled joyfully. It took effort not to gag at the sight of him. Zyion noted it and stifled a chuckle as Aden and his crew came into sight.

"Aria," he whispered, and my eyes couldn't roll hard enough at the mocked relief lacing his tone. "Your father and I have been worried sick. You vanished without so much as a trace of where you went."

"I was with Scylla Prometheus," I disclosed as the men with him watched my every move. They were also alert and watchful of Zyion, who smoothly stepped in front of me. The tension grew, making my hackles rise. He didn't trust them any more than I did.

"I was just taking the princess back to her father," Zyion stated firmly.

Aden closed the distance between us and slid his hand behind my back. "That won't be necessary. I'll escort her back myself."

CHAPTER 8
ARIA

Aden's hand on the small of my back made my skin crawl, and I had to force myself not to shake it off or step away. His men had surrounded me until I could not see anything beyond their stalky figures as they marched me toward a large, opulent entry to the palace. The eyes of the men on either side of me kept sliding over the exposed flesh as we moved past the sentries stationed outside of the dining hall.

I swallowed the uneasy feeling creeping through me as Aden's palm touched the exposed flesh on my lower back. The brush of his skin against mine was abhorrent, and again, I had to remind myself not to step away. Until I could get a better idea of how powerful they were, I was stuck playing docile princess.

It wasn't until Aden began throwing out taunts that I knew for sure that Zyion had followed us. Aden said something to the warrior about training exercises scheduled for the morning, but Zyion didn't take the bait. Lowering my focus to the floor, we moved over. I noted Zyion's black

99

combat boots, which were unlike the ones these men wore. After rolling my gaze up his muscular thighs outlined beneath the chausses, I let it linger on the cloth material between his tights.

My brow furrowed as I forced myself to keep my eyes moving up to the hauberk that reminded me of what the Templar Knights had once worn into battle throughout the Crusades. I wasn't certain what emotion Zyion had churning inside of me, but his presence made me feel safe. As if he'd defend me if the men sought to manhandle me. When I finally made it up to his face, striking turquoise-colored eyes with flecks of gold scattered throughout the irises met mine.

Aden stopped before an expansive set of double doors and issued orders for the guards to open them for us. The sound of them closing behind us forced fresh unease to flutter down my spine.

The hall we entered was immense and filled with opulence. High ceilings were decorated with stained-glass threaded throughout the stonework. Crown molding the color of obsidian ran the length of the chamber, and blood-red marbled flooring with silver veins laced throughout was under every footfall. The large stained-glass windows reflected the silhouettes of both dragons and phoenixes throughout the space.

I felt my uneasiness grow as I felt the eyes seeking to find me. My heartbeat thundered loudly in my head, even as I caught the eyes of a small child, and offered him a smile. The boy squealed with delight, which caused his enjoyment to be contagious, even with how overly tired I was. The scent of roasted meats, sweet bread, and a bevy of other savory and sugary goods had my stomach rumbling.

"I discovered the princess wandering the gardens alone, Griffon." Zyion snorted in response. "Something to add, Vicious?"

My gaze wandered to Zyion, expecting some kind of reaction to the title. If it offended Zyion, he brushed it off completely. The warrior's attention remained on Griffon, who ignored both men as he waited for me to speak. I stepped forward, but when he spotted the armlets I wore, his features tightened. Esme, on the other hand, was sitting on the opposite side of the table, glowering at me with two burly guards behind her.

I eyed the guards, then scrunched up my face. Esme merely shrugged, then grabbed a leg of meat, and bit into it, still glaring my way.

"I'm sure you're starving, Aria. Please, sit with me and eat," Griffon offered. Aden and Zyion continued to glare at one another while the king worried himself by seating me.

"Thank you, Griffon."

"His title was earned, Aria. You will address him as such," Aden reprimanded. "It is considered a slight to ignore titles. We have much to teach you, my darling."

"I do believe you addressed him by such a moment ago. I was merely following your lead, my dearest Aden," I said in a saccharine tone, which had Zyion's lips twitching in my peripheral. Griffon moved toward one of the guards, and the moment he did, I looked Aden dead in the eyes. "I'm so sorry. The lack of sleep must be getting to me."

"I am ashamed of my behavior, sweetest one," he gushed. I turned, making a face, smiling at Zyion. "You must let me make up for my rudeness. I'd love to show you the gardens. Alone, of course."

"I'd rather choke on a dick." I whirred beneath my breath. Zyion's shoulders shook, which caused Aden's face to redden. He might not have heard what I'd said, but it was obvious he knew it wasn't kind.

"What was that, darling? I didn't catch what you said over the noise of the room," Aden inquired.

"The bugs are rather thick, so after I eat, I'll be retiring for the night," I supplied. As Griffon took his seat again, another chair was brought over to the table for me. Zyion moved to sit opposite of me on the other side while Aden sat beside me, with Esme seated on my other side.

The moment my ass hit the seat, Esme hissed, "Where the *hell* have you been? I was about to make a huge scene before they explained what had happened. You fucking vanished into thin air!"

"I don't really know where I went," I admitted, still uncertain how I'd ended up sucked into a crystal. Aden had said something about my using magic openly, but that wasn't me at all. How could they not tell the difference between magic use and mana-charged enchantments? I'd bet even Fennix and Fennia could tell the difference. That thought had me wondering where they had scattered off to. I'd seen the little traitors in the garden when they'd been rubbing against Zyion's boots, but then they'd both vanished.

"You can't just disappear on me," Esme susurrated in an angry tenor. "I seem to remember you promising to stay with me."

Frustration grew until I exhaled a long, irritated puff of

air. "It wasn't as if I had a choice. How was I to know touching it would send me elsewhere, Esmeralda?"

The aroma of cooked meat hitting my nose had my stomach cramping with hunger. A sideward glance at the pile of food lathered high on Esme's plate had my attention sliding to the platters covering the table with piles of meat, fruits, breads, and pastries. Without waiting for more of an invitation, I forked a large, juicy sausage from the tray of them. Another platter had a pile of strange green berries and white berries resembling strawberries. Adding a few of them, and then a piece of spiced bread to my platter, I wasted no time before digging in with delight.

When Zyion handed me a napkin, I realized that I had an audience watching as I devoured my platter. Had I known they would all be so rude, I might have breathed between bites of the perfectly baked meal. Next, Zyion passed me a mug of ale, and when I glanced at him in thanks, I found him smirking. Yup, he was amused that I had the juice from a sausage dribbling down my chin.

Whatever.

After I'd dabbed it away, Griffon cleared his throat beside me.

"I've set you and Esmeralda up in the west wing of the palace. There are only a few others who live in that wing," Griffon explained.

"Thank you." I wasn't sure if I should address him as Your Majesty, but seeing as Scylla admitted I'd be ascending to his throne, it felt awkward to do so.

"Why would you place your daughter in the west wing of the palace? I'd prefer she be near at hand. I intend to court her," Aden challenged before biting into a slab of meat even as he pushed bread-like croutons into it as well. My eyes honed in on the way he raucously crunched it as if he lacked any manners. Of course, I had little room to talk. I had just stuffed my face like I hadn't eaten in months. Before he'd finished chewing, he continued on. "It would be much easier for me if Aria were near my chamber."

"I don't think she intends to be courted," Griffon pointed out as if conveying the message to a spoiled child.

My attention flicked to Zyion to see what he made of this argument, but his focus was on my lips. It made me self-conscious that maybe he'd felt the same way about my manners as I felt about Aden's, and I wiped my mouth with the napkin again. My appetite vanished as I chewed my lip and pretended to ignore the conversation.

"I think Aria isn't sure what she really wants or needs, Your Majesty. After all, she's been fucking our mortal enemy for months now. I'm sure the princess had a reason to be screwing our enemy's king." Aden's cold, cruel eyes held mine, revealing the true bastard behind the polished mask.

"Enough, Aden," Griffon warned.

"Why? If she is to be my bride, shouldn't I know where her loyalties are, Griffon?" Aden persisted.

"Sir or your Majesty, Aden. Remember your manners," I offered, which caused his face to turn mottled with anger. "But what's a girl to do when she finds herself the *pet* of a king?"

"I imagine a girl would be scared," Zyion said, peering across the table with a mischievous smile aimed at me.

"Terrified," I lied, dragging my thinning eyes to Aden, who rattled weakly.

The chuckle that burst from Aden's lips was harsh. "It is high time the princess learns the truth about her dragon king. Unless, of course, she willingly took his dragon cock?" My ears burned as he handed out another insult. "You said it yourself. Aria is young and inexperienced, she requires guidance on responding to her peers appropriately, Griffon." My hand holding the knife tightened, imagining running Aden through, before stabbing him through the eyeball. "We might have misunderstood the situation? King Karnavious could have taken advantage of her as she entered the Nine Realms. Either way, she needs to understand her loyalty is to us and not the dragon swine. I won't have my bride out seeking *anything* willing to bed her merely to *protect* her."

"I didn't fuck Knox Karnavious to protect myself, if that is what you're implying, Aden." The anger building inside me was boiling over. My fists tightened on the table before I slid my entire focus toward him. I was acutely aware of every person in the room, wholly focused on this conversation.

"So, you willingly slept with our mortal enemy? Do you even know the history between the bloodlines?" he spat out, as if he found the words foul. "Or that his grandmother murders yours?"

"Did Knox rape me? No. No, he didn't have to do that, Aden. His cock and my vagina met before I ever entered the Nine Realms. In fact," I slammed my elbows on the table, glaring withering at him. "Knox was the first and only man I've been with. If you're taking notes, you will want to write it down. I fucked willingly, and I liked it in case you need to know that answer as well." I offered him a smile that was all teeth.

"As for the history? I only know what Hecate wrote down, and there's nothing about any wars before she showed up. So why don't you keep the dragon dick out of your mouth? Lord knows I tried, but willingly failed on that aspect. And he's saved me countless times, without fail. But, in case you're wondering? I don't *want* to court you, or marry you. I didn't come here to align my vagina with your cock so you could get a crown as the second runner-up. And talk all the shit you want about that man, but he's out there fighting while you sit in here and worry about chairs and where your balls might bounce. Let me clarify it for you. I'd rather peg you in the ass than fuck you, Aden. I came here to meet my father. To learn about the prophecy, then head back to fight because, unlike you, I'm not afraid to fight."

"Damn," Zyion said, choking on his drink as the entire room remained silent with what I'd stated.

"See, Griffon? She's uncouth, like the womb she crawled out of." Aden's face was smug.

"Actually, she's more like Scylla. She'd have knocked your teeth down your throat, then reached in to get them out," Zyion argued, forking a piece of meat to pop in his mouth.

Griffon cleared his throat as if something had gotten stuck in it. My gaze flickered to Zyion, who had a genuine smile on his lips. The look shimmering in his eyes was fascination—or something close to it.

After picking up the mug of ale, I downed the contents and then, once again, accepted a fresh napkin from Zyion and dabbed the corners of my lips. I realized too late that it was actually his from the traces of bergamot and lemongrass clinging to the fabric. Aden's glare burned into the side of my face, but I refused to entertain any more of his slanderous comments toward me.

"I'm exhausted," Esme announced, which caused my eyes to flick to hers, seeing the laughter burning in them.

"I'm exhausted as well. It's been a daunting task to reach the kingdom, father," I admitted, which seemed to soften the tension building in the surrounding air. "I'm sure it's why I'm so forward and cranky."

"I've been a horrible host, Aria. I should've sent a meal up to your chambers. The path here does leave you relatively weak by the time it spits you out at the entrance of the cave. Forgive me, but it's been a long time since we've had guests in the kingdom." Griffon's tone held worry, which made me shrink.

"I'm certain after we've slept, we'll be better company," I offered in excuse. "Isn't that right, Esme?"

Violet eyes narrowed on my face before drifting to give Aden a withering look. "I fear I'm beyond tolerable tonight."

"It's settled then," Griffon announced loudly as he clapped his palms together. Everyone save for Esme and I stood, so she and I hastened to stand as well. I noted Esme swaying on her feet, so I hooked my elbow through hers and awaited direction. "Eva, show the ladies to their chamber."

"I'm heading in that direction to retire for the evening, Your Majesty. It would be an honor to show the princess and her companion to their chambers," Zyion offered politely. Grabbing a new mug of ale from a tray, he polished it off before standing and pushing his chair in. "By your leave," he said with a flourished bow to Griffon.

"Don't be late to the sparring session at dawn, Vicious. I intend to have a rematch to make up for today's folly."

"If you want me to embarrass you again, Aden, you need only ask," Zyion stated with arrogance burning in his startling blue depths. He didn't move, as if he was waiting for Aden to dismiss him.

"We'll see who emerges victorious in the morning. I intend to show the princess how a real prince defends her." The tight-lipped glare he exuded sent my brows up to my hairline.

"I'm not here to court you, Aden, or do anything else with you. But have a good night, or whatever you have planned." Closing the space between us, I leaned down so I could whisper against his ear. "And, for the record, loyalty is earned, not given heedlessly because of the blood someone houses. You'll be disappointed if you expect me to give it recklessly." Spinning on my heel, I left Aden to stare angrily at my back. Disrespect was evident, and I was acutely aware of it. It told him I wasn't afraid of or worried about him. I didn't see him as an equal—but, then again, he wasn't.

CHAPTER 9
ARIA

Zyion strolled behind me as Esme walked next to me through the huge corridor. I could feel the weight of his gaze burning into my spine most of the way to the chamber. The only sounds were the soft falls of our footsteps against the polished flooring and the swish of my gown as it rustled against my ankles. Then Esme released a soft sigh of annoyance, and Zyion glanced over to her.

"It isn't much farther, Esmeralda."

"Thank goodness," she whined in a sour tone. She was still upset about my abandoning her. It didn't matter that I hadn't done it intentionally.

We rounded the corner and a large set of double doors came into view at the far end of the hallway. The moment the guards standing on either side of it spotted us, they stepped forward to pull them open for us to pass. The corridor we entered was fragrant with fresh-cut flowers, which resembled strange-looking lilies, that had been placed in vases with glowing fish. It created a lovely

111

contrast between the grass-colored stems and the luminance of the animal.

Zyion paused before an unremarkable door and spoke in a rich, dark resonance that slid over my flesh like velvet. "This is my chamber. If you need help or find yourself in trouble, you can hide in it." Frowning at my strange reaction to his tone, I chewed my lips.

I fidgeted, full of nervous energy, as his sharp stare steadily moved between my face and Esme's. When neither of us spoke, he folded his arms over his wide, muscular chest.

"You don't trust me. That's fine with me." At his snide tone, my eyes narrowed. "As much as Griffon wishes it otherwise, ladies, no one trusts you, either. You are outsiders. And you?" He looked at me pointedly. "You are fraternizing *with* the enemy. Who you do shit with? That's on you. That's your business, but there's a lot of history and shit to unpack between the original two bloodlines. It isn't something some people will forgive you for doing, princess. A word of advice? Don't piss off Aden. Your father promised him the throne through marriage. That's because even Griffon realizes it's the only way the people here will ever accept an outsider as their princess."

"With all due respect? I don't care what they have promised him. The throne isn't why I came here. I'll tell you the same thing I told Aden, in case you missed it the first time. I'm here to learn who my father is and what I am to become. If Griffon promised Aden a throne, that's on him. It isn't on me. Prior to my arrival, I specified that I wouldn't be coerced into anything. I meant it. The land chose me before you found me in the maze. It has accepted my claim to it as well. So, I dare any of you to see how far I'll allow you to push me on this. I promise you it won't be far at all. I doubt Aden could handle me at my weakest, let alone when I have the power of the land behind me." The last part tumbled out before I could think better of disclosing the information. An amused smile played across Zyion's lips as he unfolded his arms.

"If that's true, then neither of them can argue your claim to the throne. Still, you'll face pushback since every woman in this kingdom wants a chance at Aden." A look of disbelief stamped over his sharp, regal features as his smile turned cocky. "I'd be careful with whom you disclose that secret to, princess."

"They can have the pompous prick and stop calling me princess. It sounds dainty. I assure you, I'm no such thing." Offering him a playful smirk, I decided I didn't hate the glimmer of amusement in his eyes. "Did you actually intend to show us to our room? Because we're not the damsels who need to be saved—in fact, we're the monsters other creatures fear, but even monsters need to sleep sometimes," I stated boldly, hiking a thumb toward Esme.

"I promise you, we're all monsters here, Aria." He didn't allow me time to reply before moving toward a large, decorative set of doors down the hall.

Zyion threw them wide as he entered the chamber. The scent of lemongrass and lavender tickled my nose as I followed him inside. They'd painted the spacious foyer in a soothing shade of Tiffany blue. Plush, white furniture sat in the center of the space. More vases of fresh flowers adorned the smaller tables, as well as one in front of the settees, creating a cozy and inviting atmosphere. The furniture was evidently chosen for its comfort rather than its looks.

"Is it to your liking, *princess*?" Zyion taunted.

"You don't like me, do you?"

Esme ignored us both as she walked toward the large French doors leading out onto a grand balcony. The moment she opened them, the gentle sound of nature flooded the room. The warm evening breeze drifted into the surrounding space, soothing the chill of my bones. The air carried the scent of briny water, wood smoke, and damp earth, and I took a long inhale before turning my whole focus back to the male in front of me.

"Does it matter if I like you or not?"

I moved around to the couch so I could sit and sank into the soft cushions. "You said that, if we found ourselves in trouble, we should come to you, Zyion. In the next breath, you made it sound as if you prefer we didn't trouble you. It cannot be both. So, which one is it?" Yanking my legs up beneath my bottom, I settled deeper into the cushions of soft material.

Zyion tilted his head to one side with a smile playing over his lips. "You don't know who I am, but you will, Aria Primrose. Eventually, you'll understand why I'd prefer you run to me if you're in trouble." With that, he turned on his heel and marched from the chamber, closing the door behind himself.

"He's pleasant," Esme muttered from the doorway. "Now, what the fuck happened?" Her eyes dared me to lie to her.

"I met Scylla Prometheus," I admitted in a hushed tone. Esme's lips parted in shock before she clamped them together, glowering at me. "The crystal I touched? It sucked me down a rabbit hole. I was literally in a chamber filled with nothing but portals. After choosing one, I landed in the woods, where a stag with flowers adorning his horns spoke to. Then I found an atrium. Scylla was there, waiting for me. She claimed she was the one who set the prophecy into play. Scylla Prometheus sacrificed her life to ensure I existed." Esme plopped down across from me, looking more troubled than angry.

"You know that makes you sound crazy, right? You know what? Forget it. Aria, I don't like how Aden is assuming you are his for the claiming." I had to agree with her on that one. Both his words and actions were sketchy.

"He matters so little that I'm not worried about him, honestly. Ember will eat him without thinking twice about doing so. Besides, Scylla performed a ritual tonight, and the Kingdom of Fire chose me. In doing so, I felt the land today when I merged with it. Not this one. The emotions belonged to the true Kingdom of Fire. Some people there aren't truly dead, which is rather disheartening. They're waiting for a ruler to return before they'll willingly rise. The land doesn't want *this* realm saved because it's not part of the Nine Realms. When Griffon created this one, he unknowingly ended countless lives within his homeland."

"You're certain he wasn't aware of the cost of creating a realm?" She inquired hesitantly.

Kicking my legs out from beneath me, I rested my elbows on my knees and then leaned forward to steeple my fingers in front of my face. "No, I don't think he knew—at least not at first. I think Griffon created this one, and it triggered the knowledge of the cost to be written in the tomes of the library. It's why it hid that knowledge from me when I was planning to create one to hide the witchlings in." Goose bumps spread over my arms as the realization hit me. I'd have to explain it to him if it were the case.

"But there's also a chance he knew the cost," she countered before resting back against the soft cushions. "I could sleep for a year straight on this thing." The groan that escaped her lips was both relaxation and exhaustion. "I know you want to give him the benefit of the doubt, Aria, but Griffon isn't stupid."

"No, but if no one had ever created a new realm before, then the witches and others who helped make this one wouldn't know the price. Knox knew the cost because he told me, which means I'm guessing he learned the hard way. I'm not foolish enough to think blindly with my heart."

"So, what is our plan here?"

"A wise man once said that in order to secure peace, one must prepare for war," I mumbled tiredly.

"Have I met him?"

"Who?" I frowned at her question.

"The wise man who said it? What is his name?"

"Metallica," I whispered, suppressing the smile tugging on my lips. "Unfortunately, you've not met him yet."

"So, we pretend to be naïve women like normal? Or, do we gather intel and use it to go to war if need be?" The skin on her forehead creased as she stifled a yawn.

"Not exactly." I snorted at her analogies. "We don't allow them to know we're smarter than we are. Be watchful of those around us, see if they're watching everything we do. But yes, we play damsels. After all, women are such weak-minded beings. How will we ever survive without the brawny, caveman mindset ordering us about?" I asked in mocked fear.

"We could eat our way out of here. Even after the meal, I am starving. I didn't want to make a scene by eating like some monster indulging my feral side." A pointed look in my direction had us both cracking up laughing.

"I was freaking starving, Esme."

Her eyes rolled before she exhaled forcefully. "Not judging your table manners, bitch. But if there's anything else you need to do here? Take me with you."

"I'll try my best to grab you next time. I'm certain you'd —oh, I forgot to tell you about the strange animals, bestie!" I carefully considered. They'd been out in the garden, that much I knew. "Here foxy . . . shit, I forgot their names already. Damn."

Esme's eyes popped up as her head lifted from the cushion. "Not your bestie after you ditched me with your dad, and who is foxy?"

"A Foxtyre and Catteris. Fennia wanted to keep me as a pet for some life debt, while Fennix wanted to off me. They were cute, but I don't think I'm a good pet owner. Unfortunately, I can't seem to keep track of either of the little shits."

"You can't be serious. You adopted pets while you were off visiting your dead grandmother? On second thought, don't answer that. I sound crazy enough saying it out loud."

Nodding, I stifled a yawn. "It sounds insane, right?"

Sitting up, she looked me straight in the eyes and gradually slid her attention to the door before sliding it back to me. "What the hell is up with the grumpy asshole?"

"I don't know. He doesn't like me, I guess," I said with the same thought churning in my head. "I met him in the garden after I'd met with Scylla. He stopped me from wandering into Aden and his friends, who were discussing me as if I was a piece of meat."

"That dead-hellhound-bastard!" She flicked her hair before turning and loosening an ear-piercing scream. Esme leaped from the sofa and barreled into me, forcing me to fall backward against the couch. "What the fuck is that?"

The door to the chamber burst open, and Zyion entered it with a sword drawn. My eyes met his as his dark eyebrows lifted and he passed the mess of limbs we'd become. He didn't stop until he reached the balcony doors, then closed them. Next, he checked behind each of the closed doors as I watched from beneath Esme. Had he been sitting outside our door or something? He sure as shit hadn't returned to his own room. Not with how promptly he'd responded to her scream.

"Get off me, Esme. We're saved," I mumbled irritably.

"What happened?" Zyion demanded. His turbulent gaze searched my face while Esme gradually released me and pointed at Fennix and Fennia, who were now seated on the sofa where she'd been sitting.

"She isn't animal friendly," I explained.

"Those are not animals! Those are the shit my mother threatened me with, making me behave," she hissed, as if it would actually keep them from hearing.

"They're cute," I argued in their defense. Zyion continued to regard me as if I'd gone insane. "What? Scylla said they chose me. That they were mine now." Zyion's lips parted as he glanced at the critters. "She said they'd show up when they wanted, and leave the same way."

"And what did Scylla say about you, Aria?" he asked. His tone held an intangible quality, and when I didn't react, his eyes narrowed.

"That I should be careful who I trust with my secrets." Tapping my forehead, I smirked at him before rising from the settee. "Oh, wait. That was you. Shouldn't *you* be sleeping instead of eavesdropping on us defenseless girls? Or is that what gets you off, Zyion?" I asked in a soft, seductive voice. "Don't lie to me because I'll know if you do. Is that even your name, Vicious?"

Zyion stepped closer to me, which prompted Esme to rise behind me. His eyes didn't leave my face as I lifted my hand, running a finger over the curve of his jawline.

"My name is Zyion Vicious, Crowned Prince of the Vanir, Head of the Queen's Guard. It isn't Zyion of the Blah-blah-blah, Aria, Princess to the Kingdom of Fire. You may address me as whatever the fuck you want, ocean eyes, so long as it isn't blah-blah-blah. Understand?"

"Not quite. Is it two blahs or three?"

Zyion rattled quietly, and the sound had Ember stretching from within me even as Esme slammed against the floor. I rattled back, but instead of him reacting as Aden or Griffon had, Zyion's eyes began glowing sea-green with gold scattered within them. My eyes also glowed similarly when I was turned on, or pissed off. I swallowed past the unease, and his brows shot up as the color drained from my face. 'Abort' was all that screamed through my head.

"Bloody fucking hell," he growled as turned and

stalked from the room, slamming the doors with a jarring *thud.*

"What the fuck just happened?" Esme demanded from her position on the floor.

"I don't know," I admitted and then jumped as she screamed again. This time, Fennia and Fennix were rubbing against her. "They're harmless."

"You don't know that! My mother said if you feed them after dark, they turn into monsters!"

"Someone's mother watched *Gremlins,*" I mused. "Let's get some rest. I'll take the critters with me so you don't have to worry."

"With them in here?" she demanded, with horror dripping from each word.

"Of course, with them inside. Where else would they sleep?" Her eyes widened at my words, forcing me to fight the smile itching to tug the corners of it up. When she didn't respond, solely staring at the critters, I spoke softly, for her ears alone. "You remember when we first met?" At her sharp nod of confirmation, I continued. "I need to do that again. If what I think is about to unfold, then I need to see Knox. There's something not right, but I can't put my finger on it, Esme."

"I felt it too," she agreed as she sidled closer to the wall, peering at the sleeping creatures. "It's malevolent of nature. I didn't feel it from Griffon, but the moment the men entered the hall? I felt it crawling over my flesh. As if something was learning me intimately."

My eyes widened at her words. "I meant with the world, but you need to elaborate on that, Esmeralda." As I watched, she once again began chewing on her thumbnail.

"You're not the least bit tired?" I asked, which caused her to release the hold her teeth held on her thumbnail. "Spill it, now."

She whispered so softly that I had to strain to hear the words. "I don't know what the hell it was. Your uncles, brothers, and Aden's men flooded the hall. Griffon sought to steer the conversation away from you, but this man kept asking things. Things he didn't need to know. When Griffon refused to entertain his direction of conversation, I felt needles poking into my head. As if he was stealing the answers from my mind. If I hadn't been so fucking exhausted, I would've known what was happening. Instead, it took me entirely too long to force him out of my mind. But I'm not even positive it was him who did it, Aria. I lost half the night from whatever he did to my mind."

"Fucking brilliant," I muttered.

"I'm sorry."

"I'm not upset with you. It wasn't like you willingly allowed whoever it was into your mind. As I said before, we stay together. If we have to leave this place quickly, it will be much easier to succeed without having to track each other down. If you feel it again, tell me and I'll counter it, Esme. No one fucks with us while we're here. No one. Not even the grumpy bastard who is listening outside the door. Do you hear me? I wouldn't suggest you fuck around. I'd hate to show you what it feels like to find out how much of a petty bitch I can be," I called, but wasn't certain what I expected in reply. I grinned fiercely at her bewildered look, tightening her features.

"Is it me? Did I do drugs while you were gone? Because I'm pretty sure you came back a lot weirder than when you left here. Dead grandma, strange pets, random grumpy asshole . . . what's next?"

"I have a rendezvous with another asshole." Lowering my voice, I stepped closer, pressing my nose against her soft, obsidian strands of silk. "Watch my body until I return? Pretend you're asleep, but do try to not fall asleep until I return?"

"Fine, but if you moan? I may stab you. My libido's been stuck on overdrive since we entered this realm. It's another thing that is worrisome. My skin is crawling with awareness, but what is it aware of? Who the fuck knows? I feel as if I need to inhale every scent until I find the perfect one. It's freaking me out, Aria."

"If I wanted to sniff everyone and everything, I'd be a little freaked out as well." There was only one scent I wanted to inhale, and I couldn't find his unique scent within this realm. "I'll be quick. Once I hear you snoring, I'll begin."

CHAPTER 10
ARIA

The moment I heard Esme's soft footsteps coming to my chamber, I slipped from the bed and searched for magical incantations. Once I checked that there was no other magic in the room that could affect the spell I was going to perform, I breathed a sigh of relief and quietly returned to bed.

The first time I'd cast this spell, I'd ended up leading Knox on a wild goose case, which had ended in my meeting Esme. That seemed like eons ago. In fact, it felt like so long ago that, looking back, I could scarcely recall what life outside of the Nine Realms had been like. Perhaps it was helpful. Those inside the human world had the luxury of being oblivious to the war brewing so near to them. Being oblivious wasn't the worst thing to be, honestly.

Softly laying back onto the bed, I let my nails slide free to cut deeply into the palms of my hands. A hiss left my lips as magic began filling the air of the chamber. Using my blood, I drew the runes to allow my mind and spirit to release from my physical body. My lips parted as the words smoothly leapt from my tongue, spilling the incantation that would force my spirit to the place I held within my mind.

Opening my eyes, I smirked until the heavy beat of Hollywood Undead "Everywhere I Go" filled my ears. Frowning as the lyrics pumped through the space, I stepped out from behind the bookshelf and froze, eyes going wide and jaw dropping open.

In the center of the space Knox normally dominated, Lore was holding a heavy tome and hopping from one foot to the other. At "their titties," he dropped his head back, rocking his chest as if they were what the song spoke of instead of his flat, pierced nipples. My palm landed over my lips when the middle of the song hit and Lore tossed the book aside to dance.

My shoulders shook as he rocked his hips, throwing his arms into the air before bringing them down as if he were holding something there. Or someone? Who knew what was unfolding in Lore's head?

"Drunken pussy!" he shouted, causing my other hand to slap against my lips. "The Lore . . . weenie . . . he loves to show!" His body was glistening with sweat as if he'd been dancing for longer than what I'd witnessed so far.

Instead of embarrassing him, I joined in his mindless dancing within Knox's sacred chamber. He stumbled over the lyrics he didn't scream, apparently not knowing the actual words. The way he moved told me he was aware of the benefits of his brother's library. Secluded space undisturbed unless the library chose otherwise. Not to mention, it played some pretty great tunes. Lore was evidently not new to the song, either.

Having not been in our realm for a considerable amount of time, they could not enjoy any of the clubs—not that there were any in Haven Falls, but that wasn't the point. He leaned back and then began swiveling his hips in a tantalizing slow motion. The man had moves, that much was obvious, but I'd also seen him use his lines on ladies before. Lore was more than smooth. He was seductive with his humorous outlook on life. He had a way of making a woman's full-on belly laugh, which was priceless in this world.

"Gods damn, Aria?" he squealed as I danced around him and mimicked his hips.

"Hey, Lore. Are we warming up?" I asked, winking as his cheeks reddened with embarrassment. The song came to an abrupt end, which forced a pout to my lips.

"Oh, don't stop on my account. I put duct tape on my inner feminist to enjoy the song with you."

His eyes sparkled before he shoved his fingers through his straight, silky platinum hair. A smile tugged at his lips before turning up into a dazzling one. Some poor woman was going to be fucked when he fell head over heels for her.

"You're back?" he asked as he slid his regard to the tome. "Thank fuck. I've been combing this entire place for a way to find you." His words caused my heart to flutter with worry that something had happened in my absence. At my panicked face, he shook his head before holding his hands up. "What's wrong? Are you hurt? Who hurt you? Do you need mouth-to-vagina?"

My eyebrows shot up in surprise. "Mouth-to-vagina?" This guy was a wordsmith. God save anyone who said otherwise. I'd die on this hill for him. "Where's Knox?" I questioned, as confusion swirled like a tornado through my head.

"Training the lads in the courtyard," he explained, nodding toward the open balcony.

Straining my ears, I heard his dark rasp that wrapped around me like silk. A smile spread over my lips as I strode to the balcony to peer out the glass, unwilling to waste a moment longer before setting eyes on the bastard who consumed my soul until it withered without him. I threw open the doors, rushing onto the balcony, then scanned the busy courtyard, which they'd converted into a makeshift training ground, and found him almost immediately. My eyes zeroed in on the ravens that covered the side of his torso and then slid up the sinewy back muscles exposed to the sun's gentle kiss.

My pulse thundered inside my head at the delicious sight of him brandishing a blade. The way every muscle moved as he parried Brander's aggressive attack forced my thighs to clench. It seemed like Knox had mastered every aspect of war, as he took each step with calculated precision. Killian moved in behind Knox as the onlookers chatted excitedly. Both Brander and Killian swung their deadly blades toward Knox, stilling his name on my lips.

They forged the man from the same mold in which they'd fashioned the gods of old. I wouldn't alter a single thing about him, even if I could. Knox was the sharp edges to my softer ones. He was the chaos that fueled me. Neither Knox nor I knew we'd become addicted to each other. This man had become my other half, which both excited and terrified me. Knox was embedded so deeply within my soul, that it fucking ached.

Knox shut out the world when he was close to me. He made the idea of becoming a monster less terrifying than it was. I had been terrified of housing a creature, to begin with, knowing how easily I could become unhinged. But Knox taught me there was a balance to maintaining humanity while freeing the monster within. With him, I didn't have to fear Ember hurting him. Lennox handled her easily.

The night we'd shared together before I'd left had made it harder to leave. I'd wanted to stay in the security of his warmth, and the protection of his arms. But I couldn't, not if we wanted to end the threat against all of us. It wasn't just about me, or I'd have considered doing exactly that. The thing was, there was an entire world depending on us. I couldn't lay about in bed with him, no matter how badly I wished to do so. Plus, I needed to put the bitch down for what she'd taken from me, from us.

The man wasn't just my enemy through one bloodline, but rather both. If I hadn't been born in the human world, how differently would I see Knox's plight? Would I have lived as oblivious as those within the new realm were?

I'd survived an upbringing that would've broken most beings. It was what had sharpened my claws to lethal points. In that place, they had never accepted me for who

—or what—I was. From the first moment I could remember, I'd never felt at home in that place. My whole life, I'd wondered why its entirety exuded wrongness, depriving me of the ability to fully appreciate its merits or flaws, but it was because it wasn't my home. This man, he alone, made me feel at peace. Knox might have been brutal and I was certain we weren't past all the bumps in our road, but I knew I didn't want to walk down it without him beside me.

A flash of brilliant color forced my eyes from the perfection of my mate. In the garden beyond the circular courtyard, women were using fans to battle the afternoon heat. Swallowing past the need to rip their spines out from their mouth, I watched one rise from her seat. Slowly, she ambled closer to the men without a care for the deadly swords they were using. Grinding my teeth as she paused next to the younger men, she dropped a canary-yellow cloth on purpose.

At the same moment she'd dropped it, Knox disarmed both men in a calculated, skilled move of swordsmanship. The woman, who was even now moving closer as she waited for Knox to retrieve her swath of fabric, toyed with the bodice of her gown. My teeth sank into my lip as my back twitched and my nails pushed through the flesh of my fingertips.

Knox bent to retrieve the scrap of fabric, giving the woman's greedy eyes a chance to devour the sight of his shirtless chest. Instead of holding his hand out, he turned to say something to one of the men, and the woman stepped closer to him. My heart clenched as I stepped back, allowing the shadows to swallow my presence. When he turned back, her palm reached for his chest, but Knox stepped back from her.

The woman didn't take the hint. Instead, she smiled enticingly as he lowered his head. My mind whirled with suspicion as I wondered if he was staring at the cleavage the bodice of her gown put on display. Nausea churned in the pit of my abdomen as I felt the floor crumbling at my feet. Her hand snaked up, running over my guy's chest.

"Step away from the king, Fay," Killian snapped, which forced her eyes to flash with anger. "I won't ask you again. When the king tells you to step back? You fucking do as he commands. King Karnavious isn't interested in the flesh you're peddling here. Now, step the fuck back."

Fay, who I was guessing was a courtesan, didn't appear to care about Killian's warning. Her hand remained on Knox's chest, which forced a rattle to rip from my throat. Knox's head swung toward the palace in which I stood, creeping up the side of the tower until his gaze clashed with mine. The moment our eyes locked, the world fell away. Silence enveloped us as only we existed within the surrounding space.

It was what told me he wasn't just a man I enjoyed being around. It created an entire storm within my body. It rolled through me in violent waves, as if he was a hurricane sweeping over my shores, battering anything in its forceful, destructiveness as he made landfall. My nipples pebbled. Heat unfurled in my abdomen, and then flowed to a pulse located in my clit. I felt my spine arch with a gentle curve as if every part of me belonged to him, and him alone.

Stepping into the sunlight, I continued rattling in

warning. It grew louder until the woman's focus settled on me as well. She retreated, showing she had at least two brain cells in her head. The sugary tang of her fear carried to me on the gentle breeze, enticing to the beast within me who wanted her blood for touching what belonged to us. The smile on Knox's lips caused everything inside me to grow taut with lustful need. A smile played on my lips as my palms braced on the wooden railing of the balcony. Knox sauntered toward me, which sent my need, fear, and anticipation to new heights. The combination was heady, yet undeniably erotic as I followed him until he vanished beneath the balcony railing.

Losing sight of him caused my heart to ache at losing sight of him. I'd enjoyed drinking in the hard muscular body that was tense from straining from defending against the men trying to disarm him. Covered in a fine sheen of sweat, it had fucking glistened beneath the suns warm, heated rays.

Knox without a shirt on was criminal. His entire body was deliciously hard edges, smooth lines, and inked to utter perfection that I could stare at day in and day out for the rest of my existence. Hell, I didn't blame Fay for trying to lure him between her thighs. If I were her, I'd want that man too. Only, he was mine, and if she thought she'd take him from me, she was wrong. Dead wrong. Because that was what she'd be if she touched him again.

The woman had slithered back to her group on the edge of the garden, and I doubted she knew how lucky she was that Knox hadn't responded to what she'd been offering him. My attention slid to Brander, who offered a wave with a boyish grin on his kissable lips. Killian, being Killian, confidently folded his arms over his amply muscled chest, nodding a silent hello. A bevy of shirtless men sat in front of Greer, listening intently to whatever he was currently telling them with wonder stamped on their faces.

"Fucking hussy," I whispered, which caused Greer's head to lift.

"Peasant, so nice of you to call upon our king," he shouted before a genuine happiness filled his eyes. "I hope you shan't be too long away from us?"

My smile faltered at his choice of words, but the sound of scraping below distracted me from pondering it. When I looked down to see what was causing it, my jaw dropped. Knox was scaling the tower. Fear shot through me as the man literally scaled the tower to reach me.

"What the hell are you thinking? You can't climb the damn tower, Knox!" I demanded in horror. "Are you insane?"

"Not at all, Little Monster," he called up in a raspy tone of pure lust that enveloped me like a blanket. "It isn't the first time I've scaled one to reach what I want. Is it?" His eyes sparkled with humor at the horror stamped on my face.

"Brander? Have you not told your brother that he shouldn't be scaling fucking walls? He's the king!" I shouted.

Brander shrugged indifferently before calling back, "He's the king, Aria. No one tells a king what he shouldn't do. Besides, it would only encourage him to do it more."

Knox's hands landed beside mine seconds before he leaped over the railing. I yelped as his palm connected to my throat, jerking me into the hardness of his frame. Butterflies erupted in a kaleidoscope of movement when his flesh pressed against mine. Then he forced my head back, smiling like a predator who'd captured his prey.

"Fucking hell, you're beautiful, Aria. Here I thought I was imagining the sound of your pretty rattle at first. But then, I caught your lovely scent on the breeze," he rasped even as he forced me to walk backward into the chamber. "Why the fuck do I smell another male on you?"

"Knox," I whispered as an uneasiness washed through me.

"Aria?" he growled as his hand tightened on my throat. "Is there another man?"

"No one would ever be you, Knox," I replied as honestly as I could.

"That didn't answer my fucking question."

"I've not been with anyone else. No other man has ever had me except you." His mouth crushed against mine in an earth-shattering kiss of possession. Knox's fingers tightened on my jawline, forcing me to open to his deliciously brutal assault. With his kiss, Knox claimed ownership of more than just my mouth. He claimed my fucking soul.

Knox destroyed any resolve I might've had. The man was a storm that battered against my defenses and forced them to break into tiny shattered pieces. His other hand slid down my back to cup my ass before he lifted me as if I weighed nothing at all. I slid my tongue against his as a lusty moan bubbled from my lungs, only to be captured by his starving lips.

The moment Knox pulled away, he rattled until my spine arched. Sliding my fingers through his silky strands, I whimpered at the feel of his thick cock rubbing against my center. Closing my eyes, I allowed myself a moment to just feel the utter domination he held over my senses.

"I've missed you," I admitted huskily.

"Have you?" he asked with something worrisome in his tone. "Because if I smell who I think I smell on your flesh, you and I are going to have fucking issues."

"What the hell does that mean?" I pulled back, and he allowed me to slide down his frame.

"Who the fuck are you hanging out with inside that realm?" he demanded with anger churning in his oceanic depths.

"I'm not following you. Are you asking if I'm *fucking* someone else? Because I'm not. You're the only man to know me in that way. Am I with others like me? Yes, but you know that already. So, what is it you really want to know?" Knox, jealous, was a terrifying thing to behold.

"I would like to know why the fuck I can smell The Dragon Killer on your flesh, Aria. Tell me why Zyion's scent is *all* over *my* woman."

I frowned at the title he'd referred to Zyion by. The Dragon Killer. As in, Zyion specialized in killing them? Brilliant. Of course, I'd end up running right into someone Knox hated. Our family histories made it inevitable. When I stepped back, biting my lip anxiously as my cheeks warmed, he prowled forward. Sleek and lethal, like the predator he truly was beneath the veneer. The anger and betrayal stamped on his face forced my heart to race.

"I've met Zyion Vicious, Knox. But I didn't allow him to

135

do anything other than escort me to my room," I explained with confusion whirling through my mind. "It wasn't as if he walked up to me and introduced himself by that title when we met."

"Did he do more than escort you into the chamber? Or was he a gentleman and left the pretty princess at the threshold to her private chamber?" His tone sent a chill racing down my spine. "Because I shouldn't smell him on you at *all* if he escorted you to the door. Instead, I can smell his touch on your supple, smooth flesh."

"I've already told you I haven't fucked anyone."

I seethed at the accusation he'd thrown at me. Was I completely innocent? No. I had eyeballs, and I'd checked Zyion out. But I wasn't dead, which meant I could appreciate a hot body or man, without touching or throwing myself at them. I wasn't cheating by just appreciating an attractive person. Fuck, I'd checked Esme out, and we were platonic—unless, of course, you asked Ember, who swore I was Esme's best lesbian. If anyone said they didn't look at someone as hot or as masculine as Zyion was, they were lying, even to themselves. It didn't mean I wanted him, though.

"Good," he snapped before he slammed his hand against the wall as my back struck against the hard surface. I hadn't even realized I'd still been backing until I'd come up against the wall. "Keep it that way. He's a murderous prick." Excitement beat through my mind, even as the weight of the past pressed against my chest.

"So are you, Knox, and so am I," I whispered softly. They exhausted my mind by obsessing with the past and needing to throw dirt at one another. Why couldn't anyone let it go? Or get over it, and move on? As long as they'd learned from it, couldn't they overcome it? "If he murdered people during war time, then that isn't on me. If he gets off on murdering dragons? Then that's on him. It isn't like I'm there to find a mate. I have one, remember? He's a conceited, tenacious, obtuse barbarian who occasionally has the brains of a gnat, but he's mine. I still bear your mark, and there's no one else's I'd want on my flesh."

"Fucking hell, woman. You drive me insane," he growled huskily, nipping at my lip teasingly. The crunching of kernels, even as the room filled with the buttery scent of popcorn, had both of our heads swinging toward the sound of chewing.

Lore, bless his heart, waved butter covered fingers toward us before swallowing. "Don't mind me. I'm here for the porn. I heard there's about to be a throw down and thought maybe this time I'd get myself a seat for the show." Lore's voice forced Knox to step back, even though he'd probably felt him there already. Not much slipped past Knox.

"Get out," Knox growled before turning back toward me. "Now, Lore. I won't ask again. The lady doesn't enjoy others watching as she bows before her king."

I lifted a brow. "Who says I intend to bow to you?" I demanded in a haughty tone. His lips jerked into a devious smile, which sent my heart thundering with anticipation.

"Oh, you'll bow for me. You'll scream too. And then, you'll fucking beg, Aria," he warned in a huskily rasp. The gravelly tone erotically abrasive against my flesh. "Here's the thing. I don't like that you're somewhere I can't get to you. It isn't enough that you're surrounded by men who aren't *nice* people, was it? No, you had to go and fuck around with the one asshole I hate more than anyone else, including your grandmother. So, if I, were you? I'd be terrified of what I intend to do to you when I capture you."

CHAPTER 11
KNOX

Aria's eyes widened at the threat. She was such beautiful prey. Taking a few steps closer to her, I smiled as she bit that lip. I didn't know if she even knew how hot she was when she did it. I didn't honestly care if she did or not. Grabbing her by the throat, I yanked her closer, enjoying the soft gasp she expelled at the rough handling. Aria enjoyed being manhandled, no matter how much she pretended otherwise.

I pushed her chin up, forcing her attention to my face. The moment she noticed the predatorial gaze, the speed of her heartbeat increased. Those lovely turquoise-colored eyes flashed with surprise before growing heavy with lust. Before she could conceal it, I caught the scent of arousal rapidly intensifying. All logical thought vanished, leaving behind only the shared raw, primal need. Our primal desires fueled the need to hunt, capture, and fuck until we declared ownership of each other.

"I don't understand why you're so angry," she admitted past her kiss-swollen lips. Her tongue jetted out

141

to lick the full bottom lip I was already imagining wrapped around my cock. Fucking hell, this woman would be my undoing.

"You don't need to understand anything." That much was true. "You left me and then came waltzing back with his scent all over you. Do you even know who the fuck you're allowing to put their hands on you?" The snarl that left my lips caused her pulse to jackhammer against my thumb, forcing my cock to spasm at the thought of being buried in her welcoming, tight heat.

Aria didn't need to understand why I was mad. She had no idea that I was about to mark her lovely body so fucking primally that she'd never even look at anyone else. Catching his scent had awoken my hunger for her, and there was no way she was leaving her without knowing who the fuck she truly belonged to. I wouldn't chance that bastard thinking she was anything less than truly fucking claimed, marked, and owned.

Zyion was a cruel, sadistic, murderous prick. He'd fucking devour her soul and leave her nothing but a hollow shell. I'd faced off against him several times, and he'd been the only one ever to meet my blade and not end up dead. Zyion was versed in more than warfare, which explained his place as Scylla Prometheus's guard. On more than one occasion, that bastard had prevented me from murdering the queen and ending the war between the dragons and the phoenixes.

Considering it wasn't a secret I'd claimed her, it was a given he was very aware that she belonged to me. It both horrified me and left me needing to get her back here, where I could protect her.

Letting her leave that morning hadn't been easy, and every day since, I'd regretted not capturing her and tying her to my fucking bed where she would've been safe. She sure as shit wouldn't be in a realm hidden from me or cozying up to Zyion fucking Vicious. Hell, the man in the cave who'd watched her pussy drip down my chin didn't concern me a fraction as much as he did.

No, Zyion hated me for more than the blood that coursed through my veins or which side of the battle I'd stood on. I inadvertently killed the woman he'd been intending to wed. She'd been a warrior, who'd led an ambush against the caravan my mother and Lore, who'd been an infant at the time, were traveling in. Eira had wanted to visit the battlefield to see our father, but also had planned to walk through the tent holding the wounded to lift their spirits. Claire Obert had died at the end of my blade, her short life snuffed out to protect my mother and Lore.

"Are you jealous?" she spat out, her eyes burning with fire.

"You honestly think I get jealous? I don't do jealousy, woman. I get fucking evil. I'm a fucking king, which means I get what I fucking want, when I want it," I retorted in a raspy hiss of sound. She was getting pissed, which was exactly what I wanted.

Aria pissed off was a sight to behold, but it would also leave her unbalanced. I wanted her off-kilter. Fear would make her run harder, faster. This girl wasn't going to forget tonight, even if it was only her conscious mind here with me. By the time she returned to her body, my markings would bruise her creamy, unblemished skin. Her pussy wouldn't just ache. It would be swollen, sore, and I'd ensure it dripped my essence down her pretty thighs.

The beings within us were primal hunters, which fueled the shells they housed. I'd hunted her pretty ass down once before in the human realm, which had forced Lennox to the surface. She'd seen my monster, sampled his ravenous hunger, and fucked him as if she had an endless desire for more of him. The time I'd chased her through water, then down the slate, I'd wanted to throw her down, fuck her soft, sweet body into submission. She hadn't been willing, even if the mark made it seem as if she was. I'd never force her to fuck me, ever. Aria's submission when it was given? Fucking undid me.

I was a cruel bastard, but I'd never raped a woman. In order to hunt her in the way I craved, she had to trust me. She had to shed her inhibitions, and she did it beautifully when Ember was near to the surface. Only, I didn't want to hunt Ember. I wanted Aria.

Aria was my girl, the one who'd fucked my world up. I didn't deserve her after what I'd done, how I'd treated her. I knew that better than anyone else, but there was no world where she wasn't mine. I'd rather burn it to the ground and walk aimlessly through the ashes until I became nothing more than a haunted, mindless corpse.

I'd chosen to earn her back, which wouldn't be an easy thing. Aria wasn't like other women of the Nine Realms. She was softer in some ways and harder in others. The woman didn't want flowers and pretty words. She wanted someone who wasn't afraid to challenge her mind or fuel her fire with knowledge.

Tightening my hold on her throat, I jerked her body

against mine, enjoying the hiss of air escaping her lush, pink lips. Rattling low with a primal tone, I studied the way her eyes sharpened, as if she was enjoying the anticipation as much as I was. Aria was bare bones. She enjoyed shedding her humanity and caving to the baser needs of our bodies. It's what had drawn me to her in the beginning, the animalistic need simmering just below the surface of the pretty veneer she used to try to hide it.

"Such pretty fucking prey," I hissed before shoving her from me, watching her stumbling to maintain her balance. "You fucked up, Aria. Did you think I wouldn't know? Or were you banking on me being oblivious to what you were doing inside that realm?" Anger burned in her stare, daring me to continue. Fucking hell she was so damn gorgeous it made my stomach physically ache to mark her.

"Know what? I don't want Zyion, Knox. I want you. If you'd fucking listen to the words coming out of my mouth, you'd know that too!" Frustration caused her features to crinkle, which only made her cuter.

"I hear your lips moving, but the only apology I want comes in the form of you on your fucking knees, worshiping my cock with that bratty fucking mouth of yours," I continued, uncaring that she was growing more pissed off at my blatant disregard for what she was saying.

While I could smell the bastard on her, I knew she hadn't fucked him. That was a scent she wouldn't have been able to hide. We both knew she wanted me. It was there, dancing in her turquoise gaze. Hell, I could smell her pussy readying for me, needing me to fuck her until we were both nothing but brainless beings trying to get deeper beneath one another's skin.

I could scent her need to run, her anticipation of my hunting her down and claiming every fucking inch of her. And I fucking would once she gave me the challenge of doing so. I'd fucking misuse, consume, and ruin, then I'd watch her rise from the ground stronger than she was before I fucked her into submission.

She took a step back the moment I took one forward. It was harder to keep the smile from spreading over my lips as the library changed, conforming to what I needed. The bookshelves vanished, and we were standing in the middle of a thick, verdant forest of towering trees. A gust of wind caught the silvery strands of her hair, shooting it up around her head like a shimmering halo. The sexy-as-fuck gown she appeared in was too sheer and hugged her lithe, captivating curves tightly.

"What the fuck?" she whimpered as she glanced around.

"You thought you'd walk in here with his scent clinging to your flesh and I'd do what? Just accept it? I warned you I wasn't interested in sharing you with anyone else. Didn't I? You're beyond my reach in that realm, but I swear to the fucking gods, you'll feel me when you return to your body. You'll feel me everywhere. Your flesh. Your pretty, willing cunt. I won't stop until you're bruised, marked, and nothing more than a mewling, crying, coming mess beneath me." Her silver brows shot up on her forehead at what I'd said, swirling gold eddies churning in her lovely eyes. The moment she turned, eyeing the high cliff the library had churned up from my fantasy, a gasp broke from her fuckable lips.

"Knox, this is insane. I came here to talk to you. I promise, there's no one else," she pleaded, ever so fucking prettily, before turning back to find me inches from her. She was a good hunter, but I was better. I was faster than she was still. Brutality was something I excelled at, which she was fully aware of. She had been at the receiving end of my rage. "Please, listen to me."

I traced the delicate curve of her jawline. She was the loveliest creature I'd ever clapped eyes on before. Aria's beauty wasn't in her flesh. No. It was in her mind. Even the way she thought was enchanting. The girl was strategic in everything she did, and while everyone else was playing checkers, she was stacking the chess board ten steps ahead of everyone, including me. She leaned into my touch, which made the next part more enjoyable. Shoving her over the edge, her eyes rounded in horror before a blood-curdling scream ripped from her lungs.

"And so we begin, my pretty prey," I murmured before jumping over the edge, enjoying the sight of her gown lifting as she plunged toward the water below.

CHAPTER 12
KNOX

Aria shifted her body at the last moment, diving beneath the watery surface. A moment before I broke the surface, I mirrored her pose, penetrating through it seamlessly. I allow myself to plunge to the bottom of the river, making it there just in time to see her push off the sleek stones and shoot up for the surface. Her toned legs kicked against the water as she rushed toward the shoreline.

I rose to the surface, only allowing my nose above water long enough to draw in a deep breath. Then I sank back underwater to watch her crawling over the silt of the beach. The moment she hit dry land, her eyes returned to the water, searching it for any sign of me. Aria didn't stick around for me to pop out of it, though. Instead, she bolted into the forest, and my body heated at the idea of hunting her.

She was about to recklessly run through the perilous forest to gauge her reflexes. Then, it was also for me to watch her stumbling through the woods as I hunted her down. Aria was fucked. There was no other way she'd escape this forest tonight. She wasn't stupid enough not to leave her body unguarded.

I'd made sure she wasn't that neglectful when I'd chased her around the realms. The moment she entered this world, I'd begun ensuring she became hard enough to survive it. Lowering her guard would result in my exposing her mistake. She'd assumed I hadn't known right where she fucking was, but I'd had her in my sights the entire time.

The way she thought, though, it had left me stunned. I'd assumed her move, but she'd been steps ahead of me without me being the wiser. I'd go to make a move, then step back, because she'd done something so mind-boggling, that I'd wanted to see her achieving it. While I was playing checkers, she'd been playing chess. She fixed the board without me realizing that she'd made a move. However, how she moved the pieces in such a strategic, merciless way was mind-boggling. It left me struggling to figure out her next move before she made it.

Aria's brain was a work of art, and the thing I liked about her most. It calculated a problem, subtracted the incidentals, isolated the target, and then went to war against her target. The woman was created to wage war, and gods save anyone stupid enough to stand between her and what she wanted. She skillfully outmaneuvered me, which I wasn't even upset about. She'd read the *Art of War*, yet it was undeniable that she was the entire book placed into one gorgeously packaged woman.

Breaking free of the shimmering, moonlit surface, I shot toward the shore, then prowled toward the forest. I didn't need to run because I could hear the erratic beat of her heart. The fragrance of her adrenaline mixed with the delicious scent of her arousal. The same arousal that would soon drip down my fucking chin.

I strolled into the dark forest, pausing as the sound of her feet crunching over the dry leaves met my ears. A smile curled over my lips as I took off after her, anticipation for what was coming humming through me. My cock twitched at the thought of being buried deep inside her tight, needy cunt. I fucking loved the way it clenched around me, sucking me farther into her haven.

Every step deeper into the woods brought me closer to her, and the veneer I wore around others steadily shed. Out here, we were animals with the urgent need to rut like beasts in the wild. The moment Aria's inhibition started lowering, I felt the primal instinct rising within her as well.

The sound of her footsteps paused, as if she wasn't certain what was happening. It sounded like she was spinning in a circle, searching for any hint of me in the area.

Our kind wasn't meant to be tethered by the constraints of humanity. The Nine Realms were filled with beasts, monsters, and those who thought themselves humanoid. None were meant to be clothed or held in constant captivity of their flesh. A beast ruled each realm, be it one who wore flesh or fur. It mattered little.

The hunt was instinctive. My base nature was driving my actions to relentlessly hunting Aria's sexy, gorgeous ass down and fuck her so roughly that she'd never get me out of her system. Never mind the fact that getting her animalistic nature to kick in would keep her safer where she was inside the new realm.

If I was right, Ember was riding within her as I hunted Aria down. The moment she felt me, she'd realize what I was doing and lend her host her abilities. Those abilities would keep Aria protected.

The scent of her sweat pulled me in, knowing she was close. Branches caught parts of her gown, leaving scattered remains throughout the woods. Pity, I'd planned to rip it from her flesh before teaching her why allowing any male close to her wasn't a good idea.

The sound of branches crunching stopped. Then Aria's heavy breathing filled the woods, which meant she was running. Pausing behind a cluster of trees, I stared at the woman who'd changed my entire world. Her silver hair was wet and glistened beneath the iridescent moonlight. My gaze raked over every curve, hungering for her, as she sucked air in greedily. The small clearing that she'd paused in to catch her breath allowed the moon to bathe her alluring form in the glow of its light The dress clung to her body like a second skin, revealing the hardened peaks of her taut, pretty pink nipples.

In my need to have her beneath me, writhing as we fucked until exhaustion, I'd missed it. Pins with the sun held a flimsy cape to the gown. Armlets, which declared her a princess to the Kingdom of Fire, adorned both of her biceps. Golden thread was woven throughout the gown, which made her look more like a goddess than a princess.

They'd created the woman to lure men to their deaths. If I'd scented the likeness to my inner beast, she'd have slaughtered me as Ember emerged from her pretty flesh.

Fuck if she hadn't been feral in her need to fuck, fight, and feed.

When I released a deep, masculine rattle of need, she spun around, searching the darkness for me. She was breathtakingly gorgeous. Her teeth worried her bottom lip, which drove me insane. The soft hiss of air from her lungs as she gradually began backing up had my cock straining for release against the wet pants I wore.

Her body tensed to run, but I shot forward, slamming into her hard. My fingers threaded through her hair before I pushed her against the nearest tree. Her pupils dilated, but her lips parted as she cried out in pain. Without warning, I released her hair to grip the flimsy fabric of the dress she wore, ripping it straight down the center before returning my hold to her silken strands. Rag dolling her body, I spun her around, forcing her against the tree until the bark pressed against the delicate skin of her cheek.

"You're such pretty prey," I hissed as I yanked the gown down, exposing her flesh to my greedy gaze. I forcefully kicked her feet apart and thrust two fingers deep into her needy cunt, realizing that it was already dripping wet. "So fucking deliciously wet for me already?"

Her cry of surprise only intensified my arousal. Aria's pussy clamped down against my intrusion, sucking my fingers deeper into her body. Bloody hell, she was perfect. I fucked her with my fingers hard, forcing them deeper as I twisted her head, knowing it would burn and add pain to her pleasure.

"Knox!" she cried out as I added another. "Fuck, that aches." Her breathy moan told me it might sting, but she liked the brutality of my fingers invading her pussy, conquering it as I taught it who really owned it and the soul of the woman it belonged to.

"Be a good girl and shut your bratty mouth up so I can hear you scream for me. You like it rough, don't you? Such a naughty little monster when you need fucked. You keep complaining, and I may even fuck your lips," I rasped as the sound of her drenched pussy caused precome to drip from my cock.

"Shit, it aches. Knox, fucking hell," she whimpered, her soft moans driving me insane as her body took what I forced into it. And it took everything so exceedingly well.

She'd floored me when my knot was deep in her cunt, forcing us together. I'd feared it'd horrify her, but she wasn't. I had never attempted to use it before Lennox knotted her pussy to force her womb open. Most male dragons didn't end up with them, at least not anymore. Fuck if she hadn't still been wild with need as she took all of it, so wantonly, too. Only some Karnavious dragons held the ability to knot without the ability to become a dragon. Until Aria took it into her ravenous, insatiable cunt? I'd felt cheated to be forced to be among those few.

"You're a good girl for me. Aren't you?" I crooned, my lips hovering over the mark she wore so perfectly. It was untarnished, which caused Lennox to release a raspy rattle of approval. Even though he couldn't sense Ember, he still enjoyed us hunting Aria down. "Say how filthy you are for me. Tell me you're my naughty little monster. Now."

"You're an asshole," she returned heatedly, her hips moving to assist me in fucking her needy flesh. My grip moved from her hair to her throat, forcing her around until her spine pressed uncomfortably against the tree. "Knox!"

"You are mine. Fucking say it before I shove you down and fuck that pretty ass of yours," I snarled back, enjoying the flash of rage burning in her pretty stare. "This pussy is so fucking wet for me. You want to be fucked hard, and savagely, don't you?" Curling my fingers to brush the one spot she couldn't ignore, I chuckled coldly as her eyes rolled back in her head. Her cunt clenched down on my fingers, even as the walls fluttered, begging for something more to fill them. Bloody hell, she was utter perfection in the rawest, truest form. "Such a good girl. Fucking hell that pussy is strangling my fingers."

"Oh, God!" she whimpered, spreading herself wider, offering me easier access to her sloppy wet cunt. And it was sloppy. If I had her against my mouth right now, her arousal would be painting my face, and I'd fucking drink her pleasure up like a glutton.

"Open your pretty fucking eyes and don't close them again. I want you to know who the fuck is giving you pleasure. Look at how well you fuck my fingers. You're fucking them like a dirty little bitch in heat who'd take whatever I offered if it got her off. Wouldn't you? You crave more, don't you?" Before I realized how pissed she was, her knee elevated, then shocking agony tore through my balls. It felt as if I'd been kicked in the gut by a stallion. Dropping to my knees, I stared up into glowing turquoise eyes with flecks of gold sparkling in them. "You want to play rough?" I hissed through the burning pain she'd inflicted.

"Have I ever asked you for mercy, asshole?" she asked in a taunting, raspy whisper. "Jealousy is beneath kings and queens." Slowly, she began backing away as if she could escape the anger she finally noticed on my face.

"You can't be jealous of something that's already yours. I'm territorial. Territorial is merely protecting what's mine, because I refuse to walk away from you, Aria. You're more naïve than I thought if you think kings and queens don't get jealous," I hissed out as I exhaled the pain she'd inflicted.

Her eyes lowered to my hand, which gripped my balls to ease the agony. Her lips parted before those sexy fucking eyes rounded in horror. A sadistic smile played on my lips, because she'd just realized how ruthless she'd just given me permission to be against that pretty, wet cunt of hers.

Spinning around, she bolted with speed she shouldn't have yet. The moon hit that perky ass of hers, bathing it in light until she disappeared into the dense forest. A smile spread over my lips as I used magic to make the first, then second branch whip against her naked, unmarked skin as beautiful breathless gasps touched my ears. Closing my eyes against the pain, I pushed from the ground and bolted after her.

Aria hadn't realized her primal self was free from restraints yet. But I could see the feral bitch unleashed in all her naked glory running wild within the woods. Yet, she wasn't screaming or whining about the limbs marking her creamy flesh each time I ordered one to do so.

I'd thought her devilish before, but my girl was a force of nature. A loud grunt sounded as a larger limb smacked against her breasts and then another against her clit. She deserved it for fighting dirty, even if I liked the type of dirty, she played by.

I had thought no woman would ever be welcomed in my life after I'd lost Liliana. Not one who could force me to be a better person. Not because I should've been one but because I wanted to be what she needed. I wanted to show her I wasn't some barbarian who didn't value her worth. I knew I didn't deserve her after the shit I'd done to her, but I'd be damned if I gave her up either.

Aria wasn't the type of woman you walked away from. There wouldn't be any getting over that girl. Greer had filled my head with shit about twin flames, which was what I blamed for my need of connection to another soul. Aria made me feel younger, and that wasn't something I would give up without one hell of a fight.

If I lost that fight, they'd be forced to put me down. I'd never stop hunting her. She and I held a deeper, more profound connection than I'd ever had before. She made me whole again with her soft touches against my sharp edges. The woman kissed my scars and wasn't afraid to get cut in order to do it. Fuck letting her go. She was my salvation. But she was also raw chaos in the truest form, and I was about to make her my queen. Ashes and ruins.

CHAPTER 13
ARIA

Running through a forest, stark-ass naked, wasn't how I'd seen this going down. Ember, on the other hand, would really love doing so. Knox had been predatory, his movements fueled by a need I couldn't understand. I'd never been so turned on, while actually fearful of the way he tracked me, like he was more beast than man. But I was down to play whatever game this was, so long as I got off before we left this forest.

My thighs ached, burning where the limbs of the trees and bushes slapped and scraped against the muscle. The ache in my side told me I'd been running longer than I'd realized.

The freedom that came with being in nature, rushing blindly through the world? Exhilarating. Though, painful when stark assed naked. I felt free here, as if my inhibitions were gone. Each step took me further into an animalistic state and allowed me to run harder, faster. I didn't want him to catch me, but only because I'd kneed him in the balls. Knox was pissed. The proof drifted in the air in waves. I felt his need to hurt me, to throw me down and rut into my body without a shred of mercy.

I'd never asked him for mercy before, but this time was different. There was something primal about his hunting me down tonight. He was pushing me toward something, but I wasn't certain what it was or why.

The moment I escaped the heavily wooded forest, I found myself staring at a cliff wall that did nothing but make dread snake down my spine. Climbing it seemed impossible until a branch snapped behind me, and then I was properly motivated. I leaped toward a low-hanging rock and then pulled myself up the ledge. My fingers ached and the scent of earth and pine clung to my flesh from the trees I'd barreled blindly through.

I was halfway up the cliff when Knox loosed wicked laughter below me but far, far too close to be from the ground. I chanced a glance, finding him standing on a small ledge a few steps away. His chest was covered in a fine sheen of sweat that glistened in the moonlight. Unable to tear my gaze from his delicious muscular body, I chewed my bottom lip and drank in every sharp edge of his physique.

"See something you like, Aria?" he asked in a raspy tone, flooded with lust.

"Most definitely," I admitted, uncaring if he knew how much I wanted him. "Too bad you're being an asshole, which means I'll need to pass regretfully." Without waiting for his reply, I began climbing faster, my body racing to go over the crest before he caught me. Something warm wrapped around my ankle, yanking me from the rocks I'd been clinging to.

I grasped out wildly, seeking anything to hold on to in order to prevent toppling to the ground. Knox leaped to the next ledge, hauling me with him by my fucking ankle. The most I had time to do was hold my hands out in front of me to keep my face from smashing into the rock as he dragged me up the cliff. At a small crevice, he paused, lifted me up by the leg, and then flicked my clit with his skilled tongue.

Adrenaline rushed through me, even as pleasure drove a moan from my parched lips. My spine arched as he dragged his tongue through the center of my core, growling as he teased, taunted, and took what he wanted from me. The position forced my mind to battle against the pleasure and fear of falling to my death. Knox's wicked laughter against my pussy told me he knew exactly why my moan turned to a whispered cry of fear.

"Such a pretty pussy you're offering to me," he murmured before he jumped to another ledge as I screamed. As he moved, he continued to ravish my center. Knox was dragging me up with him, while inching me toward another type of ledge all together.

"Knox!" I cried as his other hand released the rocks to grab my free ankle. He wasn't licking anymore. His mouth was ravenously fucking my flesh. He licked the fissure of my center before sinking his tongue so deep inside that it battered against the g-spot. "Fuck!" This was how I died. In a fucking dreamscape with Knox's tongue in my cunt while he dangled me over a thousand-foot drop. If this was it, it wasn't such a horrible way to go.

"If I were you, I'd hold on, pretty monster."

Hold on, was he fucking serious right now? His hold on

my ankles tightened as he swung me, even as I grabbed blindly for something to hold onto.

It continued until I was right side up, then he released me, even as my hands shot out, needing to anchor myself against him. My nails found flesh, sinking in as the scent of coppery tang stung my nose. A clawed hand gripped my throat and shoved me against a flat boulder. My hands slammed against the smooth surface right as his landed against my ass, stinging the already sore flesh.

"You asshole, mother-fucking, cunt-sucking, dog-fucking, dickhead!" I snarled as he came up behind me and drove his thick, lengthy cock deep into my pussy. The scream that ripped from my lungs was filled with shock, pain, and longing. Fucking hell the bastard was huge.

"I'd watch that mouth before you end up with me fucking it, woman. Fucking hell, your cunt is trying to strangle my cock." He wasn't being gentle. It was brutal fucking. Knox hadn't eased into my body. He'd forced himself in to the hilt and battered against me until all I could do was take what he dished out. Reaching back, I sank my nails into his hips, and he threw his head back, rattling until my spine arched. "Such a good girl," he purred once the rattle eased.

My eyes rolled back in my head as he continually bottomed out within me. It was painful. It was erotic. It was fucking everything I'd never known I'd needed as he jerked me back against his chest. My moan turned into a scream as the sadistic bastard began crawling up the cliff with his dick still inside me. Every move he made jostled his cock, sending waves of pleasure overriding the fear.

Knox's laughter against my shoulder told me he knew

what he was doing to me. The bastard was getting off on the scent of fear and arousal oozing from my pores. His body caged me in against the rocky terrain, scraping the soft flesh of my chest, cheek, and abdomen as he dragged us both to the top.

The moment he had me on solid ground, he withdrew and then used my throat to effectively spin me around. My knees threatened to give out as his eyes, which were spattered with diamonds shimmering in the ocean-hued depths, dragged down my scraped, battered body. Then he was shoving me backward so hard I struggled to keep my feet beneath me.

"Beg for me like a good girl. I want to taste your pleasure as it drips down your lovely, taut thighs for me. Get on your fucking knees and get this pretty ass in the air for me. Now," he ordered, but I wasn't surrendering to him. If he wanted me, he could come fucking get me.

Spinning on my heels, I darted for the brush. I made it three steps before Knox's body collided with mine. Fingers threaded through my hair and turned my head before shoving me down against the earthen floor. It hadn't hurt, but I was certain he wasn't actually trying to hurt me. The other hand gripped my abdomen from between my thighs, which pushed my knees apart before gripping my hips. His cock entered me hard, fast, pistoning into my body with need driving each thrust. A strangled scream tore from my lips as he grew, making my walls flutter as he got larger as he pushed into my opening.

The wet sounds of our bodies colliding echoed in my ears as his masculine scent of bergamot, sage, and whiskey coerced my eyes to grow heavy with need. My breasts ached as they lurched forward and backward with the velocity of his angry thrusts. I felt him growing more, whining as he forced me to take what he gave.

"Knox," I growled against the earthen floor, unable to make my head lift from where he held it pushed into the grassy knoll. "Fucking hell!" The pain and pleasure were overwhelming. The adrenaline and pleasure rolled through my abdomen, slamming against my clit with a palpable pulse. "Oh my god!"

"I'm your fucking god, Aria. You worship me. No one else, Aria." His words came out gravelly as he brought me up so he could palm my breast, squeezing it. "These beautiful breasts are mine. Those pouty fucking lips are mine. This wet pussy? Fucking mine. Your perky, pretty ass? Mine. Your lethally strategic mind? That's mine too, Little Monster. Every part of you is beautiful, and its mine. This dick? You can have it. It can belong to you and only you, but I get every part of you, woman."

"Your cock is all I get?" I demanded as my hands landed on his thighs behind me, digging into the flesh of both.

Cold air touched the breast he'd been squeezing before I'd even realized he'd released it. His hand moved to my throat, applying enough pressure to cut off the blood flow to my brain. The entire time, he didn't stop pistoning into my flesh, fucking me with brutality and skill. My walls constricted to expel the too-large cock driving me to stretch to fit him. Stars dotted my vision, but his hold on my throat relaxed enough to allow air to reach my lungs to feed my brain.

"Wrong fucking answer," he hissed against my ear,

warm breath fanning it as he once again tightened his hold. "Your delicious pussy knows who it belongs to. Doesn't it, pretty monster? You feel my cock marking your walls? I'm writing my name on them so you remember you're in my coverage area." I blinked as he threw what I'd said the first time he'd captured me back in my face. It was actually sweet he even remembered what I'd said. "Your body knows who it belongs to, doesn't it? I feel it clenching down, holding me so tightly in its embrace. Fucking hell I love how well you take me." His arm slid around my stomach as his hold on my throat turned painful. Before I could argue, not that I could, he stood. Knox walked toward a tree, making my stomach touch against it before the band of his arm released. The hand he held around me grabbed behind my knee, pushing it up so he could get deeper into my body.

My body started shaking from lack of oxygen, but if he noticed, he didn't show it. His cock withdrew until only the tip remained at my entrance. One hard, merciless thrust sank him to the hilt within me, and I had to brace against the tree as I danced on the edge of bliss and nothingness. Pain and pleasure blurred as he finally allowed oxygen to enter my greedy lungs. Gasping, I sucked it in ravenously.

"If I want to use your pussy and make it weep for me, what's your answer, Aria?" The gravely tenor of his voice scraped over every one of my raw nerve endings.

"Hard pass," I hissed between gasps of air. No way in hell was I saying yes to anything that stopped this wild beast from rutting me.

"You like being manhandled," he whirred before his lips brushed my shoulder. "I love how you feel clenching tightly around me. I love feeling your breath hitch as I pound into your drenched center with hard, pounding thrusts. You love me fucking you. Don't you? Outside of our animalistic needs, you might be a fucking princess outside of here, but in here, you're a fucking predator like me," he whirred before his lips brushed against my shoulder. The thought of his teeth embedded in my flesh sent excitement rushing through me. Arousal flooded toward my entrance, offering him a silky wet fluid to use to fuck me harder. "I see. Naughty girl wants my mark. Is that it? You want my teeth?"

"Please, Knox," I begged, uncaring how fucking desperate I sounded.

I was naked in the woods, being railed against a tree. Dirt and gods knew what else was in my hair. Then there was the fact that he held my legs spread apart so he could do whatever he wanted to my pussy. It was either bark scrapping my tits or rocks, and I was pretty sure my own cum was dripping down my leg as my body begged for more. But, what more could he fucking do? I wasn't sure I wanted to ask, let alone find out.

"Tell me you're mine." He pulled out from my body and stepped back.

I toppled to the ground, gasping for air as my pussy clenched with the need to be filled. He was fucking joking, right? Turning my head, I glared at him as he stood there gloriously naked, stroking his thick, proud cock. Licking my lips, I enjoyed the sight of his magnificent, powerful physique. Fucking hell, the bastard was beautiful.

"Say it, or I'll fucking edge this pussy all night long?"

Dropping my eyes to the precome dripping from the

tip, I considered my next move carefully. Did I really care if my pride was tarnished if it got me fucked until it wouldn't matter? If I knew he wouldn't stop until my body was one solid ache of sated pleasure and my mind was mutton stew? I would actually be totally fine with any of that. But he'd win, and that wasn't something I was willing to allow. Not yet, anyway.

"How about you get the fuck on your knees and I'll teach that bratty mouth how to say what it's told to, Aria?"

Rising to my feet, I slowly prowled toward him. Those hypnotic, ocean-colored eyes narrowed, which meant he was trying to gauge my next move. Standing before him, I licked my lips before pushing my tongue out, which caused his entire face to darken with desire.

Slowly, I began to lower myself before him, but the moment my body was crouched, I shot forward. Grabbing him between his powerful legs, I flipped his body over me, but Knox didn't go down as I'd intended him to. Instead, he landed on his feet. One minute, I was the aggressor, and the next? I was pinned beneath the full weight of his heavy, hard, unmoving body.

His knees pressed my legs apart seconds before he was fucking me again. I'd been wrong. He hadn't been brutal before. I screamed as tears burned my eyes and pleasure blossomed in my abdomen. Knox's hands landed on my wrists, gripping them painfully before he forced them behind my back, capturing both in his large viselike grip. The other slid up my spine, threading through my hair, which he used to jerk me back, leaving my body suspended in midair between his cock and his grip on the silky tresses.

"You want to fight me or fuck me?" I glared up at him, which caused his lips to slide into a smile, revealing those devastating dimples. "Have it your way. I'll fuck that fight right out of you, Aria Primrose." The way he spoke in a husky, gravely tone had my pussy clenching as he brutalized it. His knot formed, which caused my eyes to widen in uncertainty as he continually pulled it out, only to drive it back in with each hard, splendid thrust forward. It caused a delicious stretch every time it entered, then exited.

Tears flowed down my cheeks, but they weren't from pain. They were from the sheer beauty of the primal brutality of Knox. He'd snapped whatever tethered me to my human flesh, fucking me right out of it as he forced me to submit. My arms ached all the way to my shoulder blades, but I wouldn't ask for mercy. Instead, I took what he dished out, fucking loving every filthy moment of him abusing my body.

The only witnesses to the debauchery unraveling were the stars, forest, and earthen floor he fucked me on. I came hard and it hit me so fucking brutally that the kaleidoscope of colors that burst into my vision had me babbling incoherently. The sudden euphoric feeling caused my brain to misfire, even as everything became overwhelming. I could hear my sobs as I begged for more, for him to ruin and destroy me. To ruin me. To savage every inch of my flesh until I could no longer discern who I'd been before I'd been his.

"So fucking beautiful when you're coming undone for me." His words barely registered as I trembled violently through the climax rocketing through me. "I feel your pretty cunt grasping my knot. You like my cock, don't you?" Releasing my arms, Knox forced his cock from the hold my pussy held on to it with. "You made a mess on my cock," he chided before shoving me forward.

I hit the ground, and my lips parted as a whimpered cry escaped from them. Before I could even move, he grabbed my ankles and pulled me up by them so he could enjoy what he'd done, forcing arousal to drip from my cunt.

"Someone's *very* messy. I think I should clean my messy girl up, don't you?" he asked, which caused my eyes to round at the thought of more pleasure. "I fucking love how sweet your pussy tastes against my lips. So fucking wet for me. Such a good girl offering to let me taste your delicious cunt."

Knox strode toward a large, flat boulder and sat before yanking me up and hooking the backs of my knees over his shoulders. He blew a heated breath against my sore, wet cunt as one of his hands slid around my abdomen, holding me in place, and the other began traipsing through the arousal coating my pussy.

His tongue slowly began an intricate dance across my cunt. He gradually but surely built tension in my core as he lavished the center, ensuring to tease my clit with every lick, and methodical stroke of his tongue. A coil built in my belly, threatening to spring loose as he took his time coaxing my release to the edge.

He was driving me mad with the need to come, but I knew he was fully aware of what he was doing. Each powerful flick of his tongue was calculated as he intention-ally licked over my lips, center, and then moaned. It created a delicious vibration that landed against my clitoris with devilish intentions. Knox was a master at edging me to the brink of madness. I fucking loved it, but I hated it just as much.

I rocked against his ravenous mouth, moaning and whimpering whatever he wanted to hear. Fuck being prideful, I wanted him to push my next orgasm to end me. The wicked rumble of his laughter had my eyes closing as it created friction against my center. The rattle of approval had arousal rushing to my entrance, forcing a whimpered cry from my lips. It wasn't merely a little warmth gathering there, but rather enough to feel it trickling from my entrance. Knox was greedily cleaning it, as if he approved of how drenched he was making me. When I tried to push myself up to ride his mouth, his arm tightened over my abdomen, banding against it.

I tried to sit up, to haul myself up to ride his glorious lips until I came all over his face. Needy whispers exploded from my lips as he chuckled at my feeble attempt to take control from him. The arm banded around my abdomen tightened, even as his tongue pushed into my cunt, forcing a loud, sultry whimper of defeat from my lungs. Knox fucked me, as if his tongue was a cock instead of the muscle within his mouth. His name dripped from my lips as a soft cry of exclamation tore from my throat as it flicked my g-spot. The bastard was writing his name upon it, enforcing his claim of ownership.

"If I ask who this—"

"It's yours motherfucker! I'm yours, all of me. I'll do whatever, say whatever, as long as you fuck me," I babbled, uncertain if actual words were falling from my lips. "I'll worship your dick at its altar if you just fuck me. Just wreck me, Knox. I'm yours, every part of me belongs to you and only you. I am yours. My pleasure. My pain. My soul. All of it is yours already. I need you to destroy me, now!"

"Good girl," he praised before pushing from the rock, then carefully grabbing my wrists before allowing my body to slide down against his. I'd assumed he was going to make me prove it to him, but he pushed into my body instead. "Knox," I moaned through the pleasure and pain as it washed through me like a shot of morphine. Knox was a drug that you never wanted to eradicate from your system. He forced me through highs and lows. This man caused my brain to be in a state of euphoria when he battered down my defenses, then claimed me for his own.

"Fucking hell. You are so fucking perfect," he growled. Knox captured my chin with one hand, wrapping his palm against my jawline and pushing his thumb between my lips. "Taste how deliciously wet you are for me. So fucking good for me. Fucking hell, woman. You undo me."

"Please!"

I closed my lips around his thumb, tasting my arousal upon his flesh, as his cock continued to piston into my core. My legs wrapped around his waist, then I began meeting his thrust willingly.

"You are such a lovely creature, Aria. I wish you could see how wild you look being fucked into submission. Your hair is a gorgeous mess of chaos, and your flesh is painted red from strain, scratches, and my hands gripping every inch of your exquisite body. Your delicious cunt is red from being stretched from my cock, sloppy wet from the arousal it created in order to take all of it deep into your needy flesh." Knox repositioned so he hit the sweet spot attached to every nerve in my body. The friction it created caused desire to flare within my body as fear bit into my mind. "I love your scent mixing with mine, proving you're my girl."

"Knox," I whispered, hissing as the orgasm began swelling through my abdomen, driving straight to my clit.

"You're my girl. Only mine, Aria. I won't fucking lose you now, not after everything we've been through together. I couldn't live through it. Do you hear me?"

My whimpered moan was smothered by his thumb slowly fucking my mouth, and I hadn't even realized he'd been moving until I felt a silky, feather soft fabric against my back. Knox leaned over me, slowly withdrawing his thumb before his lips crushed against mine.

The kiss wasn't a kiss at all. It was him declaring ownership of my entire soul with his lips, his tongue, and heated mouth. His tongue dueled against mine, dancing in an ageless, endless kiss. His palm cradled my cheek as the other braced his weight above me. Each whimpered moan that escaped, Knox eagerly drank into his lungs. His cock slowly moved within me, as if he were trying to be gentle. The kiss turned harder, needier as my hands moved, cradling his face, and his hips began pumping harder, faster against my body.

When he tensed in climax, I shot over the edge of oblivion with him. It was intensified by the euphoria humming through my veins. This bastard had coerced me out of my flesh, while making me shed all inhibitions as I evolved from merely thinking as a human. I'd felt a bevy of emotions in such a short time that I was both over-whelmed and excited. Breaking from the kiss, Knox watched me shattering into a million shards of glass, which he continued holding until I slowly put myself back together.

"Bloody hell, woman. You're so fucked. There's no world in which I would ever let you go." His eyes searched mine with something I hadn't seen in his eyes before. Vulnerability. "Do you understand me? I will bring the Nine Realms to its fucking knees if that is what it takes to keep you with me, Aria. I'd rather live in ruins than spend eternity without you at my side."

"As if you get a choice?" Leaning up from the bed, I kissed him softly. "There's no one else I'd ever want beside me, Knox. Broken pieces and sharply cutting edges, I'd still choose you. Always. That isn't a question you ever need to ask me. I'm yours," I promised as tears rolled from my eyes and a smile played on my lips. "Do *you* understand *me*?" I countered, feeding his words right back at him. It wasn't the right words we'd needed to say to one another. Neither desired to speak or hear those words until we were physically holding one another, or at least, I didn't.

Knox and I had survived too much to want anyone else. Not in the way we craved one another so viscerally profound that it caused an ache to my very bones. This cruel, savagely brutal creature was mine. I'd destroy anything or anyone who thought to take him from me. I loved him more than I actually cared to admit it to even myself. Knox Karnavious, the same sadistic prick who'd sent my entire world toppling to the ground like ruins of an ancient temple, was the man I wanted to spend my forever with. If I didn't end up with him, then I didn't want to end up living. He was the other half of my soul, and without him? I wouldn't be whole.

He'd known I wasn't actually here, which was why he hadn't marked me as he'd promised to. The marking inside a dreamscape only offered pain. As I remained on the bed, a chaotic mess of soreness, I watched the man I'd once considered my enemy beginning to pull away from me. Had his thoughts followed mine into dangerously dark, turbulent lengths he'd go to keep me? Because I know now why love was worth fighting for. He'd taught me that lesson along our trek from where we started out, to where we were now.

If I could go back to the girl I'd been when he'd found me, I'd tell her to be fearless in her pursuit of what she'd become. I'd reassure her that his sharp edges were worth being cut on to taste the pleasure and emotions only he could invoke. If I could tell her one thing, it would be that his broken pieces were the missing parts of her soul.

"Have they crowned you queen yet?" he asked as he pulled from my body, leaving me cold without his heat.

"No," I admitted.

"You need to be very careful there, Aria. We think they might be planning something against you. There's a lot we need to talk about, as well."

"Aden is hellbent on claiming me, but I can easily handle him." I felt heat covering my chest as he left me barren and adrift in the sea of his churning ocean-colored stare. "I'm not worried about him, or anyone trying to claim me, for that matter. I'm yours, Knox."

His throat bobbed, as if my words scared him. It caused a hollowness in my chest, as the thought of me mistaking his intentions rose inside my mind. I wanted to be here with him, and while I wanted to save the realms, I was sick of everyone questioning my relationship with this man. He was the only thing I'd ever reached for to keep for myself.

"I know you can handle him, but that's not what I'm worried about. I think there's another part to the prophecy. Something they left out on purpose. I've been scouring every book inside this place to find a door to gain access to the new realm. I think they're inside that realm with you. It means you're in danger."

"Are you worried about me being hurt, or are you worried about me betraying you, Knox?"

His face closed down, shutting me out. "I'm worried about them trying to kill you to prevent you reaching for your birthright. You're young, which leads to blindly following the wrong people, Aria. Like Aurora, who led you right to her mother."

"I know there's those within it who don't want me leaving with the crown. And while I'm ten steps ahead of them and not blindly following anyone around, there are unknowns in the scenario. It works in my favor that they think I'm meek and dainty, which is the first and last mistake people make about me. You did, didn't you?" At the smirk he awarded me, I continued. "They're under the assumption I'm not a threat, which is what I've allowed them to think. You taught me that."

"I taught you many things, woman. It doesn't change the fact that you're on your own there. There's a lot happening around here, which I could use that brilliant brain of yours to help me fix." Grabbing sweatpants, he pulled them on before moving to the chest of drawers, pulling out a gown for me.

"I felt the land, Knox. But it wasn't the new realm

Griffon built. It was the actual Kingdom of Fire. I don't know why it is calling to me, but I felt the pull to go to the land there. It brought me one step closer to my birthright. Once I have it, I'll return to finish what I started here."

"I don't like you being there," he admitted. "The prophecy can get fucked for all I care. We can find another way to end Hecate. It doesn't have to be you." His words caused pain to clench my heart because it seemed as if he didn't think I could stop her. "You not being here where I can sense you? It's driving me crazy. I can't feel you at all anymore, which means you can't feel me." The tightening in my chest lessened at his tender words. "There's a lot more we've learned, as well."

"Like?" I asked as something jerked within me. "Fuck. Something isn't right."

"What the fuck does that mean?" he demanded, rushing toward me.

"I don't know," I admitted as pain sliced through me, compelling a scream from my lips. My claws extended as Knox reached for me, only for his hand to pass right though. "Knox?"

"Fuck. Aria!" he snarled as I felt myself falling.

I came to with the taste of blood oozing from my lips. A masculine whine met my ears, and I opened my eyes to see a shocked pair of azure-colored ones staring at me. The scent of fear and arousal oozed around me, making my nose wrinkle. Zyion chuckled softly, and Aden's arm dripped blood down my chin. The rattle I released wasn't friendly, not even a little bit.

Aden's hips pumped, and the scent of his come soaked into the fabric of his trousers. Behind him, multiple guards had backed Esme into a corner and were keeping her there. Blood trickled from a cut on her forehead, causing anger to explode within me. Zyion whistled, wisely stepping back from where I had pinned Aden to the ground, vehemently.

Releasing his arm, I licked the blood before standing up, smelling Knox on my flesh. I shouldn't smell him anywhere within the room, yet I did. It was the same berg-amot, sage, and whiskey that I'd grown to love about his unique scent.

"If you don't take your fucking hands off her, I'll chew them off and fuck you in the ass with them. Understand me, gentlemen? No one puts hands on my best friend. Anyone fucking moves, I'll let Ember out to play—" They stepped away, releasing her. "Smart boys. You," I hissed, peering down at Aden. "What the fuck did you do to piss off my inner beast?" Licking his blood from my lips, I eyed Zyion through narrowed slits before turning back to Aden. "Answer me. Now."

"You were fucking screaming in your sleep. At least, we were under the assumption you slept. Esmeralda was slumped over your unmoving body. She prevented us from reaching it as if she'd assassinated you, Aria." He sniffed, holding his savaged arm as it slowly began mending. "Obviously, we should've known you'd abandoned the kingdom to slither back to that bastard dragon you're fucking."

"I don't remember giving you permission to be so informal in my presence, Aden," I shot back. "And I suggest you tread carefully. It isn't smart to piss my beast off. She's ravenous, and you? You look like a snack, which would hold her over until she can hunt for her dragon. You won't fucking see me coming, either. Now, get the fuck out of my chamber. Don't enter it again unless I've vacated it, little boy." His eyes flashed with murderous rage, which had Ember adding a rattle of warning to my words. A flash of fear lit within his, sending him scattering toward the door along with the men he'd brought with him. Turning toward Zyion, I found him watching me with pride shimmering in his gaze.

"You're not weak. That's good. It might save that pretty neck of yours. If I were you, I'd tread carefully. Not all here are thrilled you returned, princess." With that, he left the room, leaving me covered in Aden's blood.

"What the hell did he mean by that?" Esme demanded, shoving past the wall of guards. When I shrugged, she exhaled. "I fell asleep. In my defense? It's been days since you told me you'd be right back. Then, add in your fucking body flopping around as you moaned. For the record, it's creepy as fuck. That was days ago. You left to enter the dreamscape, and when you didn't come back, I made up excuses for your absence. It's been days, but it wasn't until last night that you started screaming. I guess it wasn't really screaming. It was like this," she said, then proceeded to grunt loudly, which had my lips twitching as mortification burned my cheeks.

"I get it," I conceded. "That means time is changing rapidly within this realm. Either way, we need to get what we came for and get the fuck out of here. We have to do what we came here for and get back before Hecate has a chance to fully heal."

"What the hell is a lollygag?" she asked.

"It means to be idle," I offered in explanation.

Stretching my arms, I winced as my eyes widened in shock before I could conceal it from Esme.

"Were you fucking him? Oh," she said as her hand landed against her forehead. "That explains the noises so much more." Snickering, she marched toward her chamber. "I'm going to bed. Babysitting your corpse was exhausting. Oh, by the way?" She paused, turning to look at me. "Ember is awake when you're not within your body. Luckily, it was easy to appease her with meat. But you might want to explain to your father why you needed an entire deer delivered to your chamber. Also, you're cleaning up the mess she made. I refuse to do so, even if she tossed bones at me."

Blinking at her in confusion, I felt Ember snickering within me.

"You went to Dicker, and he dicked you down. But did I get to feel it? No. Did I randomly hump dicks?" She paused long enough to make me nervous before answering, *"No, but I could have. I'm a growing girl. Need lots of Dicker to get faster and bigger so we can do epic shit, like, well . . . I don't know what. But I know we're going to be the best epic lesbians together, Aria."*

"Yeah, Ember. We're going to be the best lesbians one day. Thank you for not fucking random dick. If you behave, I'll let you hunt Knox down and claim him. I owe you that for protecting my body and Esme while I was away." Her purr slowly built within me as I moved to sit on the edge of the bed.

I'd left Knox abruptly, which meant he'd worry about me. If time moved faster than it did there, that was one thing. However, I wasn't certain if it was this place or the library that had altered time. Something had changed it, which meant I needed to figure it out. If I didn't, he'd be coming here one way or another. It was Knox, there wasn't anything he wouldn't or couldn't do when he put his mind to it.

CHAPTER 14
ARIA

I'd wasted the early morning hours, fearful of Knox worrying about me. He wouldn't realize I was fine, not unless I could somehow get a message to him. Aden had forced me from him, then acted offended when I'd attacked him. He shouldn't have been in my chamber, let alone touching my vulnerable body. But I had departed from Knox unexpectedly, and I had informed him that something was amiss. It left me fearful of how he'd respond.

Aden had haunted my dreams afterward. He'd chained me to a post like a rabid animal, who he tossed kibble and bits to while onlookers cheered him on. Knox was in the crowd, laughing along with the others. It had enraged me enough that I'd woken from it, unable to return to sleep.

As I'd watched the sunrise, the worry dissipated, but not entirely. The knock on the door before the sun had fully risen didn't help in that regard. A bevy of ladies had announced that we were to be readied for the day's events, which had soured my mood. Especially when they'd stated Aden had sent them up to ensure I was presentable.

They'd stormed the suite and then began filling this realm's medieval version of a clawed foot tub before scrubbing us raw. The dress they had handed me was a lacey crisscrossed pattern with thin straps. The larger straps of ice-blue lace on the bodice covered my breasts and created an almost pushup bra effect. They wrapped a thin silver band around my abdomen before fussing with my skirt until it hung provocatively off my narrow hips. Twin slices in the flowing chiffon fabric allowed my thighs to peek through every time I took a step. My hair had been braided with an iridescent ribbon threaded through the silver strands. After primping, prodding, and forcing us into finery, the women who'd stormed the chamber began cleaning up.

"I never agreed to be tortured!" Esme snarled from the other room.

The women in the chamber with me giggled, which had been going on for the better part of the entire ordeal, and then handed me the armlets. Accepting them, I placed them onto my arms, then chanced a peek in the glass set beside the table.

"Your Highness," one woman, named Corin, called. "Your crown."

"I don't wear crowns, Corin," I stated, leaning a shoulder against the doorframe of Esme's room. They'd somehow got her into a dress similar to mine with a V-line bodice and skirts that brushed the top of her feet. Her hair was still loose, flowing in inky, dark ringlets down her back. "It's enough, ladies. You should feel accomplished by managing this much. Esmeralda doesn't enjoy wearing gowns, even if she looks beautiful in them."

"Beautiful? I look like I lost a bet with a seamstress who wrapped me in yards of fabric!"

A soft chuckle left my lips. "You do not, Esme. You look like a fairy princess."

"Seriously? Fuck being a fairy farting princess!" she snarled as the women backed away with anxious energy oozing from them. "I never agreed to wear a gown!"

"Thank you, ladies," I acknowledged before fighting a smile as Esme picked up the mirror from the table and studied her reflection. "You are safe with me. It's okay to be beautiful and womanly. I'd eat their faces if they thought to touch you without your permission. You know that." At my reassurance, she slid her violet stare in my direction.

"I look like a princess?"

"I wouldn't say it if it weren't true," I pointed out as I turned toward the sound of footsteps coming down the hallway. "They're growing impatient."

"Who the hell does he think is summoning you?" Esme grabbed the silk cape they'd offered her to appease her modesty as she headed toward me.

"Someone who hasn't been told no before. That would be my guess." The entryway doors opened, and I turned in time to see Eva walk in, wearing a leather uniform. Eva's eyes slid over me before sliding it to Esme. Then she gave us a slight nod of approval.

"I'll be escorting you to the field today." Then her attention fell on the creatures stretched over the settee. "Where did you get *those* things?" Her tone hinted at unease, causing my lips to twitch. "Who did they adhere to on your way here?"

"I found them before I found Scylla. I think they're cute, plus, they seem able to fend for themselves." Shrugging at the horror stamped on her face, I licked my lips. "Could you maybe tell me why our presence is needed elsewhere today?" The ladies who'd bombarded the chamber had said Aden insisted they dress us, but I'd heard another say that the king had sent them. If anyone knew why we were being forced to be up at this ungodly hour, it would be Eva.

"Griffon thought you'd like to see and learn about our traditions. Today's tournament will be a good starting point. Plus, you'll be able to meet a few of your brothers today. Vane, your oldest brother, has returned from scouting the mountain ranges. He's eager to have a sister, or so he claims. Aden also wished for you to be present for his rematch against Zyion," she explained. "You shouldn't entertain any salacious thoughts for Zyion Vicious, Aria. He's problematic, and his reputation is as obscured as his past is." Folding her arms over her breasts, she dared me to argue with her.

"Why do you all seem so hung up on something I have no interest in? Does no one even care that I have no interest in making Aden my anything? Even if I had entertained it at one time, I don't anymore—not after I heard him talking about only wanting me so he can gain the throne. I'd rather a callous bastard be at my side than some bastard who thinks to manipulate me." Eva opened her mouth to argue, but I held my hand up to prevent it. "Save it. I'm over everyone telling me who I should be interested in or who I shouldn't. That's not even on my list of shit I'm worried about. The politics don't concern me right now." They did, but I wasn't about to give her any secrets. I also wasn't willing to defend my love life to anyone here. There were much more pressing concerns than who was ringing my devil's doorbell.

"We shan't keep the men waiting."

"Shan't we?" I somehow returned with a straight face.

"No, she shan't. Come," she ordered as she left the chamber without waiting to see if we followed behind her.

"Shan't we?" I wiggled my brows at Esme, who snorted.

"You are using it wrong, Aria." At the door, she paused. "I shan't go before you, Your Majesty."

"But that was correct?" I asked with a frown pulling on my lips. Esme laughed as we rushed down the hallway in the thin sandals that they'd given us to wear. The thin silver chains wrapped around our calves of our legs before attaching leather bands high on our thighs clinked softly.

The guards bowed to Eva as we neared the doors exiting the wing, which we'd placed in. One of them paused as he rose, his eyes growing doe-like as he took in Esme. Turning toward her, I smirked as her cheeks reddened at his obvious gazing at her beauty. The other one cleared his throat, alerting the other to his gawking at her. Once we passed them, Esme turned back and let out an unladylike snort.

"Do try to pretend to have manners," Eva stated offhandedly.

"We'll do our best not to embarrass you, Lady Eva," I muttered sarcastically.

Eva spun around so swiftly I had to come to an abrupt halt. "Are we a joke to you?" It filled her voice with emotion, which made my smile drop.

"No, of course not." I swallowed past the lump growing in my throat. Offending her hadn't been my intent, but being deprived of sleep wasn't helping my mind consider anything other than the delirium setting in.

"Do you know what it has been like for us? We've been forced from our homes, lost loved ones to both dragons and witches, and told to wait around for the one who's supposed to save us all. But you don't seem worried in the least bit about our plight. You merely see a thriving civilization, which is what Griffon wanted you to see. That's what you see from the outside, looking in. You don't see the pain the dragons inflicted when they eradicated entire bloodlines from existence. The people you're supposed to rule over? They'd buried their loved ones lost at the hands of the man you . . ." Lowering her eyes, she lifted them with tears swimming in them. "It doesn't matter what you said. I honestly don't care if you are with him personally. But others see it as a betrayal against those they've lost during the dragon wars. Griffon knew the land would accept you, but even though it has, it doesn't mean the people will. You don't have to know the history to know this: Dragons fight dirty, even to this day. They broke the rules of engagement when they defiled the queen's tomb, tossing her remains around as if she'd been nothing. Royals have always been, and will always be, off-limits."

"That isn't on me though," I pointed out. "I get that there's a lot of history between our people, but they didn't teach us anything inside the Tenth Realm that didn't pertain to Hecate or her being the savior of the land." Eva's shoulders dropped before she exhaled, nodding decisively. "Tell me about Zyion."

"Zyion was Scylla's Head Guard. He dishonored Scylla when he left her side during a skirmish. When he returned, she'd had her throat slit from ear to ear. Dragons were responsible for her death, of course." Her eyes lowered as her mouth turned into a white line of tension. "His version of the story is that he'd chased off an enemy, then returned to find her, along with all of his men, deceased. The Queen's Guard is forbidden to abandon the queen, but he did so on that day. No witnesses were available to confirm or deny what happened. A queen died on his watch. So, if you're asking if you should trust him? The answer is no. Zyion Vicious isn't worthy of guarding anyone, let alone the next queen to rule our kingdom. He also has a sinister side. One very few have lived to talk about it afterward. Those who do are normally the ones he's shared a bed with. It's that he's cruel and has a violence within him that isn't tamable."

"I'm not interested in what he does behind closed doors. But if they think he murdered the queen, why would they allow him to remain here? Obviously, they don't think he is to be trusted, as you just pointed out."

"Because he's invaluable against dragons." Eva spoke of him with reverence, telling me she'd been one of those 'bedmates' she spoke of. "Once we're outside, do nothing to draw attention to yourself until we reach the dais. Griffon will be there waiting for you both. The match will begin once each warrior is granted an item of his choosing from a maiden. Please, don't upset Aden any more than you've already done."

"Didn't realize we were heading into some medieval shitshow," I muttered beneath my breath.

Esme snickered, and scenes from *A Knight's Tale* played inside my head. We exited the corridor, then took winding steps down to the main floor. Throughout the entire hallway, paintings depicting battles, or Scylla with a man, who I assumed was Tirsynth, in various poses. I didn't get time to study any of the images before Eva whisked us into luscious gardens. Passing a large, exquisitely crafted statue of twin phoenixes in flight, which was surrounded by children. One of the tiny girls looked up, smiling as I met her stare. Returning her smile, I noted the mothers gathered behind her, who all watched me with curious gazes.

As Eva approached the wide, heavily guarded gates, they were flung open to allow us to enter a heavily populated area filled with vibrantly colored tents. Each one appeared to be selling goods or wares of varying items. Cool air drifted over my shoulders, then forced goose bumps over my flesh as the scent of savory meats, sweetened berries, and excitement drifted on the breeze as we moved through the multitude of tents. Eva stopped at a tent with a large table filled with brilliantly colored strips of fabric and plucked up a sheer silver strip for me and then a crimson and onyx-colored one for Esme.

"The royal coffers will pay the coin," she told the merchant. "Esme, silver represents the Royal House of Fafnir. Red and black indicate the House of Prometheus."

"I'm a Prometheus?" she asked without accepting the slip of fabric.

"You are. You both are, but only one of you holds the bloodline of Scylla Prometheus."

"So, if I'm a Prometheus, then who is my father?" Esme asked, her lips tugging at the corners when Eva eyed her guardedly. "He doesn't want to meet me, does he?" The dejection in Esme's tone forced tightness in my chest.

"Leopold Prometheus isn't a nice person, Esmeralda. I wouldn't take it personal. He's not a loving father, either. It's not like you're missing out by his aloofness of his offspring. Leopold is Tirsynth's brother, and also your father. Griffon sent Leopold into the mountains a few nights ago. Considering the number of women within the towns outlining the forest, I don't expect him back for at least a few more days," Eva explained, offering us both the thin, frizzy pieces of fabric. Leading us through the crowd, which turned to stare as we progressed through it.

"There are other townships inside this realm?"

"A couple, Aria. Though we do try to convince them to come here. Some prefer to live away from the din of the larger towns."

"So, why isn't my hair silver? Or my eyes blue?" Esme asked, her forehead creased with the emotion she felt at discovering her father didn't care.

"Tirsynth's descendants inherited black hair and violet eyes of Prometheus. You house the blood, obviously. Scylla had only two children with Tirsynth—Griffon and Hagen, who has threatened to challenge him if he vacates the throne for you, Aria. You're to steer clear of Hagen and his sons. The same goes for Tirsynth's bastard-born children Baldrick, Talon, and Castain. They're minions of Hagen's."

"Okay," I agreed as the sounds of blades crashing

together reached my ears. It mixed with the shouts and cheers of men and women, as if they were watching a tournament. I caught glimpses of the onlookers between the gaps of the large tents we passed. Only after we had passed the last few, did my eyes widen and my lips part in surprise. "Holy shit."

Hundreds of men and women battled with various weapons on the greenery. Dragons observed the field intently, watching the combatants. Phoenixes sat on high perches, their colorful wings stretching but as mute as the dragons standing beneath them. Eva ignored the cries of those waiting to be let in past the guards, preventing them from entering the stands. She moved us toward an actual dais placed at the front of the arena.

Noises from a horse forced my head to turn, studying the way Zyion tended to the large, intimidating stallion. He had his back to me as the mammoth beast pushed its snout against his shoulder, continuing to make the sound. Those marine-colored eyes narrowed, then scanned my face, then narrowed with a worrisome emotion. If I had to guess at the emotion, it would be enmity. My teeth worried my lip as that annoying thread tugged, forcing me to examine it closer.

"I see daddy dressed you up all pretty, princess." Zyion's voice was like whiskey as it flowed over me. "Do you normally allow the men in your life to dress you? Because, if so, I look forward to doing it soon." It took me a moment to realize he was too far away for me to hear anything he said. Stopping in my tracks, I swung my stare toward where he'd been, but he was already gone.

What the hell? How the hell?

CHAPTER 15
ARIA

Zyion being able to communicate inside my head was unnerving. It left me fumbling for how he'd done it. It had also awakened Ember, who was even now trying to make me go back to the warrior so she could sniff him. The beat of my heart thundered violently against my ribcage as the din of noise elevated at our approach.

"Go back! I need to smeeeeell the creature!" Ember demanded.

Mentally shaking her, I refused. *"It's not happening. He was inside our head. Inside it, Ember!"* My body stopped mid-step, and I faltered as heat singed my ears. *"Did you try to take control of me?"* I asked inwardly.

"If you don't go back this instant, I'll strip off this torture device you allowed them to dress us in, and I'll shake your tiny ass all over the field while you're stuck inside my head!"

"You wouldn't," I hissed, which had Eva turning to eye me questioningly. *"I swear to everything holy, Ember. If you so*

195

much as try to undress us on this field, I will sew my vagina shut! Completely shut. Do you hear me? No dick will ever be up inside this vagina if you do that to me."

"Aria, I love you. You know that. I need to smell it. It smelled sooo good and tasty." The sound she released from my lips was sultry and erotic. Eva came to a stop in front of me as Esme gave me serious side-eye, lowering it the moment I glanced at her. "Tell her we shan't be speaking of this. Do it or I'll lick her!"

Shaking my head, I flinched from the internal image Ember sent flashing through my head. "You know you're acting like a two-year-old. Right? This isn't how people ask for things."

"Ask if I care, then tell her what I said! What is he?"

"My inner slut says we shan't be talking about this." Eva's mouth opened, then closed as she slowly scratched her silver head. "I don't know what he is. I don't know what anyone is. Remember? In fact, I don't even know what the hell I am. What I do know is that you're being childish and we have a mate. He can smell however the hell he wishes to, but he must do it away from us."

"Because you like his scent too! You like him. I know you. Remember?" Her taunt was childish as she berated, argued, and continued being a wanton hussy.

"Then you know Knox and Lennox wouldn't be keen on us sniffing another male. Sniffing people is frowned on. I can't go around just sniffing—" My nose turned as Zyion passed by me, his lips curled into a wicked smirk.

"You stopped in the middle of the field and everyone is watching you argue with her," Zyion's honeyed voice stated, once again from inside my head. *"Eyes forward, princess. Let her smell me so that you don't cause a scene."*

"He smells yummy, Aria. That creature smells . . . masculine and powerful. I want to lick him and call him ours too," Ember stated dreamily.

"We don't lick people."

"That's a lie we are told as children, Aria. I wouldn't be opposed to being licked in certain . . . places . . . but not by you," Zyion rasped, causing me to misunderstand him.

"I am not licking you!"

"Calm down, princess. I said not by you. It wasn't an invitation."

His husky laughter sent a shiver down my flesh. Turning to look at him, I dawdled as I began walking once more, uncaring that people were staring at me as if I'd gone bonkers.

"How are you inside my head?"

"I have my secrets. You have yours."

"Aria doesn't give us dick. Can we play with your dick?" Ember asked, which had a low, rumbling rattle sending heat surging through my system. *"Mommy wants one."* I winced as Lore exited her mouth.

"Mommy? Really, Ember?"

"If Lore can be a daddy, then I can be the mommy." My mouth opened and closed, but I couldn't really argue her logic.

"I don't think your mistress would like me allowing you to play with my cock. She seems prudish and would probably taste sour, creature." At his words, I swung my head to where he walked silently beside us. *"Don't worry, Aria. It's okay if you*

don't enjoy dick. You're not really my type, anyway. It's totally okay if you prefer the ladies. I do, myself."

"I like a lot of dick, thank you *very* much!" I snapped, only to realize I'd done it out loud. *"Kill me now."* Everyone who was close enough to hear the comment had frozen in shock. Zyion and Ember's laughter filled my head, but I refused to acknowledge him.

"What? We love dick. Big dicks. Aria even handles dick in beast form, and she does it well. One time, she and Dicker hated fucked—"

"Enough!" I snapped at the two of them. *"Ember is enough to handle inside my head without you encouraging her, Zyion. And not that it's any business of yours, but I do love cock. Esme jumped on top of me last night. It wasn't sexual."*

"They're totally best lesbians."

"It's best *friends, Ember! We're not like that together. It isn't sexual. I mean, she's very pretty and all that, but we're platonic."*

"They cuddle together, and one time, Aria held on to Esme and wouldn't even let her fall off the cliff. Boring. We could've climbed down and eaten her if she'd just let go," Ember pouted, enjoying having someone to listen to her.

"Is that so, Ember?" Zyion's timbre was rich, decadent, and warm with humor. *"I'm certain your mistress had a good reason for keeping Esmeralda alive. Besides, I doubt Aria knows how a woman should be eaten. When I do it, I personally start slow on one thigh before ensuring the other is given the same attention. Once her legs are trembling, I move to her molten center to see if she tastes as sweet as she looks."* I swallowed hard as my stomach twisted and embarrassment flooded my cheeks. *"Once I get an* in-depth *taste of her center, I find*

the one place inside her that's attached to every nerve ending in her body and caress—but only gently at first." Sweat trickled down my nape as I felt his eyes narrowing on me as my face exposed horror. *"When she trembles, I move in for the kill."*

"Do you hate fuck? Aria likes to be choked, controlled, and she even fights as she fucks. Plus, our jaw seems to impress men," Ember pondered, which caused me to choke on my tongue.

"Ember, shut the fuck up. He's stranger danger. Did you learn nothing when we ended up stolen and tossed in the prison of the unwanted beast king? Stranger danger is bad, say it with me. We have a man, and no, I don't know how to do shit with a woman because I love dick. Knox's dick, to be clear."

"He's not a stranger. Zyion has a dick, which makes him not stranger danger. Even I know his name, Aria. In order to be strangers, you have to not know his name. Duh," she said, drawing out the *h.*

"I really wish I could walk away from this conversation."

"Aria?" Eva called from behind me, which forced me to spin around toward her. "We're here."

We'd actually passed the dais because I'd been oblivious to everything else around me. Zyion had kept walking as if he hadn't been bothering me at all. Griffon cleared his throat, and I fidgeted as I tried to assess what I was supposed to do here.

"First thing you should do? Calm down, princess. Breathe. Face your father, not me," Zyion whispered inside my head. Did I trust him enough to lead me through this? *"You need to learn to trust me. To the right of your father in the green vest*

is his brother, Hagen, he's going to try to murder you. He resents Griffon for the blood he carries and wants you removed before your claim to the throne can be heard. The men, if you can call the pricks that, who are seated beside him are his bastards. They are faithless assholes who blindly follow Hagen around. They also want the crown you were born to wear on that dainty, lovely head of yours."

"You think I'm lovely?" I whispered as if we'd be overheard inside my mind.

"I'm not here to feed your ego. My job is to keep you alive. Pay attention, Aria. Baldrick is the man on the other side of your father, seated in your throne. You're going to walk to him, pointedly look at him, which should remind Griffon that a princess's place is beside her father, the king. Move."

I started toward Griffon, ignoring the curious looks of the men seated around him. Once I reached them, I turned and aimed a look of expectation at the man in my seat. Silently, I prayed I wasn't being led astray. Sweat began to bead at the back of my nape as the man glared up with malice burning in his violet stare.

"Baldrick, you're seated in my daughter's chair," Griffon stated, pride shining in his eyes. "Move to the lower row and take your brothers with you. Today, my beautiful daughter is selecting a hero for her people to cheer on."

"I'm sorry, but I'd rather not," Baldrick returned.

"He asked you to move your ass. When the king says to do something, you ought to do it, now." Crossing my arms over my chest, I refused to cower before the man who so openly challenged Griffon. "And you'll address him with the respect deserved of the throne he holds."

"And what happens if I choose not to?" Baldrick sneered.

A smile played on my lips as Ember peered out at him, which was hard to miss. "You could fuck around, but then you'd find out what happens. I get that you think that because I have tits and a vagina, I am beneath you, but I promise that I always come out on top." Unfolding my arms, I made sure he saw my claws lengthening. The guards slowly began shifting closer from where they'd been standing at a distance behind Griffon. My hackles rose as the men on the opposite side of my father rose as well.

"I don't need to explain what happens when you disrespect the king, gentlemen. Do I?" Zyion's question sounded from directly behind me. "The seat of honor belongs to his wife or a daughter. Do you have reason to refuse the princess her seat?"

Baldrick stood with anger trickling off him. "Vanir blood doesn't make you royalty, Vicious. My blood is that of our true kings. You think this traitorous whore can save you from your sins? Your time is near. I'll be there when it happens, and I expect my pound of flesh."

"I'll be waiting for you to come try to collect." Zyion's body had heat drifting from it in gentle waves. As if, like me, he couldn't fully control the warmth of his inner core. Zyion remained behind me until the asshole had begun moving down a couple rows. Once I stepped closer to the seat, he rebuked me inside my head. *You don't sit until your father rises. It's customary for the men to rise for a woman to sit, princess.*

"And they say chivalry is dead," I returned with a hint of

laughter in my voice. *"To be crystal clear? I'm very taken. Happily, so."*

"Says the girl who allowed spiders to nest in our vagina? What's so happy about that?"

The men around Griffon stood before he, himself, rose. Once everyone had, I nodded at my father with a small smile playing on my lips. Zyion offered his hand as I turned, staring into his gaze as his lips moved before lowering to my trembling fingers.

"He will not harm you, Aria. I will not allow it." His promise resonated inside my head until my inner thoughts blasted through my head. I wasn't afraid of the man. But my response to this guy? That worried—no, it terrified me. *"That isn't something either of us can help, I'm afraid. Don't worry, though. I will do my best not to touch you unless it is required of me."* Zyion turned on his heel and took the stairs to the field two at a time. *"I am not interested in you, princess. 'I love you' is nothing but a death sentence when it's whispered from my lips and my job is to keep you alive. Your issues, and that of your creature are on you, not me. If it helps, you're a natural at this. It's almost as if you were born to rule this kingdom."*

"Do you normally talk to yourself, Vicious?" I countered, but I felt the thread tighten painfully as I called him what the others did. *"You don't like that name. Do you?"*

"You can call me whatever you like, Your Majesty. Except for blah, blah, blah."

"Don't be an asshole, Zyion. I'm asking you a question. If you and I are linked, I prefer we know what the other likes to be called."

"Just call me daddy, mommy." Sarcasm had dripped from his tone.

"As if I'd call you my daddy?" I countered with a deepening frown, sliding my regard to where he stood, bathed in shadows, observing me from within them. *"Oh, daddy! I'm a very bad girl. Come spank me,"* I teased, but it came out in a rasped tone. Zyion pushed off the post he'd leaned against and scrubbed a hand down his face.

"You are right. Probably shouldn't call me that moments before I'm to request your colors, vicious princess. I can't wait to see what you're like as our queen," he purred roughly.

"My colors?" I questioned, turning to find Griffon watching Aden talking to three women. Three women were making asses out of themselves, vying for his attention, but he was too focused on me to notice. It felt as if he'd been staring at me, trying to get my attention for some time.

"The strands of fabric you hold. Your colors. You hand them to whichever knight you wish to honor with them. They tell the crowd which warrior to cheer for."

"Why wouldn't they choose that themselves?"

"It's a tradition. Don't worry, Aria. I don't actually expect you to give me yours. The last one to honor me with her colors was your grandmother, but I failed her. Aden would be the better choice to offer your colors to. He's an honorable *knight and* favored *by your kingdom."* There was a heaviness in the way he'd spoken about Scylla that had my stomach dropping. If he and I had this strange connection, did he have the same with her? Was their relationship more than queen and guard? Before I could ask, Aden began making his way toward where Griffon and I sat.

"Aden will be honored to accept your colors, daughter," he said with a stern look on his face.

Esme and Eva chose that moment to sit beside me, which made me frown. They'd both vanished after my embarrassing outburst, which Zyion and Ember had forced me into. Their departure made me wonder why they did so.

"They're not part of the royal bloodline. You are. Unless you're directly in line for the throne, you have to come in from the back of the dais. You have much to learn. It's a good thing you have me, since those who were supposed to teach you don't seem to be doing so." Zyion was moving up the left of the dais while Aden climbed the other. The beat of my heart picked up with each step closer each man took. *"Rise and turn to the left. Offer Aden your colors."*

I stood as instructed, turning toward Aden, who looked at me with excitement. His stare slid over my shoulder, then returned to my face with a smugness that irked me.

"My princess, would you honor me with your colors?" He asked, before bowing in a flourished move.

"I'd be honored if the princess would honor me with her colors as well." Repeating his words, Zyion expressed interest, but there was no expectation in his tone.

They both waited for my choice as Griffon cleared his throat, nodding toward Aden as I considered my choice. The moment I turned toward Zyion, a ripple of shocked murmurs moved through the crowd.

"What are you doing?"

"If my grandmother trusted you with her colors, then I will strive to do so as well. Don't disappoint me, Zyion."

"You can't do that!" Aden hissed.

"If you didn't want me to choose, then you should've given me a choice. Personally, I've always preferred the underdog." Stepping closer to Zyion, I grabbed his large, rough, scarred hand and placed the material in his waiting palm. Then I returned to my chair, smirking at the rage simmering in Aden's eyes. "Good luck, gentlemen."

CHAPTER 16
ARIA

The crowd remained silent as Aden and Zyion began moving toward the field. My focus remained on Zyion and the incessant tug of the thread that seemed to run between us. I endeavored to calm the thread, to get it to stop its overtly agitated insistence I pay attention to it. I didn't want to disturb him, not with the mounting intensity of the crowd building. I wasn't sure what had been between the men, but there was unquestionably bad blood between them.

A man in black robes rose to his feet as Zyion strode straight for him. The man smiled, but whatever he saw on Zyion's face made his joy falter. He grabbed a silver breastplate with red phoenixes on it and then assisted Zyion into the heavy armor. The gorget that protected his throat and neck was obsidian and had a blood-red cape attached. Once he'd finished adding the arm pieces, he pushed the pauldrons onto his shoulders. Zyion stood to accept the helmet, which covered his entire face in etched silver with a thin slit over the eyes.

Aden's armor seemed to be for show, since it lacked the thickness of Zyion's armor. His cape was silver instead of red, which I was certain held some meaning, and his breastplate was as shiny and untried as his helm with red and white feathers. He was a knight in shining armor who had never seen a true battle.

Overall, Aden's armor looked more minimal-like compared to Zyion's, who exuded a lethal, merciless presence on the field. After both men received their blades, Zyion glanced up at me with a worrisome look churning in his stormy blue depths.

"You should've handed Aden your colors, woman."

My eyes narrowed. *"If I'd wanted to hand them to Aden, I'd have done so. I didn't choose him because, if I am expected to choose the winner of the match before the fight has even begun, I'd choose you. Aden? He's weak of mind and conviction, and he'd also ruled by his emotions."* The sound he made inside my head was heavy with disapproval, but he didn't deny my observation. *"If it weren't a choice, you should've told me that plainly."* A soft rattle of approval rushed through my mind. *"Besides, I don't have time for men who dance around shit or play word games. If you expect me to discern or read your cues without offering me a reason for your madness, then that's on you. I don't intend to sit around here wasting time when Hecate is healing as we speak."*

"I think I prefer your silence rather than listen to you." My brow creased as he stopped in front of a small dirt circle in the center of the vividly green field. *"Do you honestly think your uncles will allow you to walk away from this realm? I assure you it won't be so easy to leave here. You are the true heir to the throne. No, you're choosing to ignore the alpha male they*

tossed at you. They picked him because he's easily controllable and simple-minded. Do you think they will allow you to live if you don't do what little girls are told to do? You weren't supposed to have a mind of your own. They wanted a puppet, one that they could control. You're ruining their plans."

"They think I'm a lamb." Establishing my place above my uncle had done nothing but heighten their scrutiny of me. Let them think I was a delicate, weak-minded thing. It would be their mistake. The last one they made.

"You are a lamb. You should carry a weapon, Aria," Zyion hissed, and the rebuke in his tone rubbed me raw.

"I may have been once, but that was long ago. I was forced to become a lion, and predators don't need weapons when they are one."

Aden lunged with his blade drawn, swinging on Zyion with hard, quick blows. Zyion deflected and guarded against each strike. Far sooner than I expected, Aden became winded, and that was when Zyion moved, advancing on Aden with hard, bone-jarring hits. Aden's lack of blade skills and training were apparent when compared to Zyion's. Anger fueled Aden's fight. Emotions held no place in a sword fight—or any fight, for that matter. Emotions made you sloppy, and careless warriors often ended up dead. The moment they began, cheers and screaming erupted throughout the air. Each move drove their excitement, ending with them growing louder until it became almost deafening.

Aden lunged, and Zyion stepped back, masterfully deflecting each blow meant to disarm him. Every parry Zyion made was precise and forced Aden to riposte each swing. The merciless assault Zyion led had Aden backing away as each blow landed with a thud against his blade. Aden blocked each clash of his blade, but Zyion didn't appear to be working hard.

The fight continued with one pushing the other back, before they'd switch and the aggressor would be forced to defend. The sharp clang of steel meeting steel filled the air as sweat trickled down my neck. It sent the scent of adrenaline, excitement, and fear fluttering on the breeze drifting through the stands, increasing the cries of those watching the maddening match. No one cheered for any color throughout the match, and the tension ratcheted higher every time the two men clashed.

Zyion continued, thrusting his blade forward at Aden, sending him back onto the verdant field. He executed each movement with precision, as though he had mastered a dance instead of swordplay. The dragons and phoenixes made noise, which forced my attention toward them, frowning as the dragons made a loud keening noise. The creatures even seemed excited about the fight, which was good for them, I guess.

I could tell the moment Aden barely escaped a few of the attacks he wielded by parrying with the blade he held, that he was tiring. Zyion waited for Aden to lift his blade, then spun in a move I'd never seen a warrior use against an opponent. His blade sliced through the air and sent Aden's to the grass covered field a few steps away from him.

Aden lunged for the blade, and Zyion didn't move to end the battle. Instead, his eyes slid to mine before drifting to Griffon, who had been studying me instead of watching the fighting on the field. Griffon's expression tightened before he jerked his head in some kind of unspoken order.

Zyion allowed Aden to retrieve his blade, which had my lips pinching in disapproval. I wasn't sure if Griffon had told Zyion to throw the match or to end it, but either way, his interference was granted. Zyion shifted, slamming his blade against Aden's in an aggressive, precise, and powerful block.

Aden continued slashing against the blade Zyion wielded and then feigned right, but Zyion must have been expecting it because he sidestepped and then swung. Aden parried, but Zyion was so incredibly fast that Aden had little time to recover before Zyion's blade slammed against his helm, sending both Aden and his blade to the ground. Zyion turned, staring at me as the crowd released a collective gasp.

Aden retrieved his blade for a second time, but Zyion's attention remained on me. What the hell was he doing? It didn't waiver as Aden approached his back or as Aden's blade landed against his armor. Through whatever thread connected us, I felt Zyion tense as Aden pulled his blade back and then lunged forward. Horror flooded me as the tip of Aden's blade pushed through Zyion's lower abdomen, and I jumped to my feet. The eruption of cheers from the people watching drowned out Zyion's grunt of pain.

Griffon rose, his hand elevated in the air. Aden pulled his blade out and stepped back as Zyion dropped, leaning forward. He lifted his blade as Zyion's gauntlet crashed against the earthen floor, hauling up the blade until it aimed in the air. His blood curdling war cry filled the air as I felt my magic rushing to my fingertips.

"Enough!" Griffon snarled over the crowd, but their

cheers overtook even his shout as their excitement heightened with the promise of blood.

Almost in slow motion, the sword swung down, and my magic flooded out of me, racing toward the two men. Before steel met flesh, my magic was there, a force so impenetrable that Aden's blade shattered against it. Zyion's silvery head swung toward me and the thread stretched ominously, almost in warning. A warning I ignored as I glared at Aden, waiting for his attention to move from his ruined weapon to where I stood, glaring down at him. Throwing the broken sword onto the field, he shouted for the squire to bring him another.

"I don't need you to save me."

"Did I ask if you did? No, I didn't. Aden meant to remove your head."

"And what if he'd done so? I didn't ask for your colors or your fucking help, for that matter. Do you think I cannot protect myself? You should heed those who warn you not to intercede into matters not of your concern, Aria."

"My concern? First off, I don't take orders from others. Did I say you cannot protect yourself? No, I didn't say shit about your prowess with a blade. I just watched you concede defeat to a worthless opponent who you could have easily destroyed several times throughout that mockery of a match. So, what I'd really like to know is why you threw it instead of teaching Aden the lesson I wanted to see him learn? Why?"

"Who I allow to win isn't your concern. Nothing I do should worry that lovely head of yours. Aden bested me. Deal with it, princess. Here's something you should know about me. I hurt people because I'm good at inflicting pain. There's nothing I wouldn't do for those I love. That's both a curse and a privilege I

bear. *I'm not a knight in shining armor, nor will I ever be one. I'll let you down, just as I've done to everyone else who placed their trust in me. Do me a favor and stop thinking I'm something I'm not.*"

"Retrieve your colors," Baldrick sneered from the row in front of us. Violet eyes narrowed on me as his mouth twisted into a malicious smile. The man was repulsive. "It appears your knowledge of warriors is as lacking and misguided as your taste in lovers, girl."

Rising as the entire congregation scrutinized me, I strolled onto the field beneath the angry glare of both men who'd fought upon it. Zyion stumbled to his feet with an uneasy look tightening his features. Aden's scowl was cruel as it followed me. The moment I was near to him, Zyion tore the ribbon from his chainmail and then placed them in my hand. His fingers enveloped mine, gripping them firmly before he released the hold and stepped back for Aden to move closer.

"If you want a proper warrior? Then Zyion Vicious isn't it. I should bypass protocol and come to your chamber to teach you what a real man truly is. Your treacherous body wouldn't be so easily drawn to men of ill reputation after you'd been bedded properly. Or do you enjoy betraying your kingdom as you fuck our enemy, whore?"

The malice rolling off Aden left me stumbling for how to respond. He'd fooled me with his kind words and encouragements outside of this realm. I'd fallen for the facade he'd displayed, but then I'd had no reason to distrust it. Zyion, clearly hearing what Aden had said, simmered with silent rage. Moreover, malice grew within him as Aden continued to slander me in his presence.

"Well, look at that. You know how to shut that poisonous mouth of yours up after all. Don't worry, darling. You will soon learn what your mouth is made for. Hand me your colors, bitch."

Lifting the hand that held the ribbons, I waited for Aden to step forward. The moment he did, I spit in his face as I released the colors. Wind sent the thin length of fabric floating to the drudgery as I inched closer, unafraid to face the bastard. The moment it landed, and Aden moved to pick it up, I sent a random bolt of lightning down, striking inches from his hand. Smirking as he stared me down, I winked.

"You won nothing, Aden. Zyion allowed you to best him. By my count, he could've ended you seven times throughout the fight. He let you appear to be the better warrior. So, go ahead, take your fake win, but come at me, and you won't walk away from the encounter. You aren't man enough to teach me shit, prick. I fucking dare you to come to my chamber with ill intent. Try to get that withered little cock anywhere near my mouth? And I will bite it off and spit it into your viperous mouth. Then you'll taste how disappointing it is as you choke on it. And I assure you that my beast would enjoy dining on your flesh. Plus, the bitch is ravenous for raw meat, and you're looking like a snack. The only saving grace you have is that you're not worth the bloodstains that I'd have to wash off my flesh after she'd eaten your face."

Turning toward Zyion, I seethed at the sight of the blood dripping from his side. He could've prevented the injury if he'd wanted to do so. Instead, he'd allowed the pompous prick behind me to appear victorious to the masses.

"You, you can go to hell too, asshole." Stepping back from him, I turned on my heel and strode from the field, pissed at both men.

Aden hadn't won. Zyion's superiority in power, skill, and calculation was obvious to anyone with eyes. He'd had ample opportunity to end the fight, but Zyion chose not to take them. Why? Why had Griffon given him a sign to concede? Something was gravely off here, which didn't bode well for me.

"Aria, stop!" Zyion's voice exploded inside my head.

"Screw you! Whatever the hell is between you and Aden, it shouldn't involve me. If you want to get stabbed by some weak little pussy, that's on you. However, I don't have to stand around and watch you do so. I'm too exhausted to deal with men swinging their pricks around to discern whose dick is bigger," I growled, passing people with my quick, angry strides to escape the onlookers. I hadn't come here to be thrown into the middle of a dick sizing contest, nor would they force me to indulge either of the barbarians competing for a fucking swath of colored fabric.

"Fucking stop for a moment, woman!" Zyion's words held urgency, but I was too angry to give a shit. *"Aria!"*

"Why the hell should I listen to you? Do you want to berate and belittle me some more? I know what you can do. How about you and Aden go play with your swords and just leave me the fuck out of it?" I demanded, but then my feet stumbled.

The hair on my nape lifted as a dark, oily magic fluttered across the field and a cloud blocked out the sun. The wrongness in the surrounding air was so oppressive it stalled the air in my lungs.

Air grew thick with tension around me. My ears popped as pressure built inside my head, and the hair on my arms rose with the power smothering me. Not knowing where the threat was coming from, I stepped back, scanning the surrounding faces, and I backed into something solid and unmovable.

"It's just me, princess," Zyion whispered so softly I strained to hear his words. "We expected an attack, but this is more. This isn't just an assassination attempt on your life."

"Excuse me? It sounded like you *just* said you expected an assassination attempt on my life." What the fuck was even happening?

"May I eat whatever it is? I'm a growing girl," Ember asked in a sincere tone, hoping Zyion would sympathize with her plight.

"If you wish, Ember, I can send someone out to hunt deer for you if you need me to do so," he promised her in a softened tone. It made me wonder if he knew she was talking about consuming people.

"Did you hear that? He said he'd hunt for me! I'm in love!" she purred.

"No, he said he'd send *someone to hunt. Do you know that, traditionally, men are satisfied through their belly or their sexual desires, not women. Ember? You're not a male, so stop the antics. And for the love of everything holy, stop going all deer-in-the-headlights just because some asshole offers you meat of any variety. Now, shut up. We're kind of in a situation here."*

"You know she's feral, right? She's likely a lot stronger

than you are. I think I'd prefer—" Zyion's words stalled as we both felt the incoming attack.

A man with his head covered with red and black colors, and armor carrying the royal house coat of arms rushed at us. I threw magic toward him, which resulted in him being shot with a violet bolt of lightning, and then sucked into the ground, leaving only his armor behind.

"Impressive, princess. You bonded with the land?"

"I did," I confirmed. "Stop calling me princess. I promise you I'm *not* delicate or breakable. In fact, I'm more like a bomb with a short fuse, just waiting to detonate."

Several men burst from the tents that surrounded the field. I stepped forward, but Zyion's arm wrapped around me, yanking me back against the hard armor he wore. Lifting my hands, I slammed my magic against them, enjoying the crunch of their bones as it pulverized them beneath the meteor-like ball of power. Zyion's hiss of shock was satisfying.

"Where is the King's Guard? Fuck! It's a coup." Zyion turned, looking at me, then at the men wearing the same armor as him. "Guard Griffon, it's a coup," Zyion called to the men rushing at us wearing similar armor to his.

My head whipped toward where Esme had been, discovering her gone. Fear sliced through as I turned, looking for any sign of her. The wind slapped my hair against my face as worry tightened my chest.

"Where's Esme? Esme!"

"No one is after your friend, Aria."

"You think I care? She's not a great fighter, and she's an even worse swimmer. And this? This looks like shit creek without me to keep her from drowning."

"She'll be okay. I saw her with Eva, who will ensure she gets out." His tone held a trust that I didn't share. "I should've trusted you enough to warn you about what we feared would unfold here."

"Jeez, thanks for admitting it as we're being attacked?" I muttered as he turned with me and then grabbed my hand to yank me back toward the middle of the field that he'd fought Aden on.

The sounds of screams erupted from the stands, causing my stomach to drop as I looked back toward the stands. Esme! I'd left Esme in order to hand off my colors, and now she was gone? I knew I should've stayed in bed.

I tried to pull free of Zyion's hold so I could go find her, but his grip was unrelenting. Still, I searched for her in the stands where I'd left her, but they had devolved into a melee of fists and swords and people fleeing. Worry ate at the pit of my stomach as Zyion continued to pull me farther away from where she should've been.

"So much for this place being peaceful," I whispered, realizing I hadn't spotted Eva yet either. "I can't find her." Panic gripped my throat.

"Your friend's safe, Aria. They aren't interested in her. She didn't come for the throne."

I gave him an unladylike snort. "I neither wanted nor intended to claim any throne. Scylla informed me it wasn't an option to walk away without it, though."

Frantic shouting erupted to our right, but Griffon's scream compelled Zyion and me to turn towards it. One of Baldrick's sons was standing behind the king, an arm banded around his chest and a dagger pressed to his neck. A small rivet of blood stained dripped from where the blade pressed to flesh, dripping down and staining the king's collar.

"It's a coup?" I wondered out loud. "I did not see that one coming."

"That bloody, treacherous bastard," Zyion snarled. "Baldrick will give the order to Sain to murder Griffon before we can reach him." The panic in Zyion's tone was as genuine as the fear perfuming the surrounding air.

Amused by his conclusion, I aimed my assault on the man brandishing the blade against my father's throat. Sending a prayer heavenward, I brought the single violet-colored bolt down from the sky as lightning struck from the angry gray clouds above us. It slammed into the stands where the guy held the blade to my father's throat.

The single bolt caused the sharp scent of ozone to drift to me on the gentle breeze. Next, I invoked the wind, which forcefully rushed through the crowded dais. Everyone caught in its path lurched forward or stumbled to maintain their balance, and those who couldn't stay on their feet were sent to the ground or fell from the stands.

The skies strobed lightning, which was punctuated by thunderous claps of thunder. Wind continued rushing through the area as it forced those on the dais to crawl as they sought to escape or move toward the king. I eyed each man, trying to discern his intent before I brought violent, angry bolts rushing toward the next man who sought to end Griffon's life. It was a beautiful symphony of chaos as they struggled against the onslaught of my wrath.

I hadn't even had a chance to know my father or have an entire conversation with him, and they were attempting to end him? I'd be damned if they murdered him before I'd gotten the information I'd come here for. I wouldn't allow them to steal that from me.

Slowly, people figured out where the new waves of violence were coming from, and started backing away, shoving at those who were too slow to move. I wanted to scoff because, had I wanted to end them, I could have. They were perfectly safe so long as they weren't trying to murder anyone. Though, I probably looked like a badass with my hair whipping against my face and the skirt of my gown tearing under the onslaught of cyclones spinning near where I stood. Violet veins pulsed beneath my pale flesh as the magic within me waited for my next target.

"Damn, woman." Zyion gripped my hand and started toward Griffon. My vision blurred with the turbulent storm of power humming through my body. I felt myself being dragged toward where Griffon now knelt, his eyes locked on the sight of my immense power oozing from my soul. Baldrick crept closer to where Griffon remained perched on his knees, staring at us. My heartbeat thundered along in time to the bolts crashing against the ground. The scream that tore from my lips was drowned out by the clamorous storm fueled through my emotions.

"Can you take him out? Aria, can you just hit him?" Zyion asked as Baldrick lifted his blade before he swung it wildly at Griffon's exposed throat.

A horrified wail ripped from my lungs as I yanked against Zyion's hold and then directed several wide, lethal bolts of lightning down at Baldrick. Forcing my mind to ignore the battle raging around me, I continued sending bolt after bolt of violet light at the bastard who thought to depose the king. Baldrick dropped, flopping around on the ground. Zyion rushed toward Griffon, shouting for anyone who could hear him to protect the king.

By the time Zyion reached him, several warriors had already closed ranks around the king, creating a circle of defense. The relieved smile on my lips fell as a strange whistling noise reached me. I turned just in time to spot something shooting through the air toward me, too fast for me to dodge or deflect. Then pain exploded against my skull.

I went toppling over into the greenery of the field as blood filled my mouth. Blinking past the light that flooded my vision, I whimpered in pain as blood trickled from my lips. My equilibrium was akin to when I'd downed a fifth of tequila and tried walking afterward. Crashing against the ground, I lay there, unmoving, as the ground began to shake. Acid rushed through my veins, burning its way through my system as agonizing pain consumed my mind.

The wind blew my hair into the air as if something large had landed in front of me. Forcing my palms against the field, I screamed at the agony burning through my body. A massive shadow spread over the area, and the booming rattle that silenced everyone on the field was loud enough to steal my hearing for a second. The men and women, who weren't already prostrate on the ground, dropped to their knees, bowing their spines and yielding to the demand for submission.

The creature landed with one clawed foot on either side of me, and it was a struggle not to black out in sheer panic. Rolling onto my back, I gazed up in horror at a massive black dragon, which was dripping saliva over my torso as it stared down at me as if I were a snack. It radiated unbearable heat that pinked my flesh, and there was no way I was sticking around to see what it wanted. I flipped back onto my belly and began crawling to escape being smashed beneath the beast's large, razor-clawed feet.

An angry rattle vibrated the earth, and as the beast lifted its clawed talons, I pitched myself to the left, blindly rolling as fast as I could to try to avoid being crushed. The second I was free, I was on my feet trying to stumble away even as the world blurred around me.

The dragon turned on me, opening its mouth of serrated teeth to reveal a black maw of endlessness. A spark ignited and the surrounding air turned into an oven. Its rattle became a high-pitched scream, a heartbeat before searing flames engulfed the men who'd been sneaking up behind me. Their flesh melted from their bones, and a look fresh horror at how effortlessly the dragon made the panic rise within me.

A scream bubbled inside my chest as the thought of being burnt alive consumed my mind. I saw past men being charred or melted into puddles of melted armor and gore over the surrounding field. On shaking arms, I continued to crawl away from the colossal beast, laying waste to the men who'd foolishly charged it with their weapons drawn.

I closed my eyes against the nausea fisting my stomach. Then hands grabbed onto my waist and hoisted me onto the back of a large, emerald-green dragon. As it launched into the air, I screamed and scrambled for something to grasp on to. I met the sea-green eyes of the man who I assumed placed me on the back of the dragon, and he chuckled as he stepped back.

The leathery wings flapped powerfully against the air, bringing us higher and higher with each beat. Fear gripped my heart like a vice as I continued searching for something to hold on to in order to prevent falling to my death.

"No-no-no-no," I whispered as I turned, ready to beg for the green-eyes man to get me off this thing. My plea died a quick death when I watched him become a dragon. "Nope. This isn't happening!" Within seconds, I was too far from the ground to even consider jumping. Everything looked like ants scattering on the ground below.

"Where the fuck are you?" Zyion demanded. *"Aria? Answer me, woman!"*

"I'm on *a fucking dragon! Oh my god. Get me the fuck down! I'm going to fall, Zyion. There's nothing to hold on to. What the hell do I do?"* I demanded as tears threatened to choke off my words, which was sad considering they were in my head. *"How do I get down from here?"* Panic was overwhelming me, which was causing my breathing to be erratic. I was on the back of a dragon, being *dragon-napped*! How was this my life? A year ago, I hadn't even known dragons existed, and now, one was stealing me and Ember was cheering the beast on!

"Unless you can fly, Aria, you stay the fuck on the beast's back. I'll find you."

"Zyion! I'm going to die!"

"If they wanted you dead, you'd be dead already. They want you alive, which means they won't drop you. Don't piss them off before I can get to you, princess."

CHAPTER 17
ARIA

I was flying on a dragon! It was my only thought as I clung to the large scales with a death grip. When the dragon dropped without warning, I screamed so loudly it burned my throat, but the wind snatched away the sound. I wasn't sure if the beast was pleased about tossing me onto its back, but its flight with me on it wasn't reassuring. A smaller, light blue dragon flew in its path, and the dragon I clung to veered left. Then I was screaming again as it aimed its large, wicked-looking snout downward and dove toward the ground.

I desperately clung on, but then the dragon rolled, dumping me off its back and sending me into a freefall. My arms waved futilely at my sides, and the wind bit at my skin forcing my eyes closed as I fell faster and faster in an uncontrolled tumble. My mind refused to focus on anything other than the quickly approaching ground and just how dead I'd be when I hit it. On the heels of that truth, a strange sense of peace flooded my mind. As if colliding with the ground wouldn't be the worst death to experience.

The air that had been slamming into my face ceased, which forced a whimper from my lungs. My eyelids parted gradually as fear slithered through me, revealing an emerald green dragon, which wasn't the one who'd taken me. Several more were flying V formation below us. I'd torn the skirt of my dress in the gales of wind I'd unleashed, which left my legs naked as I hung from the beast's deadly claws. Lowering my head, I stared into the crimson irises of the black dragon. The green dragon flipped without warning and sent me flying onto the back of a sapphire dragon.

Pain from landing on the hard scales burned my side as I struggled to right myself. My skull was still buzzing with piercing discomfort, which left me gasping for a reason. Placing my palm against my head, I found it covered in warm liquid. That explained the pain, at least. It didn't explain the blurry vision or inability to move without feeling as if I'd drank an entire bottle of tequila.

"Still with me, princess?"

"Who the fuck are you?" I demanded weakly.

"Your fucking savior," hissed the gruff, scratchy voice.

"Calm down before you give the girl heart failure. I'd hate to explain why she didn't make it back with us, brother," another dragon growled, sending my anger rising. *"And you, I'd calm yourself because the ground is a long way down."*

"Calm down? You just fucking dragon-napped my ass! In case you missed it, I was fighting just fucking fine before you showed up and damn near pulverized me beneath your claws. You also almost melted me! Plus, I was fucking winning. You took me without permission, which is kidnapping!" I snarled, which had a few dragons making sounds similar to snorts. "Did you just snort at me?" The question escaped as an incredulous hiss of sound.

"You were not winning. That head wound? It's laced with enough nulling serum to prevent you from casting anything for days. You were about to be assassinated by your own fucking brother. Do you honestly think that if we'd been offered your death, we'd allow you—a Prometheus—to fly on our backs? I assure you I'd rather do anything else than allow you or your kind anywhere near my back, woman."

"A what now?" I demanded, fighting against the nausea rushing through me.

"You're magicless," one dragon sniggered. *"Fucking birds."*

Undoubtedly, he was not a fan of my bloodline, which wasn't exactly a surprise. No one held a grudge quite like a bunch of dragons and phoenixes, that was for sure. I forced my body upright, peering one way, then another to take in the mammoth sized dragons who'd saved me. Inside me, Ember was howling like a banshee, which meant I wouldn't hear Zyion if he spoke.

"I'm flying! I love them! Aria, we are flyyyyyyyyyyyyyyyying! Zooooom. Weeee-weeee-zoooom! I am a freebee. We're finally flying!"

"Ember, I can't hear myself think, let alone hear if help is forthcoming. Stop screaming! And for the love of God, stop fucking saying you love everyone! Someone might actually think you mean it." The dragons laughed, honest to God, laughed at us. *"Oh, shit. They can hear us!"*

"We can all hear your mind and that of your inner beast.

227

Zyion already knows where we're taking you, Aria Hecate. He requested we remove you from the current situation unfolding at the palace. We cannot allow you to stay there until your coronation and ascent to the throne. But women are all the same fickle, impulsive creatures. You never listen to reason and blindly run toward danger blindly."

"Can we eat that one? He'd fill us up," Ember asked through a bout of rage which shot through me and it was getting harder to focus around the disorientation from whatever they had shot me with.

"We're not eating a dragon. I'm pretty sure that would stick to my ass."

"At least something would be stuck to it, maybe even in it," Ember pouted. *"I bet he'd stick to your thighs too. Then we'd have something between them. You'd remember we have a vagina, which is also starving!"*

"You didn't get enough dick when you let Lennox take us in his beast form? Because I'm pretty sure he wrecked my vagina!" The moment the words echoed inside my head my face flamed with embarrassment.

"Lennox?" the grouchy dragon asked. *"Lennox Karnavious?"*

My stomach sank as the large, obsidian-colored dragon turned red eyes toward me. The oval- pupils set in cat-shaped eyes inspected me meticulously.

"Are you a ravenous slut for cock, princess?" he asked, making the word princess sound like a slur.

"Excuse me? I've had one dick in my entire lifetime, asshole. I don't think I meet the criteria to be one. Not that a woman who enjoys dick is anything other than a woman. Why is it acceptable for a man to have sex with thousands of

women, but the moment a woman takes more than one lover, she's slandered and thought of as less for enjoying her sexuality? Women have needs too, which oftentimes aren't met by men who can't figure out how to handle her body's needs. We like getting dick, and there's nothing wrong with that."

"Unless you're stuck inside Aria, who only likes Knox's cock. To be fair, it's a really nice cock. And he kissed me." She sighed dreamily. *"Lennox wouldn't kiss me, but Knox did. I like Knox. I'm going to make him a daddy."*

"Thanks for oversharing, Ember."

"That's what best lesbians are for, right?"

"I don't think—"

"You play with my vagina when you try to get off," she stated as she interrupted me.

"Yeah, but it's my vagina too," I argued.

"Semantics."

"Do you two normally spend your days arguing about your vagina?" Zyion's honeyed voice asked, which caused my ears to prick.

"You asshole! Why didn't you just tell me you called in dragons? I wouldn't have been hyperventilating!" I snapped.

"Because there are ears everywhere, princess. Do try to lessen the talk about your personal needs. Most of the men up here haven't been around a woman in a while. Had the Prometheus line known they were here, they'd have hunted them down and killed them."

The Dragon Slayer was friends of the dragons? Because that shit made total sense.

"They'd fucking try," One dragon snarled.

"They'd lose." Another hissed.

229

"Great, more chest beating cavemen. Just what I didn't need."

"Perception is everything, princess. If they fear your reputation, they don't seek to fuck with you.

We descended through the clouds, and I felt my head growing heavier. The dragon I rode lowered its head, and the wind crashed into my face. A shockingly painful amount of pressure pulsed inside my skull, and I was knocked back on the creatures' scale-covered spine. The obsidian dragon shot forward to act as a windbreaker, which was probably the only reason I didn't topple off the beast.

"She's fucking human, Ronin. Be careful with her or she will die before we reach the peak of the mountain range."

"Fucking hell," I whispered thickly. Lifting my hand to touch my temple, I peered through the spots dancing in my vision as the surrounding clouds began darkening.

"I'm going to pass out." It seemed inevitable. The pain rushing through my head joined with the burning acid still humming through my veins. My body went heavy and weightless simultaneously and I listed hazardously. A bevy of violent curses filled my mind even as my vision blacked out and sucked me into the velvety bliss of nothingness.

I woke to a hard bed beneath my cheek, and when I tried to sit up, the room spun around me. It forced me to place the back of my hand against my lips as my breakfast threatened to come back up. Holding on to the blankets, I fought against the room spinning around me.

"Delicate little thing, aren't you?" Asked in a deep, scratchy voice.

Turning toward the owner, I frowned when I found Knox leaning against the wall. "Knox?" I whispered, swallowing back the saliva building in my mouth.

"Basilius Karnavious," he informed coldly. "You'd be Aria Hecate, the little lost princess everyone can't wait to get their hands on."

"Aria Primrose Hecate Prometheus Karnavious," I amended for him.

"I wouldn't lie to me, woman. You won't like me if you force me to cut out that tongue. It would be a waste to take it without feeling what it could do first." He folded his powerfully muscled arms over his chest, glaring at me.

"I'm not lying to you. Knox Karnavious is my mate."

"That's almost believable, except I'm his brother and I know better. Next lie?" His words were a rasping purr of promise and threat. The eyes so similar to Knox's slid to the doorway as another man with similar blonde hair and oceanic-eyes strolled in.

"She talking?" the newcomer asked.

"Indeed, she is. In fact, the princess claims that she's married to Knox." Basilius and the new guy laughed. "I don't think Knox would enjoy her spreading lies of marriage, especially when she's a Prometheus bitch."

"Knox wouldn't touch a Prometheus female, not even with Killian's cock. Save your lies for someone willing to buy them because we sure as shit don't, little girl." The owner of the voice seemed younger than Basilius, who continued to stare at me as if I was a meal he wanted to devour.

"So, what's your story?" asked a third man I hadn't noticed before. Still moving slowly, I turned just enough to look at him. He was sitting on the bed, devouring me with ravenous eyes.

Like Basilius, he had an uncanny resemblance to Knox, and I came to the conclusion that they must be brothers. The realization that they didn't know what had happened to him or Liliana made sense since they'd been cut off from the Nine Realms, but I had my own puzzles to focus on. The last one in his line who'd held the ability to transform into a fire-breathing dragon was their grandmother, which meant something in this realm allowed them to take their dragon form. That made me question whether Hecate had intervened or if there was an internal constraint within the Nine Realms that hindered their ability to transform into beasts.

Ember was studying each male as if they were a meal she could devour. But her gaze continually returned to Basilius, even as she rattled. Although my guess was that Basilius looked and smelled like Knox, Ember undivided attention laser focused on him, remaining there entirely too long to be considered anything other than improper.

"It's not him, Ember. Cool your shit."

"But how do you know? Could it be him for like a long enough time to get off?"

"Absolutely not." I snorted, which had Basilius's eyes thinning.

They were dressed in poorly sewn pants and tunics that were threadbare and too thin to conceal the coiling muscles beneath the fabric. The brothers were clean shaven, save for Basilius, who had the same facial hair Knox had on his sharp jawline.

Dark, wispy ink covered his muscular arms and danced

up his throat to his jawline, which was the only difference he held from Knox. As if he sensed me staring, his lips curled into a self-assured smirk that made my thighs clench against the imagery of him between them that he created. His dark head tipped and his oceanic-colored eyes leisurely returned the favor, growing hooded as they caressed over my breasts before landing on my exposed thighs.

"You came here from another realm. I'd like to know which realm it was?" he asked without taking his eyes from my naked thighs.

"The Nine Realms."

"We know there's nothing left of the Nine Realms outside of this one. We haven't hidden in these mountains for the scenery, woman. I was in the Kingdom of Fire when it fell to your grandmother. I felt Norvalla falling as well and saw the flames Hecate left in her wake as she laid waste to my home. Lie to me again, and you won't like what happens."

"You're wrong, Basilius. I've stood in the palace of Dorcha myself. I've even been to the castle in Norvalla. Knox, Brander, Killian, and Lore can all tell you the same thing I am. Hell, even Greer's cankerous ass could tell you while he insulted you."

"Greer would never insult a blood-born prince of the Karnavious line," Basilius rasped. He rattled, which caused mine to roll out in a sultry, silky vibration of noise. "Why don't you answer a straightforward question for me, love? Why the fuck don't *you* smell like the other women of your breed? They reek of embers and cinnamon. You on the other hand, smell like desire and feminine sexuality that is strangely intoxicating and one hell of an aphrodisiac. I've smelled nothing like you before. Your rattle? It isn't like theirs either. In fact, it's sultry and addictive against my ears." Basilius strode closer before he knelt in front of me, staring up into my wide eyes. His palm landed against my cheek as he murmured seductively, which forced my own to whisper through the room. A wolfish smile played on his full, kissable lips as he continued.

"So, what are you? Because I'm not an idiot. Zyion Vicious wouldn't bother himself over some spoiled little princess. A sadistic prick like him? He'd eat you up and spit you out in one night without feeling bad about doing so. After all, he did murder your grandmother for King Karnavious. He also kept me and my brethren a secret from your father, Aria. But you? He didn't keep *you* a secret from *us*. In fact, he told us right where you were on that field and made sure we had a clear path to you. So, what the fuck makes you so special?"

"No, I wouldn't," Zyion's voice sounded as if it coming from the hallway.

I fought to hear over the thunderous beat of my pulse pounding violently inside my head. When I attempted to draw magic to me and nothing came, my stomach bottomed out. I'd been stupid to trust that Zyion was helping me. He'd wanted me to think he was on my side.

I scooted back from Basilius, who continued studying my face as panic clawed its way up my chest and wrapped its sharp nails around my throat. Footsteps sounded down the hallway, and the men turned toward the empty doorway, smiling. The blood drained from my face as the male I'd expected to save me from them entered. Zyion smiled when he found me awake, but his eyes sparkled with calculation.

"I hope the princess wasn't too much trouble, gentlemen. She's rather a handful, but nothing we can't deal with. Aria, I apologize for misleading you into thinking I was something I wasn't, but I can't have you running to daddy once you've learned what's truly unfolding in this wretched, miserable realm he constructed. Now can we, gentlemen?"

The men chuckled in response before Basilius responded.

"We were just having some fun with her. Plus, we were making sure you'd told us the truth, Dragon Slayer." Basilius's eyes roved over me, then flicked back to my face. "I can tell you one thing. The little princess isn't a bird, as you said she was."

CHAPTER 18
ARIA

The duplicity of Zyion's façade left me grasping for how to escape my current predicament. It just proved that I couldn't trust anyone, ever again. My instincts apparently sucked. So much for him being a man of his word, or being the Queen's Guard, not that I was the queen yet, but semantics. They had somehow nullified my powers, leaving me with only my wits and hands to defend myself against them. Basilius was staring at my thighs while Zyion whispered something in his ear. I strained to make out what he was saying, but my heightened senses were gone as well.

"Fine," Basilius uttered without moving his attention. "Let's discuss this over ale. She isn't going anywhere tonight. There's nowhere for her to run, anyway."

Without a word to me, they gradually filed out of the chamber, closing and locking the door behind them.

As if that would stop me.

I couldn't bear to linger here while they conspired and Esme's safety remained uncertain. I'd assumed she was because Zyion had informed me that she hadn't been their target, but his word obviously meant nothing.

Knox would never let me live it down that I should've listened to him and remained within the Nine Realms instead of adventuring off to the unknown.

The moment I stood, the room spun and saliva flooded my mouth in warning. I took a deep breath, filling my lungs with the scent of too much masculinity with earthy undertones. Slowly, I moved to the window, which looked as if they might open, and calculated how far the drop was. My lips pulled into a thin line as I took in the drop I'd need to make to the ground level.

I tilted my head, listening to the footsteps and men's laughter fading as they moved farther away from the chamber. Once the sound of a door closing met my ears, I immediately rushed for the windows, only to discover I was higher than I expected in the air. The sun hadn't set, which meant we hadn't flown too far from the city.

It gave me hope of escaping, which had me trying one window, then another. Each one refusing to budge. Hadn't they ever oiled the fuckers? At the last one, I frowned, then frantically searched the room eyeing a wooden chair beside the bed. Cautiously moving to the wooden chair, I paused to tilt my ear, hating that my senses weren't there.

"Ember?" I waited, then frowned. She was just there. *"Ember, it's sort of important."* Nothing. *"Thanks for being there when I needed you, not best lesbian!"* I'd thought the last one would get her moving.

The window was thicker than I was used to, but that should be a problem. As I lifted the chair, my body swayed, which forced me to set it back down for a moment. What the fuck had they really done to me? How had they even known what to use to nullify the land's power? Somehow, they'd neutered me and that was terrifying considering I was in a strange land, with no one coming to save me.

Squaring my shoulders as I battled for strength, I hoisted the chair up and slammed it against the window. It bounced off the pane and sent me sprawling on the floor, which made Ember snort. She had felt my inner turmoil, which should've worried her since I didn't panic often. Instead, the bitch was snickering at my sad attempt to escape the bevy of men who'd been looking at me like I was a snack and they were ravenous.

Rising to my feet once more, I gripped the chair and slammed it against the window with all the strength I had left.

It didn't so much as crack the thick glass. I was fighting to keep myself from freaking the fuck out or allowing the inner turmoil, betrayal from Zyion, and worry for Esme to flood it to prevent him from deciphering what I was currently doing.

The third attempt sent glass shards and larger pieces scattering to the floor. Ignoring my lack of equilibrium, I tossed the chair aside and rushed through the window as footsteps thundered toward the chamber. The shards of glass still stuck in the sill cut into my thighs, but I didn't give myself permission to stop. If I did, I wouldn't have enough strength to move again, and I needed everything I had to pull myself through and balance on the thin edge of the wood outside the chamber.

The door slammed open, I glanced back to watch as

Zyion, Basilius, and the other men burst into the room. Then I leaped toward the ground.

I landed with a bone-jarring crash, and forcing myself to get up was easier said than done. Still, I managed to get to my feet just as Zyion's head appeared above me. The sound of cheerful voices was closer than I cared for, but it didn't stop me from running as fast as my wobbly legs would go directly into the fray of them. The building was built of stones, and if I was right, they'd covered the roofs with branches from the pine trees to camouflage them. It was actually genius, but not productive in my rescue.

The men and women who had stopped to stare at the strange female who just jumped from a window gave me pause. But then shouting started from inside the house, and propelled me into a mad dash toward the edge of the forest. I was halfway there when I started mentally berating myself for not finding some shoes to wear.

"*You know, if you allowed me control, we could move much faster,*" Ember chided.

"Now you're fucking available? If I let you have control, I wouldn't be a fucking snack. I'll be a sample you let everyone taste, hussy!" I muttered and then winced as something cut into the heel of my foot. Without pausing to extract the object, I charged through a thicket of trees and then came to a skidding stop, flailing my arms to maintain equilibrium as I stood precariously on the cliff's edge.

The cliff overlooked a deep ravine with a rapid river rushing through the center. A scattering of pebbles rolled over the edge and I lost sight of them long before they hit the water. Fucking hell it was a long way down. A branch snapped, forcing my eyes to prick as I looked between the tree line, and the fall. When I glanced back at the rushing water, defeat sank its teeth into my mind. My heart thundered agonizingly against my breast as I spun around as men's voices neared.

"Told you she wouldn't get far, Vicious." Basilius's deep, silky baritone was clear as he pushed past the branches.

"Aria, don't be stupid," Zyion cautioned, his face tight with worry.

One of Knox's look-alike's snorted and watched me with cold ocean-colored eyes that were filled with mockery. "As if she'd have the balls to actually jump. No one is stupid enough—"

Spinning back around, I leaped recklessly over the edge, not willing to wait for them to overtake me. I'd faced death enough to know he didn't want me. Not yet, at least. The chilled air hit my face, and my hair rushed up as if trying to become wings. Quietly, I uttered a prayer before sucking a deep breath into my lungs and spinning midair so that my feet would break the surface of the water.

The landing was painful and forced my legs up against my abdomen. Everything screamed as agony rushed through my thighs, stomach, and chest. The moment my feet touched the bottom of the river, I kicked off it and started for the surface. The water was shockingly cold, but I did my best to ignore the pinpricks of pain that dug into my flesh. Breaking the surface, I slowly began moving my limbs, treading water as I moved in the current.

A loud splash jerked my focus toward where I'd gone into the water, watching as Zyion entered the water seconds before Basilius and the others followed. Using what little energy I had left, I began putting effort into swimming toward the shore. Beyond the bank, a dense forest lined the canyon, which would allow me some coverage to hide from them. Crawling onto the shore, I ignored the pain in my extremities as I rushed into the forest, gulping air into my lungs.

I hid in the foliage and ripped off a piece of my gown's skirt, throwing it in one direction before taking off in the opposite. Shouts began echoing through the forest behind me, forcing me onward. Scanning the dark shadows of the thicker underbrush, I searched for somewhere to hide. It wasn't until the sound of leathery wings whispered above me that I started running, tilting my head to scan the tree-tops to figure out where the dragon was.

The silhouette of an enormous dragon was outlined through the low-hanging clouds. Of course, they'd use their beast forms to hunt for me. I hadn't even considered that before bolting from the room they'd locked me in.

The trees were larger than the Redwood Trees in California and Oregon we'd once visited. I paused behind a wide trunk to catch my breath, leaning against it as I sucked air into my lungs. Above me, the dragon rattled before circling above the tree I hid behind. Since I was rather unwilling to wait around until it figured out I was here, I forced my legs into motion, pumping them harder and faster, each stride taking me farther away from the men hunting me.

I could hear the branches snapping beneath their weight, every crack of wood causing my heart to pound faster. A loud, thunderous banging sounded above me as the dragon rushed toward the ground through the trees, shredding branches in its descent. It landed right in front of me, so I slid on my ass between his four limbs, coming up behind him. Not waiting to see if he melted me into a pile of goo, I continued forward the moment I was back on my feet.

The dragon released an ear-piercing shriek and heat licked up my spine as he whipped around and chased after me. Who the fuck brought dragons for foot chases? If I lived through this, I was fucking designing shoes, because screw these soft slippers. Where had they even gotten the idea from? Princess Academy or some shit? Tears burned my eyes as my legs screamed from running. Branches whipped against my arms, welting the flesh as I forced my body to continue forward.

"Aria, fucking stop! We will not hurt you," Zyion snarled from in front of me.

How the fuck had be gotten in front of me? I skidded to a stop before sliding around the trunk of a giant tree. The bark and rocks bit into my arms as I felt anger colliding with despair. This was bullshit. I didn't even want to think of the 'I told you so's Knox was going to feed me for this shit. Eyeing the thick brush, I slid onto my knees, then crawled through it until my arms felt nothing but air. My body lurched forward without warning, tearing a shocked cry from my lips as I landed with a painful crash onto the ground. Darkness swallowed my vision as I landed on something sharp. The coppery tang of blood filled the surrounding air. A growl broke from my lips as I desperately tried to figure out where I'd landed.

It had to be a pit or cave. I groped blindly before grabbing on to something hard and rounded. My stomach churned with unease as I felt two empty sockets and what was likely teeth. Smothering my scream of horror with both hands, I inched backward while scanning the darkness.

Arms wrapped around me before Zyion's gravelly voice whispered, "Do not make any sudden movements. You'll be safe if you listen to me."

I wanted to roll my eyes at him. The last time I'd trusted him, it had disastrous results. Something moved beside us, and Zyion forced me behind the shield of his larger, more powerful body. The sound of the dragon's rattling overhead incited a challenge from the unknown entity in the dark hole with us. The hairs on my arms rose as crimson eyes opened, glowing in the cave's darkness.

"Move back slowly, and go as far as you can, Aria. It cannot hear us. It hunts prey by tracking movement," he warned. Rocks moved in front of us, which caused my head to turn slowly in the direction I'd heard the slide of rocks.

"What the hell is it?"

"It's a wyrm," he stated, as if I should know what the hell one was?

"What the hell is a wyrm?" I demanded through chattering teeth.

"If you don't know, now isn't the time for me to explain what is in the dark, damp cave with us." I frowned as I strained my eyes, searching the darkness for the wyrm.

"Do you honestly expect me to trust you?" I challenged myself to keep my mind off not knowing what a wyrm could possibly be in this realm. I'd never heard of them, let alone anything that could hunt only by sound.

"I don't care if you believe me or not, Aria." His tone was clipped and sharp.

"Screw you and screw this," I hissed as I began feeling behind me, only to place my hand on scales. "There is something behind us."

"Not behind us. All around us," he corrected. "You're shaking."

"Is now a bad time to tell you I'm claustrophobic?" I whispered through trembling lips. His snort was the only reply to my question. "What are we waiting for?"

"For the Karnavious brothers to figure out our current predicament and cause a distraction so we can escape without being ingested by the wyrm. You shouldn't have run from me, princess. There are monsters in the forests that feed on our kind."

My anger spiked at his insinuation that this was my fault. The balls of this bastard! "Did you honestly expect me to sit around and wait for you to murder me? Or do whatever it was you and those assholes intended?"

"It would've saved me from having to jump into a fucking cavern with a wyrm. There are things happening in this realm that you're not aware of."

"No shit? I totally didn't catch that, Zyion!" After a moment, I actually asked what else, in case the coup wasn't the worst shit happening. "Like what?" I protested emphatically, wondering if he was making up the wyrm to keep me pliant. It was clear that something was among us, but its nature was yet to be determined.

"That was your eldest brother Vane who attacked you today." Pausing, I turned, feeling a twinge of regret that I wouldn't be bonding with him after all. "What is actually worrisome, is that he knew how to bring you down and nullify your magic. According to my sources, he intended to stab you through the heart, then set you on fire to prove to the people in front of his father, and those gathered at the training field, that you're not a Prometheus. If he'd succeeded, we're uncertain your beast would survive the attack, or even rise. You're not connected to your inner beast. I improvised with what I had in order to prevent Vane from succeeding."

"Why does everyone want to kill me?" I asked irritably.

"You really can't whisper worth shit, can you?" His question forced my eyes to roll.

"And them attacking Griffon?"

"The coup wasn't in their plans until Hagen learned of the assassination plan. He wants the throne, and there's nothing he won't do to achieve his goal."

"And your plan to save me was to have me kidnapped by dragons?"

"I did whatever the fuck I had to do to ensure you lived. If that makes me your villain, so fucking be it," he growled as something slammed against the ground above us. The creature currently surrounding us shot into the air so rapidly that my mind didn't process what had happened until Zyion's arm wrapped around me and he jerked me back against the heat of his body.

"What are you doing?" I squeaked.

"You're fucking trembling because you're freezing. The temperature is about to drop without the wyrm's body heat inside this cavern, and there's no way we can climb out of the hole you got us into. That means we're going through the tunnels to escape from it. Now, I'm going to need you to stop asking questions and fucking move. They can't beat the bastard, which means we have moments to escape before he returns."

"I'll be fine once we leave this cavern. Let's go." The cold was unnerving, but so was the irritable prick behind me.

"Stay close to me, and if you hear anything moving? You need to freeze in place immediately." Zyion turned away from me—or, I assumed that was what he did. Discerning anything was impossible in the pitch-black darkness we were trapped in. "We're not dying here, princess. Understand? Few things can kill a phoenix, but wyrm's happen to be on that very short list." I seized the tunic he wore with a tight grasp. "Oh, look at you good girl, you can listen," he murmured with sarcasm dripping from his tone

"Don't say that to me," I grumbled irritably.

"Why? Is that what your dragon calls you when you're beneath him?" he queried. His tone implied he knew what Knox said to me during our turbulent bouts together.

I chose to ignore him as we crept sideways through the damp tunnel. Scraping sounded behind us, which forced me to freeze in place. Warm air shot from whatever was in front of us, blasting into our faces. The horrific scent of it combined with the heated breath drifting over my back had my gag reflex kicking into overdrive. My fingers remained locked onto Zyion's back, twisting his tunic as fear rocketed through my mind and forced a soft whimper from my throat. This was how I died. I felt the gravity of it in my bones.

CHAPTER 19
ARIA

Zyion was faster than I was. He yanked me backward and then forced me to the ground before the sound of his sword scraping against the scabbard filled the cavern. My fear and horror shot up my throat, choking off the sound of my scream. Something wet and warm splattered over my face as I crawled backward, trying to give Zyion enough room to fight without me being in the way.

"Run, Aria," Zyion demanded through clenched teeth seconds before he released a howl of pain. The echo of his sword clattering to the cavern floor alerted me to the seriousness of the situation. "Fuck!" he snarled as the sound of something being slammed against the wall sounded within the darkness of the cavern.

Closing my eyes, I told myself I was a fool for what I was about to attempt. Still, my hands were blindly searching the ground around me for the blade. The sound of his body being slammed around didn't hide the soft click of claws against the stone. Something else was in the cave with us. Finally, my palm landed on the cold steel, and I heaved it up before swinging it recklessly through the air before me.

"Zyion?" I screamed.

A scratching sound against the ground started in front of me, which allowed me to slide the blade forward. There was the telltale resistance of the blade piercing flesh, and I prayed quietly that I hadn't just skewered Zyion with his own sword. The sound of something rushing toward me forced me to aggressively swing the blade with every remaining ounce of strength I had left.

"I am not dying here!" I snarled as tears fell from my eyes. My arms shook under the weight of the sword, and I hated it. "Fuck you! Fuck you, motherfucker! If you want me, come get some!" I sobbed as I slashed the blade once more. Something solid hit the floor. Not daring to stop, I continued bringing the blade down in wild, angry, fearful slices until light burned across my vision, forcing me to stop. I blinked persistently to allow my eyes to adjust. When they refused, I lifted my arm to shield them from the blinding light. A hand slid down my arm to my hand before tugging the sword from my hold.

"You killed it, princess," Basilius assured. My focus lifted to where he stood across from me on the other side of the wyrm's lifeless corpse.

When I saw the monstrous thing, the blood drained from my face. The wyrm had something that resembled a dragon's head, but that was where the similarities ended. Its serpent-like body was covered in scales. Sharp, dagger-like teeth were glistening in the light's eerie glow. Strange antler-type horns speared from its head, still moving even in death. Essentially, the wyrm lacked limbs and wings but possessed a mouthful of razor-sharp teeth. Swallowing the uneasiness I felt in its presence, I flinched from the multiple rows of wicked looking teeth in its cavernous maw.

"Zyion?" I called out as I turned and then searched his body for injuries. His chest was coated in blood, but otherwise, he seemed fine. I expelled an unrestrained sigh as a loud exhale left my lungs and my fear for him was eased. "Idiot, did you see that thing? Why would you even think of fighting it?"

Zyion awarded me a lopsided smile and a lifted brow, but I ignored his smugness. I told myself I'd only worried because him dying would have left me alone in this damn cave. My legs threatened to give out as the adrenaline exited from my system, leaving me weak. Zyion reached out, holding me up even if it was a bit awkward.

"Worried about me? Careful, Aria. I may start to think that you actually like me." His heated breath fanned against my ear as I gripped a handful of his tunic, uncaring that it was soaked in blood.

"As if I'd waste my emotions on you, Zyion. You're mildly tolerable to be around—at best." He'd physically pushed me to safety while putting himself right into the line of danger. He'd known I wouldn't have been fast enough to get out of the way, and he'd chosen to protect me by sacrificing himself. "Thank you for not letting that thing kill me," I murmured, slowly lifting my hand to place my palm against the hard muscles of his chest. When I looked up at him, I hadn't expected him to look surprised.

If I had to guess, Zyion hadn't ever been thanked for his selflessness before.

"I merely did what anyone else would do." I noted the lines on his face, even as more formed around his lips. Zyion reached up to scratch the back of his neck, then shrugged. "Has no one taught you how to use a sword?"

"Well, no. Normally, I don't need weapons. I am the weapon." Which had been true, but apparently my brother had found my kryptonite. Luckily, Zyion didn't point out that I was currently helpless and vulnerable.

"We have to remedy that after we've helped you ascend to the throne. Come, we have a lot to get done in a short amount of time." Zyion slid his arm firmly around my trembling form and helped Basilius hoist me over the remains of the wyrm. "You continue to impress me, Aria Prometheus."

"Honestly Vicious, I'm still shocked she even tried to protect you. I thought that, for certain, she'd let you rot in the bastard's gullet." Basilius smirked as he gripped my hips, pulling me from Zyion's hold and jerking me into the heat of his body. Like Knox, he was a veritable furnace of heat. I shivered against his hold as the scent of bergamot and sage tickled my senses.

"She's a savage little thing. Isn't she?" Zyion asked as he jumped over the carcass. "If I hadn't watched the light burning out of Scylla Prometheus's pretty eyes, I'd think Aria was her, returning to seek revenge against me."

"Does she know it was you who murdered her grandmother?" the younger version of Knox queried with a wolfish grin burning in his eyes. Either his whisper skills were as shitty as mine, or he'd meant for me to hear it.

"Do you wish to keep your tongue, Acheron?" Zyion hissed, disapproval tightening his sharp, masculine features.

"Just asking if she's aware of what your part in all of this is, Vicious. Eventually, she'll figure the truth out." Basilius turned and pegged him with a look of censure causing Acheron to step back. As I observed, the air grew thick with tension, thick enough to cut through with a knife. "Whatever. I'll meet you guys back at the keep. I'm heading out on patrol. Don't enjoy the pretty princess too much without me. I adore crazy bitches."

"Why do you adore crazy bitches?" I was curious why anyone would enjoy a woman being cracked in the head. His lips curled into a smile that reminded me of Knox's.

"Crazy bitches hold nothing back. They fuck like they're unhinged. I'm fucking here for that shit." He strode closer before dragging his fingertip over my cheek. "Are you crazy, princess?" His eyes darkened as they lowered to my lips. My tongue jutted out, licking them, which caused a rattle to slip from his.

"Aren't we all a little crazy at heart?" I returned, answering him before turning back, staring at the others. "The thing is," I said, turning back to stare at Acheron. "My type of crazy? It comes with an entirely different brand of insane. Stick around me long enough, I'm sure my crazy will come out to play," I muttered as Zyion pushed Acheron's hand from my face.

"She's about to be queen. Show her the respect deserved for the position, Acheron," he growled protectively. The tone held warning, causing Basilius to study Zyion and his reaction. A look of amusement played over his face, so alike his brother. "Let's go before she catches her death from the cold."

"Fucking weak ass birds." Ronin, who hadn't even bothered to make his presence known, muttered.

I followed Acheron down the dark tunnel we'd been moving down before the wyrm had caught up to us. Zyion's stare burned into my spine as I listened to him and Basilius talking. The footsteps behind us got further back, as if purposely adding distance between them, and myself. Straining my hearing, I shamelessly eavesdropped on the conversation between Basilius and Zyion.

"You already know how this will end, Vicious," Basilius warned in a hushed tone. I let him think I couldn't hear him.

"She's different for me," Zyion replied just as quietly. "Scylla ruled by the loyalty to the kingdom her mother handed down to her. She wasn't given a choice in who she'd wed, as you know. Aria is not ruled by loyalty to the Prometheus line, either. She won't allow Tirsynth to rise to power or release him from the ground. Not once she knows the truth about him. Griffon is naïve to think his brothers give one fuck about propriety or a bastard born daughter foretold to rule in order to save the realm. Vane sought to murder her before he'd even met her. The queen tied my fate to hers when she forced me to sacrifice what I wanted most, as well as the other thing. I feel Aria on a level I've never felt another before. Scylla forcefully embedded this girl into my soul. She's the one, Basilius. This girl will become the queen, born to destroy the darkness shrouding the Nine Realms."

"Are you certain it isn't your cock that feels her? She's

pleasant on the eyes, and the fire burning in her glare would make any warrior take notice of her. Not to mention, she is the mirror image of Scylla, who you once loved."

"I loved my queen, Basilius. But I was never in love with her. Her mates wouldn't have thought twice if she'd taken me to her chamber, but she never trespassed against the bond we shared. I'll not mince words here or tell you that Aria isn't intriguing, but she has a mate outside of this realm, which means her heart belongs to him and him alone. I am merely her protector. My job is to guide her on her path and ensure the rightful heir ascends the throne and lives long enough to claim it as her own."

"Your honor is commendable, but I've seen you look at her. I've seen you blindly leap into a wyrm hole to protect her, which wasn't done out of loyalty or duty. You are so fucked if you think you'll be satisfied with merely protecting your queen. When that happens, you'll bury another queen. Only this one? She'll take your heart to her grave with her, my friend."

"I won't allow her to burn out or go mad as Tirsynth and Scylla's daughters did. They thought the world owed them, which resulted in it refusing them with its magic. The land has already granted power to Aria, and it did so long before she left the Tenth Realm. She is the son who was promised, but Scylla ensured no one was looking for a daughter born with the sun smoldering in her soul. She was never told of her parentage until she returned to the realms." Zyion not only spoke with tenderness but also with reverence. He believed what he said. "She will set the world afire, and those who oppose her reign will burn if they try to stop her."

"Where does that leave you, my friend?"

"My destiny's tied to hers through the Fates. I am connected to her in a way that cannot be undone. The girl's different, which is unsettling. She doesn't order people about, she's kind to lesser classes. She's actually refreshing after being stuck serving assholes. Aria doesn't expect this world to hand her anything as Scylla's daughters did. Their downfall was their sense of entitlement because of their status as royals. Aria on the other hand? Without first earning their respect, she won't expect anyone to merely bow to her. Scylla made sure that Aria wouldn't so easily bow to the whims of others." My ears perked up at his words as my stomach churned, twisting with misery from the truth buried in them.

"That girl had to learn how to survive from birth because her mother attempted to steal the power Aria housed. So where does it leave me? It leaves me guarding her back from the bevy of blades seeking to end her life, because she is the key to unlocking this prison that they've held us in and returning us to the fight brewing inside the realms."

"You and I both know there's nothing left of our home," Basilius hissed.

"Oh? Didn't you hear? Aria's the key to unlocking the walls forcing us to remain here. The moment she exits, the entire realm dissolves and then our prison holding us in will open, my friend. As I said, she's our salvation and for that, I'll die on my sword before I allow another to touch one silken strand of hair on her alluring head."

CHAPTER 20
ARIA

The village we traveled to wasn't the same as I'd run from earlier. They built this one in a cave, which forced the dragons to veer left and then right through a slender rock formation. A wide entrance allowed them to fly into the cavern, which was filled with lanterns covering man-made bridges reaching throughout several tiers. In the center of the large, open cavern a wide walkway reached from one side to the other.

"Welcome to the City of Dragons, princess," Zyion stated, even as he slid from the back of Basilius, who'd been the only dragon willing to carry both of us for the long flight to the hidden city. "Basilius and his brethren who ended up trapped here built it while our people were blessed with a mirror realm of our own."

"It's amazing," I admitted before wincing as a familiar voice called out from above. I spun around, peering up three tiers as Esme and Eva waved from above. "You brought Esme here?"

"You wouldn't have remained here without her.

There's a lot we need to discuss, Aria. It will not be a quick conversation." Zyion's eyes held mine before lifting to where Esme was shouting down from above. "It is best that you follow me. You need warmth, and your gown is beyond repair."

Zyion walked through a hallway, which threaded throughout the cavern. Thousands of tiny glowing lights filled the walls, as if they'd captured millions of lightning bugs, then released them. Once we'd passed the long, winding corridor of small hand carved doors, the cave opened into a vast oasis. The same tiny flickering bugs were within the large, intricate structure. An entire city had been built into the earth, which stole my breath. The damp, earthy scent drifted around us, soothingly. The air was chilled, but then we were inside an underground cavern.

Zyion didn't stop long enough for me to appreciate the view, forcing me to run to keep up with his longer legged strides. We moved over a rock formation, which they'd utilized as a bridge, which allowed a glimpse over the edge, which had a fast-moving river running through the lowest level of the cavern. Around the edge of the same level as the underground river, a pathway with strips of drapery covered what I assumed were doorways. Following directly behind Zyion, while still inspecting the wondrous city built into the vast cavern, I didn't notice him stopping before me. I plowed into his chest, then jerked back as his hands shot out, steadying me.

"I wouldn't get too close to the edge. I'd hate to drag your corpse from the river below. The cavern won't disappear before I've provided you with warmth and something suitable to wear. There will be plenty of time to both explore and appease your curiosity after we've spoken," he chided, before pulling back a crimson tapestry with images of dragons and phoenixes in flight sewn into the fabric in silver thread. "Ladies first," he purred as I ducked beneath his arm, entering into the room.

The chamber we entered was obscured by darkness. The dim light from the lanterns outside offered just enough to discern the layout of the chamber. I remained in place as Zyion released his hold on the curtain, closing the room off from the outside. I swallowed down the uneasiness of being alone with him created in my abdomen. Zyion didn't seem to hold the same worry, entering behind me and promptly vanishing into a doorway, or what I assumed was one, only to vanish.

I didn't move, uncertain if he'd expected me to follow behind him. The fact that Acheron had insisted I'd find out about what Zyion had done created uncertainty within me. I had my suspicions about what had occurred, but I needed answers. Answers that only he could give me.

"Are you nervous about being alone with me, princess?" he questioned from behind me, which almost had me jumping out of my own skin. He'd managed to catch me off guard, which wasn't something people normally did. Knox was the only one who managed to sneak up on me.

"Actually, yes. I don't know you well enough to be alone with you, Zyion. Plus, I don't like whatever is connecting us. It's bothersome." I hadn't meant to admit it to him, but he unnerved me.

"And you think I'm enjoying being tethered to you?" In

his voice, I heard pain and anger, which caused the skin on my forehead to crease. "I don't know if you're ready for the answer. Neither of us were asked if we wanted to be connected to one another. If Scylla had asked me? I'd have declined being connected to anyone ever again, but that wasn't the case. You'll soon be the Queen of the Kingdom of Fire. That means I will be your protector and champion. It's not a job I'll take lightly, either." He turned me toward him, which I allowed.

It felt like he was peering into the depths of my soul as he held my gaze. Silently, I studied the turquoise irises within his eyes, noting the flecks of gold that shimmered within the tranquil color.

"Why should I trust you?" I asked with hesitancy, warring through my emotions. "You failed my grandmother." I noted the way his eyes closed before opening, flaying me open with the pain I witnessed in them.

As I waited for his reply, his emotions closed down and the thread pulling us closer felt frayed. Almost as if he was trying to rip free of the link.

"You shouldn't trust me, Aria. In fact, you shouldn't trust anyone until they've proved their intent toward you. I didn't fail my queen, either. If you'll let me, I'll explain why you feel the thread tethering you to me."

His words caused a flurry of butterflies to whisper through my belly. Though not like Knox created, it was a more worrisome flutter. Was Zyion pleasing to the eye? Definitely. Was he Knox? No, which meant I needed to sever the thread binding us together.

"Why should I trust you if what Basilius said earlier is true?" I asked, needing to know why he'd murdered her and then allowed the others to think he'd betrayed her.

"Are you asking me if I killed my queen? The answer isn't pretty, princess. I killed my queen."

The long pause between his words sent my heart thundering powerfully in my ears as it thumped against my chest. His tone was the only thing holding me in place. There was pain in how he'd admitted what he'd done.

"Tell me why you killed my grandmother," I commanded. Anger clashed with fear, causing an odd combination of emotions to churn through my stomach.

"If you give me a chance, Aria, I'll tell you everything." Nodding for him to continue, he snorted before moving to a wooden table.

On it, there was some sort of wooden holder, which had been whittled into the shape of a phoenix in flight. Zyion placed a tea kettle on the smooth wooden base. In the small cupboard beneath it, he pulled out a basket of herbs, then a small rounded piece of glass.

"I am not a savior. Hell, I'm not even a good person, but I've never pretended to be one, either. You are good. I can sense the goodness that clings to your soul. You're not a murderous bitch who kills without warranting death. You came here without the intent of taking your birthright."

"How do you know that?" I countered, watching him as he added herbs into the small strainer, which he then put into the other rounded glass item he'd brought out.

His head lifted as a small smile played on his lips. "Because, unlike others, I can feel the intentions of others. You're easy enough to read without me needing to use any abilities, though. Esmeralda is the same as you are. Neither of you came here with ill intent, but it doesn't alter the others, who don't wish to see a stranger placed upon our throne." Zyion waved his fingers beneath the strange kettle. My forehead creased as the water began boiling in the glass of the upper chamber. "Scylla changed your mind, didn't she?"

"In a way, yes." Pausing, I considered how much I should disclose of what I'd discovered on my own.

"You can trust me, Aria. I am honor bound to protect you with my life, as you witnessed in yourself earlier. Scylla chose me to be your protector. It wasn't a choice I willingly agreed to, which is why she forced it upon me."

"Ouch," I whispered as the tether within me tightened. His head dropped forward, as if he was deciding how to word something. "I don't have time for vacillation, Zyion. There's a war unfolding outside of this realm. The people need me, so if you have something to say, say it now."

"I didn't think you'd ever actually be real. I was the commander of Scylla's armies, her personal guard. I am damn good at fighting, strategic in battles, but I am not a good person."

"Good at killing dragons as well?" I carefully studied the smirk spreading over his lips.

"Absolutely," he rasped, which caused me to pause, considering him carefully. "I take it you mentioned me to your lover?"

"He's more than just my lover," I corrected sharply.

"Oh, yes. I forgot. Correct me if I'm mistaken, but he's not your husband any longer. I heard he allowed them to annul your marriage. If it had been me, I'd have murdered the entire assembly before I allowed them to remove vows spoken before the gods." His words caused tears to swim in my vision before I pushed them away. "That was uncalled for, Aria. I was good at killing dragons, but we were at war against them. I didn't *enjoy* killing them, if that's what King Karnavious told you. In fact, I am the reason his brothers survived for this long within this realm."

"He thinks they're lost to him," I admitted, not forgiving him of the low blow he'd hit back with.

"He had good reason to believe they were. As you've noticed by now, we have both within our line. Dragon and phoenixes both are born to the Prometheus and Fafnir lines. When this realm was created, they weren't our enemies. Griffon is king, but his reign depends on his brother not seeking to depose him. Hagen never forgave the dragons. His son Aldred was slain in a battle against them, and he has made it his personal mission to slaughter any dragon in the Karnavious bloodline. Your connection with them sparked the uprising that occurred today. He and your brother Vane, they nullified the power the land feeds you." Turning to the percolating tea, he pushed the upper basin of boiling water over, which sent the boiling water into the strainer, and then the water steeped in briefly before trickling to the glass teapot.

The heady scent of earthy undertones with citrus filled the chamber. My mouth watered as I continued to study the trickle of dark water as it journeyed to the glass below.

"These herbs are from my homeland, Alfheim."

"Scylla was from Vanaheim, though. Right?" I countered curiously.

"Correct," he stated, smirking when I chewed my lip, waiting for more. "I was a gift to your grandmother from

Freyr. The Vanir and Aesir were often gifted and captured in raids on one another. Freyr, who bound me to Scylla before she was even born, raided my village. Since I held Aesir blood, warriors trained me to fight tactical battle strategies, and once I'd mastered warfare, they then sent me to the harem of an aging elf lord who couldn't satisfy the needs of his concubines. There, I mastered the art of . . . *loving*. After, they gave me to Frejya. She forced me to drink the flames of Muspelheim."

"The primordial realm of heat and flame? She forced you to drink flames?" I asked in a horrified tone.

"It is the same flame her daughter housed, which I needed to be immune to in order to serve at her side, but also to protect her. They tethered my life to hers, after all." *As a slave.* He didn't need to elaborate the last part. I felt his anger of being one within me.

"Your grandmother wasn't born a phoenix, Aria. She was born of a dragon, but never took dragon form. When the Queen of Dragons first changed, then burned through our realm, Scylla refused to retreat. I searched for her for a long time. On the sixth day, she rose from the ashes. Your grandmother was gloriously lovely in her rage, which compelled her to transform into what she became."

"The first Rise of the Phoenix," I said with a sad smile. "On the seventh day, she demanded those who'd perished join her rising. One by one, they rose as if born from the ashes. On the eighth day, they erected the palace. A palace which was created from the sand and ashes forged into glass, from the intensity of the dragon's flame that consumed the lives who failed to rise." I felt a shiver racing down my spine as he nodded, but there was agony in his eyes that told me he'd lost someone in that battle. "On the ninth day, the Kingdom of Fire rose from the same sand they'd waged war on."

"Your love of reading anything you can get your hands on is paying off, princess." Zyion poured a cup of tea, then added something sparkling from a jar he'd retrieved during my recital of the Rising Phoenix.

"I get the history, but I don't understand why you killed my grandmother."

"She forced me to make a vow to her days before it happened. I didn't agree, which caused her to remind me of how she'd received me. I wasn't merely a slave, Aria. I was magically bound to do as she ordered, even if that meant doing things I didn't want to do." My face tightened with disdain, which had him slowly exhaling. "Scylla only reminded me of my position in her life twice. Once on the night I was sent away to spy on the Karnavious dragons, then again when she bid me to do the unthinkable."

"I'm going to need you to tell me more than just that, Zyion. I need to know why you and I are now tethered together."

"Fine, then you can drink as I explain from the beginning of your creation. The tea may make you a little dizzy as the land fuels you with mana. Unfortunately, I cannot remove the bitterness of the tea leaves. It cannot be altered or it won't undo the nasty binding spell Vane nullified. The link between you and the land won't be removed again." My lips parted, but he shook his head slowly. "I don't know how he managed to do it, but once you drink the tea, he won't be able to use it on you again. You'll be immune if he attempts any magic on you, princess."

Accepting the tea, I lowered my lips to it, blowing on the steam spiraling up from the delicate glass cup. A small sip revealed the bitterness Zyion had spoken of, which caused my stomach to rebel against indulging in any more of the tea.

"If I were you, I'd drink it one drink instead of sipping it, Aria."

Moving away from me, he leaned against the wall, crossing his arms to wait for me to do as he'd instructed. Once I had, he began to explain from the very beginning.

"Scylla was skilled in the old ways of foretelling the future. She'd asked the seers if a champion would be born to end the suffering of her people. The answer was grim when it came. No one was coming to save us from the monster who'd created darkness in the lands. There was no balance to the dark swelling over the realms. Scylla asked what she could barter to create a being of light. One to push the darkness from our land, returning the balance lost when Hecate was sealed inside the Nine Realms."

"Her life for mine," I whispered against his palm.

"Not just her life, Aria. Scylla used seidr. A type of magic that can determine the outcome of the future, while shaping it as well. In order to achieve her prophecy, she needed something from both the Vanir and the Aesir, which, when combined, would make a worthy sacrifice that not even the old gods could ignore. No one else knows what I am or where I came from. They only know I served Scylla because she was of the Vanir. I am not of her people, Aria. I was born with Aesir blood within my veins. My sacrifice couldn't be the same as hers. I had to forgo what I wanted most."

"What did you want most?" The question escaped with sadness crushing my chest.

"I wanted to find love with a woman of worth, to watch her grow round with my child growing in her womb. I wanted to have a family of my own. I sacrificed any chance of that to bring forth one who would drive the darkness back into the shadows so that the light could once again shine in the Nine Realms, which is my home." Tears slipped from my eyes as heat seared behind my nose. "Are you crying for me, princess?" he asked, stepping closer, even as he wiped away the tears falling down my cheeks.

"I hate knowing that Scylla gave her life for mine and that you sacrificed being a father for me." It was the truth. I wasn't worth the sacrifices they'd made. What if I fucked up? Then they'd have done it for nothing.

"I am of the Aesir, Aria. You hold a piece of me within you. As you hold a piece of Scylla, as well. We bless you with both of our tribes from our sacrifices, which forged you into life. They forced part of our blood into the Fate's cauldron, which was then threaded into the fabric of your soul. It's one of the reasons you're warlike, but still delicate and graceful. Griffon may have created you, but he did so because Scylla ensured the child, his sire would hold the mana she and I removed from ourselves. The thread you feel? It's because you house a part of me within you—the part that gives you the ability to love that dragon of yours so faithfully. Scylla gifted you with the power to remake the land."

"That's why I feel you within me?" I whispered as my mind whirled with the overload of information.

I was relieved that it wasn't something more profound,

such as a mating connection, but it also made sadness swell inside me until my heart ached with it. He'd given up his chance to become a father in order to save the Nine Realms. All he'd gotten in return for that sacrifice was me.

"I don't want your pity, princess." A soft glow filled the room as he stepped back and turned away.

As the light grew, it revealed a large room decorated in shades of onyx and ice-blue. In the center of the room was a massive arrangement of pillows placed like a bed, which flowed along the wall. A small table sat beside it, and a tapestry of knights mounted on warhorses with their blades held high covered the entire left wall. Across from it, nude women were sewn in various stages of undress, all of them sunbathing beside a massive waterfall. Narrowing my eyes on the imagery, I smothered a snort.

"Don't like my tapestry?" Zyion asked as he reentered the room, holding a silk gown. At least, I assumed that was what he held.

"Inside the Tenth Realm, men have similar posters of women inside their rooms. I was merely comparing the men of the Nine Realms to the one I derive from." His eyes skimmed over the naked women before slowly settling back on me.

"You don't derive from the Tenth Realm, Aria. We forged you in this very cavern, which is also where she asked me to take her life. The only difference is that it was in our realm when it went down. Get dressed so that we may continue this conversation without you causing a stir because your creamy thighs are on display." He tossed the clothes to me before exiting the room through the door we'd come through. "Fucking Vanir blood."

I sighed. At least now it made sense for him not to like me. If I'd sacrificed my chance of love and children to procure his prophecy of unraveling, I'd hate him, too. Absorbing a lot in a short time was necessary. I needed to get back and seal Hecate in her actual body before she healed from what I'd done. If I waited too long, we'd be back to searching for a way to weaken her enough to be able to force her into her original form again. She wouldn't be stupid enough to face me again without taking precautions. If I fucked up the next time I faced off against her, I'd be dead and those who'd sacrificed so much to ensure I existed would have done so for nothing. I couldn't allow that to happen.

CHAPTER 21
ARIA

Dressed in the soft, ice-blue colored gown Zyion provided, I sat on the bevy of pillows loitering on the floor of the chamber. I hadn't realized Scylla had single-handedly created my existence and destiny. Hell, I hadn't even known it was possible for anyone to create another's destiny. Undoubtedly, no one spoke of those who had once flourished with power in the Nine Realms. Hecate had changed the history of the realms to center on her and only her. If you spoke of those who'd ruled the kingdoms within the realms before her time within it, she considered it a slight against her. Punishable by torture, or even death.

Both Zyion and Scylla had sacrificed parts of themselves for my existence. It left me baffled as to how to absorb what I'd just learned because it was so different from what I'd been taught. The ones who'd sacrificed for me merely allowed the Fates to see to my rearing, or whatever. It meant everything I'd learned since coming here was basically useless.

I could comprehend that they'd changed everything pertaining to the prophecy. At least they didn't expect us to wait for a child to grow into the savior. They'd claimed to have protected me by altering the stories, which had ended in repercussions. Hecate hadn't stopped seeking to ensure the prophecy never came to fruition. Hell, she'd forced her own daughters to lose their sons to prevent one from being born. The information was overwhelming, and was hard to decipher how much of it was real, or more lies by those fed promises by false gods.

The sound of footfalls outside the chamber forced had me folding my legs beneath my bottom and sitting up straight. Then the curtain back, revealing Esme. Her violet eyes scoured the chamber, then settled on me. Eva strolled in behind her, slowly scanning the room.

"Fucking hell," she spat out, wide eyes filled with wonder as she walked over and plopped down beside me. "This place is insane. Could you imagine if we created something like this for the orphaned witches?" Exhaling past the heaviness I felt at learning the cost for my existence, I grinned to ease the tension it would create if Esme felt my sadness.

"I would be nice to have such a place for them to hide." My head moved between both girls, Esme, who was excited, and Eva, who looked ready to throttle someone.

"You left me, which wasn't okay. I mean, I understand you didn't have a choice and all that, but next time you get kidnapped? Take me with you."

"Do you think I willingly mounted the dragon intending to be spirited off for a joy ride?" The moment the question escaped, I wanted to take it back. Her lips twitched with the threat of laughter shimmering in her violet gaze, smiling.

"Don't answer that, Esme. Fine, next time a dragon seeks to snatch me up, I'll make sure you come along for the ride."

"Hey," Esme exclaimed, holding her palms up in mock surrender. "You don't need me with you to ride dragons. You can come all you want with the dragon, but if I were you, I'd only attempt that while on solid ground." Eva snorted, and a quick glance in her direction revealed she was trying not to laugh.

"You're an ass," I muttered.

"You're forgiven for leaving me behind. Besides, it wasn't as if you wanted to do it, right?"

"Have I ever left you behind if the choice was mine?" Her cheeks jerked as a dazzling smile spread over her lips. "Besides, you'd have thrown up if you'd been on that creature's back. It was as terrifying as it was exciting."

Esme rested on the pillows, sinking down into their softness beside me. "Dragons actually stole you right in front of everyone. Honest to god's dragons, Aria. I wasn't sure what to do at first, other than gawk as a man tossed you onto the beast's back. Then, the entire shock of what was unfolding around me sank into my thick skull. I was lucky Eva was there to grab me from where I'd hidden behind the dais, or I'd have ended up rounded up with the others who were chained to one another, then forced into carts. It was insane."

"Thank you for protecting and getting Esme to safety, Eva." Her silvery head tipped, but it was the only acknowledgement she offered. "How did you two get here?" My question caused Eva to push from the wall before she fidgeted. As if she wasn't happy about being here.

"Zyion insisted I bring Esme to you. It was more of a demand. I assumed it meant he'd found you, but was unable to return to the palace." A soft rattle escaped her throat, exposing her unhappiness about being here at all. "If I'd known he was bringing us to the enemy, I wouldn't have come." There was tension in her jaw, which had the muscle pulsing. "We should be focused on getting back to Griffon and assisting him with whatever is occurring back at the palace. I don't think you're fully grasping the precariousness of the situation, or where Zyion brought you to, Aria. We're standing in a city that no one knows about, with men who are our enemies." Eva began aimlessly pacing in the cramped, confined chamber. "This place shouldn't even exist. I've trained and fought against the Karnavious dragons and bloodline my entire life. Yet they're here, inside our realm that was created to escape both them and the witches."

"I don't think they are as bad as you assume them to be," I mumbled with frustration growing at her inability to put the past where it belonged. In the past.

"If you think that, then you're foolish and naïve. Do you honestly think they intend to let us walk out of here without a fight? Because if you do, then you're much more naïve than I'd assumed you were, Aria. They're our enemies, and even if you don't perceive them as a threat, I assure you, they are. I get that you are fucking their king, which you assume makes you untouchable. It doesn't, as his predecessors before him have done, King Karnavious will turn against you the moment he'd done slaking his thirst with you. Do you think you're the first phoenix to ever bend over and let a murderous dragon abuse them? You're not, nor will you be, the last. But if you intend to be the queen that our people need, you'll need to put them before you carnal, salacious needs. A queen does what is best for her people, even at the cost of her own needs or covets." The sharp barbs cut deeply. Her narrowed, accusing stare burned into my flesh as she waited for my reply.

"Why the fuck can't anyone keep my vagina out of their mouth?" I snapped, then winced as I heard muffled laughter.

Whatever thread holding my mood back, snapped. It was one thing to insult me, it was a whole other thing to imply I being used. I'd have fucking known if I was. I wasn't some star-struck teenager with a crush on a celebrity. To also insinuate that I was placing my lascivious needs above others? No, fuck that, and fuck her talking shit as if she knew me.

"Why stop there, Eva? I came here under the impression that I'd be welcomed by everyone. You yourself told me my father and his people couldn't wait to meet me. But that's going well for me, isn't it? I believe you wanted me here to prevent Griffon from being deposed. Then there's Aden, who wants to marry me so he can take the throne to see if he could use my powers! You knew what he wanted, yet you promised me I'd be safe from that archaic bullshit, which was just another lie you fed me!" I snarled, shaking as the veneer I'd worn since arriving flaked away under the flames of my anger. My hair floated around my head and the sun marking on my forehead reflected in her eyes, which were rounded in horror.

"Oh, Eva. Did you honestly think I didn't see the bull-shit? The moment I got here, I was a rancid taste on the back of my tongue. So, which one of us is the asshole here? Me, who walked into a mess and has shitty taste in men? Or you, who knowingly walked me into a realm laden in landmines just waiting to be stepped on?" Eva swallowed before opening her mouth to argue, but she must have decided whatever she was going to say wouldn't change my mind.

"I didn't mean to come off so harsh, Aria," she finally offered. "You don't know what we've been through. Some of us? We lost everyone in the war. I lost everyone but my brother, who sacrificed me to save himself. Aden is my brother, but not one I cherish. Our relationship is very difficult."

"It's a sad story, but we all have one, Eva. You aren't any more special than I am. I prefer you not lie to me, and I'll respect you more if you tell me how you feel instead of talking shit behind my back." There are a lot of things I could overlook, but lying to ease my mind wasn't on that list about coming here wasn't cool. Though, I could see their side of it, too. The truth was never pretty, and it was normally hard to swallow, but that didn't mean it was acceptable to withhold it.

Eva's posture stiffened with annoyance. "Whatever this is, let's get on with it. I don't intend to stay here a moment longer than I'm forced to do so."

"If you want to leave, I'll help you escape," I offered,

shrugging when her eyes narrowed with frustration. "But I'm not going with you because I don't trust you."

The thing was that I liked Eva. I enjoyed her no-nonsense attitude. She had balls, which were needed to survive in this world. But I wouldn't allow her to trample over me, or talk down to me. I'd been through hell to be here, which meant I wasn't leaving until I got the answers I'd come here for.

"Your father could be hurt, or worse, dead. You've not asked about him once since I walked in here. Do you not even care about him?"

"I don't know my father enough to necessarily care what happens to him. In case you've failed to notice? My time inside the Nine Realms has been spent being betrayed by those who I trusted and loved. You know the one person who was honest about his intentions for me from the minute I got to the Nine Realms? Knox Karnavious. Unlike those who share blood with me, who smiled at me and lied about everything that's happened throughout my life. So, please excuse me if I don't waste emotions on someone I don't know and who hasn't given me any to trust him."

Okay, so he'd been an honest asshole who'd wanted to enslave me. But he'd still been honest about his intentions. He'd lied about plenty of other stuff before I'd ended up here. There's been a bit of duplicity, but he'd told me he wasn't letting me go. The others they were nice to my face, only to stab me in the back when I turned away.

"There's an honest reply," she whispered sadly. "I'm still leaving. I won't stand around waiting for Hagen to parade Griffon's corpse through the city streets."

"I thought Baldrick was the one leading the coup?" I offered.

"Hagen was the one behind it. At least he is now that you disabled Baldrick and his son from being much help until they're recovered." Eva exhaled. "We have to go help your father."

"Griffon isn't dead," Zyion's deep, silken voice declared from the doorway. How long he'd been standing there, I had no idea. "You might not want to continue pointing out options for those enemies you're speaking of, either." Drawing the tapestry back, he allowed Basilius, Ronin, Kael, and Acheron to enter the room before following them into the chamber. "If you choose to leave, no one will stop you. I think you might be interested in what I'm about to say, though."

Pain ripped through my forearm as Esme's claws bit into my flesh. Swallowing the gasp of agony, I trailed her terrified stare to where Basilius was leaning against the tapestry-covered wall. He also was zeroed in on her. The bastard looked as if he wanted to either fuck or fight her. The smell drifting through the room caused my hackles to rise. The masculine pheromones of sage, bergamot, leather, and oak made my stomach churn. Worry slammed into my chest at the thought of Basilius being one of the men who'd attacked her village. It would explain her sudden panic and single-minded focus on him. The way he took her in was worrisome. He held a prurient curiosity, plain to read in the oceanic colored eyes, churning with captivated interest currently directed at my best friend.

Eva growled, forcing attention to where she'd backed up against the wall. Warmth drifted thickly throughout the space. It created a disturbance as the men's earthy scents warred against the softer, more feminine air inside the chamber. Eva's snarl turned to a seething rattle.

The desire to force Eva to bend and fully submit was almost overwhelming. If the men had a similar reaction, they concealed it well. Not one of them so much as spared her a glance until she pushed from the wall. Then the brothers turned their attention toward her—all except Basilius. he remained focused on only Esme.

My hand slid over where Esme held my arm, but I didn't pull her hold away. She quivered. Her scent showed it wasn't out of fear. It was something different. Something sexual, if I had to guess. Her violet-colored irises turned the color of newly polished amethyst with silver flecks scattered throughout them. A hint of feminine arousal filled the air, forcing Ember to shake with laughter. Clearly, I was missing something she hadn't.

"We have bigger issue to address right now than your obvious hatred of the Karnavious Princes. I don't care how you do it, but shut it the fuck down for now." My eyes darted between the two as I felt Eva's magic steadily electrifying the air. The moment Zyion used his powers, he smothered the entire room with its velocity as it oozed around him. His mana forcefully sent a shiver rushing through me. Staring at one another, their swelling powers threatened to unleash in the crammed confines of the chamber, which would bode ill for those of us trapped amid their quarrel. "Choose now. Stay and learn what is to come or leave and run back to be imprisoned with your king. I don't have all fucking day to butt heads with you, Prometheus."

"You are a traitor. An oath breaker! I fucking stuck up for you, and you've been hiding dragons? You are nothing more than a bastard who failed to protect the greatest queen this world has ever, or will ever, know," she snarled. I tensed as something tickled my brain, creating an itch that forced everything inside me to feel off. It was almost as if Ember was trying to force a hostile takeover of my body, but she was calm, as if she was relishing the show.

"Am I? Because I took an oath to fulfill my queen's every wish, including her *last wishes*. Until we complete everything she began, I am stuck ensuring her sacrifice wasn't for naught. How about you? You follow a king who wasn't even fucking crowned in the land he claims to rule over. This realm we're in? It might feel like home, but this place isn't the Kingdom of Fire. You and I both can sense the difference. Tell me, does this place feel like home? Or do you feel yourself weakening as everyone else here does? This realm shouldn't exist and even it feels the wrongness of existing. Tell me, and I wrong?" Eva snorted, her eyes simmering with rage, threatening to unleash the magic she strained to keep controlled. "I know. How about you ask Aria what the cost is to create another realm?"

The price of a realm? I hadn't been able to pay it. I'd taken one innocent life and almost lost it, but an entire realm? His eyes slid to mine, locking as heat crept up my throat to strangle me. The boy I'd killed with my grief flashed inside my mind, his haunting eyes glaring accusingly at me. Images carved inside my mind replaying, one after the next. Nausea churned in the pit of my belly, roiling as it rose, threatening to come up.

"Why do you think I'd know the price of creating one?"

Knox's words echoed in my mind, loud, angry, and coated in an ugly veracity. *"Sorry doesn't bring back the dead. It doesn't change what you did."*

Oh, how I'd needed to hold my hands over my ears, preventing that truth from reaching my heart. Not that it would have done any good. Not when I'd needed to be reminded that actions had consequences. Closing my eyes, I let out a shallow exhale and then shifted my focus to Zyion. A frown furrowed his brow. More heat flooded my senses, but it hadn't originated from me. It came from something within me that was lessening the pain I felt.

"Answer the question, Aria," he encouraged.

"In order to create a new realm . . ." I paused, swallowing memories of the parents crying and screaming in grief. "Another realm would need to fall. It would cease to exist. Those within it, they'd die as well. In short, the realm that falls during the creation of the other ceases to exist anymore. Everything inside the realm would become ruins."

Eva snorted before asking, "How can you claim such a thing?"

"I intended to create one, Eva. In desperation, I sought to create a place the children of the Nine Realms could go to escape the horrors of what was happening within them. Knox prevented me from doing so, sparing me the weight or even more guilt I wouldn't have been able to carry. He knew the cost of creation, as he'd been searching for a way to hide his people from the monstrosities unfolding in his kingdom."

"You're saying Griffon destroyed another realm in order to create this one?" she countered skeptically. As I nodded, her eyes drifted to Zyion. Distrust churned over her face, wrinkling her delicate features. "He wouldn't have done that. You know him as well as I do. Griffon is soft-hearted and an *excellent* king to our people. Even if he holds no crown upon, he's been generous to our people when he need not be so."

"He's a wonderful king, Evaleigh. In fact, Griffon is a damn excellent king. That doesn't change the fact that he allowed this realm to be built at Hagen's behest. His choice to allow it resulted in the true Kingdom of Fire to fall to ruins. His actions led to those who hadn't escaped with us perishing in the collapse of our homeland." *Evaleigh?* At his use of her name, Eva's features softened briefly. They'd been lovers, easy to catch from the way they held each other's gazes. Regret simmered between them, but I felt nothing at the thought of them nice being together. Childish, but it was how I felt.

"The first people forged the truce that ensured no other land was created outside of the nine pre-existing kingdoms. The land needs balance, or else it becomes unstable. The price for creating one is the loss of another. They gave up everything, including their own lands and citizens, to form a new kingdom, which becomes destabilized immediately after its creation. Griffon had pure intentions when he made this realm, but it doesn't change the fact that he did it or the consequences."

Eva had had tears trailing down her cheeks. "Does Griffon know what he did?" Eva's voice shook. "Does he know he sentenced those who hadn't escaped with us to death?"

"No, Griffon isn't aware of it, nor does he need to be. At

least not yet, anyway. As you pointed out, Griffon wouldn't handle the truth well. He'd break, which isn't what our people need from him right now."

That made my heart clench with a drop of hope. If Griffon hadn't known what the cost was as I suspected, maybe he wasn't like everyone else in my life. Maybe he wasn't as terrible as I'd been convincing myself he was.

"He'd want to know what he'd done."

"I never said he'd never find out. I said not yet. First, we need to worry about what will happen now that Aria must ascend the throne." Zyion's posture stiffened. "Griffon's no longer the king. Hagen ascended to the throne shortly after Basilius got Aria out of there. Vane is at his side, but it is only a matter of time before takes the throne for himself."

Of all the things to occur, being here when a coup was happening wasn't one that I'd planned to witness. Esme's claws withdrew, as if she was seeking to escape my possessed body. The moment she stepped behind me, Basilius's glare landed on me.

"Did they harm Griffon?" Eva seemed genuinely fearful that Hagen, Griffon's own brother, could very well harm him.

"I can't tell you that," Zyion admitted. "However, I've sent spies out to learn what they could and see if we can reach the dungeon where they're holding him. Right now, Hagen and his sons are scouring the realm to find where we've hidden Aria. We can't allow them to find her, not until she's ready to face them. They intend to murder her before she can become queen, ousting them through the right of the land. We're short on time here, because the moment they altered the balance of power. Without the balance, it will deteriorate quickly. That means we can either return to our rightful home or remain in the passes. That is what I learned moments ago from our spiders."

"Isn't there a process to ascending the throne? I mean, don't they have to have a parade through the streets and then gather at the abbey?" Okay, maybe I'd read entirely too many novels set in England, but I was doing my best to ignore the two shit-poor options he'd just ticked off.

"If you can overthrow a king, you can declare yourself one. It's as easy as that, Aria. Unless you have the backing of the land, but you sort of lost that for a bit. No, Griffon held it because they feared tipping the scale and upsetting the balance. But you coming here? You were about to do the same as they've done. Once you took the throne, the world would have destabilized," Eva returned icily as anger radiated from where she stood. "We should have been prepared for their deceit. We knew it would come, just not when it would. Hagen expressed his ire at her, which fell on deaf ears. Griffon was elated over his daughter coming here, uncaring that it would force us all back into the midst of this bloody, unending war with the witches."

"Then what the fuck did you bring me here for? To play A Game of Thrones? Because fuck that. I've seen the ending to it, and I'll be damned if I'm sitting my ass on a throne. It never works out for them. Ever." I stopped, noting everyone was staring at me. "And you have no idea what the fuck I'm talking about. Brillant."

He'd known my presence here would tip the scales, forcing them to return to the ruins they'd left of the Kingdom of Fire? And he'd still came for me?

"Griffon knew Aria's presence would create tension. He

knowingly ignored the issue, praying she'd take her rightful place at his side. Griffon never wanted to be king, but Scylla made him promise her he'd hold the throne until Aria was ready to take it from him." Turning toward me, he continued. "It isn't a choice you can make. You were born to become the queen, not just of the Kingdom of Fire, but the entire Nine Realms."

"So, then let's do it. Let's crown the queen and then storm that palace to free Griffon. He won't survive if we leave him there. If Vane murders Griffon, the people won't follow Aria. They'll turn to who they think they can trust. They'll turn to the prince, who ensured they did not see him deposing his own father from the throne he coveted."

"It isn't time for her to ascend, Eva. You forget, this realm isn't the Kingdom of Fire. Aria must ascend her throne in the land which chose her to rule over it, which means we are going home. Aria doesn't want nor need this land. Claiming it won't allow her to reach for her birthright."

"What about her father?" Eva demanded. "What the fuck are you looking at, wyrm?" The moment the slur left her lips, a dangerous tension to explode throughout the cramped space.

"Tirsynth ruled," Basilius offered calmly. Even if he'd spit the name out of his mouth like it was vile poison that burned. "Tirsynth was the king. He ruled over the land without it choosing him."

"Tirsynth never truly ruled over the kingdom. He merely held the title once Scylla perished." Angry, condemning eyes sought Zyion out, blame burning in their depths. "Scylla ruled and was the only one truly claimed by the land. Tirsynth invoked terror in those he lorded over and reinforced every time hung someone who opposed him. He was a tyrant who brutally broke our people after the rightful heir was murdered." Her eyes clashed with Zyion's, who nodded in agreement.

"Scylla used seidr magic to learn how to create a savior. One who could undo the damage Hecate unleashed upon the land."

"You shouldn't get to say her name. If she were here right now, we wouldn't be in this mess, fucking traitor." She stepped closer to him, and before I knew it, I was standing between them, glaring murderously at her in warning. Except I hadn't fucking moved.

"I forced him to kill me, Evaleigh Prometheus." The words exploded from my lips, even as my eyes rounded in horror. It wasn't my voice that had left my throat. "He did not fail me. I failed to realize just how much the cost of my sacrifice would be. I never imagined they'd demand such a hefty price, but once I'd set things into motion, it could not be stopped."

I was flabbergasted at the fact that Scylla, who was fucking *dead*, was speaking *through* me. What in the fuck was even happening? How was she controlling my body, my lips? I had enough personalities, damn it. I seriously didn't need another one. Especially not my grandmother!

CHAPTER 22

ARIA

"Zyion, the Vicious, was mine to shape into whatever I wished him to become. The warriors of Valhalla trained him, then spent time in the jarl's harem to learn how to please a woman. After the harem, he learned how to grow wheat, craft mead, forge weapons, and so much more." She paused, rising from my seat, which meant I was going with her, even if I didn't want to do so. My hand landed against his solid, powerful chest. "But I didn't crave or hunger for a lover, not for many eons, anyway. So, I sent my dutiful, honorable champion off to train alongside the Valkyrie. From the first moment I looked into his eyes, I knew the price he'd pay for belonging to me." I felt Scylla's presence, which I was certain Zyion sensed as well. His eyes held mine, as if he searched for me within the shell, which she'd taken control over.

"Scylla," he murmured reverently, as if he'd been in love with his queen at one time.

"My bravest knight," she whispered, leaning closer as if

she intended to kiss him. I jerked back, which had my lips puckering against the air. It was the loudest air kiss ever heard, which caused heat to spread down my face as I fought to control my body. A scream of horror broke from my lips, or tried, at least as I realized she'd fucking stolen my body. Scylla pulled back from Zyion, then leaned into the hardness of his body.

I searched my mind to try to remember if I'd agreed on a granny-soul-snatcher-three-thousand using my body. If I had, I couldn't remember. But I wasn't about to let her keep it, either. There had to be some way to stop her . . . right?

"Ember! Do something! My grandmother stole our fucking body like she owns the fucking thing! She just tried to kiss Zyion, with our lips!"

"It isn't us trying to kiss him. It's her, so technically, not our problem?" Something moved in my peripheral vision, forcing my head to turn, startling when I found a mirror image of myself sprawled out beside me, sunbathing in the grass. Quickly peering around, I discovered an entire meadow within my head that she'd formulated to lounge about in, bathing in the heat of the sun. What the fuck? Was that what she did all day? Just lazed about while I was working my ass off? *"I like kissing a lot. Knox told me he'd kiss me whenever I wanted him to kiss me. Wasn't that sweet of Dicker? He can be dense, but he has his minutes. Far and in between, though. I think he likes me more than you, you know? Because I like fucking, and you don't bait the beast into rutting us like I do. Knox likes to fuck, too."*

"Damn, I thought you'd at least look different from . . . you look just like me, Ember," I whispered as I deflated, at a loss

for how to take back control of our body. At least Scylla was a grandmother, which hopefully meant I wouldn't wake up eating a dick or riding one. Horror rushed through me as I wondered if she would be like Ember, riding within me as I fucked Knox.

This would not turn out good for me. I could just imagine riding the prick, while my grandmother offered pointers inside my head. Right then, Zyion's hand gripped my lower back, jerking me in closer as he glared at me. A sudden jolt of warmth shot through me, forcing my eyes to widen in horror. Warmth continued down my frame until I felt a foreign urge within me. I couldn't discern what it was, or why I felt it. I hadn't ever felt shit for him, other than to notice he wasn't hard on the eyes.

"Jesus, is that what it feels like when I get turned on for you? Do you feel that? Shit, no wonder you're always hypersexual. I feel feral right now, but I don't sense any of it being my desire. Does that make sense, Ember? I'm always turned on when around Knox, which means you feel this shit all the time?" I asked, struggling with an image of us riding Zyion, which I shut down quickly. The sound of Scylla's laughter and Ember's made my jaw drop. *"Oh, my fucking God! I'm becoming you? It's only been a few seconds. Holy shit. Am I already a nymphomaniac? Is this actually happening to me? How the fuck. What the fuck?"* I demanded in a panicked tone.

"Calm your tits. This is normal emotions. It's her, not you. Honestly, it took you long enough to realize you were the problem. You are the hypersexual bimbo here. I'm a good girl, just ask Dicker."

Her words caused a snort to escape before I could

conceal the reaction. *"I am not the one who constantly demands dick. Remember? That would be you."*

"Who ripped him apart? You. Who terrified me, who enjoys feral fucking? Oh, yeah. That was you, too. Who rode him until we had saddle sore between our legs . . . right, that was you too, Aria. But to answer the question? Yes, it is what I feel when you go into heat, or lust rushes through your entire body. Most idiots realize they need to get laid, but not my host. No, I have to kill something, use the blood to write it down. I have to use blood, because you went and used all the crayons on Dicker! But yet I endure it because if I didn't, you'd get all pissy when I took control and rode your Dicker until he begged me to give him mercy. It would be fun for me, but you two need breaks because you're both weak. The need rushing through us all the time. But then you deny us what we need. See the cobwebs?" she asked, pointing at her dress covered thighs. *"An entire spider family moved in to our vagina today. The kids seem nice though, only bite me if I bother them. I've even decided to name them all. I actually grandma. Think she might even get me more dick than you did!"*

"You're an asshole, Ember," I groaned loudly. *"This is so not cool, Scylla!"*

Zyion was stepped back, his eyes sliding over my face before recoiling as he realized it was my face buried in his chest. The tenderness he'd held my body with lessened, as if he was slowly coming to his senses, noticing it wasn't Scylla against him, which he held longingly. I told myself the sharp pang I'd felt as he'd realized he held me, not her, wasn't real.

"It was real. You're a horrible liar, for the record, Aria. It's okay to be a little jealous. I am when Knox holds you, but

Lennox won't do that for me. Men are the dumbest when trying to learn our needs."

"I get it, Ember. But right now? We have to figure out how to regain control of our body before we end up doing something we really don't want to do."

"Your grandmother doesn't want to fuck him. She feels as if she betrayed him. He trusted her. Then she forced him to murder the one woman he'd ever truly loved. Of course, she didn't know how he felt because guys are so stupid."

"How the hell do you know that?" I whispered the question, sensing her sadness.

"Because in this realm, I sometimes cannot hear you. There's a wrongness here that hurts me, but it stresses our connection, severing it sometimes. You've been too busy to notice my silence. Probably best since you're best lesbians with Esme, not me."

"Oh my god, are you fucking with me right now?"

"Is it working?" she countered, which had my eyes balls rolling so hard I was shocked they hadn't ringed the bell at the back of my head. "Can't blame a girl for trying." She shrugged, as if it wasn't an asshole thing to do.

"Focus, Ember. We don't have time for complaints. File them with management later." I groaned, then internally rattled, praying it was heard within the chamber. Ember added her rattle to mine, which caused the entire room to stiffen with the call to bow before us.

"That's enough of that shit, Granny-body-snatcher-three-thousand! It's rude to steal someone's body or trying to kiss someone else with the body you snatched! Give it back, now! And, for the record, I have a man! And he's a damn good hunter, too. My guy? He doesn't enjoy sharing his toys, which means *stop trying to kiss, touch, or get closer to Zyion, who smells really nice for some reason."*

"If the King of the Dragons thinks you're his toy, child? Then you need to remind him of who you are, and who created you. Zyion deserves more for what I've forced him to give up to create you, Aria. I only intended to give him a chaste kiss on the lips."

"Look, it's not that I'm not grateful. Because I am . . . grateful. But I don't want Zyion to get the wrong idea here. It's not your body pressing against his right now. It's mine. You aren't alive, remember? That means he'll confuse me with you, and I love Knox."

Shock rushed through me at what I'd just admitted. Even if it was only inside my head. I'd never acknowledged my feelings, not even to myself. Warmth sliced through me, but it wasn't from arousal. It was because it had been the honest truth. I loved that asshole.

Zyion's touch sent warmth through me, sure, but it wasn't Knox. Leaning against his body had caused a strange tingling sensation to spread through me. Not as much pleasure as it felt like a connection of awareness from the link we shared. Unlike the raw, primal arousal I experienced when Knox touched me, either. He just wasn't Knox, and that was who I craved. Zyion was gentle, but Knox? He was brutally savage against my soft body, unafraid of breaking me. It was what I loved about him most, which was he didn't see me as something breakable. He didn't handle me like I was made from glass. He manhandled me, mauled me like he couldn't get enough of me, and I liked every fucking filthy moment of the way he took me.

"*If you love him, granddaughter, then you'd best be willing to fight for him. I fear his road will not be an easy one. Neither will loving him. His grandmother invoked the anger of the gods when she sought to escape the arrangement made in order to prevent Hecate from ending their line, as she sought to do with ours.*" Icy fear encased my heart as her words slammed into me.

"*What arrangement?*" I queried even though I was uncertain that I really wanted the answer.

"*If I'm going to tell you the truth, then all should hear it at once. I've employed much of the energy I housed in order to prevent Evaleigh from coming to blows with a room filled full of dragon kind. I enjoy your presence, but to answer your question? I am within you, but it isn't easy for me to reach you, even though I am near to you, my darling. If you worry about me intervening during a tryst, know that I cannot sense what you do unless you're fearful of what is occurring. I only woke because of the tension you worried over, which allowed me to see through your eyes, and listen with your ears.*" I felt her love for me spreading through me, as if she was wrapping her arms around me. "*Be kind to my knight, Aria. Zyion was forced to sacrifice more than he was willing to at my behest. I chose you and your destiny, even over his life or happiness. He has yet to forgive me for forsaking his future for yours. I know you feel the thread linking you two together, and think it is wrong. But, Aria, it isn't wrong. It's his connection to my fire, which now burns inside of you. Whatever type of relationship you choose to have with Zyion? It is up to you, and only you to choose what it entails. You were born with the right to choose your mate, which was my gift to you for what you'd surely endure as become the monster who was needed to protect the world created for me. The Nine Realms was the first and only gift my mother gave to me, which is why I've fought so hard to protect it from being destroyed. If you truly love your dragon? Don't let him go. Hold on to him tightly."*

"Aria?" Esme demanded, slapping my face even as Zyion attempted to step between us. "Fuck off, asshole. She wouldn't have kissed you! I don't care who is trying to use her body to speak. Aria didn't grant them the right to do so," she hissed as panic-stricken violet eyes held mine.

"She's spirited, Aria. I see why you chose her to be beside you during this turbulent time. Esmeralda is also born of my blood, even if through a weaker line. She will never betray you. You should respond to her before Zyion harms her to prevent injury to your person. I've released my hold on you."

"I'm okay," I stated, not entirely sure I was. The moment I said it, my entire body jerked forward against Zyion's hard frame, then it was flung backward, forcing him to rush to catch me before I could fall to the ground. "What the hell is happening?" I demanded, even as I felt warmth leaving my body, as if the source of heat within me had diminished to nothing by an iceberg was left within me. Turning as I shivered, violently. I discovered Scylla standing beside me, her eyes filled with worry at the sight of my trembling frame.

"She will require warmth until I return to her, Zyion."

Immediately following her words, the entire room was bathed in warmth. It only took a few moments of him radiating intense heat, along with the other men in the room, before I was able to stop shivering. All the heat forced my body to slowly begin swaying, as if I were about to pass out. Zyion grabbed me, steadying me with worry churning in his stare.

"Are you okay?" Zyion whispered as he released his hold on me.

"I am," I admitted, peering at the Karnavious brothers, who were all openly gaping at the sight of my grandmother's illuminating presence, standing in the center of the chamber.

"I'm glad you listen so well, granddaughter," she stated, then winked at me. It forced my eyes to round, even as Ember howled inside my head. "I like Ember. She's very entertaining, even if she was naming spiders. She gave them ridiculous names, which I'm certain she chose merely to ensure I mentioned them to you. You should know, she's merely an extension of your true self. She's everything you want to be, but can't while wearing the flesh of a human. When you're ready to bond with her, you'll become one. Of course, she'll still need to slumber within you. You are the part of her she wishes she could be, but as you cannot wear the face of the beast, she cannot wear yours, either."

"Next time you decide to body-snatch-a-bitch? A heads up would be appreciated," I muttered as embarrassment rushed through me the moment realization of what I'd done with Zyion decided to fully sink into my brain. Stepping back, I felt him pulling farther away as well. "It wasn't me . . . before? It wasn't me in control." I needed him to understand my interest in him was entirely plutonic.

"I'm aware of who attempted to kiss my lips, princess." His words were sharply issues, and tightly clipped. They forced my regard to him, forcing my forehead to crinkle at the anger simmering in his stare. "I wasn't sure you'd ever reappear, my queen."

"I am no longer your queen, Vicious." Scylla's use of the name he didn't enjoy responding to, caused a deep crease to form on my forehead. "My time here is very short. If we're to win this war, then we must begin planning for what happens next. As I was saying before Aria began screaming inside her mind. Hecate coming to our world wasn't by accident," she explained, slowly moving throughout the chamber, which forced everyone else to snap out of the shock of seeing the dead queen in the flesh. Or as close to the flesh as she could get.

"Wow, is that your *dead* grandmother?" Esme asked, recovering first. "Holy shit. Well, I'll be damned. You aren't insane after all. Or am I insane, too? Is this insanity you told me contagious to others?" Esme stepped away from me, her eyes slowly narrowing suspiciously. As if I'd given her insanity from being around her. At my soft snort, she shrugged her shoulders with a matter-of-fact look tightening her delicate features. "Hey, I hadn't even known a person could be inflicted with this ailment of insanity, or that there was such a thing. You are the one who told me about such things, Aria." Crossing her arms over her chest, she eyed Scylla, then flicked her hair over her shoulder. "For the record, this is why we can't be best friends. You make me insanity, then I end up seeing your dead ancestors too."

"I am not making you *see* anything. You do know the entire realm can see her as well. Right? I mean, unless we're all insane, we're all looking at my dead ancestor," I whispered back, knowing it was heard by everyone inside the room. Eva stepped forward, which caused my attention to shift to her.

"Scylla?" When Scylla turned, facing Eva, a soft, heart-warming filled smile curved her at the corner of her lips. "My queen," Eva whispered, then dropped to her knees, bowing.

"Correct me if I'm wrong here, but she is dead. Right?" Acheron asked, which had Basilius nodding his head, as his narrowed gaze mirrored mine. "I swear, I did not eat any of those mushrooms this time, Basilius." Rubbing his eyes with the heels of his knuckles, he blinked rapidly, as if it would reveal the truth. "I am not hallucinating because of them, for the record."

"I'm most definitely dead. While you are most definitely of the Karnavious bloodline." Scylla's tone held aversion embedded deeply in the tone. It caused discomfort to rush through me. Turning toward the other princes, I noted they were also on edge.

"Why are you here?" Basilius asked, his fingers flexing as if he prepared to defend his brothers from her if need be.

"To tell you what is about to unfold. Aria is about to begin the war which will decide the fate of the Nine Realms. If she intends to win, then she needs to know the rest of the story of how she was created, and her purpose in the fight to come." Scylla's hand extended, touching mine with a heartwarming smile. "Before Hecate entered the realms, I'd been shown a vision of the destruction her presence would create. She would become a disease, which would then spread throughout the land. It would send the realms into a downward spiral of utter chaos. The magic Hecate houses, it caused an unbalance of power within the realms. As you all know, the land requires balance to remain stable, but without that balance?" Scylla left the question open, knowing we knew the result of the unbalance she spoke of.

"Once it destabilizes to a certain point, it will return to nothing but a maw of darkness." Zyion's words had tension cutting through those inside the chamber. "Which means the Nine Realms is slowly deteriorating until it won't exist anymore."

Zyion's words caused a buzzing to blare in my ears. If the realms were becoming unstable, it meant we'd all die. Right? How the hell had I missed that?

CHAPTER 23
ARIA

"Yes, that's exactly what will occur, and Aria's presence has sped up the process. She unknowingly removed the runic pentagram. They are what carried the mana throughout the kingdoms, dispersing it through each land. Hecate did, however, rearrange them for her own personal use, weakening the people. So, you'd have to have collected them, anyway."

My jaw dropped, and I barely restrained myself from slapping my forehead. I'd never even considered it could be something else. In fact, I'd felt brilliant for discovering the shape of the pentagram. Of course, I'd assumed it had been Hecate who'd placed it since the pentagram was so closely aligned with her magic.

"You are not at fault, Aria. But you need to return them in order to stabilize the land. Plus, you've already begun doing so, which shall offset the balance, per se. Aurora didn't realize what she'd asked of you in her need to gather power because she didn't understand that they can't be held after removal. Had she removed them, Aurora would've perished instantaneously. That part she was very aware of. It's why she had you attempt to steal them for her."

"How do I put them back?"

"Unfortunately, in order to replace them, you'll need to finish collecting them. Once you've done so, you will need to release them where you feel the pull to do so. The land will guide you to where it wants them. The elements will do the rest for you. They don't need a body or vessel to house them. That was Hecate's way of punishing rulers who'd refused to bend the knee to her claim for the throne over all of the realms."

"That's something, at least," I muttered as some of the pressure I'd felt dropped off my shoulders. "If I don't release them soon enough, what happens to this realm?"

"Well, considering you carry the flame within you, that is the heart of this realm? It dies, then the walls deteriorate. It was never created to be a permanent home to our people." My breath stilled in my lungs because the thought of displacing that many people all at once was unsettling.

"It isn't your responsibility to carry the weight of that burden. As queen, your only responsibility is to ensure they have a kingdom to go back to. The majority won't mind returning to the home they fled from in order to survive. A kingdom is nothing without a heart. When you leave here, you will take it with you." Scylla's fingers touched beneath my collarbone, pushing against my heart. "You are the heart of the kingdom. Our people will feel it once you ascend, which will draw them back to the place they call home."

"How is it possible that it will cease to exist by Aria

leaving, who just arrived, mind you, leaves?" Eva questioned, her head cocked to the side, as if she were trying to understand what Scylla had disclosed.

"Freyja created the Kingdom of Fire around seeds she'd brought here with her. Those seeds became sentient beings. Once they'd put down roots, it sealed the creation of the first realm within the nine. Aria now carries those seeds, as well as the most of the elements."

Scylla's explanation sparked memories of things I'd learned during a time of forced imprisonment in the basement as a child. Sabine had brought down books on Norse mythology and the cosmos. In that moment, the bits of information were a hundred tiny puzzle pieces, meeting to create the perfect picture.

"Yggdrasil? Your mother didn't bring you here to avoid conflict with those opposing seidr. She brought you here to hide what you were. She brought you here because she'd stolen seeds from Yggdrasil, which she then planted in the void." My mind spun with the facts being slammed against the blackboard in my brain. "She consumed them, didn't she? Freyja swallowed the seeds from the world tree to create you, her daughter." *Take that, scholars!* My grin was almost manic, but Zyion and Scylla looked at me as if I'd lost my marbles. The longer they both stared, the stupider I felt, and my smile slowly faded.

"I warned you she'd be incredibly intelligent if you forced my blood to be added to the mold," Zyion murmured, eyes sparkling with pride that caused a flurry within my belly. Not one of lust, but of worry. Had he just stated his blood had been used to mold me? Because that shit wasn't strange at all?

"Which means Aria now carries the mana of the world tree inside her. As did I and my mother before her. The seeds attached only to daughters born from mothers who swallowed them, and my mother was uncertain about the spreading process. Not all of the girls in our bloodline were born with the mana of the tree inside them. There is also the fact that many before my mother had stolen and swallowed the seeds, but only a few ever came to fruition. The seeds are selective of whom they flourish within, as well. Aria will return to the Nine Realms, which means this one will cease to exist without the mana of my soul to keep it living."

"You said they gave you a vision?" Basilius's interruption forced my eyes to snap up before sliding to where he'd leaned back against the wall. "A vision of what, exactly?"

Scylla's head turned, which caused Zyion to tense with apprehension that I keenly felt.

Clearing her throat, she lowered her head before speaking. "In the vision, they showed me how to combine two of the most powerful bloodlines into one powerful creature. A creature born of both dragon and phoenix blood."

Esme elbowed me as if she too were remembering the room where we'd watched the 4D rendering unfolding before us. My mind swirled as curiosity blossomed. I hadn't stopped wondering about the scene we'd been privy to in the library. Now, I'd get to learn of it firsthand.

"A child born of both creatures would be powerful and house the hottest flame we'd ever known. Using the cloak my mother left me, I shapeshifted into my mother, then forced two unmated individuals to come to me. A fierce dragon known as Dragharyn Dreki, the first dragon who roamed the lands, untethered by kingdom or throne. Princess Rhianna Fafnir, my own daughter, was the phoenix. She was pure of heart, but a fierce warrior." The moment she'd spoken the name, I'd felt the thread connecting me to Zyion grow taut. Scylla spared a glance in his direction but continued without acknowledging the tension churning through him. "When I first approached them, neither would agree to what I asked of them. It forced my hand to do whatever was needed to ensure they created a child. Using the binding spell, I threaded their lives together. After I had, they did what was needed. The spell unraveled, though. Eventually, Dragharyn undid what I'd done to them. Two years after Rhianna gave birth to their child, he murdered her by ensuring her flame could never be lit by me, nor another living soul."

Zyion's teeth ground loud enough to be heard. The rage he felt was both terrifying and immense as it percolated inside the chamber. It felt like I was missing something huge. Something which left everyone else other than Zyion and Scylla, lost in the dark.

"I raised the babe myself, ensuring no one else knew of her true parentage. In doing so, I'd set forth the first thing demanded of me from the old gods. Ryna never took a feral form, though. The combination wasn't compatible with dragon and phoenix. I followed the vision provided to me by seidr magic, and her fire burned hotter than anything we had seen before as promised.

Zyion's face blurred in the tears stinging my eyes, and every fiber of my being snapped taut with denial. I had to have heard her wrong.

"That's messed up," Esme interjected, her face downtrodden, as if she'd been forced to breed with her enemy. "You took her free will and used her as a weapon?" Esme's wide, horrified eyes snapped to me, widening even more if at all possible.

Zyion made a strangled sound in his throat. Long, powerful steps took him to the shelf, holding several green glass bottles. His fingers flexed, then balled into fists before repeating the action. His shoulders rose and fell with slow, practiced breaths, as if he were counting inside his head, forcing his emotions to remain in check.

"If you had to choose between doing what was right and what would save the world, what would you have done in my place?" Esme noisily exhaled and then folded her arms across her chest, glaring. "I loved my daughter more than I loved myself, Esmeralda. If I could've traded places with her, I'd have done so without question."

"You could've fucking tried to find someone else!" Zyion snarled, which had my heartbeat increasing and the hair on my nape standing on end. "You didn't even think to warn me we would sacrifice the woman I loved? That my mate had to die in order to bring forth *your* fucking savior?" My gaze darted between the two being bleeding anger and hurt into the room. Scylla, who looked wounded, and Zyion, who looked utterly devoid of mercy. "Instead, you took her from me without allowing me to say goodbye. You fucking lied to me and told me she'd chosen him." His fury forced something inside me to tighten. My breathing turned sharp and shallow, passing my lips as rapid puffs of air.

"You would have tried to alter the course of events had

I told you the truth. Rhianna was *my* daughter and the only unmated phoenix. So, I did what I needed to do in order to ensure her sacrifice wouldn't be in vain. I knew you'd fancied yourself in love with my daughter, but not that it went beyond that. How could you *not* love her? Rhianna was so easy to love." I wasn't sure if they remembered the audience actively watching the exchange, but it was as if I were watching a show about their tragic history. "I couldn't change the course without the old gods abandoning us. If I'd have tried, you'd have lost her anyway, Zyion. Of all my children or those I'd loved. Rhianna was special to me. The day she was born, it was like I'd finally found a purpose in life. She was the only child I'd ever thanked the gods for giving me. By doing so, I'd sealed her fate to mine, knowing the gods would come for her if I didn't follow through on what the visions foretold."

"It didn't have to be her, Scylla. You willingly led *my* lamb to her slaughter."

"If I'd told you they'd tethered her fate to another, you'd have fought the fates to prevent it."

"You're goddamn right. I'd have waged war for that girl. I'd have done whatever I needed to keep her from knowing the pain he forced her to feel beneath him. When you said I had to give up love, that wasn't what I'd agreed to do. She'd still have been mine, and loved me. I'd asked Rhianna to keep the secret until I'd found time to tell you myself that we were mates. True mates, Scylla. Obviously, that was a mistake. By the time I returned from you forcibly sending me away, I was told she'd fallen in love with the dragon, who'd eventually become king to their kingdom."

"If you were mates, I'd have known, Zyion. You'd have told me the truth, as you pledge to always do." Zyion reached for the collar of his shirt and jerked it down to reveal a bite right above his heart. "How? Why didn't you tell me? You were beholden to me. If you'd mated my daughter, I should've been the first one to know of it."

"Before I could, you sent me away to scour the realms for the sickness you'd obsessed over. In the meantime, you fed my mate to a cruel, violent, heartless bastard who brutalized every woman he took to his bed." Zyion fearlessly strode forward, his eyes burning with images playing inside his head. It wasn't hard to imagine what those images might have been either. If he'd been able to, he'd probably have murdered her again.

"Do you know what Dragharyn did to her? I assure you he wasn't gentle to the girl whose pretty turquoise eyes held my future and my entire soul within them," he rasped, shoving fingers through his hair. It laid his pain bare before us, raw and profoundly rooted in his soul. "I felt her pain when he ripped her cunt in his need to force his dragon knot in as deep as he could. He'd been spelled to think she was his fucking mate, which led his beast to demand he rut her because *you* fed your daughter to a rabid dragon who'd spent more time in his beast than he'd ever spent in his human flesh."

The rawness in his tone had tears burning my eyes, and my lips trembled. I didn't need to hear him say he'd loved Rhianna. He revealed his vulnerability through the trembling in his voice, in the grief embedded in his every syllable. It was in the way his eyes turned glossy and moisture pooled too quickly to be blinked away. Zyion had loved her.

"The Fates showed me they'd be compatible. In the end, she bore him a daughter. Ryna was their child. Had she lived, she'd have adored the child they'd created."

"She had promised to have my child, not his, Scylla. The gods blessed *me* with a stunning, tender-hearted mate. And you? You'd promised her that only she could choose her mate. Rhianna chose me. I'd never had any of the women from the Vanir or anywhere else fucking choose me for anything other than my cock. They didn't want your thrall staying for one second more than it took for them to get off on my dick. Rhianna, though, knew what I was, and she wanted me regardless of it. You took that away from me. You, who I served dutifully, stole all of it." Rubbing his chest, he shook his head. "Instead, I returned the same night you wed my mate to another. That night, I found her walking around aimlessly, bathed in her own blood and another's come dripping down her thighs. My mate bore the scent of another alpha, and she told me she loved him, that they were true mates. I can still hear the haunted way she declared it to me. It was how I knew something was horribly wrong." Tears trickled down Zyion's cheeks.

"I wish it hadn't been her, too. If they'd given me a choice, I'd have chosen another. To achieve what was required, my blood was necessary. I only have one daughter, Zyion. In the end, he took her away from us both."

"Dragharyn didn't kill my mate. Your actions did. He couldn't have murdered Rhianna." Though I was glad he'd done what he had to the sadistic bastard, it was still shocking to hear it laid out like that. "When I found Rhianna again, I knelt before her and placed Dragharyn's head at her feet. If she noticed the gesture, she failed to show it. I didn't see her again until I collected her broken body from the bottom of the cliffs she'd jumped from. Had you not been so obsessed with creating your precious savior, you might have noticed how endless her pain had become."

Never would I have thought he'd lost more than he'd already disclosed. Turquoise eyes clashed with mine and widened when he noted the agonizing pain exposed on my face. Squaring his shoulders, he exhaled before shaking his head. He wiped away the tears and then strolled back to the colored bottles, grabbing one before downing the entire bottle in deep swallows.

"I didn't know," Scylla whispered brokenly.

"No, you didn't. But that wasn't enough to steal my and her future together for your own goals, was it? No, you also had her soul taken to where I could never go. In the library you created with Draghana Karnavious. Rhianna is within the Library of Knowledge, forced to remain among the same beings that stole her from me." My eyes went round, and I knew my face had leached of color.

"You created the library?" I asked.

"Why don't you tell her and Eira Karnavious sons about how the library came to be, *my queen*," he hissed in a tone that scraped against my flesh.

"Before the war between dragons and phoenix began, we were allies." Scylla started. "Draghana was one of my closest friends. Before Hecate arrived, we'd created a place where the council could gather, where we could discuss things amicably. Dracarius, her husband, also used magic, though it differed from mine. We combined our power to forge the Library of Knowledge. It houses all knowledge of everything and everyone within the books inside the library."

"Is that why some people cannot see it?" Basilius asked, and after Scylla nodded slowly. he continued. "The rumors of a Keeper of the Library, are they true?" His dark, smoky voice was close enough to Knox's that I felt a tug on my heartstrings.

"Yes, very much so. We created the Keeper of Knowledge after issues began arising between monarchs. We sought a fair-minded and incorruptible being. The Keeper doesn't take sides, per se. He had no need for titles, land, or riches, and he was fair to all. The library also became a safe place for our children to hide after war broke out between the dragons and phoenixes. Children were off-limits, as were all royals from being murdered in the endless battles occurring over land. But war brings out the worst in people."

Hello, Kettle, meet your pot!

"Until you murdered my brother." Acheron asked.

"Prince Adym was mistaken for a lord who'd been raiding villages along the border and killing indiscriminately. I realized who he was only after his head was brought to me. I personally made sure his remains were returned to his parents. In war, there are no rights." Scylla's elucidation caused the men to deflate.

"I don't mean to be rude, but we aren't here to discuss the past. In case you've all forgotten, Vane and Hagen have stolen the throne and are likely planning to kill Griffon." Eva tapped her foot, as if she thought everyone would jump.

"Griffon isn't the one who needs to be saved, Evaleigh.

Right now, he's safe from harm since Hagen won't allow Vane to act. For all his faults, Hagen cares enough about his brother not to allow him to die." She turned to me. "Aria, you asked me about the arrangement I made with Draghana Karnavious. Here it is. She and I both sacrificed for one who'd be able to end the darkness shrouding the land in unnatural magic. Neither of us were prepared for the cost the old gods would demand from us."

Scylla drew closer, her stare boring into my soul as she continued. "The dragons created a second savior as a backup plan to eradicate Hecate, but Draghana died before revealing who the Fates answered for her sacrifices." She lifted her eyes to mine while wringing her hands in front of her. The look churning in them felt like a kick to the stomach. "I've seen your future, Aria. He wasn't in it with you. You were happy at the end of what I was shown."

"Fuck that!" I snapped, hating the pain that tore through my heart at the suggestion I had any future that didn't include that man. "No, fuck that shit. I choose how my story ends, not anyone else. Not you, not some ancient-ass primordial crones, not *anyone*. One choice can change the future. Right?"

"It is possible," she assured.

"If he isn't in my future? Then you won't have to fear Hecate destroying everything, because I'll burn it all down myself. I have not walked through hell and sacrificed our daughters for him to end up a casualty of this war. Knox is my endgame, and if he isn't? Then I will become the monster they all thought I was. I wasn't born to be vicious, but I can be against those who think to take from me. I'm neither good nor malicious, but I can be malevolent to those who trespass against me or those who walk beside me. If this world thinks of me a monster? Wait until I become one to protect the man I love. I will show them what true chaos feels like when it's unleashed by a woman." My chest rose and fell with angry, fearful breaths.

"Which is exactly why she's after him. He's your greatest weakness. He's also the only thing within her grasp that she can use against you. You are not fighting a mindless monster. You're warring against a goddess who's lived long enough to know right where to hit in order to break you down piece by piece until there's nothing left of the girl beneath the hardened armor you've crafted to wear into battle. Despite your youth and naivety, you were able to hold the light. No one ever emerges from war free of sins. You already know that, which is good, since this war you're about to wage will be brutal. As will you, my darling. I never gave you a chance to soften. Soft wasn't something you could have in order to be violent, unbreakable, and unmoving against those who stood between you and what you need to do."

"You guys wanted me here to tell me things I already knew or could have figured out myself. Why?" I demanded.

"Because had I not brought you here, you'd have died protecting those you love. Hecate was intending to make a move, which would cost you your life. It's best you're here for now, as the Fates advised." A hint of worry flickered in my mind, which forced my eyes to round in horror.

"Who did she go after?" Fear wrapped around my chest, constricting it like a corset bound too firmly.

"She didn't get to those ones. There are others you

care about." Her words caused worry to grip my throat. Even though they'd been true, they were hard to swallow.

"Monsters do not weep, and neither do weapons, my darling. The fire burning inside of you? Let it burn and win this war before more needless bloodshed occurs."

"I don't intend to just bring a war against Hecate," I admitted, and Knox's brothers snorted. Esme cleared her throat, as if she feared I'd forgotten who I was. Eva chuckled coldly, and Zyion? He was smiling, and something I'd never seen simmering in his eyes. "I'm going to bring her a massacre. I intend to slaughter whatever comes between my wrath and the vicious, homicidal goddess who thought she could take from those who could not fight back. I'm about to be the consequences of her actions."

"One day, you'll finish reaching for your birthright and take your rightful place on the throne of the Kingdom of Fire."

"I need no crown or throne. The first would only give her a location to terrorize, while the latter would give her archers something to aim their arrows at," I stated, as I felt magic growing within the chamber.

"You may not want a throne, but you were born to sit upon it. If you'll agree to it, I'd like to crown you before you leave this room, granddaughter. You were a princess when you came here, but you'll be a queen when you leave." At my subtle nod, she turned her stare toward the men, then dragged it back to where I stood. "Zyion, I'll need you to show me where I can bathe the princess and prepare her for her accession. I cannot bless my granddaughter within your chamber," she stated, looking around it with disdain tugging at her lips.

"Unfortunately, it will have to suffice. There's no grotto we can easily access, nor is there a bathing chamber. The only thing I can offer you here are my chambers, the ointment your mother anointed you with, and a tub for the princess to be cleansed of her sins in. You may use them, Scylla. But know this: once you've crowned Aria, and she's seated on the throne the land offers her, you will leave and never return when I am present. I will continue to protect her, but I will not suffer your company for a moment longer."

"I . . ." Scylla's words cut off as Zyion strode from the chamber without a backward glance. "If I'd told him, I feared he would wish to follow her into the afterlife. I couldn't lose both of them."

"You broke him, your Majesty," Eva muttered. "The entire kingdom has condemned him, slurred his name behind his back, and even those brave enough, to his face. Zyion the Vicious might as well have gone with you to the afterlife." Eva strolled from the chamber, leaving an awkward silence in her wake.

"Should I go, too?" Esme asked, which caused both myself and Scylla to turn toward her. "If you could just forget I'm here, that would be fine with me." I felt a smile playing on my lips at Esme's sudden interest in the ceiling.

"I'll go," Scylla announced. "It would seem I am no longer needed. Zyion can anoint you and attend to your ascension. I need not burden him with my presence. After all, he will be the one at your side now. I didn't mean to hurt him. Unfortunately, when the Fates choose a piece to move on the board they play upon, you can either do as they bid, or you suffer eternity at their hands. I knew when I began moving pieces at their behest, I'd lose more than myself along the way."

"Yeah." I wasn't certain what to say to her. Scylla's sacrifices caused both her and Zyion pain that couldn't be eased. She'd done it to save the world, even though it had cost more than she could bear. "It couldn't have been easy."

"Thank you for trying to ease my pain." Stepping closer to me, she pressed her forehead against mine. "Remember this, my darling. Just because you're fighting against a tyrannical evil, it doesn't mean you're entirely good. There's a thin line you cannot cross because there is no way back from it. That line is there to remind you of who you are, but more importantly, it will define who you are to become as queen."

"Where is Scylla?" Zyion entered the room, staring at me as the golden glow reflected in his turquoise stare.

"Gone," I answered, noting the flinch of pain he released. "She said you could anoint me in oil since you'd be beside me now. I don't know how to ease the pain of learning about her betrayal, Zyion. There's really nothing that would remove that type of deeply sated pain either. But, for what it's worth, I'm sorry for what it cost you to create me." Unshed tears choked my words, but the angry glare simmering from him was enough to force them back.

"You're a queen, Aria. Queens do not weep for slaves, or knights." He used this thumb to wipe away the tear trailing down my cheek.

"Queens are not told what they can and cannot do, Zyion. I can cry if I want to cry, asshole."

"You need not apologize for something you had no part in. I reacted badly, and for that, I am sorry."

"Don't apologize for your grief. There's no time limit on how long one can feel endless agony from the loss. Congratulations, Zyion. You're human." His eyebrow lifted as if he didn't fully agree with the assessment. A smirk lifted my lips as I rolled my eyes. "Part human, then?" Just then, a loud rattle echoed throughout the exterior of the room.

"Times up, they've found us. Let's go, your Majesty." Zyion jerked me toward him and then lifted his hand, allowing me to see the glittering gold oil sparkling on his thumb. "Do you promise to always put the needs of your people before your own? Nod, Aria."

I nodded.

His thumb drew a cross over my forehead before he dipped it into the glass container for more of the oil.

"Will you always listen to the cry of the land and ensure it receives what it needs to thrive?"

I nodded, and this time, he ripped the front of my gown open and painted the symbol of the sun on my chest.

"Kneel," he ordered, pushing me to my knees before him.

Zyion whispered something inaudible, and his turquoise-colored eyes sparkled with specks of gold. The same gold burned wispy lines under the flesh of his eyelids, webbing as it slid down his face, neck, and vanished beneath the long-sleeved shirt, which he'd replaced the other with. Power erupted around us so forcefully that my thoughts swam and lips parted. Esme released a soft gasp, and I wanted to tell her I was okay, but there was no way to form words around the magic. My dress turned to ashes against my flesh. In its place, a crimson dress with an ombre skirt the color of succulent tangerines covered my legs. Zyion clasped a gold necklace around my neck. On it hung a medallion depicting the sun melded with a sunflower. Next, he knelt in front of me and slid golden arm cuffs that matched the necklace up my arms until they were secure around my biceps.

Still kneeling before him, I closed my eyes as he, at last, placed a citrine studded crown on my head. When his fingers slipped beneath my chin, forcing my chin up, I didn't resist him. Narrowed eyes held mine fleetingly before moving to the side of my face. Pushing my hair from my ear, he placed the matching earrings in each of my earlobes. The moment he rose and stepped back, he offered his hand, assisting me to my feet. Flicking his finger, a mirror appeared before me. Staring at my golden reflection, I peered at the crown which had rainbow prisms within the pure, polished citrus points pushing from a thin golden band.

"All hail the Sunfire Queen. Long may she reign." His deep, soothing baritone flooded the chamber, then the sound of others echoing his words forced my chin to jerk toward the main entrance of the chamber. "Long may you reign, Your Majesty."

"Long may she reign," Esme whispered before kneeling at my feet. Zyion was next to take a knee, and then Eva.

"I'd summon the land, your Majesty. The doors

preventing your uncle from entering the city won't hold for much longer," Zyion offered.

Closing my eyes, I whispered to the land as he'd advised. Within moments, rumbling sounded from behind us. It forced me to turn, eyeing the plain throne that had appeared.

The throne, if you could even call it that, was a wooden chair with white cushions, which looked discolored. I cringed as I imagined dust filling the chamber as my ass touched the dingy thing. I inched closer, then carefully sat down, expecting the dust cloud to ensue. The moment I sat on the wide, off-white cushion, vines wrapped around my wrists, locking me into place. Panic rushed through me as it held me in place. More vines slithered around my ankles, which caused dread to trickle down my spine. A gentle whiff of suntan lotion, ocean breeze, and just-cut flowers wafted through the air around me. It reminded me of the one time I'd visited the inlet outside Haven Falls.

A vine pricked both of my index fingers, causing a shimmer of magic to encase me and the throne I sat upon. Wincing as it drew more blood, I shivered as the haze grew thicker, denser with magic. The cushion beneath me raised, alerting me to the fact the entire throne was altering from the taste of blood it had taken. Tiny phoenixes began carving into the wooden arms, then pushed out of the wood to zip around in front of my face. Greenery sprouted from the sides, expanding until fines and foliage covered the high arched back of the throne like a canopy above my head. Sunflowers began blossoming around and above me, vibrant color splashes against the emerald of the vines and flora. Roses, snapdragons, and chrysanthemums sprouted, then bloomed around my body providing silken petals against the hard, wooden arms. Every shade of the rainbow colored the throne in delicate flower buds.

Next to me, trees thrust up from the floor, shattering the rock as if it were a mere inconvenience. Beneath my feet, green grass sprouted through the cracks the trees had created, spreading until my feet rested on a soft, plush carpet of verdant grass. The small phoenixes sang as it etched other small creatures into the wood, only to do as the tiny magical birds had done before them. I ended up on a throne that appeared to be designed for a woodland princess and was surrounded by a beautiful landscape of greenery and flowers.

I refrained from pouting that I didn't have a similar throne to Knox's. Or dragons, because that would've been badass.

"Holy shit," Esme's shocked outburst forced my mind from my throne, to where she stood, wide-eyed, with her mouth wide open. "You . . . holy shit, Aria."

Eva suggested, "You should address her properly," as her gaze drifted over the throne I was seated on.

"You are truly beautiful, Aria. Unfortunately, there isn't time to sit around and gawk at your loveliness." Sarcasm dripped from his words. "We have to leave." Zyion demanded as one of the Karnavious brothers jerked back the curtain.

"They've broken through the doors and are already searching for her." Basilius pointed, then his eyes widened as he took in the sight of me and the insane throne that sat in the center of Zyion's chamber. "Gods, she actually is the queen?" His brothers chuckled, but the sound was cut off when the sound of steel meeting stone started to get louder.

"Aria, you need to call the Keeper of the Knowledge and demand entrance into the library," Zyion urged.

"How the hell do you expect me to call him?" I asked. Closing my eyes as a soft puff of hair whistled between my lips, I sought the Keeper of Knowledge. "I demand entrance into the library." Opening one eye, I peered around, frowning.

"Mean it, Aria. We're out of fucking time," Zyion encouraged.

"Keeper of Knowledge, I, Aria, Queen of Sunfire, demand that you grant me access to the Library of Knowledge. Now!" Power slithered down my arms as I turned toward the breeze drifting against my naked spine. Relief flooded through me as I peered into the familiar space of the library. Smiling as I realized I'd called it to me, I yelped as Zyion grabbed my arm and hauled me forward into the library, the others following closely behind us. The moment we were through, a collective exhale of relief followed as it closed, sealing out those who were scouring the City of Dragons for me.

"Peasant?" called a familiar voice from behind me.

CHAPTER 24
ARIA

The sound of chairs scuffling over the floor echoed through the library. I stood in place, smiling as my gaze wandered, looking for Knox. I'd brought the Karnavious brothers along with us, which was causing sounds of amazement and shock as Killian, Brander, Fade, and Greer rushed forward.

"Basilius?" Brander's tone was hauntingly soft, barely a whisper of breath to form his brother's name on his lips. "Fucking hell!" Brander pulled Basilius, who stood frozen in place as he was jerked into his brother's arms.

The warmth of watching their reunion flooded through me, even as I scoured the library for any sign of Knox. Someone pulled my arm, and then I smashed into the solid yet surprisingly soft shirt covering Greer's chest.

"I'm glad you're home, Peasant." His words forced heat to prick my eyes as tears threatened to fall.

"I missed you too, Meat Suit," I admitted, pulling back to smile at him. Something in his eyes caused worry to flicker, then gradually blossom into something akin to panic. "What's wrong?"

"It's good that you're here. You have impeccable timing." His cryptic statement caused my forehead to wrinkle. I waited for him to elaborate, but he removed the arm he'd slung over my shoulders to welcome the others home.

Standing in place, my gaze darted between Killian, Brander, then to Lore, who'd remained seated. It seemed like he wasn't thrilled with the idea of their return as he kept his back to us. He may have not known the others as well as the brothers who'd help raise him after Eira and Lennox Karnavious were killed.

Esme tugged on my gown, which forced me to turn toward her. Her huge, violet eyes pleaded. But for what, I wasn't sure. I allowed her to drag me with her through the library, then farther into it until we rounded a set of ancient white oak shelves.

"We have to murder him," she hissed.

I blinked at her murderous statement. Confusion danced through me, then slid over my face. Then I remembered her reaction to Basilius, which now seemed like it had occurred days ago instead of less than an hour ago.

"Is he the one . . .?" My question wouldn't come out. Instead, my stomach clenched as I pulled her in for a hug. "If he is the one who hurt you, Esme? I will personally bring you his severed cock."

"What?" she sputtered, then pushed me away. "Wait, you'd do that for me?" Her violet hued stare narrowed before she exhaled. "Never mind that. No, he's not the one who hurt me. He's so much worse than that, Aria. He has to die. I need it done now, though. Before . . ." she paused when my nose crinkled as my face twisted with utter perplexity.

"I can't just murder Knox's long-dead brother because he gave you googly eyes, Esme. It's murder without justification. He just came back from the dead. Don't you think it would look a little strange if he returned to being dead so soon after his return?" I asked in a hushed whisper.

"You don't understand!"

"Then make me understand why you wish to kill someone," I returned while carefully dragging my regard over her panicked stricken face. When she began bouncing from one foot to the other, I noted the pallor of her coloring. Her face was damn in a fine sheen of moisture. As if she was sweating. "What is wrong, Esme?" The air leaving her lungs was quick, short pants.

"Basilius is my mate!" She shouted, then slapped her hands over her mouth. Wide, horrified eyes turned darker than glistening amethyst as fear, to shocked horror within them. "You have to help me kill him. We can finally bury a body as you've wanted to do. Please?" Her tone shook with emotion, which caused mine to quiver with mirth.

I should have been a better friend and felt sorry for Esmeralda. But that she'd ended up mated to an asshole, who was just as broody and brutish as Knox, was karma. Esme had given me so much shit about my mate that I was enjoying her horror at being mated to his brother. Did it make me an asshole for enjoying it? Nope. Not one bit, but that was because if the shoe had been on the other foot, she'd do the same.

"Aria, are you laughing?" When the clap of laughter I

failed to conceal tore through the hallway, she huffed, then puffed as her hands squeezed into tight fists, then she began pacing in front of me. "That barbarian can't be my mate," she exclaimed. "Did you see him? He's a Neanderthal! He could be Knox's twin. For fuck's sake, help me!" Her growing frustration only fueled my laughter, which, in return, made her even more so. "You are the worst best friend ever! All this time we've been together. You've wanted to bury a damn body. Here's your chance, but are you taking it? No. Nope, not the newly crowned Queen of Ruins," she scoffed, making air quotes around the queen, then ruins with her fingers. Stopping her endless pacing, she put her back to the entrance we'd come through, planting her palms on her hips.

Basilius rounded the corner, catching my eyes as I fought against the laughter bubbling up from my chest. His gaze narrowed before gradually gliding down Esme's animated frame.

"Which you are, by the way. Nothing but ruins await us there, your Highness. But it doesn't matter, does it? Again, no. If we have to hide a body, his is freaking amazingly powerful, and solid! Which is beside the point. It doesn't matter if he's got the prettiest eyes I've ever stared into, either. Nor should I care that he'd be able to bend a bitch over and fuck her so viciously she'd hurt deliciously in certain places, but I do!" A smirk at her mess up had her groaning, loudly in protest of my lack of support.

"You mean, you don't care," I corrected smoothly.

"I couldn't care less about any of that. I mean, he also smelled fantastic, too. Dark masculinity with vetiver, a hint of sage, and bergamot? Definitely bergamot. Fucking hell. I can still smell him." My eyes darted between them, trying to indicate he was directly behind her.

"We should get back," I offered, seeking to prevent her embarrassment of him overhearing every tidbit she was word vomiting in front of him.

"Did you not fucking hear me?" Her fingers pushed through her hair before she dropped her head back, groaning in frustration. "I bet the bastard is an utter beast in bed, too. And even worse? I was too occupied fucking my hand to relieve the damn ache between my thighs while you were getting fucked! That's why my vagina is now drenched. Fucking hell. Can you please just help me murder him? I promise to help you dig whatever hole you ask me to if you'll just help me this one time. Please?"

Clearing my throat, I locked eyes with Basilius. His had narrowed while listening to Esmeralda complaining about her current pressing issue down below. He'd leaned against the edge of the entrance to the hallway where we were. The anger churning in his eyes caused my stomach to churn, as if he thought we were actually considering doing as Esme requested.

"It's called venting, which doesn't end in homicide," I offered, which should've stopped Esme from continuing. Esme didn't take hints, cues, or general directions well. Instead, she began anew. "Or murder, as you call it around here," I corrected when a deep frown forced his eyebrows to push together.

"I'm allowed to vent. The man seriously was eye-fucking me so damn hard with those pretty eyes, that my vagina threatened to invite him inside! I've never found anyone who made my vagina all tingly without even touching it yet." Running her palms over her face, she made complaintive sounds. "Why is that the one time I ask you to hide a body, you won't even consider it? Besides the fact of it being considered murder, which of course it would be. Obviously in order to hide one, we'd need to murder it first. That's obvious. As I said before, the neanderthal would just climb out unless he wasn't able to do so."

"That, and he's standing behind you," I muttered, unnerved at the fury I was witnessing in his mind. "I honestly think he believes you mean to murder him, Esmeralda." Stepping closer to her, I eyeballed him with a warning burning in my gaze. "Let's go, Esme." I refrained from asking, as the turmoil in Basilius's mind appeared exceedingly unpleasant. I wasn't leaving her standing in a scarcely lit hallway with him, alone.

"You couldn't warn me?" she hissed, which, like mine, was more of a shout-whisper.

"When my eyeballs look like they're a fuzzball, you should pay attention. I'm obviously not suffering from a stroke. Why did you think my eyes were moving to you, then over your damn shoulder?" I asked, which caused a crease in her forehead as her nose scrunched up.

"What the hell is a fuzzball?" That she'd only heard the one word she couldn't discern was frustrating. "Is it something else you expect to know that is from your world, not ours?"

"Yes," I admitted. The moment we emerged from the hall, I gazed at the men who were speaking in hushed tones. Walking toward them, I paused at the sound of a rasping purr that vibrated through me. Esme's hand gripped my shoulder, her nails digging into the flesh. "Basilius, unless you want me to rattle back, I suggest you save your male antics for after I've found Knox."

"Thank you," she whispered, then removed her hand with a wince at the blood she'd drawn.

"You don't have to thank me for protecting you. I understand the feel of that primal need currently rushing through your veins like molten lava. That's how I feel when Knox is near, which I haven't felt since we arrived." Stopping in front of the men, I scanned their faces before turning back to Brander and Killian, who watched me closely with an emotion I couldn't put my finger on their faces. "Where is he?"

"Who?" Killian asked. The guilty flush creeping up his throat made my stomach churn.

"Who the hell do you think, Killian? Who would I ask you for? Surely not a palace steward, not when I have a suit of meat on hand."

"I resent that remark," he breathed, but it lacked his normal jovial tone.

Uncrossing my arms, I let them drop to my sides. "You resemble that remark, not resent. Where the hell is Knox?" I asked, noting the heads dropping, as if the floor had become intriguing. "Answer me," I whispered as fear clamped down around my heart.

Their silence sent every worst-case scenario running through my mind. A chill snaked down my spine as my stomach churned, threatening to empty at my feet. I wanted to shake them until they disclosed to me where Knox was. Or was it because he was with someone else? The pain that thought alone caused was debilitating. Had

Knox given up on my returning to him? I'd promised I'd come back. Was there another warming his bed that I'd left cold with my absence? Tears pricked my eyes, singing them as I looked from one person to the other. My breathing turned erratic, matching my heartbeat as it battered against my ribcage.

"Somebody answer me," I demanded as my fingers curled against my palms, forming a fist.

"He's gone," Brander said, shoving his hands into the pockets of the pants he wore.

"Gone where?"

"Aria," he began, but I wasn't about to get some lecture from him before he shattered my heart by telling me Knox had found someone else, or worse, he'd married Sabine for real this time.

"Don't lie or seek to protect me. Just fucking say it, Brander."

"He's with Hecate." Brander's words might as well have ripped into my chest and removed my heart as it still beat. The echoing sound of it rang in my ears, deafening them to whatever he'd uttered after he'd told me who Knox was with. The entire room spun around me as if I'd stepped onto a carousel. But as I spiraled on it, no horse was available to prevent me from falling. "Aria?"

CHAPTER 25
ARIA

In the middle of the library, I stood as dread slammed through me. It felt like violent waves thrashing against the shoreline as the tide came in. The sound of voices around me wouldn't reach my ears over the deafening sound of my heartbeat and my screams ripping through it. Only, I didn't scream. I couldn't. It felt as if someone had reached into my throat, and stolen my ability to make a sound.

The tightness in my chest wouldn't lessen, not even as I sucked in air as I realized I'd stopped breathing. I swallowed several times to clear my throat, feeling as if something was stuck in it, blocking my airway and trapping the sounds in my throat.

Brander stepped closer, but I shook my head as my hand lifted, warning him to back up. I repeatedly opened my mouth to speak, but everything I wanted to say wouldn't escape. I couldn't find the right word to say, and even if I could, they wouldn't articulate. I fought to regain control of my thoughts, my voice, and the emotions that were presently breaking my heart into sharp, jagged pieces. Gripping my throat, I applied pressure to my breastbone, praying it eased the agony and torment I felt so fucking deeply that I feared looking down, only to discover a gaping hole from where they'd torn my heart from my chest.

"Aria?" Esme whispered, her eyes wide with concern.

"I'm sorry, Brander. You'll have to repeat that? Because it sounded like you said Knox was *with* Hecate?"

"You should sit down," he encouraged as he pulled a chair up beside him.

"I don't want to sit down," I hissed as my world shattered into a thousand broken pieces.

The entire room blurred as fear collided with terror at the thought of him being anywhere near her. It took effort to force words to leave my lips. As if I'd lost them with him. It hurt to even think he'd have gone with her, but why the hell would he have done something so fucking stupid? It was Knox. Knox wasn't stupid! He'd never voluntarily go to the sadistic bitch who'd hurt him repeatedly. He knew she'd only force him to be a slave, to murder those she placed beneath his blade.

"Tell me what happened," I grounded out through dread and the pain consuming me far more than it ever had touched me before. My nerves frayed as something within me tugged, as if fighting to gain some semblance of control over the wealth of violent emotions slashing through my flesh, flaying it to torn ribbons.

Brander's soft, sapphire stare studied my face.

Searching for what? Was he enjoying seeing me break apart? Maybe it was his kink? I didn't care, but I knew that I wanted Knox to walk through the library doors, of fuck, even scale the wall and tell me to wake up. That this was merely a seriously fucked up nightmare.

"What. Fucking. Happened?" It had taken an effort to hiss each word as I enunciated them. His head dropped forward, then gently nodded. Parting my lips, I fought to demand he tell me what happened to Knox, but Killian cleared his throat, forcing my stare to jerk toward where he moved closer to us.

"Knox sent a group of warriors to the Dark Mountains to find out what happened to the caravan which was due here, but never showed up. He figured they'd either been attacked or needed help. Those in the caravans were easily discovered and retrieved. They'd been set upon by ravagers who'd taken their food, clothing, and whatever else they had before they left them stranded on the other side of the pass. They and the group Knox had sent out started back through the passes. They'd reached the top and intended to set up camp."

He scratched the back of his head, sliding his eyes around as I stood statue still though my breathing was still quick, short inhale. Killian scrubbed a hand over his face, then searched the room, as if someone else would tell me the rest. When no one offered, he exhaled a deep, even breath from his lungs. His hand held his neck. Those azure eyes that once viewed me with hate now offered me pity.

"The moment they settled in for the night, they were set upon by a small group of dark witches. Since it appeared to be only a few, they didn't think to take precautions. Intending to dispatch them quickly, they forewent precautions or a protection shield. As they moved to attack, Hecate stepped from the group, slaughtering all but a few of the warriors, and some women from the caravan," Killian explained.

"That doesn't explain how *she* could reach Knox. If he sent them out, then why would he go to her? Knox isn't fucking stupid." Brander exhaled at my words. Then he and Killian shared worried glances.

"Hecate made an offer to trade those she'd captured in exchange for him," Brander admitted as his voice strained from pain.

Absorbing what they'd told me, I shook my head. It didn't add up. None of it added up. Knox was the king, which meant he had to remain safe from the bitch who had continuously hurt him and his people. By sending them out, he would have alerted them to the potential for attack or capture. Additionally, if they had intentionally ignored their own safety, then they had opted to risk being captured, or worse. It didn't fucking matter. Knox knew not to trade a king for a knight or a pawn. He'd chided me for doing so once as we'd played chess. I deliberately lost because losing meant we would remove a piece of clothing for each high-point piece.

"That makes little sense. Knox's very strategic, which means he wouldn't give up the king for a knight or a pawn. What the fuck was worth trading the king to Hecate for? Nothing would be worth trading Knox to that murderous bitch!" My voice cracked as anger and denial clashed, sharpening it like a blade.

"Me," Lore muttered, which drove my eyes to his back. The moment Lore turned around, a shocked exclamation of shock expelled from my lips. Horror sliced through me at the sight of numerous lacerations, all which were severely cut into the flesh on both sides of his face. There were more markings from blades slashing into Lore's flesh continuing to his throat, his chest, arms, and even lower until they disappeared beneath the soft, black sweats he wore. Nausea rushed to the back of my throat as the reality of what had happened sank in. "I'm aware that I'm not a worthy trade for the king, Aria. I told him not to trade for me. Knox wouldn't listen to reason."

The guilt in Lore's voice shredded whatever was left of my heart. Tears trickled free of the hold I'd held on them. My hands covered my lips, holding the scream that demanded passage at bay. The carefree humor that Lore always brought to the room, even when it was filled with tension or anguish, was gone. In its place was a colder, harder version of him. That alone was a tragedy.

"I didn't mean that, Lore," I clarified.

He rose gradually, revealing even more damage to his flesh, which looked as if it had been stitched up a while ago. My eyes narrowed, uncertain how he still held the scars if he'd not scarred before? Hecate had tortured Lore until it had finally broken Knox. Knox had raised Lore when the same sadistic bitch had murdered his parents. Hadn't she put them through enough? Wasn't she tired of ceaselessly destroying what was left of Knox by now?

Stepping toward Lore, I hesitated as he flinched back from my approach. Brander jerked his head sharply, as if warning me not to approach.

"What the fuck happened? Hecate shouldn't have been able to heal yet." At the confusion I felt, they laughed, as if I was cute, or maybe stupid even. It caused my eyes to narrow on the two men before me.

"Which time, Aria? You've been gone for six months. Hecate has been attacking for months. Where the fuck were you? A lot has fucking happened since you left to go fucking find yourself," Killian scoffed, his eyes accusing as they drifted over my shoulder to Zyion, who'd wisely remained off to the side.

"I haven't been gone six months, Killian. You're wrong." My argument sounded weak, even to my ears. Despite my awareness of the possibility, Knox made no mention of my extended absence upon my return. "I wasn't even an entire five days," I argued. My mind fought against the need to recklessly rush to retrieve Knox and what Killian had said. "How the fuck could you think I was gone an entire six months?" My lips quivered as the words trickled out through the narrowing of my throat.

"Because you *were* gone that much time. At least, you were for them, Aria," Zyion specified from behind me, forcing me to turn on my heel. "In the mountains of the new realm, time moves vastly differently. For you, it was only a few hours. But for the outside world, it could be weeks, months, sometimes even years."

His explanation sent surprise joining the already overwhelming emotions tearing through me. I'd suspected a few days difference, or maybe even a week. Never had I imagined it would be six fucking months. Zyion studied the pain his words caused, adding salt to the injury I'd inflicted on my return. Lowering his head, he frowned at the silence that followed. Once the tension and pregnant silence became too much, he spoke once more, offering an apology.

"If there had been another way to protect you from what was occurring there, I'd have taken it. I didn't have any way else to get you to safety, and Basilius was near enough to hear my instruction to protect the heir at all cost."

"How long has Knox been with her?" The room went silent with an uncomfortable silence, which gave me an idea of just how long she'd waited once she'd realized that I'd snuck out of the realms.

"Four months," Brander answered. "That isn't the worst part, though."

I lost the train of thought I'd held as the thought of just how long he'd been suffering while I'd been gone. My ability to speak was stolen by the claws gripping it in a merciless choke hold. Quick, shallow breaths left my lips, but I felt as if I couldn't get air into my lungs. The coppery tang I tasted on my tongue told me I'd bitten it hard enough to draw blood. Repeatedly clenching and releasing my hands into fists, I shook my head in denial.

This had to be a nightmare. It had to be, right? Everyone watched as I constantly shook my head, then began yanking off the jewelry I'd been adorned with before leaving the other realm. It felt as if it were strangling me. The crown I'd never want went sailing across the room first. Next, the earrings that jingled in my ears noisily. The palpitations in my chest incessantly beat faster, harder, until I thought it would break from my chest and run to who it truly belonged with. A tightening in my chest had my fists pressing against it, rubbing where it ached.

"I'll be right back." The words were a faint hiss of air as I moved toward my side of the library. I didn't make it over ten steps past the shelves before the tears fell. An image of Knox bloodied from Hecate, punishing him for being with me, ripped through my head. I slammed my palms against it, needing it not to be true. One after another, images flashed through my mind, as if I was being fed memories instead of panic induced scenarios. Inside my head, I watched him rutting into the goddess. His ass slamming forcefully as he turned, looking at me over his shoulder, smiling coldly. My palms flattened against my eyes, needing to stop the images from entering my head.

A strangled scream ripped from my lungs. It held every ounce of frustration, pain, and panic with it as it tore through the library. My rattle came, Ember sensing my pain as she realized what had happened, adding to the sound of grief ripping from us all at once.

"Where is Hecate holding Knox now?" I demanded with strength and resolve laden in my voice.

"She isn't holding Knox anywhere, Aria. He stays with her willingly." Brander's words compelled my eyes to narrow, even as I tried to understand why Knox would stay beside her.

"What does she have that keeps him there?"

"He's no longer Knox. He's tainted in the darkness, which he's agreed to serve." Killian dropped his stare the moment I glanced at him.

"That's not possible," I argued in disbelief. "Knox was protected from her control."

"He was," Greer corrected.

Greer's words caused my head to skip a beat. "You're saying that Hecate has Knox, and he's not warded against her?" I felt the color draining from my face. The normal shiver that rushed down my spine at scary shit was missing. My entire body shivered, then my mouth dropped open. "What the fuck!" The reins of my control snapped, shattering the armor I wore. "That's fucking fuckity, fucked up!" Stepping back, I sucked in air. Big gulps of air into lungs, refusing to hold anything. Without another word, I walked back to the shelves, then bent over, holding my middle.

"Peasant?" Greer's voice held worried, but it also had a hitch in it, which was worrisome.

"Meat Suit? If there's any other tragic fucking news, I am going to need a moment," I warned. My head was between my knees, which applied pressure, even as my eyes squeezed closed.

"I think you're supposed to sit down before trying to shove your head up your own ass," Lore's rasping voice tugged at my heartstrings.

He sat down beside where I was trying not to hyperventilate. My gaze inspected the deep gouges in his flesh, knowing precisely what Hecate had done to him. Being near him made it effortless to distinguish the claw marks of the dire wolf from its long canine incisors. My heartstrings pulled as I leaned forward, resting my arms over the top of my knees, the same as he had done. I felt the sting of tears burning behind my eyes as he released a long-shuttered breath, as if he'd been holding it this entire time.

"I'm sorry I wasn't here to help you," I whispered as I rested my head against my arms, poised on my knees.

"We're all just glad you're back now, Aria." My smile slid to his smile, which didn't touch his eyes. Lore's light was dimmer. The amber gaze he held on me lacked the normal sparkle of golden light in their starry zeniths. "The dragon needs you to save him, damsel. Occasionally, all things need to be saved, even if it is from themselves."

"Are you okay?" My voice shook as a single tear slipped free. I'd been unable to conceal the tremble of my tone, or tears from Lore.

"I'll be alright now that you're back where you belong. Knox left you a letter," he informed, then slowly sat up, leaning against the bookcase. I saw the slight flinch caused as his back went flush against the wood.

Lifting my head, I frowned as I realized why he wasn't healing. "There are no witches here." I stood, even as Lore looked at me like I'd gone off my meds. "It's dire wolf saliva. It's poisonous. Once it is in the flesh, you need a salve to remove the toxins. That's why your scars aren't healing, Lore," I simplified it when he merely narrowed those dull amber eyes on me.

"See," he muttered softly. Lore smiled, exposing the severity of what Hecate had done to him. His eyes held mine, uncaring as I stared at the damage. "It's okay, Aria. I hear chicks dig scars." He winked, but I didn't feel the same way he did.

Hecate had placed him in a pillory, then allowed a

starved dire wolf to rip his face and arms apart. Though, she'd probably used the magical restraints on it, ensuring the wolf hadn't killed her bait for the beast she really sought. I carefully lifted my hand, noticed he flinched, then shrank away from my touch. Sitting back, I gave him a reassuring smile.

"I need to know if she allowed him to use toxins, or venom, Lore." At my softly whispered words, he dipped as his eyes closed.

"Aria?" Killian called, then sat down beside me. "He isn't okay."

"I won't hurt Aria. One day, she's going to be my baby momma. Maybe sooner than I thought, since we fucking Knox." The guilt bore heavily on his words. Pain fought to roil through me, but I shoved it down. "If she can even stand the sight of me now."

"I think I prefer this version. The other was entirely too pretty for my taste," I returned, leaning closer as I smirked at the sparkle lighting in his eyes. "Who knew it was true, huh? Scars really make a girl wet after all," I lied, uncaring if he bought it or not as my fingers skimmed against the deep cut beneath the skin, where he would never heal without assistance to extract the toxin.

His hand reached up, gripping my wrist. Sliding my gaze to hold his, I offered him a smile as his lips skinned over my knuckles. Dropping to my knees, I cupped his cheeks between my palms and exhaled.

"We are going to be okay, Lore. This? This will pass too," I promised, knowing he'd come back from it. He had to. He was Lore. The one good thing I'd had, no matter which side they'd assumed I was on. "We've come a long way from when or how we met."

"You fucking throat punched me," he recalled with a genuine smile glittering in his eyes. "That's the moment I knew I loved you, Aria. My fucking dick was rock hard, even though I couldn't breathe." I laughed outright at his remark, then shook my head.

"She's a queen," Eva whispered to Zyion. He smiled, then chuckled at the sight of me on my knees, tending to my friend as I coaxed him back from the darkness.

"You're right. She's the queen. And that is her friend who is in pain right now. I knew a queen like her once before," Zyion returned.

"I need fresh mugwort, borage, saffron, and feverfew," I stated as I turned, eying the room. No one moved, which caused my eyes to narrow. "I need it yesterday, gentlemen!" The entire room moved into action. Returning my attention to Lore, I noted the way his eyes devoured me. "Lore?" Before I could react, he had me pinned against the floor.

"Pretty." His rasping purr caused Ember to rise, peering through my eyes. "I see you, creature. Even better, I smell you," he hissed eerily.

That looks like your problem, Aria. Not mine. Mommy isn't playing with . . . whatever he is. He's about to show you how daddy likes it, she snickered. I felt her stiffen as his eyes spread with thin, golden vines that spiderwebbed down his cheeks. *He's a super freaky one!* Ember began humming Super Freak in my head, which left me annoyed and worried.

"Lore, stop." His smile was lethal. It sent a shiver of

heat straight to my core, which had him inhaling the tendon at the base of my throat. "Please." My eyes closed as his scent slammed against me, forcing arousal to coat my sex. The sound of feet rushing over the floor sent worry for Lore. It also gave me hope I wouldn't have to hurt him in order to make him stop.

Basilius yanked Lore off of me, holding him as he struggled in his arms. My eyes held Basilius's gaze fleetingly before drifting to the amber eyes, which were tracking me with predatory awareness. I stepped to the side, and Lore's head swung toward me, laser sharp focus as he released a primal rattle, which had my thighs clenching.

"Incubus, and dragon. Born of Isadora and my father, Lennox," Brander muttered from behind me. Turning, I watched the strain playing on his face. "It isn't a delightful combination to watch struggling."

"What do you mean?" I asked, with Lore's demand to bow drifting against my skin, causing goosebumps to rise.

"It means he needs to fuck, and fuck often. Only, Lore doesn't stop feeding until death occurs. Once he starts to feed, even if you remove the meal he's feeding from, he can still consume her soul. In short, feeding him is a death sentence to anyone brave enough to try doing so." Brander looked exhausted, as if he'd not rested once since Knox had left.

"When's the last time you slept more than a few hours?" I questioned, which has his vibrant bedroom eyes sliding to lock with mine.

"Honestly, I don't remember when I slept last." Guilt radiated through me as I nodded. "You shouldn't feel guilty about what happened. It would've happened with or without you here. Knox would've still sent the soldiers out to find the caravan lost in the passes. Lore would have still requested to go since most were women, and you know how he is. Hecate would have still been there and captured Lore. The only difference would have been, you'd have traded yourself before you ever let Knox do so. If that happened, it would be a disaster for everyone, Aria. If Hecate got to you, it would be game over," he warned.

"I still should have been here, Brander. If I'd known going into the mountains would make me lose months? I'd have fallen off the damn dragon to stop from being flown up there."

"Back up, Aria," Killian demanded as he placed a cauldron and several herbs on the table beside it. I stepped back, but his tawny head shook. "You said dragons, as in plural? And you rode a dragon? Not his prick, but on his back?" I nodded in reply, which caused his lips to curve into a devastating smile.

"I missed you, assholes, and I was only gone days," I admitted, slowly sidling up to Killian. Stepping on my tiptoes, I kissed his cheek. "You are a good herb hunter," I purred raspily, which had Brander snorting loudly.

"I go grab the map to show her where Knox frequents, and you grabbed herbs? Yet you got the kiss on the cheek, fucker," Brander mumbled under his breath.

He spread a large map out, which drew me closer to it, knowing I'd see where Knox had been while I was gone. Grabbing the pestle and mortar, I strode to the map, then exhaled a shuddered breath.

"He went to the palace where my people are?" I whispered as a new type of pain tried to take control of my emotions. Forcing them down, I turned, eyeing the herbs. Not all had been for Lore, but I'd needed something to numb the pain.

"No, but he almost caught the girls outside of the palace. I'm not sure how they escaped, but they thankfully managed to do so before he could harm them. Avyanna, Sabine, and Soraya and a few others were there," Brander stated. "When he went to her, he presumed she'd be able to access his mind. He was wrong. Knox began leveling entire keeps similar to what you were doing. It's been a fucking, Aria. One huge, chaotic mess."

I meticulously studied the map, noting the path he took. "Does he take the same path every time?" They'd marked the large map with colored pins. Some locations had several poked into the leather, while other places had only one. Dread knotted my stomach, even as it twisted.

"Yeah, but we can discern the pattern or why he's continuously looping around this area." Brander pointed to the Swamplands, then the Valley of the Red River. Bile pressed against the back of my throat as I closed my eyes against what I knew he was doing. "Once he's finished whatever it is he's doing, then he goes back to Vākya."

"He goes to the Kingdom of Unwanted Beasts, then through the passes of the Dark Mountain. He veers to the Beltane Circle, then back to the border. Once Knox finishes those places, he moves toward the Valley of the Dead. It's everywhere he found me throughout the realms. Knox's looking for me," I whispered as nausea surged inside my stomach. If what they said was true, and it wasn't Knox anymore, then I was in trouble. "She's sending him to kill me. Hecate wins either way. Either I end his life, or he ends mine."

The mere idea of killing him sent me off the rails. As if I were a runaway train who'd jumped the tracks. Barreling aimlessly toward catastrophe. My death would never be at Knox's hands. I wouldn't allow him to ever carry that burden. I wouldn't allow the hands that once cradled me as if I was something precious to use violence to take my existence away in such a manner. The sharp, elongated incisors which had left their mark so profoundly in my flesh, that they'd embedded his claim on my soul. Those oceanic-eyes that I'd weathered the storm he'd become, tossing in their endless depths as he'd sent me drifting afloat in their treacherous waters.

Tears filled my eyes, then slowly trickled free as they slid down my cheeks. I couldn't be me and succeed in freeing Knox from Hecate's clutches. I'd have to change into something else entirely. There could be no emotions to make me reckless, or fraught with them governing my actions, decisions. Grief of losing him couldn't rack my mind, or heart. The agonizing, debilitating torment that gripped endlessly for control, would have to die. If I were to survive this, I'd need to be emotionless, untouchable. If I were to survive what was needed from me, I'd have to shut them all off. Closing my eyes as the last sob escaped, I forced myself to shut-off everything I'd been. Then, one by one, I began to compartmentalize each one, slowly eradicating them from self.

I locked it all down, including the brutal pain.

I declined to let fear in, or to have control of me. I'd be afraid later, but fear wouldn't bring Knox back.

I disengaged from the love I felt for him, expunging it from my mind and heart. Later, I'd remember how I'd loved him, which would remind me that he'd been real.

I swallowed down the hopelessness losing him forced me to feel, choking as it trickled down my throat.

I permitted anguish a fleeting second more, loathing the way it caused my mind to break, shattering my resolve, then I violently shoved it away.

I forced grief to release me, to free me from the horrid grip it held around my throat, blocking the air from reaching my lungs. One day, I'd allow myself to grieve the loss of the man I'd loved, but it wasn't today.

As everything detached, I permitted my psychosis to fuel me with new emotions. Then, I let new emotions enter. Wrath. Disdain. Abhorrence. Indifference. Bitterness. Self-loathing. Rage. Contempt. Resentful. It was all that was left now. I wrapped myself within the cloak of it, slowly allowing the new, harder, more savage blanket of emotions to adjust over my tender flesh.

I let them all crash into one harsh mindset of pure determination. I'd need the grit they'd lend me. The others could wait until I'd gotten Knox back from the evil whore who thought she could take him from me. Turning around, I discovered every single person I'd told to wait had followed behind me. They were all staring as I returned a lifeless, emotionless grin, which only made those who knew me, flinch.

I'd thought I was coming back to claim a kingdom, and prepare to end the life of a goddess. Instead, I'd be fighting against the man I'd fallen in love with. The entire room went silent around me. The cold, merciless bitch was hoping Knox would end me, and she'd get her happy ever after with my beast. I'd be damned if I allowed her to get her ending. Not if I didn't end up with my beast, and the library. I'd show that sadistic bitch just how wicked beauty could be for her beloved beast.

CHAPTER 26
ARIA

Three days had passed since I'd returned to the library. Each day I awoke in Knox's bed, reaching for him. The moment my eyes opened, a tightening would build in my chest, bubbling in the burn as a silent scream. It never escaped past my lips, though. Every morning, I'd slip into the cold, detached persona I was crafting around my poor, shattered heart. Then, I'd get dressed before doing mundane things, like stacking books until the pile stood taller than I did.

Inhaling the scent of fresh herbs mixed with a hint of lavender, I strode toward the bed that Lore lay on, unmoving. Like him, I was awash in self-loathing. It hadn't mattered if I would have traded myself for him, as Brander had pointed out with such attention to detail. The thing was, I wasn't here. Lore on the other hand. Guilt consumed him for being the one thing Knox couldn't handle watching, as he was tortured in front of him.

"This shit stinks," he muttered, then waved his moss-covered hand toward his face. "How much longer do you expect to wear it?" At the delicate brow I raised, he slumped back down against the mattress.

"You are a horrible patient, Lore." Leaning over the bed, I pulled the square pincushion moss from his cheek, smiling tightly as I roved over the oozing, putrid, black secretion continually being extracted from the multiple bite and claw marks that threatened to leave him scarred and disfigured. "How do the wounds feel today?" I questioned, reaching up to push the unbound strands of silvery hair behind my ear.

"Like swamp ass." His sparkling, golden eyes forced mine to them, then held them fleetingly before returning them to the ceiling. "Fucking hell, I didn't mean to attack you, Aria."

"Silly Lore, I know you didn't," I supplied, while offering him a reassuring smile. "I'm afraid you're going to be a 'swamp ass' for at least another day. In a little while, I'll change the moss. It should help with the smell."

The crashing of hooves over the ground sent my attention to the large, open window. Glancing at Lore, who refused to interact more than he had to, I headed toward the balcony I'd stood on when Knox had climbed up to me. Reinforcing the lock on my emotions, I stepped outside, then swallowed down the disappointment as Killian, who'd met the scouting party at the gates, shook his head.

I sucked in the fresh air before resting my arms on the railing, scanning the courtyard. The air was filled with the scents and sounds of early fall, spreading over the land. The leaves had shifted to varying hues of red and orange. The autumn breeze rustled both my hair and the leaves. Tension trickled through the air, as if the world was holding its breath. It seemed as though the realms were aware of the impending battle. The strong scent of disturbed earth from newly-dug graves slowly drifted up to where I stood.

A crash below the balcony forced my eyes to where boys were struggling to haul a cart laden with supplies. Brander had gathered supplies so that it would prepare the palace in the event they unleashed Knox upon it. He wasn't wrong about doing so. Hecate wouldn't ignore Norvalla for long. She wanted control over every kingdom, right along with every soul inside of them. That meant eventually, she'd come for them.

"You doing okay?" Esme questioned. As I turned, I noted the worry swimming within their violet pools. Leaning against the same railing, she exhaled a long, shuddered breath. "And are we ready for when he actually comes? Because you facing him isn't a brilliant idea."

"I'm still breathing. I guess that means I'm fine," I returned smoothly, turning to peer toward her. "I don't know if I'm ready to see him like this. How do you see someone you care for taken over by someone else? Are you okay, Esme?" Her jaw tightened with the question.

The sound of her bottom molars grinding against the top ones mirrored my current state of mind. Winking at her, she frowned, but slowly nodded. Releasing an exhale, I pushed up from the railing, then tapped seven times with my hands, then pulled my hands back. Scooting back into the alcove of the balcony, I leaned against the wall, watching for any trace of movement outside the gates.

"They didn't find any trace of Knox through the passes." Esme exhaled, her eyes still following the small children attempting to help the men. "Someone once told me that the most dangerous people are those who can quietly hold their anger inside. But you hold it against you like its armor, which won't force the pain not to touch you." Esme turned around to lean her back against the railing, glancing around the library before her eyes landed on me.

"Anger is useful against your enemies. Pain, on the other hand? It only makes you do stupid shit and make reckless choices," I returned, eyeing the men on horseback rushing toward the courtyard gates. Their pace forced my heartbeat to speed up, even as I refused to allow hope to enter my mind. Slowly but surely, tiny bumps spread over my arms. "They've located Knox." I didn't need it confirmed. The blood splattering their armor pretty much gave it away.

The men barely allowed the gates to open wide enough for them to pass before they were pouring through them. Raising my chin, I inhaled deeply, smelling the wrongness surrounding the returning warriors. My brows pushed together as the sharp, pungent scent of death and the coppery tang of freshly-spilled blood brushed against my nostrils. They were freshly murdered, which meant Knox was nearby.

"Close the gates!" I shouted. Too late, though. I disengaged, cautiously pulling forward before observing Esme, who frowned before standing toward the corner I'd just been standing in.

I'd wasted time in combating against the useless emotions seeking to force their way through the locked door that they'd been shoved behind. In doing so, I'd failed to notice the irregularity in their movement, or rather, the lack of their movement. Plus, if I'd been paying attention, I'd have been able to detect the decay caused by death. Soaring over the balcony, I heard Zyion's cry of shock as I leaped from it, slamming down onto the ground below.

"Gods, woman!" he snarled, then landed beside me. "You're a queen, and they don't jump from fucking balconies."

I winced at the words he'd chosen, which forced me to shake off the memories of saying the similar thing to Knox. Standing up from the squatted position I'd landed in, I sauntered toward the dead warriors riding through the gates. Killian, Brander, and the other brothers dragged their stares from us to the men entering the courtyard.

Studying the men's bloodied armor, I frowned as they returned, splattered in their own blood. I wasn't certain if Knox had killed them, or witches had, but the blood wasn't making me think the latter was at fault. One raised a sword high in the air, even as the mutilated horse beneath him reared-back his front legs. Acheron turned, his eyes widening as the blade sliced through the air, aiming for his throat.

Lifting a hand, I rolled my fingers into a fist, which sent a violent bolt of lightning slammed down into the corpse. It caused the scent of ozone to flood the air. Acheron's eyes slid toward me, rounding as his mouth opened in surprise. The next one swung wide, aiming for Killian, who bent backward, then rolled his body before his legs slammed against those of the lifeless horse's. The sound of the gate drawing closed shot through the courtyard, even as I threw up a magical barrier and pressed onward toward the corpses.

"Knox either did this, or he watched as they were slaughtered before taking control," I stated the moment I reached the men.

"How do you know that?" Brander asked, eyes colliding with mine before he'd finished asking the question.

"My first guess? The black ooze dripping from every orifice of their face, for starters. If Knox or Hecate wanted us dead, they wouldn't send someone else to make us push up daisies. One of the two is driving the corpse. They'd come here to handle it themselves to ensure it got done right. There's no way in hell Hecate isn't intending to be there when I die, either." That caused the men to grunt in agreement. "No, he sent them here for a reason. I want to know what it was." I said, then turned as I caught movement from my peripheral vision, then turned to watch as the warriors dismounted in uniform formation. The nearest corpse stepped against the barrier, forcing a hiss of magic to singe his pale, lifeless flesh.

"I've been waiting for you, Little Monster," Knox's voice rasped huskily from the warrior's oily, black lips. The head tilted, then black, sightless eyes crawled down my frame. "You look good enough to devour," he susurrated, then licked his smudged lips hungrily.

My head lowered to cover the throbbing ache his words created. Clenching my hands into fists, I felt my nails cutting into my soft palms. Raising my chin, I swallowed the bitterness burning the back of my throat as he crossed his arms, then widened his stance, as Knox usually did when we squared off against one another.

"Knox," I returned, somehow preventing the quake I felt from entering my tenor, as his name left my lips. "I hate to say it, but you're not looking so hot. Rather gothic of you, what with all that black ooze? I guess it does match your eyes, though."

He released a purring rattle making my thighs clench forcefully together. It, more than anything else, propelled a jolt of wretchedness swelling through me. Dropping his arms to his sides, he and the men behind him all stepped forward, uncaring of the barrier burning their flesh. The scent of singed human tissue caused my stomach to roil, threatening to deposit the meager meal I'd eaten this morning at my feet.

Zyion's hand touched my shoulder, which had black, empty sockets where eyes should've been, snapping to my shoulder. A low, deadly growl rumbled from the body Knox was viewing us from. His posture had stiffened, and as I watched, his nostrils flared in response.

"If you don't remove your hand from her, I'll personally rip it off and fuck you with it," The corpse warned, his lips twisted into an unfriendly sneer. My eyes narrowed as his threat shot a jolt straight to my belly. I felt a short, breathless puff of air pushing up from my lungs. Knox's eyes held a thin, blue outline, which I had to fight to pretend I hadn't noticed.

"Fucking make me, asshole," Zyion returned, which forced a shiver over my flesh.

"It'll be my pleasure, Dragon Killer. I may even shove it up her pretty, little naked cunt if you'd like to spend eternity there. I know I do," he hissed, emitting a dark chuckle. His words caused my brow to push together on my forehead. "She'd fight me at first, but then she always enjoys fighting before fucking me." Knox's head shook, which caused my heart to thunder angrily against my ribcage.

"I'm certain I can convince the little bitch to accommodate it for you. After all, she takes my fucking knot so magnificently. Hell, she even whimpers and squirms for me, even as I force it all the way against the opening of her insatiable cunt." Knox's sightless stare held my gaze before dropping, then slithered to lock with Zyion's. "Oh, that's right. How could I be so cruel? Isn't that why your little *slut* of a mate took a swan dive from a cliff?"

Zyion stiffened beside me, then lunged so quickly that I gasped. Flinging my hand out, I threw it back with a magical pull, jerking his massive frame back forcefully. The sound of Zyion's grunt of disbelief, then the second as he connected against the ground, told me he'd be fine without me needing to look.

"You protecting your lover from me, Aria?" The incriminatory pitch he used sent knives stabbing into my chest. "Don't worry, I replaced you too, gorgeous." That fucking eviscerated me. I swallowed repeatedly to keep back the bitterness that burned my throat.

"I'm sure you did, Knox," I whispered thickly, unable to prevent the narrowing in my throat that his words created, choking on my words. "Is that why you came? You want to shove her down my throat since *you* can't shove *anything* there now?" I goaded him, needing his emotions to rise. "Does she give you what I did?" His hands clenched tightly at his sides, but the black fully-consumed his eyes.

"Much more than you ever did, stupid little, needy bitch. She does shit you can't even begin to envision. But then, you always thought you were playing hard to get with me, when you were just easy pussy that was conveniently on hand to fuck." His head lowered minutely, then tilted. Black, lifeless eyes of the corpse met mine. "Ain't that some shit? A raven doesn't care about magic, Aria. Think about that. In four months, they're fully embedded with more intelligence than you've ever had. Maybe you should find a flock of unkindness and go take a flying fuck off a cliff."

The smile twisting over his mouth reminded me of when I'd first met him outside of town. The fates were viciously cruel bitches to force me to face him like this. Swallowing, I considered his words as my head tilted to the side, observing as more ooze began pushing from his orifices.

"What are you thinking in that lovely head of yours?" Knox asked as his fingers rubbed over the barrier, forcing a shudder to rock through me, even as his lips slid into a wolfish grin. "You forget, I know everything about you. I know your weaknesses, the people who matter most to you, your secrets, and what can hurt you the greatest."

"Did you come here to boast, or goad us, Knox?" I inquired, then sauntered closer to him noting the way his head tilted, studying the sway of my hips. On cue, thick black liquid cried from his eyes. I felt Zyion's alarm over what I intended to do, but turned, eyeing him with a warning gleaming in my eye. Turning back around, I challenged Knox once more.

Zyion returned to my side, offering me an annoyed side-eyed scowl of rebuke. Knox held *some* control over his mind, obviously. He was aware of shit he shouldn't know, like Rhianna and how she'd taken her own life. But he'd also had endless knowledge at his fingertips since he could devour the written word. It sent a chill through my blood, racing through my veins until I forced a shiver down, refusing to release it beneath his razor-sharp gaze. Hecate had taken both Knox, and in doing so, she'd ended up with her own Library of Knowledge.

"It's cute how you've wrapped the Dragon Killer around your finger. That pussy of yours has a way of ensnaring beasts with the promise of its sirens song it sings when its being fucked. Have you made him a father as you did for me?" Knox's words made me stagger as they sliced through me like a warm knife through butter. My eyes fluttered to prevent the tears swimming in my vision from being seen. "Don't worry, gorgeous girl. I'll ask Hecate to at least allow you to hear them cry once before I rip them apart in front of you." I felt the power he'd been gathering, wincing at my stupidity.

"You think Zyion would help me make pretty babies?" I asked, then giggled as my words caused his smile to die as they pulled into a grayish thin line. Knox's features hardened, exposing murderous fury. "I mean, since you replaced me, someone will have to fill your role. Right? No hard feelings?" I goaded, hating him a little for throwing our daughters into the hatefulness of what was occurring right now. "I bet he can fuck like a beast just as well you can, Karnavious." Turning around, I slowly swayed my hips temptingly as I moved back to Zyion, whose lip had pulled up farther on one side as he wrinkled his nose. "Can you fuck like a beast while putting a babe in my belly?" I asked in a rasping purr of sound, causing those around me to wince as if it hit them in the balls. If I had a better aim, I would have only hit Knox, but I wasn't sure the purr I used could be aimed at one person.

"I can fuck you any way you want me to. Slow, gentle, rough, or savagely. Tell me what you want, but I don't intend to stop until you're too fucking hoarse to even whisper thank you when I've finished with you." An audible swallow sounded, which took a moment to realize that I'd created the sound. "I'm down to make some babies with you, my queen." Zyion's eyes glittered with something wicked dancing dangerously in their depths. I stepped back, but a hand lifted, collaring my throat as he pulled me closer. "He's gathering power to attack," he whispered softly against my lips, making it look to Knox as if we were kissing.

A single breath separated them from touching, which sent a trickle of uneasiness through my center. He wasn't Knox, that meant he wasn't who I wanted. The irony was, the man I wanted was somewhere close enough to control the warrior he used to speak through.

"I know," I returned, pulling back, needing distance to prevent exposing that I'd felt nothing from Zyion. Nothing like Knox had forced me to feel. If he sensed it, he'd release the power he'd gathered, which would end up with someone here hurt, severely. "Good news. He wants lots of babies."

"He's fucking dead," Knox hissed vehemently. His eyes flashed with a sliver of startling blue before the strange obsidian-colored waterworks began, only this time they poured both from his eyes, and ears.

"So is she, Knox." The corpse pointed a half-severed finger at me. "She's just too big-headed to realize how fucked she's about to be. Only, I won't make her come. I'll bury that bitch so deep in the ground that she'll be banging the devil door knob to be rescued instead of for pleasure by the time I'm done with her."

Because one of us wasn't fucking pretending! Which meant that whore was so fucked that I'd ensure she never rested once I sealed her in the tomb. I'd build a nest on it, and fuck Knox nightly just so she could hear him moaning my fucking name. She'd listen every night as I whimpered, moaned, and begged for him to fuck me harder. He would, and I'd smile the entire time, knowing she was beneath us, pouting as she used the stick, which I intended to toss her before sealing that bitch in for the rest of her miserable fucking life.

"I came here to invite you to my wedding," he declared with a cold, merciless smile simmering in ocean-colored eyes, which appeared through the oozing sludge.

"Over my dead body," I whispered as the knife he'd already stabbed in my heart twisted.

"It's actually preferred that it's lifeless. After all, I promised my bride to bring her your carcass as a wedding gift. I suggested we toss you in our bed before murdering you. I wanted to fuck her while staring into your pretty eyes. Unfortunately, Hecate is very possessive of her things." His tongue drifted over his bottom lip as those scandalizing ocean-blue eyes studied my face. "I never loved you, Aria. You and I both know we wouldn't have worked out. You're pathetic, and she's a fucking goddess. You are too fucking young to know what I hunger for. Hecate, though, she gives me everything I never knew I needed." Gut. Punch. "I'll tell you what, Little Monster, you come to me now, I'll fuck you to death. Hell, I'll even make that pussy sing for me before I twist your neck until your head breaks off. I might even continue fucking your tight, pretty cunt after you've expired. For old time's sake, of course."

"How about you go tell your owner that I'm coming for her? If I can't end her life? Then she'll get what she wants. I'll burn this entire place to fucking embers and she can have you in what's left of this place. Hecate can ascend the throne in the ashes and ruins of everything and everyone she's destroyed. Hell, I'd even crown her as the queen myself. Except, that would be tricky, right? What, with her needing alive beings to house her power within? I mean, *you* could breed the nasty bitch and house her power inside of *your* children. Oh, that's right. She can't breed any more children. I ensured that when I trapped the whore in her own body. Sorry, Knox. Looks like you don't get to be her baby daddy after all." I shrugged my shoulders, taunting him to end this before I lost my ever-loving mind and control of the locked door.

"No, I won't," Knox snarled as his eyes returned obsidian, then black sludge ran as if someone had turned on a faucet. I studied the tension on his face, the contorting over the soldier's features before his hands rose, forcing me to hastily defend against the onslaught he unleashed.

I'd assumed he'd be powerful. What I hadn't counted on was that he had actively begun gathering it when he'd arrived. I also hadn't realized he'd be using my fucking magic, either. He'd more than likely began storing it as he drove the group of corpses back here. The moment our magic connected, violet light exploded in the courtyard, blinding all within it.

Knox's magic slammed against my body, then sent me flying backward through the air. I connected with the stone wall surrounding the courtyard. My skull hit against the rocks, forcing both sparks and black dots to burst into my vision.

Instinctively, I grabbed the side of my head as a surge of splitting pain pounded within. Ringing blared in my head. The second pulse of power connected beside me, forcing me to roll, turning onto the ground before pushing myself upright. Nausea swirled through my stomach, even as bile burned against my throat.

On my feet again, I swayed, then whirled around in a circle, scouring for any sign of the others. Blinking to clear the blurriness in my eyes, I continually searched for those who'd been close enough to be hurt in the blast radius of his magic.

Turning back around at the sound of footsteps, I struggled against the nausea, still trying to escape my throat while teetering on uneven ground. The warrior Knox had been speaking from was the only one still on its feet. A cruel smile twisted his mouth as he sauntered his way toward me.

"You look so much better broken, my pretty little prey." His words sent warning bells off in my head, even as groans began issuing around us. "I promised her I'd make it hurt."

"You promised you wouldn't break my heart again. I guess we're both liars now," I whispered through the tightness in my chest. "When you're buried balls deep in that

whore? I hope you see me, and wish it were me instead."
His hands firmly grasped the bodice of the gown I wore,
yanking me against the corpse's frame.

"I always see your face. Every thrust into her cunt? I
dream about you, and doing this," he rasped, then
wrapped his hands around my throat. "When you get to
your next life, I'll be there too, waiting to end it as well. Tell
our baby girls daddy says hi," he murmured before his lips
skimmed over my forehead, and his hands sealed around
my throat.

Knox's hands were merciless. Just as they'd always
been. Light exploded in my vision, blinding me. Pain shot
through my entire frame as a sadistic laugh burst from my
lips, wrong, yet unmistakably loud enough to ensure he
heard it. What he didn't hear was the blade slicing through
the air behind him, which removed both of our heads.

Dropping the blade, I rubbed my fingers over the hand-
prints left over my throat. The body on the ground I'd
created from magic gradually began to vanish, leaving only
the warrior's corpse, and decapitated head, which was still
grinning. Bending down, I gripped it by the hair, holding
it up.

"You don't know all my tricks, Knox. I've learned a lot
of things since I've been gone. And you don't get to call me
your little monster while you're standing beside that
whore. I'm coming to get you back. Sometimes, it's the
dragon who needs a queen to save him. Fuck being a
princess when you can be a queen who creates such beautiful chaos. I hope your girlfriend is ready for me. Because I
am," I hissed before tossing the head into the air, as the
world flashed to white as lightning struck the skull, as it

shattered into tiny pieces of grizzled, charred flesh and bone.

Peering through the cloud of smoke, I caught sight of Killian, speckled with brain matter. I winced and offered him an apologetic smile. Thunder cracked above our heads, resoundingly. Forcing him to flinch, then tip his head back to scan the cloudless autumn sky.

"How the fuck did you do that?" Zyion's garbled words forced my eyes to his bloodied face. His turquoise eyes darted between the dull image I'd crafted from magic, to me, then back again. "You don't think you should tell us your plans?"

"I am not allowing mistakes to happen. It's Knox, and whatever it takes, I'm getting him back. If you expect me to tell you all my secrets, you're about to be disappointed, Zyion. A girl doesn't indulge others with her secrets. It would be a tragic miscalculation to assume I would do so." His face tightened, then he jerked his head once, showing me that he could live with it. "Now, we have to figure out how to get him back, and undo whatever the hell damage she's done to him."

"You don't think we haven't scoured the entire library for answers on how to remove the shit oozing from his eye sockets?" Brander's words were laced with anger, but identifying Knox's voice from a corpse had been a challenge for those who'd known him. At my narrowed stare, he shook his head, then planted his palms on his hips and bent forward, breathing shallow. "That may have been him merely driving someone else? But he has the same shit running down from his eyes, nose, and occasionally, his lips."

My stomach somersaulted at his words. I'd tried once to remove that toxic sludge, but they'd killed the witch before I could know if it had worked. I didn't know if I could remove it while leaving the person alive. Of course, if they were dead, I wouldn't be able to save them regardless of removing the sludge.

CHAPTER 27
ARIA

The funnel of power Knox unleashed through the corpse caused an influx of wounded people in the library. Bitterness adhered to my tongue like the nauseating taste of poison. It felt like a blade was continuously being stabbed into my chest, puncturing my lungs. Air refused to fill them, which made it impossible to breathe. No matter how much I wanted otherwise, emotions clawed their way free, ripping through me until they dove into the cavernous, hollow void of misery which had replaced my heart.

It had been one thing to be told Knox was beneath Hecate's control. It was wholly another thing to see it with my own eyes. Knox's comments about our daughters, or any child I'd have, thoroughly left me shaken and disturbed. The glimpses of him I'd caught throughout the exchange shouldn't have torn me asunder, but it would be a lie to say they hadn't.

My gaze roamed around the room, noting the small groups huddled together. Brander and Basilius, who both were close in age, sat across from one another. Esme stood behind Brander, sewing the gashes of flesh back together that he'd received from Knox's attack. It showed that even he couldn't mend everything without a little help.

Basilius, on the other hand, glared at Esme over the top of Brander's head. A murderous rage simmered over his face, thickening the air with tension. Esme, on the other hand, appeared unaffected by the daggers being thrown her way, even as she sewed Brander's back with tight, clean stitches.

Eva was tending to Zyion as she spoke to him in hushed tones. His eyes flicked to me and then slid back to Eva's face. It told me I was more than likely the topic of conversation. They hadn't resolved whatever was between them. Eva's attraction to him had not diminished, even after she had accused him of being a traitor. Her head lifted once more, this time worry tightened her lips into a hard, white line. For someone who hated him so much, she sure spent a lot of time pining after her *traitor*.

Killian sat with Acheron, Kael, and Ronin. Acheron reminded me of Lore—carefree with a serious side he turned on at the drop of a hat. Kael had the same boyish good looks as Gideon, and a kindness that was impossible to conceal from the world. Ronin, he was silent and broody, always examining everything and everyone around him with an expressionless look on his face. The three men looked more like Knox than the brothers I'd been around. Lore's soft chuckle forced my focus to shift, sliding over his moss-covered face.

"You aren't inspecting my brothers for a potential mate, are you? Because Daddy had his application in early, for the record. Knox isn't coming back from this, is he?" The stabbing pain in my chest began anew from the pain flashing over Lore's face.

"We're going to need a miracle, but who knows, right?" Tears singed the back of my nose, as heat pushed down my face.

"What was the point of searching for him? He's gone. That *thing* that was here, that was not my brother," Basilius growled in a rough resonance that had Esme visibly trembling.

"We needed to know if he was alive," I admitted, which caused all conversation within the library to stall out.

"Is he?" Lore asked, cutting through the tension my words had created.

"Yes." I felt my throat narrowing as the truth of it scratched its way to my tongue.

Killian exhaled a weighty sigh, then crossed his inked arms over his chest, tucking his fingers between them and his chest. "Look, Aria. I want Knox to be alive, too. But you saw the black shit leaking from every fucking orifice just as much as we did. That isn't my best friend. That was a fucking corpse with Knox's voice dripping from its lips," he scoffed.

"Killian's right." Brander placed his hands on the table in front of him. The blackish-blue strands of his hair were disheveled from constantly raking his fingers through it, ever since the confrontation with Knox. The bags beneath his eyes were dark, which made him look older, if at all possible. I wasn't even sure how old Knox was, let alone any of his brothers. "It's a hard thing to accept, but it's even harder to hope he's in there. Not when he's willing to murder his own people or brothers."

"Can't say I don't agree with them," Esme stated. "He intended to kill you, Aria. Knox wouldn't do such a thing."

"No, Hecate intends to force him to kill me," I argued. "That black shit? That's her fucking darkness. I watched the beginning of her introduction into the realms. Hecate released the same ink-colored droplets from her own eyes. It's her magic, which allows her to take control of whoever it slithers into, literally. It's a part of her, which means she's inside those who hold the darkness." I'd watched it slithering up the woman's leg in the 4D rendering, the same as Esme had that day in the library. "She created the witches to harbor her dark magic. It spread like a virus."

"Hecate didn't create witches," Acheron argued as his nose crinkled. "She brought them with her, or so we were told."

"No, she didn't. The gods imprisoned Hecate here because she reached for things that weren't hers to take. The only thing Hecate could bring was her oak staff and her dire wolves." Lore issued a smothered whine at the mention of the wolves. I calmly sat beside him and ran my fingers through his hair. "When she arrived, she released her own darkness and used it to taint other creatures to become useful to her. That's why witches can breed with any creature as well. The darkness can be spread through sex from a mother, to that of her unborn fetus. In short, those who have even a sliver of her oily, dark magic in them, are what eventually became what you guys call witches. They're not, though, not really. They were the inhabitants of the realms before she showed up and infected them."

"You're certain?" Brander questioned.

"I'm more certain of that than I am of my ability to drink water," I confirmed. "You remember the witch Knox killed when I was in the water?" He gave a slow nod as his lips pulled down at the corners.

"The one in which you sought to free the tainted ooze that Ilsa controlled her with . . ." Brander sat up straighter, his eyes widening.

"Exactly." I chewed my lip and glanced down at Lore, whose eyes were glittering with adoration. "I'm fairly certain that if they've held it within them too long, the host can't sustain life after she withdraws the darkness. Those born with it in them? They're different from those forced to consume it. They're infected with the taint she unleashed to build her own army, but she uses them as a power source. She is only as powerful as the numbers standing beside her, literally. The fewer witches in the realm, the weaker she becomes. Luckily for us, Knox went on a witch-killing bender before he forced us back here."

I'd never thought to be happy about what Knox had done. Not that they all deserved to be slaughtered. That wasn't the case with the ones who hadn't ever asked to be born with her magic inside them.

"How do you know he's even still alive without actually seeing him?" Killian cocked his head, then leaned forward, lacing his fingers together as he rested his hands on the table. "How can you know that if none of us could discern it?"

"Easy. The idea of having to kill Knox forced me to use

my brain instead of my emotions. The moment Zyion touched me, Knox fought to the surface to threaten him. Knox was there, but the more he fought her, the more darkness she forced into him. He was struggling to tell me he was still there. That means we've got to figure out how to get him away from her. Once we have, I can attempt to draw out her darkness from him."

"In order to do so, you'd have to get close to him," Zyion scoffed. "I don't know if you're aware of this, but I'm not easily taken down. He didn't just hold power, Aria. That was a direct line from Hecate that he merely drew from. I'll add that he was using a corpse like a lackey, which still caused a lot of damage. If you face him, he could kill you. Shit, he could kill all of us." The tone he used caused my flesh to cover in goosebumps. His hand lifted, rubbing his temples as if he had a headache.

"I'm aware of the cost, Zyion. It's Knox, though." Closing my eyes against the stares of worry filtering from the faces within the room, I shook my head. "I'm going with or without you guys. I can't leave him there knowing he and Lennox are trapped in his head. She's forcing him to remain at her side with magic. Knox isn't there because he needs or wants to be there. He traded himself for Lore, for fuck's sake." My voice broke, and the fingers gently moving through Lore's hair were pulled down and laced through his. "I'll fight for him. I'll fight for him with my last breath, if that is what it takes. I can't just leave him to that fate. And, if I can't have him, she can't either. Knox would rather die than be forced to remain endlessly by that bitch's side. So, if I can't save him, then I'll set him free."

"What if he kills you and we still don't save Knox?"

Lore asked, with sweat beading on his brow as the fever burned within him. "Because I can't live with being the cause of losing you both, Aria." Chills chased up my spine at his words.

"It isn't your fault, Lore. If it hadn't been you, then it would've been someone else. Hecate doesn't necessarily want me dead, which is what I'm counting on."

"Bullshit, Aria. Knox intended to strangle you out there. If you hadn't cloned yourself with magic prior to his arrival, he'd have ended you."

"No," I argued as my tongue snaked out, licking over my lips. "Knox was fighting her, which probably set her off. He said he wouldn't. Seconds after that, even more darkness oozed from his eyes, nose, ears and mouth. Like she'd turned a faucet on. He also said *'Ain't that a bitch? A raven doesn't care about magic, Aria. Think about that. In four months, they're fully embedded with more intelligence than you've ever had. Maybe you should find a flock of unkindness and go take a flying fuck off a cliff.'* It didn't make any sense. I mean, the ravens are his eyes and ears . . . fuck. I missed it." An icy chill curled up my spine. "Has Knox been with her for four months or less? Longer?" I demanded urgently.

"Why does it matter?" Brander countered.

"Answer me!" Panic thrummed in my words, quivering as it gripped my heart and throat in an unforgiving hold.

"Three months and three weeks?"

"Three months, three weeks, five days and six hours," Lore muttered.

"We don't have time to wait around doing nothing. Knox was trying to tell me that. Ravens gain their intelligence four months after they're born. He was warning us of how long he had left before he ceased to exist with her darkness inside him. There's also the reference to the unkindness. When you left earlier today, Killian, did you notice any ravens?" I asked, with a rock sitting in my stomach.

"I did," he admitted while he straightened in his chair. "In fact, one sat on the courtyard wall, which I found rather strange. Normally, they go to the birdcage Knox built for them. It's where he keeps the ones he raises. They're taught never to be seen around the palace. It prevents anyone from connecting the ravens back to him."

"Perfect," I whispered through a smile curving my lips. I whispered, "He'll be lost forever if we don't do something soon. That isn't something I can live with. With or without your help, I'm going to the citadel to confront Hecate."

"You're not going alone," Esme piped up. "Even though this is a terrible idea, you're my person. I'd hide bodies with you any day." Esme caused heads to turn toward her, confusion stamped over their faces. "If you go, I go. If we go down, then let it be together."

"Together," I whispered, as my throat constricted with tears.

"Where you go, I go," Zyion stated. His worry at the idea of me putting myself in danger made his words a harsh whisper.

"Oh, for fuck's sake. I'm in, even though this is a shit idea." Eva's tone mirrored Zyion's, but I figured she was "in" just so she could watch his back.

"I'll go," Basilius muttered even as he glared toward Esme.

"I'm in too," Killian announced. "He's my best friend.

Knox is also my family, which means no way in hell are you saving him without my help. I wouldn't be able to live with myself if I didn't do something to help him."

"Count me in too," Brander grumbled, shaking his head. "I can't believe you noticed he was aware of anything happening. We hadn't gotten close enough to him until today."

"No, Brander. The king doesn't take unnecessary chances with his life. If shit goes south, we can't chance losing the king too. Norvalla needs you more than he does right now."

Brander's eyebrows pushed together as he snorted. "If shit goes south, you'll need me. What do you plan to do if people are hurt, you'll have no one with you who can mend them enough to get back here."

"If shit goes south, Brander, we will not need a healer to mend our broken corpses. Knox is one of the strongest beings inside the Nine Realms. He's currently being driven around by a complete sociopath."

"He's my brother," he continued. The look of hopelessness in his stare almost caused me to concede. Knox's voice inside my head reinforced my resolve.

"A king doesn't go into a battle with the odds stacked against him. Knox would tell you it isn't your job to come for him, Brander. You handle an entire kingdom, and he's one soul within an entire realm of souls who both depend and rely on you. If we don't return, they're going to need their king to lead them to safety. You can't do that if you're dead."

"I'd go, but I'd only be a hindrance." Lore grumbled. His face turned away as if embarrassed. The angle caused the moss to slide from his cheek, revealing perfectly, undamaged skin. "Besides, they'd smell me coming from five realms away."

"Lore needs you more than we do, Brander. He needs the moss removed. Once you've removed it, burn it. The toxins are still active, so don't touch them without some kind of protection. Those who are coming with me, you have thirty minutes to grab or do whatever you need to before I open a portal to the keep on the edge of the Red River."

"Are we going to pick up what I think we're picking up?" Esme asked with a hopeful tone.

"It's time to announce our return and then bring them here. If shit goes bad, they'll need someone to protect them."

CHAPTER 28
ARIA

Powerful wing gusts caused silvery strands to whip across my cheeks. The scent of tangy copper triggered my heart to still before it hammered, pounding against my ribcage. No sound originated from the ruins of the castle that we'd left Soraya, Siobhan, and Avyanna secured inside. Fear sought to hold me in its embrace as I took in the damage done.

"They're okay, right?" Esme's trembling lips caused my stomach to knot.

"I don't know, Esme." I wouldn't lie to her or myself. I advanced cautiously, examining the rubble for any sign of bodies littered beneath the heavy stones. *"Ember, I'm going to need your help here."*

"Why? Is best lesbian, Esme about to cry? She can use your titty to wipe them away, not mine."

"Do you hear any heartbeats beneath the stones?" I questioned, unwilling to argue about Esme with her, not when I was so close to screaming in both denial and grief.

"There are several beneath us. All beating quickly, in fear.

387

Esme's sister is one of them, Siobhan. I also hear the horny girl's increasingly nervous heart thundering louder than the one that woke me as it rumbled." Guilt washed through me, which forced my eyes to narrow. It wasn't *my* guilt that I was feeling.

"You didn't make a sound when I confronted Knox," I pointed out, only to close my eyes as more guilt and shame drifted through my mind. *"I am not upset, Ember. I wouldn't wish to see my mate like that, either."*

"Not my mate. I can't feel my mate anymore. I haven't felt him since we returned. It's as if he's just . . . gone. I don't know how to feel. My insides are twisted, achy, and it hurts me."

My lips released a sad, grief-filled whimper that was part rattle, part-whimper, which had a chorus of similar sounds coming from around me. Ember's inner turmoil became turbulent and washed through me in violent waves.

"He's a storm, one I'd willingly weather to have him. He could drown me in his rain and I'd willingly sink into the turbulent waters to feel him. Aria, I don't want just anyone. I want Lennox back."

"I know how you feel. I can't feel Knox, either. It's like a void has replaced him within my soul." It was a brutal and gut-wrenching truth that revealed itself. *"I miss him too. Both of them, Ember. Right now, we have to ignore the pain. Bury it deep inside until they're free of Hecate's hold. Emotions do not belong in battle or wars. I promise you this, we're going there, and we're creating a perfect storm of chaos to get him back. That means we have the get the others so that we can go get our Dicker back, and his sometimes psychotic, aggressive, sexually-depriving inner beast. Then we bury the*

bitch so fucking deeply inside her tomb that she ends up in hell."

"You had me at bury Hecate, Aria. No need to keep going. Tell the men to stop breathing hard and making salivating noises over my sexy, feminine noises! Gods, can't a girl just whine a little without every alpha wanting to mount her from behind?" She appeared to be amused with herself as she teetered. *"You'd think they'd let a bitch grieve her mate in peace before trying to imprint her depresso, but very sexy, ass."* Ember released a loud rattle, which freed the scent we'd been holding back from the men.

"Seriously?" I asked, only to realize I'd done so out loud.

"I knew she was different, Vicious. You *smell* that, gentlemen?" Basilius asked, which caused a soft rattle to release from Esme's lips. "Just guarding *your* queen, huh?"

"If I were you, I'd stop there," Esme warned. Basilius turned, peering at her over his shoulder. If sex had a look, then he'd just fucked her. His eyes darkened, smoldering as they dragged down her body leisurely, down her frame drinking in every inch of her. By the time he'd finished, I was positive that he'd memorized each tiny detail to mind. Esme, bless her heart, released a low rattle once more— though her trembling betrayed a submissive and timid creature. "Got a problem, asshole?"

"I'd be very careful, Little Bird. I'm not afraid to teach you some manners."

The feral stare he aimed at her caused my eyes to widen. Basilius built a deep, lustful rattle in his chest, then released it as he prowled closer to her. Esme jerked, then crossed her legs as if she were about to piss herself.

"Dayum! Your best lesbian is about to be mounted. I'm pretty sure her mate is about to fuck her harder than karma. Is it wrong if we watch? Because I'd enjoy watching her scream, even if it isn't from me inflicting pain."

"We are not watching them fuck. And she's my best friend!" I hissed internally.

Ember's cackle of mischief caused my focus to shift back to the issue at hand, which wasn't Esme's mate intending to teach her who was the more powerful one in their relationship. If you could consider her wanting to murder him, while he wanted to murder her pussy while choking her, one.

"Fine, whatever. Fair warning, if the submissive one gets dicked down before we do, I'm going to be very dramatic. I will also cause a scene, just so you're aware. If I were you, I'd really start thinking about getting Dicker back, and by Dicker, I mean we need to get dicked down before that sad, neglected hole closes up and you piss out of your nose or some shit."

"Are you done? You're embarrassing me. Did you forget they can actually hear you?" A few of the surrounding men chuckled, causing my cheeks to redden and Killian to glance around as if he'd missed something, but I didn't offer an explanation.

She snickered and then rattled, forcing it to break free from the hold I'd sought to maintain it with. *"You, I'm sorta like your emotional support animal. You might be the unicorn, but I'm the dragon! Rawr!"* Ember made the most unsexy sound in the history of roars, ever.

"You don't even know if you're a dragon, jackass."

"You don't know that I'm not," she rebuked.

My eyes slid to a shadow within the woods, which sent

uneasiness rushing through me. "In the woods," I whispered to those near me. Slowly, I started around the debris that was littered on the ground from the once-impressive courtyard. Zyion and Eva closed in around me, even as the others spread out, looking for a way in while covertly scouring the wards.

"And even I don't know you're not a dragon, I wouldn't call you an emotional support animal. You'd be more akin to a rabid animal, who enjoys being banged harder than a screen door in a hurricane and eating bloody meat."

A pair of horns lifted from a bush that had the men chuckling. Before I could say anything, Acheron shot forward with inhuman speed.

"Don't eat Avyanna, Acheron!" I screamed, which caused Ember to release a full-on belly laugh from within me. "She's a friend, not food!"

Acheron didn't seem to hear me, and I watched in horror as he leaped over the bush and landed on top of her. The ear-splitting scream she released had him standing upright and then backing up with his palms raised to show her he hadn't meant her harm.

"Told you we should've eaten her before someone else did. But do you listen to your emotional support animal? Nope. Now he's going to eat her, and we won't grow big enough to have wings!" Ember complained, then shook within me. It caused the thing on my spine to rearrange, which forced a worried look on my face.

"Ladies, we're scouting, not pouting," Zyion rebuked, which caused Ember to snort.

"I'd be scouting your dick, but ours is waiting for us to rescue him," Ember pointed out. *"And he's not the smartest,*

but he's an excellent hunter. Plus, he kisses me and fucks Aria so hard that she sleeps soundly, and I don't have to hear her inner mind complain nonstop about everything that could go wrong on an endless loop."

"Seriously, you hear my thoughts, too?" I muttered in frustration. Was nothing I did private?

"No, nothing. That's why I'd make the best emotional support dragon."

"I see you gave yourself an upgrade already. Why am I not surprised," I said pointedly, *"that you already upgraded yourself from an 'animal' to a 'dragon'? Wait, how come I can't hear you when I'm the one riding bitch in my body? And is it your thoughts I'm always hearing? Because that would explain so much! I guess I probably sound the same to you sometimes?"* I asked, then remembered I couldn't see through our eyes when she was in control. If it was her inner thoughts, and not her actually speaking? That would explain why she was so horny all the time, or her endless complaints of hunger.

"That is your creature speaking directly to you, Aria. You cannot see through her eyes because you're not feral enough to peer through the eyes of a primal predator," Eva said *inside* my head. My hackles went up, but Ember preened. *"It's not your fault. None of us see through the eyes of our beast well. Mostly, it's shapes or outlines. Occasionally, they want us to see something and allow our sight to merge. You've been cutting Ember off, which I'm assuming you haven't realized."*

"Honestly, I didn't even know I had a shut-off switch from her accessing everything." Eva was about to be my best lesbian . . . best *friend. Fucking* Ember.

"Aria apparently wants to be your best lesbian now, Eva. But if you teach her how to shut me out, I'll fucking eat you."

"Probably not the best retort after the previous statement, Ember. Plus, I enjoy both men and women. So, if you want to eat me, I'm not opposed to meaningless sex." Eva's words caused my head to snap toward her, even as my eyes thinned and my lips tipped into a deep frown. My nose revealed the deep, scarlet color that spread from my ears to my chest.

"Um, thanks, but no thanks? I like my meat, Eva," I squeaked, which caused those around me to snicker.

"Am I missing something?" Killian asked, a frown line deepening between his brows. "Do you need me to hunt for you, Aria? I know Knox would if he were here, but I can do so if you need me to."

"I can take it or leave it personally. It isn't worth the heartache caused by what's attached to the other end of that pole. Meaningless sex, on the other hand, I can leave before they wake, which bypasses them becoming clingy bastards." Eva's words caused my shoulders to shake.

"What the fuck?" Acheron's angry shout jerked our focus from Eva's rant to where Siobhan, Avyanna, and Soraya were hitting him with large sticks. "Fucking stop hitting me! Fucking banshees!"

"You were trying to eat her!" Soraya scoffed, kicking his knee, finally sending him to the ground.

"And that is why we didn't eat her, Ember. Because friends are not food," I chirped.

"You should probably stop them," Esme muttered.

"I will in a moment. He deserves it for calling us *women* as if it is a slander against us." Crossing my arms over my chest, I laughed at the sight of the girls all whacking Acheron. Even as he threw his arms up to cover his head protectively from the branches they used to belt him with. Laughter threatened to spill from my lips at the sight of the large dragon prince on the ground, getting walloped by my girls.

"This is what you wanted to retrieve for a fucking fight?" Eva asked, horror gripping firmly to her tone.

"They're witches, Eva. Not monsters. And, yes, because if it goes down as I think it will, we're going to need to a few people with the ability to portal out of the Kingdom of Vākya." Strolling forward, I felt Ember's uncertainty. *"You have an issue with them, too?"*

"My issue isn't with them, Aria," she breathed. *"It's with you doing this while we're well . . . pregnant."* Ember had whispered the single word, and it sent me spiraling down into a dark, horrid void of fear.

I stopped dead in my tracks as bitterness roiled in my belly, scorching the back of my throat as I leaned over at the waist, throwing up. *"You fucking asshole,"* I whispered thickly. *"Damn it, Ember. Goddamn it! I told you no, didn't I?"*

Everyone around me stopped, staring as I up-chucked what little I'd managed to eat this morning. Fear pierced my heart as Ember's words echoed through them, repeating what she'd just disclosed. Pregnant? Now? Fuck! Glancing around, I met the pitying stares before groaning with horror and embarrassment.

"I'm sorry. But I promised Lennox I would so that he didn't force you to open our womb for him. Honestly, I didn't think it would happen so quickly after we'd lost the little girls."

"Don't. Don't even say it right now. It changes nothing. The

rest of you listening? I swear to my soul that I'll rip your fucking heart out if any of you mention it to Killian or Esme. For now, we aren't going there. I'm staying the course. Without Knox, I don't want to be a mother. Not in the middle of a bloody, brutal fucking war."

"Avyanna, Siobhan, and Soraya? It isn't nice to beat the welcome party," I called, before wiping my lips off with the back of the cloak I'd worn, and rinsing my mouth with water. My eyes drifted back, finding those who'd overheard Ember's confession peering at me, with both worry and pity clear on their faces. The sound of the girls' happy squeals forced me to turn toward them as they barreled over the clearing, racing right for us.

"You're finally back!" Siobhan said, hugging Esme to her. "I feared you and Aria had ended up trapped there. You'd never believe what's been happening here."

"Yeah, well, we lost track of time, I guess you could say." Esme grinned widely, tightly hugging her sister to her.

"It wasn't Knox who attacked you," I admitted, cutting their reunion short.

Soraya stepped beside me as Avyanna moved to the other side, observing the sisters still clinging to one another.

"I saw his eyes," Soraya snorted. "I'm so sorry, Aria."

"He isn't dead." I argued in a cold, angry tone. She turned, staring at me. "If we can reach him in time, I think I can try to remove the darkness before she can fully claim him."

"Aria," she said as her head tilted. "You don't know if that witch would've survived. No one knows how it would have ended. I'm sorry."

"Well, I have a better shot if I try than if I don't. Besides, I have a plan to get Knox away from Hecate. It's not an easy one, and it's going to be dangerous. If he engages Zyion, I can get close enough to attempt drawing out the darkness. I think I can force her darkness to release him. The issue is that he's not exactly aspiring to be rescued. He's under her control. If that doesn't work, we'd need to find another way to trap him. One that would hold him long enough for me to figure out how to force it out."

"You didn't think I might *need* to know I was the bait?" Zyion asked, as his and Eva's eyes rounded with shock.

"I intended to once we'd actually discussed the details." His head lowered, then elevated with an anxious look over face. Scoffing at my plan, he dropped his attention to my middle, frowning.

"You want everyone to risk their life for Knox, who may or may not already be gone? Aria, he could literally be a corpse and you wouldn't even know it."

"I saw the blue in his eyes, Soraya," I snapped, glaring at the ground while slowly counting inside my head for patience. "Knox took control of a warrior's body, then rode through the palace gates while driving it earlier today. He told me he was in there, and I need to see if it's true. I have to know he's not trapped in there, waiting to die."

"Okay," she whispered with a short exhale. "I'm in. However, Avyanna and the kids need a safe place to go. We've gained a few since you left *six* fucking *months* ago." Hurt was buried in her tone.

"For us, it was only a couple of days. We did not know we were gone that long. I'm sorry for not foreseeing it as a possibility. Trust me, no one is as sorry about it than I am right now."

"How is that even possible?" she countered as her forehead puckered in confusion.

"That's a longer conversation than I'm prepared to endure right now," I muttered. "Let's get the urchins to the library, then we'll head out from there."

CHAPTER 29
ARIA

I stood in the shadows, my eyes skimming over the towering, foreboding walls of the citadel. We'd cemented the plan and set out to execute it, praying we didn't end up executed ourselves for daring to trespass on their home field. We'd stopped along the way at various grids, tossing corpses aside, shattering Hecate's connection to them. She wouldn't dare allow anyone else to mend the grids, not when it would give up her secrets.

Hecate's grid was an extension of herself. It contained her weaknesses and strengths that she'd genetically designed to strengthen her further, making the details one of her closely-guarded secrets. Wiping out one would hurt her immensely, leaving her weakened as well. I'd counted on Hecate physically feeling the grids she'd fueled with the lifeless witches, which then would force her to inspect them.

I'd left her too weakened to manage a body jump, which meant she wouldn't leave the citadel. As I'd told Brander, you didn't allow your most valuable piece to leave the protection of an impenetrable fortress. You sent your strongest, which meant she'd send Knox. He was also one of the most powerful, feral beasts in the Nine Realms, which, if you had the option to wield against another, you did so.

"If it comes down to you or him, he's dead," Zyion hissed. "I didn't sacrifice my future to watch you throw it away for him. You are the future of the realms. Without you, our sacrifices were all in vain."

"You hold the course. I'll hold the light." I pivoted and met his hard gaze. "I'd rather burn the Realms to ashes and leave her nothing but the remnants of the land she coveted so much." Swallowing the pain, I exhaled a calming breath. "I have a reason to live. One that I promise you is going to force me to do everything in my power to ensure that I stay alive."

Zyion's face softened before he dropped his head forward. "You are no longer alone, Aria. If need be, I will stand beside you as you raise them. Not as your consort or your king, but as your friend." Zyion's words made my eyes watery, which wasn't what I needed right now. I needed to be composed, or I'd end up fucking everything up and losing Knox.

"There he is," I murmured, watching Knox and Hecate stroll to the edge of the gates.

Hecate waited with hopeful eyes, which caused my stomach to churn. Knox stopped, lifting lifeless eyes. His movements were jerky as he went back to her and leaned over, his mouth waiting for something. She leaned closer to him, kissing his lips—that didn't kiss back. A line formed in the middle of my eyebrows. The entire time she lathered his mouth with her tongue, Knox didn't reciprocate the kiss at all. Narrowing my eyes, I heard my jaw pop from straining, as he stood like a zombie waiting to be released.

"Did you see that?"

"That was peculiar. He didn't return the kiss," Zyion uttered. "Obviously, she didn't get all of him." Zyion's words sent a wealth of hope slicing through me. It at least confirmed I hadn't merely seen what I'd wanted to during their exchange.

The longer I watched, the more uncomfortable it became. Hecate didn't seem to care that he wasn't returning her forced affection. A tight ball built in my abdomen, spreading out as hatred simmered in my soul. My fingers curled against my palms, forming tight fists at my sides.

"She doesn't seem to care that he's merely . . . *there*. He's a mindless killing machine that she sends out to do her dirty work. That fucking bitch doesn't understand the storm in his vibrantly-colored eyes is the most beautiful thing to stare into as fury coils in his belly. Knox is the type of tree that stands tall within a forest as the wildfires burn everything around it." I wanted to scream and send down fireballs and lightning bolts, until everything around and inside the citadel died in anguish. To watch all of them burn until their flesh melted off of their face, then limbs, until their corpses fell lifelessly into the sludge of their rottenness. The murderous emotion forced a jolt of fear at how easily I'd do something for the man I loved.

"I think I now understand what they meant. We may survive this war, but will we be able to live with the trauma we inflict during it?" It felt as if someone had punched me in the gut and then drove me to the ground, continuing to assault me. A shuddered breath pushed from my lungs, compelling me to slam the door on my emotions, staring at the man I loved.

Zyion's head tilted, then turned as his eyes lingered on the sight of my salty tears trickling down my cheeks. "The thing about war is this: it will absolutely change you. How it changes you, though? Well, that is something only you can decide, Aria." Pushing the back of my hand against my lips, I fought to suck in fresh air. "If you do not wish to become a monster, then why are you running toward the fight? If I ever confided what I've done in the queen's name, you'd never look at me the same. Scylla might've removed the shackles, but her promise of freedom tastes like bitterness and ashes."

Forcing myself to return my gaze to Knox, I watched as he strolled out of the gate, turned, raised his hand, then swiftly brought it down. The gates lowered, sealing the only entrance to the citadel closed, while also trapping Hecate inside the wrought-iron bars. My teeth clenched as Knox turned, revealing black, lifeless eyes.

"You fear becoming a monster, but here's the truth. You need to become a monster in order to face one. There's no middle, it's everything or nothing. But being a monster? It's not who you are. It's what you eventually become when those around you continually push you away from what you desire most. I didn't give up everything I've ever wanted for some dainty, little spitfire. *Descensus Averno Facilis Est.*"

"The descent into hell is easy?"

"As is always so, falling is the easy part. People never talk about the descent, other than to expose weaknesses. That's why when you crawl your way back from hell, you bring all of the demons back with you. You make them yours and then send them out to show them how you rose from the fall. *Ancheronta movebo.*"

"I shall release hell." I wiped the tears with the back of my hand, staring as Hecate studied Knox's posture as he moved toward the mounts. "He's not like others, Zyion."

"I not only know exactly how he fights, but also how powerful Knox Karnavious is in mind, body and skill. If I didn't think he was such a bastard, I'd tell you that you chose well when you picked him for a mate. He's worthy of such a resilient woman, admittedly. Except, I absolutely know he's a cruel bastard." Bitterness seeped through his words.

"Stay far ahead of him, no matter what you hear. If he turns back or gets a hold of me, you are not to kill him. Wound him if you must, but we all walk away from this alive. I'll accept no less."

"Spoken like a true queen," he acknowledged with pride.

"He'll head north."

Zyion examined the tree beside us that revealed the gusting wind disturbing its leaves. Facing forward once more, his head angled, scrutinizing Knox, who stood by a sizeable steed.

"Please elaborate on why you assume he'll head north."

"Knox is a true hunter. The wind will carry scents. It'll make it more difficult for anyone to remain concealed if it continues. Knox hunts with the wind because he prefers not to waste time finding his prey, he'd take it down fast and easily."

I'd noted things like that. When I was in the cage, he'd gone south with the wind. It had allowed him to expediently produce sustenance without wasting time. The time he'd hunted several animals, the wind had beaten against the eastern side, proving he'd gone east, with the wind aiding him in tracking prey.

Those memories of the little things sliced through my mind, gutting me as I stood, watching him mount the horse with fluidity, without hesitation. Knox never hesitated in anything he did. It stood to reason that even when he wasn't in control, he'd still be efficient and steady. So then why hadn't he returned her kiss? The stallion reared back, as if even it felt the darkness of his passenger. Knox nudged the horse with his knees, then turned it, heading north as I'd predicted.

"If you love him, don't let him go. Ever," Zyion's soft words drifted to me from where he stood, forcing the reality of everything he'd lost down my throat. "True love never dies. Even if a person who once felt it, did."

"You'd have to cut off my legs to make me stop fighting for him. I love him, and I never got to tell him how I felt about him." That realization stung the hardest. I'd had the chance to say it to him, but I'd hesitated.

"Then after we've saved him? You should tell him how you feel. Tomorrows not promised. In times of war, death is waiting for us all to make one wrong move, or to have the slightest hesitation in judgement or battle. When it comes, it doesn't hesitate like we do."

"You are smarter than you look, Zyion." A smile spread over my lips, even though it failed to reach my eyes.

"Pain is a lesson we never forget." That one hurt, too. I didn't want to learn the lessons they had educated him on.

"Too easy, Knox," I muttered through the constricting in my throat. Spinning on my heel, I moved toward the others, who'd remained back, preventing too many scents from being carried on the breeze. "North, to the Valley of the Dead."

"How fitting," Soraya muttered.

"I don't need to tell you guys that this will not go as planned. There's no way to calculate what he'll do once everyone's scents surround him. My guess is that she's allowing Knox and Lennox to combine skills, but she's still in there, watching for any familiar interference. Knox's only weakness is family, which he's spent his entire life protecting from her."

"You're a weakness," Killian added softly. "If I had to guess what his greatest weakness is? It would be you." His words caused my insides to heat, even as a sad smile fluttered over my mouth. "Especially when you dress like that." His stare dropped to where the skirt I wore clung to my hips. "You know, he's going to see red at you wearing that outfit."

"Let's hope it's once he's in control of his own mind."

"You're practically naked, Aria. I can see your legs," Eva pointed out as she slipped from the portal, grimacing at my outfit. "What the hell are you wearing?"

"What is wrong with my legs?" The library had provided me with a razor, which I'd gladly used.

Gliding my palms against the lacey, rucked skirt. I'd

405

matched the skirt with a vintage lace-embroidered bustier. It would make it easier to run if needed. I divided my hair and braided it into two smaller ones, then threaded them into one thick braid that hung down my back. The boots I'd pictured were Doc Martens, which were safer and less likely to slip off if I needed to run from Knox, if things didn't pan out.

"When he goes for one, the others move in, then out when he goes for another. I'll make sure I'm close enough to ward off the magic, but as your saw last time, he's fucking fast. I'll be faster now that I know he's drawing from her." Verbalizing where his power came from sent ice rushing through my veins.

"If Killian is right, then Zyion's presence near me will trigger Knox, which will make him struggle against her control. Once he does, he should go for Zyion, which will buy some time. If he doesn't, we'll need to switch courses quickly. Zyion, if you keep Knox in the line of salt around the location we've set at the grid, I will be able to draw the darkness out. Though, I honestly don't know how long it will take or if it will work on the first attempt. If that's the case, we go to the next, because once engaged, I believe he will follow us."

"How will we know if it worked?" Esme questioned.

"I'm not sure. He'll either go down, regain control of himself, or die. I've only attempted it once, and as far as I know, I'm the only one who's ever attempted to do so before. It left me tapped out of almost all my magic when Knox broke the connection."

"Has there been an entire day since you entered the Nine Realms, where everyone isn't trying to kill you?"

Killian asked, which caused a smirk to twitch over my lips.

"With Knox, yes," I responded sadly. He was my protector, even when he thought of me as his enemy. Sure, I'd had to worry about his moods, but they'd been triggered by the chest, mostly.

"Trust me, he was killing something," Killian scoffed before releasing a soft chuckle.

Chewing my lip, I considered the backup plan, which wasn't ideal. "If shit goes wrong, I'll run. He'll follow me. That's where you ladies come into play. You ladies will open a portal, then you'll open another far enough away so that you can easily escape, but be sure to maintain sight of the first one. Once you're through, you will do the same thing again. If Knox cannot be contained or freed, we'll continually move until the men and Esmeralda can create another salt barrier. Soraya, you'll open the first. Siobhan, the second. If Knox gives chase, I'll use the first as you two enter the second, immediately setting the next one. There will be seconds between jumps. I cannot stress this enough, but you cannot stop for anything."

"What if they don't get there before Knox catches you?" Esme asked thickly. "Aria?"

"Then I do whatever it takes to keep us both alive until someone reaches us," I whispered, though the heat scorching my eyes and behind my nose.

"That's the worst fucking idea I've ever heard," she acknowledged, with tears rolling free. "I won't let him kill you."

"You won't interfere, Esmeralda. That's not happening." My voice shook with my fear and worry of her intervening. "I cannot afford to have my attention divided. Knox will fight. He has to. If not, she'll make him kill me. It will make it less troublesome for her to fracture his mind and then finally destroy his soul."

"I can't sit there and watch you die. Knox is faster, stronger, and he's being driven by a murderous bitch who seriously wants you dead." The tears in her throat were so thick that they almost choked me instead of her.

"You won't have to," Killian assured. "We take him down. Then she removes the darkness from Knox. If we have to go with Plan B, I'll ensure he doesn't harm Aria, Esme. I'll do what he ordered me to do in order to save her and our people." At Killian's reassurance, Esme's eyes drifted to him, which caused Basilius to rattle with possessiveness.

"I think the *fuck* not," I snapped sharply, as a rattle tried to claw its way up my throat. "Killian, I am saving Knox. You need to at least allow me to try to save him. He'd come for me, just as he'd come for anyone else here if they were in trouble.".

"Knox wouldn't want that for you. He'd want you to live, even if it meant letting him go, Aria. If he killed you and somehow survived? How do you see that playing out?" Killian countered with a plea burning in his eyes.

"No. No, Knox has to live. He has to because I can't breathe without him." The words trickled from my lips, as gasps of shuddered breaths forced their way through the pain gripping my throat. "He's going to be a father. Hecate doesn't get to win. Do you fucking hear me?" My voice trembled with agony and paralyzing fear. "Hecate doesn't get to win this time. She's taken everything from Knox. I'll be damned if she takes his life away from him, too. Stick to the fucking plan. I give you my word that if shit goes sideways, I'll get everyone out. We'll regroup and figure out a different way to get him back."

"You're pregnant?" Killian asked through narrowed eyes. "Aria?"

"Ember told me right before the girls began hitting Acheron. It changes *nothing*."

"It fucking changes *everything*. Women don't go into battle pregnant!"

"Yes, they fucking do. A woman's life is a never-ending war, Killian. Women fight from the moment they take their first breath until they breathe their last. They've gone to war plenty of times before, and I will be no different from the women who came before me. I can fight her pregnant. I have to do this. I took precautions to ensure that what happened last time doesn't happen again." Shaking my head, I straightened my spine and looked around at the faces before me.

"I shouldn't have placed you in a box with the women I know, Aria. You're truly nothing like them, but Knox wouldn't come back from harming you. He *wouldn't* come back from it if you're harmed, or worse, you died."

"I am no damsel, Killian. I'm going to go save my fucking dragon. With or without you. That's your choice to make. I've made mine."

"You've come a long way since the naïve, soft girl we met not long ago." Killian smiled, his eyes sparkling with mirth.

"Plan B is I run, he chases and I don't stop running. Ember can escape him. She's aware of the problem at hand. In the abandoned village three miles south of here, there's a well. It's spelled already, and it's deep. If I can get him in it, we can use it. Plan C will be nuclear. Do you all understand the plan?" When they nodded, I felt a prickle of fear at the idea of running from Knox. He was a better hunter, better runner, better fucking everything than I was.

"What aren't you saying?" Esme asked, her perceptive stare festering with worry.

"It's not just me who needs him back," I admitted. "Knox has had access to the Library of Knowledge, which contains a detailed history of everything that's occurred, every creature's creation, their weaknesses. By taking him, she's taken the library, as well. Since he was a child, that has been his favorite place. He's an archive in which she can continually pull information from, against all of us. It holds both the phoenix and dragon histories, but also what can wipe the races out? If she maintains control? We're not fucked. We'll all go extinct. So, no. She can't keep the repository of knowledge he holds within his mind. Even if his soul dies, the knowledge and shit that aren't a part of his soul, like memories, remain."

"That's why Julia never remembered me," Soraya uttered.

"Exactly why she didn't. Julia's soul left long before Hecate killed her body." Smiling sadly at her, I felt Ember adding warmth to tell me she was there. "We tie emotions to faces instead of souls. But we are merely souls in outer shells, which often leave when they become too much to carry around. You said you sister was gentle, so she didn't stick around long enough to feel the pain Hecate would've forced her to feel."

"You're lying, but I'll take it," she said tightly. "Lies are what we feed on nowadays. While we pray for better ones to find us."

"Lies, or days?" Esme asked with her eyebrows shoved together.

"I'm not as good as Aria with the whole 'speech' shit," she scoffed with a soft shrug. "I was giving it a whirl."

"Do me a solid, Soraya, leave the speeches for the queen?" Esme snorted, even as she put on a brave face, smiling. Soraya bumped Esme's shoulder, which sent Esme into Siobhan, who leaned her head against her.

"You bitches know we're all going to die. If we don't, Aria is going to go back to demanding I help her hide a body." Soraya and Siobhan's stares slid to me at Esme's statement.

"It's a metaphor. We're not actually digging a grave to hide a body. That would be way too much work when Ember could just eat the evidence." At my explanation, Esme's mouth dropped open.

"This is why we can't be best friends." Folding her arms over her breasts, she offered me a withering stare.

"I thought you two were so close because you were lesbians," Acheron offered while scratching his head as confusion stamped over his face.

"What?" Esmeralda demanded.

"That's what Aria's creature said. That you two are the *best* lesbians."

Esme's eyes swung toward me, rounding wider as she absorbed what he'd said. "Are you fucking me?"

"Are you offering to . . . wait, what's happening here?" I replied, trying to figure out what she'd meant. "I mean, honestly, Esme? I like meat. I'm a carnivore. Of course, if that's what you prefer? Then I'll support you wholeheartedly on your vegan diet of that pink, meatless taco. Shit, I already have a rainbow unicorn jacket, so I'm dressed for the job as your bestie already!" Her nose scrunched before her head tilted to the side.

"So, this *isn't* a joke?"

"Oh, I see." I grimaced as color burned my cheeks. I was so only eating lettuce for the next fifty years to punish Ember for this shit. "No, you're supposed to say '*You're* not fucking *with* me.' See, that's why it's important to pay attention if you intend to steal my slang. Either that, or you'll continue walking around, asking people to fuck you."

"What did I say?"

"Are you fucking me?" I asked and fluttered my lashes dramatically.

"I seriously didn't ask you to fuck me."

"Did too," Acheron argued.

"Ladies and Acheron, if we don't leave soon, we'll lose him," Eva said, forcing us back to reality.

I stared at Esme, who returned the look of fear flowing through us. It took work to push down my emotions and offer her a reassuring grin.

"Who wants to live forever, anyway?" I asked.

"Us? Remember that, Aria. You don't want to be captured or die. In fact, since you're pregnant, you need to promise me you'll be smart and stay safe," she said through alligator tears, as her lips quivered and her face scrunched into something akin to the Hunchback of Notre Dame.

"Damn, you're not a pretty crier. How have I never noticed that before?" I asked, which had her stopping mid-sob. Affronted, she wiped her tears away. "I will not die today. Nor am I going to be killed by her. That's not how my story goes. Let's go bag us a beast, hmm?"

CHAPTER 30
ARIA

The wind raged around the valley, violently hammering against the trees surrounding the location of the grid. Powerful gusts flowed from the mountains, then brutally advanced into the Valley of the Dead. Angry, dark clouds rumbled as the threat of rain clung heavily in the air. Clouds encased the world in an eerie darkness, forcing the land to seem foreboding even as the sensation of malevolence slithered over my uncovered flesh.

The ominous feeling swirling through my stomach caused goosebumps to spread over my flesh. I felt the sensation of being watched, forcing the hair to raise on the back of my nape. If the tension and anticipation of an attack were anything to go on, the others felt it, too. A clap of thunder caused me to jerk before exhaling a shuddered puff of air from my lungs to steady myself.

A savage bolt of lightning shot across the sky above us, bathing us in indigo light as the scent of ozone and dead vegetation burned my nose. Following behind it, a deaf-

415

ening boom of thunder echoed through the valley, rolling down the mountain. Forcing those around me to search the dark corners of the forest for any hint of Knox hiding within them.

"Something feels off," I muttered. "Do you feel that?" Beyond the storm, there was no sound other than the storm at all. Almost as if something had spooked the wildlife into silence. Turning, I stared at Zyion, whose words were being swallowed by the wind. *"Ember? Can you see him or feel him close by? I can sense him staring right at me. But I can't, for the life of me, discern where he is."*

"He's hunting us, Aria. Knox is deciding the best way to isolate us from the others. I can taste the threat thickening in the air, drifting with a heavy intent of predatorial violence. I don't think we should be here. He wants us dead. Our mate wants us destroyed."

"Not our *mate, Ember. He isn't our mate right now. He's being controlled by Hecate. There's no Knox or Lennox inside his mind right now. Nothing he does will be his choice. I need you to understand that he's not in control any longer. I also need you to promise me something."*

"Anything," she replied with a heaviness I'd never heard from her before.

"No matter what happens, you get us out of here. Be ready to run if shit goes south. He's not in control, but she'll use all his heightened speed and senses to catch us. I need you to ensure he doesn't."

"I will do my best, Aria. But Knox is much faster than we are."

"I know he is."

"They are stronger this time. This time, they're not only

yours and Knox's babes, they're ours. All of ours. Do not fear for them, for they are indestructible. Lennox and I planted the seeds, but you and Knox will grow them. He needs to come back to us. We need him too. No one else will kiss me, Aria." Ember's fear of never being kissed again registered low on the list, but it still made tears swim in my eyes. I knew explicitly how she felt. I wanted him back, too.

The shadows bathed the forest in a chilling cover of darkness. Knitting my eyebrows together as I peered into the shadows, I felt them rounding as the bolt of lightning sliced through the sky, revealing the form standing directly across from me. Under the cover of darkness within the obscurity of the trees sheltering him, Knox stood. The dim silhouette outlined only by the blinding, white light of the bolts zipping through the clouds above us.

My heartbeat stalled and then began beating against my ribcage at a dangerous pace. His eyes slid down my frame, and where I'd once felt only desirable heat from the action, now there was only iciness that scraped down every single inch of my frame. No words escaped my lips in warning. A chill shot down my spine, even as Knox stepped out from beneath the forest.

Knox's movements weren't hurried, as if he had not a worry in the world. Each powerful stride brought him closer to us. My fingers curled into my palms as they formed a tight, nervous fist at my sides. The closer he got, the more I felt the need to run away. His sightless, black eyes remained anchored on my face the entire trek across the clearing.

"Are you planning to fight me, Little Monster?" he purred, the sound like silk against my mind.

"No," I uttered while scanning his eyes for the sliver of blue, needing to know he was in there. The idea of someone else having control over this man was inconceivable. He was one of the most powerful beings within the Nine Realms, but yet she'd got to him.

Knox's mouth tugged up on one side farther than the other. The wickedly dark smile softened his entire face, as impossible as it seemed. My heart wrenched as his head tilted. The familiarness of the look threatened to destroy what remained of my heart, without him there to hold it together.

"Well, I know you're not planning to fuck me. So, what have you planned for us to do out here?" His eyes drifted to my clenched fists and then drove back to the anguish apparent in my face. "Oh, my sweet, gorgeous girl. Are you intending to murder me? Even if you take my life, she'll continue using my worthless corpse."

"Not if you fight her," I begged, not caring how pathetic or desperate I sounded or if Hecate heard my words. "Help me fight her and rid you of her influence, Knox. I can save you if you'll let me."

"I don't want to be saved. I prefer Hecate's bed to yours. Her skill's unmatched for pleasure."

"Like when you kissed her on your way out of the citadel? I get it, Hecate, that you got him, but that oily slime you forced into him doesn't compel him to do what you really want. from him. Does it? He wouldn't even kiss your poisonous lips back."

The sound of a sword sliding through a scabbard ripped through the air. My eyes widened as the flash of steel aimed for my neck. Unable to move, I watched as

Knox's blade rushed toward my throat. The thundering echo of the blade against the hard steel of another sword vibrated in my bones, rattling my teeth.

Killian's fingers wrapped around my upper biceps, biting into the flesh as he jerked me backward in time as the sparks from the colliding blades, barely missing me. With frightening strength, Knox slashed his sword toward Zyion's blade as he deflected and blocked each angry, aggressive blow.

Realizing he couldn't get to me without going through Zyion first, Knox squared up to him, then swung with alarming speed and accuracy. Zyion blocked, his arms shaking with every blow. Together, the men danced with agile, sleek moves that looking more like a dance than a battle. In perfectly balanced steps, they both moved forward, then back, striking blades as sparks began adding a pulsating glow from the echo of steel colliding against steel.

Each strike made my heart race a little faster. To win, Zyion had to take Knox into the salt barrier, where he would have to rely on his defensive skills to fend off Knox's aggressive, lethally-aimed strikes. If Knox took Zyion down, that was it. He'd mercilessly slaughter Zyion, as there was no humanity behind the creature wielding the fortified blade that he attacked with.

If Zyion went down, I'd be forced, along with the others presently watching the vicious assault, to flee for our lives. Knox had to be forced into the circle, or at least one of the others we'd spent endless hours placing in case he couldn't be walked into this one easily. Zyion pushed Knox forward,

419

but for every one step forward, Knox pushed him two steps back.

Stepping closer, I lifted my hands, fighting the worry over the battle waging before us as I tried to find the end of the thread of darkness, or something to grab on to. I needed a way to unravel the layers Hecate had needed in order to control Knox. No matter how hard I searched, I continually came up empty. It was as if she'd forgone merely adding the slimy layers, and poured it into him, instead.

"Do you honestly think I'd allow you to have *my* girl?" Knox snarled vehemently. His eyes crying the black sludge in rivers of tears.

"Fuck you, Karnavious."

Realization that it wouldn't work as we'd expected, tightened painfully around my heart like a vice, squeezing until my heart fluttered. Each violent strike clattered like a war drum into the night. How much longer could Zyion endure defending before being forced to go on the offense?

Closing my eyes, I tried again to find a way to unravel the insane amount of darkness within Knox. Hecate had either anticipated I'd try to remove it, or she'd felt it when I'd attempted to remove the darkness before. Each attempt drained the well within me, as if I was merely feeding Knox my power. It was worrisome, forcing me to back out, even as frustration washed through me.

"You think I'll let her live? You're smarter than that," Knox taunted, his words bitter with acid burning me from each thing he said.

"I am smarter," Zyion returned.

If he didn't start taunting Knox back, we'd never force

him to the surface. What the hell was he waiting for? An invitation? I'd told him to use whatever he needed to incite and provoke Knox harshly. We had to force him to fight against Hecate's hold. Alone, we'd fail to eviscerate her from his being.

"You don't have it in you to fuck Aria the way she needs it, Vicious. That little slut takes a beating and still begs for more. She'd fucking eat you up and spit you out, little boy," Knox sneered. While I wasn't concerned about the world's opinion of me, I also didn't want it to be disclosed. "Hell, she even took my entire knot into that greedy cunt of hers and liked it like the filthy whore she is. You think you'll ever be able to *fulfill* her needs? Nah, that's right. The first girl you loved? Didn't that bitch swan dive off of a cliff? Total header, right? Oh, I remember now. The idea of returning to your tiny pathetic prick after having a real dragon made her want to die, right? She knew you'd be unable to quench her thirst for a real man so she did what was needed to escape you."

Zyion's strike against Knox's blade sent him back, forcing him to dig his feet in as he smoothly countered it. Knox's fingers tightened against the pummel of the blade, as sweat trickled down my back. My nails pricked against my flesh as my stomach roiled with tension. Knox swung then lifted his foot, kicking Zyion in the chest, sending him staggering back a few steps. The color fled from my face as I watched Knox bring his sword back, then swung it with a killing blow. Zyion turned just in time, missing the blade connecting with his chest by a hair's breadth.

"Do you remember the second woman? I do. I remember her screaming for you as I ended her life. And she did, Zyion. She pleaded for me not to kill her, too. But I ensured she sang for me before I allowed her to find the blissful nothingness of death. That whore sang like an angel as she took every fucking inch of my blade through her supple, tender flesh. So, do you honestly think I'd entrust my whore with you? You'll never have her, Vicious. At least, not while I still live." Fear fluttered through my awareness as the vicious determination on Zyion's face, as his body grew taut and rigid with murderous rage.

"I already fucking have her, Karnavious. I've had her many fucking times, and I'll have her many fucking more now that you're out of the way. And your girl? She sings so fucking pretty when I'm inside her. Fucking hell, it is so deliciously beguiling to want her to continually sing her sweet, lustful song again so soon after I just had it humming around my cock as I fucked her throat, raw. Your girl even sang my praises as she purred against my lips, promising to be a good little slut and let me use her however I'd like once we've finished up here. Of course, I wouldn't say she sang like an angel, but she did gag prettily as I forced my entire cock down her throat. She's exquisitely primal. That is why you like her so much, isn't it? She doesn't just give you her submission, she makes you fucking take it from her."

My eyes fluttered in shock at his words, even as Killian's gaze burned into the side of my head. I had told him to use whatever he could to bring Knox to the surface. There hadn't been time to specify what would be out of line.

Turning to glance back at him, I exhaled before whispering, "I said whatever it took, Killian. Do you honestly think I'd have fucked Zyion and then brought him home with me to meet Knox?"

"You best hope he doesn't remember what Zyion just said, Aria. Knox has spent his life hunting Zyion because he's the one who removed the head of Dracarius Karnavious. Knox's grandfather and the former King of Norvalla. You brought him right to him too," he hissed back with his eyes on the duo currently fighting. "If he thinks you fucked him, there won't be any coming back from that."

"That pussy of hers?" Zyion asked. "It's fucking delicious, isn't it? She let me fuck it like I owned it. I enjoyed every whimpered gasp as I stretched her tight pussy out to ensure it knew who it belonged to, though. That girl is vicious, and knows how to fuck, I'll give you that much. However, that knot of yours must not be as impressive as you think. Getting into her cunt wasn't an easy feat. Her walls were a snug fit, but easier once I'd had a few good, hard, lengthy bouts of breeding her. But I wasn't hearing Aria complaining about the length or width of my prick, Knox. But I assure you, before I'd finished with her, my seeds were planted and growing in her womb. She's going to make me a daddy."

Knox stumbled, but as quickly as he did, he recovered. The sound of his steel crashing against Zyion's rang out through the darkening night. Every move was fluid, graceful, and driven by murderous rage. Horror entered my mind as the men became blurs of movement, each aggressive slice faster than my mind could process or my eyes could even register.

I'd known Knox moved with an impossible, inhuman speed. But I'd never considered it being employed in a sword fight. Zyion still met every swing with a defensive blow. Zyion was tiring from the relentless blows vibrating through his arms. Knox parried, then sent his blade thrusting forward, piercing Zyion's shoulder. His scream of pain tore through the night as horror shot through me faster than any bullet could have.

Zyion stepped back, freeing himself of the blade, then just managed to lift his blade to defend himself as Knox brought his sword down. Horror tore through my mind as Zyion tried to regain his footing with angry, deafening blows colliding against his blade. The moment Zyion was on his feet, Knox knocked Zyion's blade aside with a downward sweep of his own.

As if the sky heard and felt the horror unfolding beneath it, it released a deluge of rain. A lightning bolt ripped across the darkened space above us, then forked as it spread out in several directions. A white light filled the scene, even as a sharp crack of thunder followed behind the flashing light. Several more bolts shot like arrows throughout the night skies, one after another. Thunder mirrored the beat of a war drum as the world went still around us.

Knox brought his blade down with lethal accuracy. A cry of frustration tore from my lips as I sent my magic toward both men, sending them soaring backward and away from one another. Both men collided with the murky, wet ground. Only, Zyion didn't get up as quickly as Knox, who wasn't the type to ever stay down.

Knox planted his palms against the earthen floor and pushed up with practiced strength, throwing himself back onto his feet with the gracefulness of a cat. Then he glanced at Zyion, who was searching the area for any sign of Knox, and looked back at me with fear. Knox's head turned, following Zyion's stare until it landed on me. The moment it did, horror gripped my heart, working to rip it free of my chest. One step toward me, then another. My footsteps mirrored each step he took forward. My lips parted to issue a warning, but no sound escaped past the knot swelled in my throat as a vicious smile twisted over his mouth.

"Aria, run!" Zyion snarled, which jerked me from the shock of what was unfolding.

Knox was going to catch me. Hecate would then force him to end my life, right along with the lives of his unborn children. Adrenaline shot through my veins, forcing a surge of desperation to bite into my mind. Turning on my heel, I shot toward the dense forest.

CHAPTER 31
ARIA

The entire forest seemed to come alive the moment I entered it in a dead run. As if the storm felt my battling emotions, it hammered down on the entire wooded lands. The air shook with loud rumbling as branches persistently snapped beneath my feet. An earthy scent of pine needles, dampened earth and moist timber battled against my senses. A bolt of lightning shot straight down, crashing into a tree in front of me. The branch it hit clattered to the forest floor, seconds before the entire tree shook against another crackling bolt of violet light. Another explosion sounded behind me, forcing the entire forest to shake.

My legs pumped hard as I flew across the forest, knowing that if I stopped, he'd kill me. Zyion hadn't been able to back him into the salt circle, which wouldn't have held anyway. Not with the rain washing it away as it melted the grains. The only light offered within the dense pines, was bolt after bolt of vivid lightning that mirrored camera flashes.

A dead tree blocked the path, forcing me to veer to the right. I caught sight of Knox, alarmingly close behind me. Ember's warmth spread through me, and my legs pumped faster, harder to put distance between us and him. In the darkness, I struggled to distinguish between the escape path and any barriers that were in my way. I didn't dare stop to attempt opening a portal, not with Knox so close on my heels.

I rushed over a hill and hit a slick patch of mud that took my feet out from under me, sending me head over feet and pain tearing through my body. I spun incessantly, crashing violently with boulders, tree limbs, and other debris as I rolled down the steep incline at a terrifying speed. My head smashed into a sharp rock jutting up from the muddied ground, which caused a desperate shriek to rip from my lungs. The worst part was that every roll revealed Knox rushing down the sharp incline on sure-footed steps.

The moment I reached the bottom, my back slammed against something sharp, sending searing pain down my spine, burning the entire length down to the tips of my toes. Raw agony wrenched through every fiber of my being, as a metallic taste filled my mouth. Forcing my limbs to work, it felt as if I were being dragged up from a grave instead of the hazardously treacherous ground.

"Ember!"

"On it," she whispered, then shot energy to each limb, forcing the raw, undiluted adrenaline to fuel my body. *"I can't take control!"* she snarled, panic tearing through her voice as black dots filled my vision. *"Run, now!"* Her terror shot through me, forcing me to burst into a sprint as the

sound of branches snapped right behind me. *"Something is stopping me from being able to force your control to yield to mine."*

"Come on, Aria. Let's fucking play," Knox taunted. His words sent a silent scream bubbling to my lips, but it never broke free. "I want to hear just how pretty you sing choking on my fucking knot, slut!"

Tears pricked my eyes, blurring my vision. Fiery agony burned the muscles of my thighs. Every breath was a struggle to draw, and pain pulsed through my side, letting me know at least one of my ribs had snapped. Anguish sparked in my skull, the center of pressure expanding like a spider web as it stretched across my skull, firing down my neck and spine.

"Faster. You've got to fucking move faster, Aria!" Ember's scream forced me to pick up speed, even as she forced an inhuman burst of speed to tear through me.

Calming my mind, I whispered the incantation for the dead army to rise. The sound of fists pushing up through the ground began resonating thru the area behind me. Sending a signal, I imposed the necessity for them to slow the predator who was relentlessly hunting me. Hindering his ability to reach me. The sound of something being sent sailing through the air forced confusion to flutter through my mind, until the lifeless body of a man slammed into the tree in front of me.

Holy fuck!

Knox was throwing bodies of the dead *at* me! Another crashed into a tree a few steps ahead of me, and I leaped over it, darting between the trees as the sound of another flowed into my ears. The odor of coppery tang coming from my wounds sent worry of how badly I'd hurt myself, humming to my brain. Spinning at the sound of something coming toward me fast, I ducked right as a decapitated head whizzed past.

Knox's eyes held mine as he gripped the edge of his shirt, peeling it up from his chest and then over his head. Prowling toward me, I watched the corpses rushing toward him, but where they'd been intended to hinder, they'd become his weapons as he plucked another head off as if he was picking a fucking flower. Nonchalantly, he stepped out of their reach. Tossing one skull in his hand, he pulled his arm back and sent it forcefully toward me. I evaded it, finding it narrowly missed its target, my breath, jagged puffs of air that stung my lungs.

Rain persistently pelted my heated flesh, shocking with its icy-cold chill that weighed me down. Searching the surrounding area in the darkened woods, I didn't see any of the others within sight. Panic surged through my psyche, realizing I'd ended up rushing in the opposite direction from the abandoned town. In my urgency to escape capture, I'd ended up tumbling down the hill, losing the ability to discern which way to run. A frightening awareness of being lost in the woods with Knox, who wanted to murder me, sent paralyzing fear to my mind.

"Did you make him the same promises you made me?" he asked, as his head angled to the side, studying my face. He tossed the skull in his hand, as if it were a ball and not a bodiless head. "See, I thought you were falling in love with me. You made me think it so effortlessly. Didn't you? Those lethal, enchanting lips of yours spew nothing but vitriol and empty promises when they flap. Hell, maybe after I've finished using the others, I'll rip those pretty pink lips off and shove them into that ravenous cunt of yours. Would you like that?"

"You have to fight it, Knox. You're the strongest, most stubborn asshole I know. If anyone can push the bitch out, it's you! So fucking fight her! *I* need *you*. Do you hear me? I fucking need you! I can't do this without you. I *love* you. I've always loved you. Come back to me. Don't make me do this. I don't want to do this," I pleaded as giant, grief-stricken sobs rocked through my chest. A scream tore free as he sent the head right for mine.

Spinning on my heel, I dashed the opposite way of the verdantly green moss covering one side of the tree I'd paused beside. He snarled as his rattle forced my stomach to contract before reacting to the enticing familiarity. My nipples hardened with the vibration he created. The next rattle was worse yet. His predominant pitch rocked me from my head to my toes.

I refused to stop fighting to live. Our bond was indestructible, even in the face of Hecate's influence. Thwarting his ability to control my body's response, I used my magic to project the song playing inside my head. "Arcade" by Duncan Laurence blasted through the woods. It echoed around us and carried on the wind.

My lungs burned as if I was inhaling razor blades, slicing them wide open. I prayed the sound would alert the others of my current location. Every time my foot landed against the twig-carpeted floor of the forest, it drove agonizing pain up the length of my leg. My arms moved with every step I took, pumping through me as I felt

Ember's frustration coming through to flood my mind with her helplessness.

I was weakening. That my feet were gradually becoming harder to lift from the ground told me I was in trouble. "Under Your Scars" by Godsmack echoed through me, filling the space between us. Butterfly wings the color of night, fluttered in my vision.

Turning my head at the deafening crack of a branch snapping behind me, I caught a blur of movement out of the corner of my eye. Then he collided into my body. Knox's arms were steel bands around my waist. A scream ripped from my lungs as he twisted us both through the air, as we spun from the sheer force with which he'd collided against me.

The turbulent, spiraling assault flung my body, sending it hitting hard against the ground in an excruciating, bone-jarring crash that knocked the breath from my lungs. The landing was cruel, making me roll numerous times as dangerously pointed branches gouged into my skin. The sob that burst free from my lungs sent blood splattering from my lips.

I forced myself up, but dropped back as anguish tore through my frame. I heard Knox's heavy footfalls, which were progressively moving toward my motionless, broken body. Tears of defeat swam in my vision as he bent down, then gripped my ankle, using it to forcefully flip me over onto my back.

"You look lovely with all that blood covering your exquisite body. I think it's my favorite color on you. It brings out the defeat burning in your pretty, blue eyes. Is that defeat simmering in them? I think I prefer it shining from them, as well."

I couldn't get words past the regret swelling in my throat. Failure slid over me like fire ants biting into flesh. Forcing air into my lungs, I flinched as he stooped, threading his fingers through my hair. Lifting me by it, a shriek tore from my lungs. Knox straightened to his full height and brought my body flush against his hard chest.

"Did you allow him to touch what belongs to me, Aria?" In his voice, a dark warning whispered raspily within the air. The longer I remained silent, the more threatening his darkness became.

"No! Never. I'd never let another touch me. It's only ever been you. Knox, please fight her. Fight her for us. For you and me. I love you. I love you so fucking much it is tearing me apart. You're my everything. You're all I've ever wanted. No other has ever held my heart, only you."

"Is that so? Ironically, I'm also intending to rip you apart. First, I want to know how bad it hurts knowing you've fucking lost, little girl."

"I'm not done yet! You stupid, selfish cunt," I roared, kicking him in the balls. A strangled scream of thunderous rage burst from his lips.

My hair slid from his grip, and I landed hard on the ground, but there was nothing left of the fight within me. A tormented cry of infuriation tore from my lungs, even as he rushed toward me as I clumsily attempted to stagger back to my feet. Strong hands locked around my upper arm, then plucked me from the ground, forcefully shoving my spine achingly against the hard trunk of a nearby tree.

"Fucking bitch," he hissed as his mouth lowered against mine. My eyes fluttered close seconds before it drifted against mine, his heated lips touching mine with the softest kiss. A ravenous, whimpered whisper of grief and longing vibrated from my lips, devoured voraciously from his. "I hate you for letting that bastard touch what is only mine to know." His teeth captured my lip, applying enough pressure that I gasped from the burning pain. "Fight me all you like, Aria. I am your jury, judge and executioner." His tongue delved between my lips, finding mine, then kissed me until I felt myself steadily falling down into the endless well of despair.

He'd kissed me. Fucking kissed me with the same lips he'd touched motionlessly against Hecate's. But where he'd failed to return or join in her kiss, he'd devoured mine as if he were starving for more. Just as he'd told me, he was my jury, judge and executioner.

Knox drew back at the sound of feet thrashing over the ground, reverberated around us. His dismal obsidian pools drifted from the men rushing toward us, then slid back to lock with mine. A wicked chuckle exited his lips, turning menacing, sinister.

"I'm going to need to borrow some of that vast magic you house. Don't worry, I don't intend to give it back. Let's be honest here, you no longer need it because you're fucking dead. You just haven't caught up to that idea, yet." Knox's lips parted, then pressed against mine as his arm extended, aimed his palm at the men charging toward us. Then a spasm shot through me as he began sucking the magic directly from my soul. The agony cruelly tore through every inch of my body, sparing nothing as it pushed through me.

Fear, failure and grief settled within me, weighing against my chest. He'd ripped my power straight from my lips. He consumed it aggressively, unconcerned with how it ripped me asunder. My feet had left the soil before I realized he'd collared my throat, fingers digging into my jaw as he lifted me.

The men collided against a barrier Knox had erected. Ice shot through my veins, as surely as if he'd injected it there himself. He'd siphoned too much magic, draining me to the point I felt nullified.

"No!" Esme's horrified shriek forced my eyes to flutter closed. "Aria, fight him!"

"She can't," Knox purred, his nose rubbing against my cheek. "This is *your* savior? How pathetic." Knox cruelly gripped my arm, then gripped a merciless hold on my throat. He continued, lifting me until my feet dangled, searching for the ground. "Are you ready to sing for me? I bet you'll sing so fucking pretty when I rip your heart out." He tossed me to the ground, which sent the air from my lungs in a whoosh of sound.

"Fight me, motherfucker!" Esme snarled, as her eyes flooded with tears streaming freely down her cheeks. "Fucking fight, Aria. Please. Oh, gods, please get up! I fucking need you. Do you hear me? Fight him!"

"Aria, do it," Killian demanded, his voice strained. "Knox wouldn't want you to be a fucking martyr. Fight. Do what you do best and kill him!"

I couldn't fight against him even if I wanted to do so. He'd taken all of my reserved magic, draining me until only a tiny whisper of it remained tethered in my center.

"Aria," Siobhan whispered, kneeling down at eye level

with me. "Bring it down. Remove the shield so we can do what you cannot bring yourself to do. Without you, everything is lost. We lose you. There's no reason to keep fighting. Don't let her take that from us. We need you as much as he does."

Crawling over the wet, rain-soaked floor of the forest, I moaned as his booted foot slid beneath my belly, rolling me onto my back. Staring into the sightless, murky eyes, I exhaled, knowing it was coming. My chest rose and fell with the strenuous, quick gasps fighting to bring enough air into my lungs to form words.

"Knox, it's Aria!" Killian cried, his hands singing against the barrier preventing him from intervening.

"Get up, Aria," Zyion demanded. "Get the fuck up. You're stronger than this. I know you are. Now fight back, damn it."

It was better that way. Even better if he'd block them all from witnessing what he intended to do to me. Not that I'd get so lucky. He wasn't fighting against Hecate's control, not that I could tell through the blurriness of my vision. A shuddered breath left my lips, sending bubbled blood speckling against the pale flesh of my skin.

"I know who the fuck she is. Don't worry, Killian. Once I'm done removing her heart, I'm coming for yours next. And you?" Knox pointed his finger toward Zyion. "You, I'm going to rip apart piece by fucking piece for touching her. She is mine."

"I didn't touch her!" he snarled, his eyes wide with helplessness as he watched Knox tipping his head back, smiling.

"Even so, you'll both die screaming for me," he purred in a raspy tenor.

"Get up! Aria, fucking move! Let Ember help you!"

"She can't help her. Ember, like Lennox, is blocked until it pleases Hecate to release them from her hold. After all, she's the queen now."

What he'd said issued fear into my soul, carving through the sharp, unkind fingers of unconsciousness, reaching for my coherent mind, seeking to consume it with nothingness. Compelling my mind to clear, I forced my scent out, reaching for Lennox.

"Snuff" by Slipknot burst into the surrounding air, even as he stared down at me through eyes, bleeding blackness. The smile spreading over his mouth forced words to issue from mine.

"I love you, Knox. I'll always love you. For this, I forgive you. Don't carry the weight of my death with you. Let me go when you escape her hold. You will. I know deep inside of me that you're going to beat her. Because you're Knox. I know it's hard right now, but eventually, you'll win this fight. You're my darkness, which allowed me to shine brighter because of it. As your queen, my job is to save you. Even if the cost is my life for yours. If you cannot sit in the light with me, then I'll come into the darkness with you."

"You're not invited." He laughed, but it was cold, merciless. Knox straddled my body, then sunk to his knees, trapping me between his powerful thighs. "It turns out that I don't actually need your corpse. Hecate didn't want you in our bed sharing it with us, Little Monster. Instead, she wants your heart as a symbol of my undying, endless devotion to the woman I love." Holding up his fingers, lethal, back-tipped nails pushed thru his fingertips one by one. "Are you ready to sing for me?"

"You'll only remove the storm, but you'll never touch my chaos. In the end, Knox, we're nothing more than stories. Some tragic, others formed from the sweetest lies, then the ones written about strength and courage against insurmountable odds. Ours, it's going to be a tragic love story that will never die. Do you hear me? I *will* find you in this life, or the next. I'll always come back to you. You are my sweetest ever-ending of cruelly savage, brutally endless eternal love. You are my evermore." My breathing had become harsh, painful whispers of air as it fought to escape my lungs through the damage of my esophagus. "You fucking kill her. When you're free and you've set the world ablaze with your fire, I want you to rip her fucking head off before you force her back inside that tomb."

"If I were you, I wouldn't come looking for me in any lifetime. It won't end the way you want it to," he hissed, then shoved his nails through the wall of my chest, burying them deeply into my flesh.

The world spun around us, even as a new, punishing ache flooded my chest with acid and fire, scolding my flesh. Every muscle seized at once, muscles, my lungs, soul-destroying pain as fingers clenched around my heart.

"Any last words?" Knox asked as Esme's broken, heartrending sobs flitted through my ears.

"I forgive you for your broken, sharply-cutting edges. I love you, and that'll never change. Not even in death," I whispered around the blood flowing from the corner of my lips. "I'm coming for you, bitch. And then I'm coming to burn everything down until you're nothing but a fucking rat seeking shelter in a trench—" A blinding light erupted, driving a shocked cry from my lips.

Everything around me faded, as the blinding glare compelled my eyes to close against its illuminating light. The world spun around me, as if they had forced it from its axis, and it was now careening toward a downward spiral. My lungs screeched from the dizzying agony. It caused black dots to flood my eyes, striking against the light burning around me. Numbness came upon me ever so slowly, pulling me deep into the freezing embrace of nothingness, far away from where the tormentingly hot, piercing blade of anguish could reach me.

CHAPTER 32
ARIA

Weightlessness filled my mind, body and soul. Consciousness refused to come, even as a scream of distress rang from my lips. I felt his claws in my chest, still. Had we died? Had he ended my life, then gone back to Hecate? My eyes refused to open, even as I cried, sobbing violently within my head.

Images of what had happened flashed through my mind, trickling through it on an endless, spiraling carousel played on a loop. Blood covered my face, my chest, Knox's hands. The flash of blue before he'd pulled it out, stuck out among the other images. Had he fought her for me? Or had she merely allowed him to see my demise unfolding?

Voices whispered all around me, forcing me to fight the hold of the land. I needed to know what had happened to Knox. Why didn't I hear him talking to the others? Where had he ended up? Fearful flames licked over my mind, consuming it as I fought to regain consciousness.

The sound of voices had my brain ticking, as if it were a clock. My vision was obscured by blurriness, as if I'd lost the ability to see. My brain struggled, as if it were misfiring. I felt free of the worry of dying, but did that mean I'd died?

An image slowly began forming in front of me. Something large, something with a halo around it. Fucking hell. I had died! My breathing was erratic, as if my chest hadn't healed correctly, or maybe it hadn't healed at all? Blinking frantically past the film covering over my eyes that blocked me from seeing or discerning what was in front of me, I gasped as the picture cleared.

Knox's sleeping face came into view, forcing my heart to stutter, then beat hastily at the sight of him. Pain drifted through me as awareness slowly flittered through my mind. Had I saved him? Or was he simply caught between the land healing me, which had shoved him into the light?

Reaching up, I touched him with trembling fingers. Parting my lips, I tried to speak, but nothing came out. The simple movement forced agonizing pain to slice through my chest. Sliding my other hand to the hole he'd created, I felt nothing but smooth, supple flesh. Tears wet my lashes, then rolled down my cheeks as I moved my lips, brushing them against his.

"Knox?" I forced out, my voice scratchy from screaming. Knox didn't move, which sent icy-claws tearing into my flesh.

I could hear the whisper of voices around us, each one fearful of what had happened. Hecate wouldn't let him go without a fight. It was possible she was fighting the land to keep hold of him. He looked peaceful, though. Which sent horrible thoughts racing through my mind.

For hours, I went in and out of consciousness. I struggled against the land's powerful hold on me. Each time,

Knox never responded or awoke. The fourth, or maybe it was the fifth time I awoke, I checked for a pulse, sobbing in relief when I found one.

The warmth of the light we were suspended in was soothing. It persistently healed me, each time my eyes opened, I felt a little more whole. Knox still hadn't moved by the time I dropped, thudding against the ground with a painful gasp ripping from my lips.

"Knox," I repeated his name for the hundredth time. "Wake up," I whispered, sitting beneath him as he hovered weightlessly in the air.

Knox was suspended in the air, even after I'd been released. A frown line formed between my eyes, creasing the skin there. Tears continually streamed down my face, forcing myself up on my knees. I raised shaky hands to touch his face. With my heart in my throat, I pushed his eyelid back, feeling instant relief as it revealed the whites of his eyes.

"Aria?" Esme's worried voice had my hand jerking back from Knox's eye, turning to find everyone standing behind me.

"I . . . did you die too?" I whispered, hardly able to speak past the scratchiness of my throat.

"We don't think so? The light came as he began pulling your . . . his hand out." Esme only added more to the confusion inside my aching head. "You've been suspended by the land for over a week."

"You scared us, Aria," Zyion stated, his eyes slowly roving over my face.

Scanning his frame, I noted the bandage, which was obvious without a shirt covering his chest. I wanted to ask if he was okay, but my thoughts drifted back to the battle, flashing through my head on repeat.

Peering around, I noted the clearing was a large chamber. It wasn't the forest where we'd previously been when I'd lost consciousness. How the hell had we been moved?

"Where are we?" I asked, returning my focus to Knox, who didn't move at all.

"We're in a chamber inside the library. I don't know what the hell happened, but we're here. You fought him, but you—weren't doing so hot. He'd put up a shield, or Hecate had. We're not sure about that one yet. However, it dropped, which allowed us to get closer to you, but a light shot through the ground, and everyone close to it ended up here."

"It transported us to the library?" I asked, even more befuddled than before.

"Yeah, one of the larger chambers, from what we can tell."

"That's ... weird."

Knox's face was slack, as if he'd died. It freaked my brain out, even if I knew the land was healing him. Why was the land healing him? Unless what Scylla said was true. If Draghana had indeed made a sacrifice, then there was another who could fight against Hecate, another part of the prophecy. Knox could be the one she'd been sacrificed to create. Had he known what he was?

"Peasant," Greer's soft, calming tone forced me to spin toward where it had sounded.

Greer's eyes were rimmed with red, as if he'd been crying. Trying to stand, I whimpered as the searing, red-hot pain burned through my chest. Falling over, I barely prevented my face from connecting to the floor of the chamber as I pushed my palms down flat against it. The entire room spun around me. It caused my head to bob around drunkenly. Sitting back down, I tried not to add any more injuries.

"Slowly, Aria," Greer offered, then knelt in front of me. "You've been floating in the light for a few days. You need to give yourself a moment."

"Why isn't he waking up?"

"We don't know. We didn't know why you weren't, either. My guess is, the damage was more extensive than any of us realized it would be." His explanation made sense, but didn't ease the claws tearing through my mind. "Try to calm down. You've endured a lot of pain. Enough that we've listened to your screams through the walls for days now. Even asleep, you screamed in agony."

"But Knox didn't," I pointed out, watching his face crumple. Turning back to take in his form, I forced my legs to support my weight. "Because we don't know if he survived what she did to him. Right?" My heart squeezed painfully as I let the thought enter my mind. Hecate could even now be forcing more darkness into him. "Right?" I demanded again, wanting an answer to why he wasn't coming out of it, since the land was tied to only me. Or was it?

"The moment the light shot up through the ground, I witnessed the darkness slithering out of him. Snake-like things, which then vanished in a cloud of smoke. As if they couldn't survive being in the direct light, or the light the land released." Killian offered, his hand touching my shoulder, then squeezing in silent reassurance.

"We should draw you a bath, then get something into you, Aria," Greer said carefully, worry sharpening his expression. "Unless you don't wish to leave him."

"I want Knox to wake up," I whispered as tears gripped my throat, choking the words off. "I don't fucking care about me right now. I'll be fine once he's awake." My words caused a bevy of worried whispers, which I ignored.

"We're all just as concerned about you, Peasant." He tipped his head, the worry turning to uneasiness, then fear for my health. "An hour ago, we didn't even know if you would wake up. You've been like Knox for days, too. Knox is healing, but you can't save him if you're exhausted or become sick from neglecting your own needs."

"We all want Knox to wake up. Knox wouldn't want you to make yourself sick by ignoring your needs. Do you know if you . . . did you miscarry?" Brander's eyes dipped to my middle, then drifted back to my face.

My hand moved to my abdomen, frowning as I felt a sob rock through me. "I don't know." A new worry joined the growing list of them. I'd not even thought about them after seeing Knox's unmoving form.

"Then we should assume you didn't lose them until we know otherwise. That means you need nourishment. He's not going anywhere. We've had someone constantly on watch within the chamber since you both appeared inside of it." His words were comforting, but I needed Knox to wake up. "Your shift is covered in blood, and there's a rather large hole in it, Aria."

I glanced down, finding the top ripped. Dragging my fingers over the gaping hole Knox had put in the fabric, I jerked my head back, drinking in the calmness of his face.

The moment I reached for him in the light, he spun over, his head at an awkward angle from the light spinning him so his back was to the floor. Stepping closer to him, my hand slid over his naked chest, skimming over the sleek, hard muscles. Heat drifted over my palm, proving he was still alive.

"Knox, I need you. You have to come back to me," I whispered, then lowered my head, placing my lips against his. "I love you. I can't fight her without you beside me. You're my fucking anchor. Without you, I'm adrift on a churning sea. Come back to me, monster." Kissing his lips, then forehead, I turned, uncaring, who watched my foundation crumble.

Knox was my fucking air, and without it, I couldn't breathe. He'd kept me grounded, as if I'd become unhinged without his strength. I didn't want to lose him, nor could I survive if he was gone.

"Do we know if Hecate's aware that he's . . . gone?" My words cracked, refusing to come out as anything but broken.

"I've been keeping watch of the citadel. It's a bevy of activity. There's been an endless parade of dark witches converging into the city, then entering the gates. Hecate hasn't been seen since we saw her with Knox inside the gates." Zyion leaned against the farthest wall, his eyes scanning my face.

"Basilius, can you take dragon form?" I asked, even as my mind grasped onto a way to get inside the citadel.

"Yes. We all can," he confirmed.

Bowing my head, I studied Knox's sleeping face. If I exposed the dragons, would she come at us twice as hard?

Absolutely, but only if we lost. Pushing my fingers through his hair, I tried to consider what he'd want me to do. What would Knox do if he were the one in my position? He'd rain down hell on Hecate until she went to ground.

I couldn't kill her outright. Not without draining her endless supply of magic. That meant I had to figure out how to begin disassembling her extensive network.

"What are you thinking, Aria?" Killian asked, his tone holding trust.

Could I lead his men into battle? I wasn't the warrior Knox was, nor did I have the ability to lead with unfaltering strength. I did have the mind for strategic warfare, or so he'd continually told me that I had it in me. But would they follow me in and trust me not to get them killed? Turning toward Killian, I smiled.

"I think it's time she learns that we hit back, and we hit back harder when we're wounded. I just need time to figure out how we do so without losing anyone else. We'd need to hit hard and fast without her realizing we were coming. You said she had dark witches gathering at the citadel?"

"Hundreds of them," Zyion confirmed. "As if something is about to happen."

"Or she's about to attack us," I whispered, even as my stare drifted back to Knox.

If Hecate was gathering witches, it was more than likely she was planning an attack. Her target would be something big enough to warrant gathering attention to herself. The only threat to her right now, was us. Which meant she was coming here, to where Knox was healing. That wasn't something I could allow.

I couldn't allow her to reach Knox a second time. In no world would I allow her to take him from me again. Instead, I'd need to come up with something quickly, and stop her from ever stepping foot outside of the citadel. But they were right. I couldn't do so if I was weak or depleted.

"I'll take that bath, Meat Suit."

CHAPTER 33
ARIA

The bath had cleared the remaining fog from my head. I'd spent the majority of it searching for a way to prevent Hecate from realizing Knox was incapacitated, if we attacked. She'd said she only had to remove one of us in order to win. It's why she pitted us against one another. That meant she couldn't know, or she'd fight harder.

I stared down at Knox's face, tears rolling down my cheeks. It terrified me that he had not awoken from the land healing him. Knox wasn't the type to go down, ever. I'd never even seen him hurt before, which was part of the reason I was freaking out. Knox didn't get wounded, shit, he didn't even complain about being tired or hungry. I'd never been down that long before. I was normally healed within a few hours, but he was heading into day eight. Pushing the silken, dark blond strands from his face, I exhaled a shuddered breath.

"Come on, Knox. I need you to fight for us. You're in there, I know it. I'd feel it if you were gone. If our love was gone, I'd sense it," I whispered through the tears burning my throat. "You are so much better at strategizing than I am. I'm more of a 'burn it all down' kind of girl."

"He's going to be okay, Aria," Esme whispered, slowly stepping from the shadows. "I know you want to rush in and attack, but shouldn't we wait?"

"For what, Esme?" I asked, turning toward her. "Should we wait for Hecate to come here? It's one of the only strongholds still standing. If she reaches the gates, we won't be able to defend it against the army of witches she's gathering. Hecate thinks we're weak, she'll use it to her advantage."

"So, we go and attack, and what? Rise from the ashes?" Esme's tone was worried, her eyes breaming with it as well.

"I'm not planning to rise from any ashes. This time, I'm planning to make them," I hissed as I let the bitterness on my tongue sharpen my words. "If I can't have him, then I'll burn this world until all that remains is the ashes of the love we once had. The love she destroyed, and stole from me. I'll show her the flames of my anger, which is all that remains inside me."

I hadn't been a monster before, not entirely. I'd clung on to the optimistic, soft-hearted girl I'd entered the Nine Realms as. She had to die in order to become what the world needed. Knox had been right: the world hadn't needed a hero. Heroes had too many rules to fight against villains and come out on top. In order to fight a monster, you had to become an even bigger monster.

"What about the others? Do you trust them enough to

go into battle beside them?" Esme questioned as her lips tugged into a frown.

"We either learn to work together, or we watch this world burn. I can't do this alone, Esme. Not anymore. I've been fighting alone for my entire life. I'm not the only one hurting here, either. It's time to make the sheep into lions, and unleash their anger upon the one who fueled the flames. If we're to win, then we can't falter. We hit her hard, and we hit her fast with no fucking mercy offered. After this battle, we'll have a choice to make. It's no longer going to be a question of what would we do to end it." Pushing my fingers through his hair, I felt the tears swimming in my eyes as I grieved the girl I'd been.

"Then what is the question?"

"What won't we do to end it," I whispered, even as I shoved the old me in to a nameless, unmarked grave within my soul.

"And if we end up dying?" Violet eyes brimmed with worry, even as she brought her thumb to her mouth, chewing the nail while waiting for my reply.

"Spoiler alert, Esme. In the end, everyone dies. Death is inevitable. If your number is called, there's no escaping. This moment will define what comes next for this world. We can either rise and take everything back, or we can serve on our knees. I don't know about you, but I don't intend to bow before anyone. It's time for Hecate to feel the same pain she's inflicted upon the creatures of this world. This time, it's personal for me."

"We could die," Esme blurted out. "I get that we have to die sometimes, but I'd rather it not be soon. If we die, she wins."

"She's already won, Esme. Without Knox, I don't know if I can kill her. She said with one of us gone, she couldn't be killed. Scylla mentioned Draghana Karnavious making a sacrifice for another savior. What if she figured it out before us, and that's why she forced us to fight against each other? Hecate wanted us to fight so she didn't have to, which meant she's afraid. I think she's still wounded. That's why she went for the one thing Knox would bargain his soul for. It's why she went after Lore. She knows he raised him, and that while he's a brother, he's also a child he raised from infancy." It did raise the question of how Hecate had figured it out, but then if Knox had been privy to the truth, she'd more than likely plucked it from his mind.

"What happens if Knox—"

"Never wakes up?" I finished, when she'd hesitated to ask the question. "I don't know, Esme. I know if he doesn't wake up, I won't only become the monster this world needs. I'll become the one it seeks to put down after I've destroyed Hecate."

"Let's hope it never comes to that," Killian said, alerting us to his presence. "Brander said he'd like to speak with you. I think you'll want to hear what he's come up with." A trickle of fear rolled down my spine as I turned to look at Knox.

"I'll stay with him, Aria," Siobhan offered as she moved into the chamber behind Killian. Her eyes slid over Knox's slumbering form, then drifted back to me. "Don't worry, he'll be okay. He's the king, he always bounces back."

That was my worry. What if this time, he didn't? What if Hecate had taken steps to ensure he couldn't come back?

She'd sent him to kill me, but what if she'd considered that he might not win? If it were me, I'd have done everything possible to prevent the chance to lose. My only hope was that she'd been cocky.

Kissing his forehead, I leaned against his ear to whisper. "You're going to be a daddy. Do you hear me? You have to come back to me. There's no one else who can teach them to be as honorable, selfless or savage as their daddy. You're my ever after, Knox Karnavious. We're written in blood. Remember? It's time to wake up and help me bathe this world in blood, as you promised me, we'd do." Placing my forehead against his, I sent a silent prayer to any benevolent god listening, to bring him back to me.

"You're still pregnant?" Esme asked, dropping her regard to my flat abdomen, then rolling it back up to my face.

"I believe so," I muttered. Was I still pregnant? I didn't know, but I hadn't felt any cramping, nor had I bled. There was no pain or pressure like last time, and Ember had been silent since I woke. So, until I could confirm it either way, I'd continue to hope I was.

"Do you think you should maybe sit this fight out?" Lore asked, but whatever he saw burning in my eyes caused him to clear his throat and then scratch the back of his neck. "Right. I didn't think you'd want to do that, but I can't help but think about the last time."

"Last time, I was betrayed by those who walked me into the battle. I no longer follow. I lead, which means I won't take any unnecessary chances when I lead us against the citadel."

"I'll gladly follow you into a fight, Aria," Killian said

firmly, which caused a tightening in my chest. "You know I was never your biggest fan. But after watching you with Knox, I know you're not trying to fuck us over. He wasn't wrong when he said you would be the queen to his king. I couldn't imagine someone else better suited to be the woman standing beside my king, my brother in arms, and my brother."

"Thank you, Killian. You're not so bad either, you know?" I returned. "I'm ready to see Brander, if you want to take me to him." I glanced back at Knox's unmoving form, forcing myself to allow Killian to lead me through the palace, then to Brander.

CHAPTER 34
ARIA

Brander wasn't in the library. Instead, Killian walked me through the halls crowded with people. They stared at us as we walked by, everyone seeking to catch a glimpse of the unseated queen, was my guess. Aurora and Celia had worked together to ensure I'd been removed from Knox's life. They'd annulled our marriage by coercion, which had deposed me from the throne. Every step I took was met with whispers said behind hands or withered glances that refused to hold my eye. A ruthless smile played on my lips because I spared them not a moment more of my attention.

Killian entered the throne room, which caused my heart to sputter. There, upon the raised dais, sat the throne of skulls. The one which used to give me nightmares. The same one he'd promised I'd watch grow. Behind it were piles of skulls that I'd sent him. I wasn't sure what was more romantic; that he'd kept them, or that he'd built a matching one for his queen.

"We took a vote, Aria."

Brander's words pressed my stare to where he stood beside his brothers. Killian moved over to stand beside the brothers, who were all gathered together beside the thrones. Swallowing down the uneasiness, I tilted my head, smiling as I realized it was what Knox normally did when I spoke.

"And what was up for vote?" I asked without the curiousness I felt at hearing that they'd voted.

"We think you should ascend," he stated, which caused even more confusion to flitter through my mind. "Knox is the king, even if he isn't here. You're his queen. Not by marriage, or by force, but by choice. Dragons mate for life, as you know. You're his mate, Aria. Regardless of status, papers, or banners being read, you are the other half of his soul. I'm not strategic. If you need a healer, I'm your guy. But I don't have the mind to play war games. In order for us to allow you to lead dragon warriors into battle, you must ascend the Throne of Dragons." Brander nodded at the thrones, smiling tightly.

"I'm already a queen."

"That's true," Zyion stated, smirking as he studied the thrones. "But nothing says you can't hold both of them. As long as your interest doesn't clash between kingdoms, you can rule them at the same time."

"I would prefer Knox make that choice," I whispered before biting my lip and moving toward the thrones. Running my fingers over the symbol of the one I prayed was Freya's, I smirked. He'd built a second throne, but he'd also done some remodeling.

The floors were white, which I knew he'd used to paint them red with the blood of those who crossed him. He's done a three-skull tier around the center height, around the entire chamber, each skull held an obsidian burnt cross in the center of the forehead. On a pedestal, there was a large, misshapen skull. Drawn to it, I paused at the name scrawled on the paper beneath it, written in blood.

Garrett, Former King of Unwanted Beasts. Sentenced to Death by beheading, by the blade of the High King of the Nine Realms, crowned King of Dragons, Knox Karnavious. Crime: Touched the Queen of Hearts, Aria Hecate Prometheus Karnavious.

My eyes pricked with unshed tears. Most people got flowers or jewels, but not me. My guy brought me the skulls of those who'd trespassed against me. Knox knew the way to my heart, that much was certain.

"When?" I asked, spinning to look at the men.

"He hunted him down the week before Lore was captured. Knox said he wouldn't allow anyone who'd promised you harm to remain in any of the Nine Realms. There are more, but if we're to strike, we need to crown you and announce it to the people." Killian answered, smirking when he noticed the smile I couldn't hide, which spread across my face. "He said you'd be pleased with his offering."

"More than pleased," I admitted softly, then glanced once more at the bastard who'd tried to rape me.

"I know you'd like to wait for Knox, Aria. But we don't have time to wait for him to wake up. Zyion reported movement within the citadel. Hecate's about to make a move. She's not wasting time. Only the Queen of Dragons can lead us into battle. We cannot follow the Queen of Phoenixes, it's against the laws of our sovereignty. Until Knox changes it, our hands are tied. We're willing to follow you into battle. You're literally Knox, but with very nice tits." Brander stated.

"Knox intended to make you his queen when you returned," Mateo stated, his dark eyes roaming over my face slowly. "I see no reason not to crown you now. When he wakes up and he's finally worn you down and made an honest woman out of you, we'll do the formal ascent." My heartbeat increased as I moved to the queen's throne, running my fingers over the smooth, off-white skulls.

"Your mind works like Knox's does. Everything you do is strategic and thought out entirely. You don't lead people into battles you don't intend to win. You're always five steps ahead of your adversaries. None of us have the ability to wage war as efficiently as you can. We are able to fight, or dominate on a battlefield. But the fine-tuned parts that need to be planned out? That's always been Knox. He's not here to plan for the unexpected. Knox always has one way in and five ways out. That's where you come in on this one. I have a map of the citadel, as well as the surrounding area. I can get us in, but if shit goes sideways? We're going with it, Aria. Unless you choose to lead and allow me to do what I do best." Brander's eyes held mine, a silent plea burning within them.

"Fine. Tell me how to do it." The moment I said it, a crown landed atop my head.

"I think this one suits you best, Your Majesty," Greer stated, forcing my lips to twitch.

"Is there a crown of dicks on my head, Meat Suit?"

"Would I do such a thing?" he asked innocently.

"Yes," I replied.

"You're right, I would. Unfortunately, you needed an actual crown to rise to the Queen of Dragons. This one seemed like the best fit for you," he informed. "The material is black steel, mined from Dorcha. It's rock that has melted beneath the dragon's flame. Not much of it remains nowadays, but there was enough in the vault to create this one. The diamonds set into the black steel are mined right here in Norvalla. Knox filed the points, himself. He wanted it to be perfect and trusted no one else to do it." Greer pushed wayward strands of my hair behind my ear, smiling as he wiped away the tear that tipped over my lashes. "He'd want you to lead his brethren against Hecate. You know her weaknesses. He also knew that no one else would ensure they return here safely once the battle was over, except you."

"Thank you, Greer."

"You'll have to wear his mantle. We didn't have time to have one made for you," he informed. Wrapping the obsidian mantle over my shoulders, he clasped the raven heads together, smiling proudly. "I always knew you'd be his queen. At first, I hated that it would steal your innocence. You had such a beautiful soul, and were so soft when we first met. I knew you'd have to kill that girl in order to survive this world."

"Are you trying to turn me into a blubbering mess?" I asked pointedly, smiling as he kissed my cheek.

"No, you shouldn't cry. Tears are for later, My Queen. Right now, I need your ruthlessness, and that chaos you bring so freely upon those you destroy. You hit her for me, at least once."

I stared at the throne, hating that Knox wasn't here to approve my ascension. I'd never dared to even imagine sitting on the throne of Norvalla. Even when I'd been his wife, it had seemed pointless. Now, he wasn't here, and I was about to agree to protect and defend his people in his absence. Taking the step toward it, I sucked in air as I read the inscription on the back.

Aria, beloved Queen of Dragons, Queen of Phoenixes, and rightful ruler of the Nine Realms.

"Who—"

"He did," Brander stated. "Knox would want you to be his queen, we all know it, probably even knew you were before he did. Knox doesn't do anything without thought, which means he wanted you to become queen. You already were, even without the crown to back your claim."

I stood there, staring at the throne he'd built for me, breathlessly wishing he were here to ease the worry. Knox always forced the world to go silent around me. As if nothing else existed other than the two of us within the universe. I craved that with him, the ability to shut off the world and just exist with him beside me.

A hand touched my shoulder. It made head turn, finding Brander beside me. His eyes, beaming with pride slowly moved over my face. "I am proud of you, Aria. If you'd have asked me when I'd first met you if I saw you ascending the throne to rule beside my own brother? I'd have laughed at you. You've come so far, and matured into a beautiful, chaotic woman. There's no one else I'd want to sit beside Knox to rule our kingdom." Grabbing my hand, he brushed his lips over my knuckles. "Long may you reign beside your king."

Lore stepped into Brander's spot once he'd stepped back. Golden eyes sparkled as a wide grin spread over his face. "You know how I feel. I'm always here for *whatever* you need. I joke around a lot." He shoved his fingers through his platinum hair, frowning. "You know that as well. But really, Knox has been through hell. When he's with you, he smiles, Aria. He fucking laughs. He raised me. Before he met you? I could probably count how many times he'd laughed throughout my life on one hand. You make him happy, which is all I've ever wanted for him, really. It's what we've all wanted . . . I mean, *other* than an extending jaw. Obviously, any man would want a girl with one of those. You're going to be the best queen this realm has ever had. I know that because I know you. You're kindhearted, and you're . . . well . . . you're you. I'm going to be proud to say you're our queen. Knox would be too, if he could." Leaning over, he kissed my forehead. "If he doesn't wake up? I'm willing to be their daddy. I won't make you call me daddy, either." Killian swatted him, which caused the men to chuckle. "Hey, the girl needs to know she has options."

"Move along, Lore. Let the real men have a chance with the girl." Brander's taunting tone had Lore rolling his eyes.

"Thanks, Lore. I'll keep you in mind if I end up with daddy issues." My joke caused his eyes to shimmer with sparkles of gold dust.

"Aria, you know how I feel," Killian uttered, his head tilted, a frown marring his brow. "Knox is my best friend. I came here at five years of age to learn to train beside a prince. I hated him at first. He was the reason I'd been forced to leave everything I'd ever known or cared about. Knox was never a child. He's been groomed to rule since the day he took his first breath. I've been with him the longest, other than Greer's cranky, old ass. I was glad he married Liliana, then brought Sven into the world. But I stood beside him when he buried them, and you were right. He buried his heart beside them in that crypt. Until you resurrected it, then brought him back to life. With you, he's a different person. I watched him trying to hate this enchanting woman, who gave him no mercy. You didn't take his shit, Aria. You gave back as hard as he gave it, and that was entertaining to watch. It wasn't all you did. You made Knox into more than just a king. It was like watching him age backward, from ruthless king, to the lad who snuck out to frequent taverns. I guess what I'm trying to say is, you make him into a better man. For that, we're all eternally grateful you came into our lives. If he doesn't wake up, choose me. I promise not to make you call me daddy," he said before leaning over and kissing my cheek.

"He'll wake up. Knox doesn't know how to stay down."

"Thank you, Killian."

"Peasant," Greer stepped up, eyeing Killian until he released my hand, moving away to stand with the others. "You know I was a total asshole the first few times we met."

"You don't say?" I asked in a mocking tone, my hand flying to my heart. "Don't break my heart, Meat Suit."

"You'd have to actually have one, first." He sniffed, lifting his nose into the air, before slowly lowering it, grabbing my hand in his surprisingly warm ones. "The first time I saw you outside of the house in Haven Falls, I knew you were innocent. Both of mind and heart. I also knew Knox intended to force you back into this world. A world that would chew that beautiful, innocent girl up and spit her out. That wasn't something I wanted for you, ever. You've blossomed from the naïve, soft, delicately made girl into a savage." He stood there while I waited for him to continue.

"And?"

"Uh, that's it," he paused before adding, "I do wonder about something though."

"Yeah?"

"Did you ever start tipping the naked men prancing around you, more than a dollar?" His lips jerked up as my mouth opened in horror.

"I was in my pajamas, Greer. It was all that I had on me. Besides, I should have flicked a quarter at the bastard. He wasn't even worth the dollar."

"Indeed, he was beneath you. I already knew you'd become a queen. We just didn't know you'd become ours. Had I known, I wouldn't have changed anything. Knox was always a singular creature, even when they brought in others to force him out of the library. His love of reading came from Eira, who taught him to read in that very library. But when he's with you? He doesn't seek to escape the space he's claimed for himself. I think that's when I knew you'd be his. Because he'd never allowed anyone who wasn't of the bloodline to step a foot deeper into that chamber, other than his best friend. So, while you may feel reservations about waiting for him to wake and place you on the throne, know that we hold none. He'd want you here. If he didn't, he wouldn't have cleaned the skulls you so generously kept piling up at the gates. And he sure as hell wouldn't have written your name upon it, Peasant. He may be too prideful to say it, but we all love you. You've a way about you. Annoying, slightly obtuse, and an over-dramatic actress between the sheets, but it's a way, I guess."

"Don't forget how I light up the room when I enter it," I advised.

"That's called arson, Peasant. And it's frowned upon. Heavily, I might add. You should sit, and try not to burn anything down."

I turned, staring at the other brothers who were smiling, approval shimmering in their eyes. Exhaling the air from my chest, I sat on the throne, placing my hands on the skulls of the armrest, peering out at the men. Greer handed me the Sovereign's Orb, and then the Sovereign's Scepter which had a crystal quartz composed of the highest quality I'd ever seen. My heartbeat thundered violently against my ribs, threatening to break them.

"All hail the queen," Brander announced, his voice echoing around the entire room.

As they shouted it, people began entering the chamber, bowing with worried eyes. Those who'd whispered behind their hands met my gaze, then lowered it in shame. A cruel smile spread over my lips. I wouldn't be cruel to his people, but I wouldn't trust the fuckers farther than I could see any of them.

"All hail the mate of Knox Karnavious, rightful Queen of the Nine Realms, crowned Queen of Dragons, and Queen of the Phoenixes. Long may she reign!" Killian shouted, his eyes beaming with pride. One by one, the brothers lowered, bending their knee as they recognized me as their rightful queen. I'd hold off on celebrating until Knox was beside me, supporting my place on the throne, with him as my king. "And lord have mercy on anyone who disrespects her, for her mate will not."

CHAPTER 35
ARIA

The map of the citadel was spread out over the table inside the library. Brander hadn't explained why Knox chose this room, other than it was his favorite place inside the entire palace. There wasn't a way to spy on those within the library, without it detecting them. Therefore, no one could ever discover their strategies, secrets, or the plans they made within it. I hadn't even considered that it was a living, breathing sentinel for him.

Knox had loved it, which was why I'd slept in his bed without him. It hadn't been easy to leave his side, even for the night. Unfortunately, they were right. If I wanted to be well enough to take care of him, then I also had to take care of myself first. If I wasn't healthy, then I couldn't defend him while he was weak.

I'd heard the men speaking when they'd thought I'd fallen asleep last night. The queen's job was to protect her king. It wasn't merely to lead them into battle. It was because they knew I'd protect him with my last breath.

And I would, I'd sooner die than allow anything to happen to Knox.

He'd endured a lifetime of pain, and been endlessly tortured, and still, he fought against it for those who hadn't felt the blade of loss. He'd stood in the darkness without anyone ever knowing he held the monsters at bay. Knox was raised like a sentry of hope in the darkness he'd survived, wearing it like a cloak around his shoulders.

The other kingdoms merely existed, enduring under oppression. They'd chosen to bow before the self-proclaimed queen, who had returned their loyalty with endless death and destruction. Yet Knox, even as a prince, had taken a stand against Hecate's demands, and proclamations. But it came with a price, one he'd paid ten times over in his own sweat, tears and blood.

"You have the table, My Queen," Killian said firmly.

Blinking slowly, I chewed on my lip, uncomfortable with the title. "Hecate is weak, but she's trying to appear strong."

"What makes you think that?" he asked.

"It's what I would do if it were me. Appear strong when you are weak, and weak when you are strong. Sun Tzu, *The Art of War*. 'In order to keep the appearance, one must use deception to prevent an enemy from knowing when one is wounded, or when one is at the precipice of great power'. Hecate called many dark witches to her. Why would a goddess need them if she wasn't weak?"

"You're right, she's just like him, brother. His mate even quotes from the same book he does." Basilius smiled as Brander, Mateo, and Lore all made a sound of agreement. "Where am I and the other dragons supposed to be?"

Reaching for the wooden dragons on the board, I put his beside my queen piece and then the others around the citadel, out of sight.

"Am I not needed in dragon form? Or do you wish her to kill me?" he countered.

"When we first met, I thought you were Knox. You could be his twin, Basilius. She doesn't know what happened to him, or that's what I'm hoping. If we can make her think she saw him, then she won't seek to figure out where he is."

"Do you not think she's the reason he isn't waking?" Acheron asked, his turbulent, blue eyes studying my face.

"There hasn't been anyone who has returned to themselves once the darkness has been forced out of them." Exhaling the pain that saying it out loud caused, I continued in a confident tone. "Knox will be the first, if he comes through it. Unfortunately, there's no way to know if there will be damage, or such until he wakes up."

"*If* he wakes up?" Ronin asked, which caused nausea to churn in my stomach.

"Exactly, but right now, we should focus on the battle strategy. If I could figure out how to bring him out of whatever state he is, I'd have done it already. For now, we focus on taking Hecate down, which will buy us time to find a way to save him. If she's the reason he isn't coming out? Then putting her to ground will lessen the hold she has on him right now."

"Okay," Ronin agreed, his head tipping when I waited for him to acknowledge if I'd answered his question.

"He'll be happy of your return, gentlemen," I offered before looking at the faces around the table. "I'm worried about him too, but worrying doesn't help us win. I'm going in there, and when I leave, it will be with both her crown and her head. Hecate has to be shown that if she comes for us, we'll come back twice as hard. I promised her that I'd run to ground until she felt like a rat, burrowing in the gutter. When I made a threat, it wasn't idle chit-chat anymore."

"How do you plan to get everything into place without her knowing we're there?" Esme asked, her eyes on Basilius. His were locked on her, naked heat simmering in their oceanic depths, so much like Knox's.

"Using the water element, I'll create a dense fog to provide cover. The citadel sits at the junction of several rivers flowing throughout the realms. Hecate used the rivers as a conduit, forcing each river to flow and carry the realm's magic right to the major grid hidden beneath the ground within the courtyard of the citadel. Fog is a common occurrence there, according to Zyion. As well as Soraya and others who've frequented it before. It shouldn't raise suspicions."

"Can you make it thick enough to hide dragons?" Acheron asked, his brow forcing into a worried crease. "You'd have to be pretty damn powerful to make it thick enough for cover."

"That's not something we worry about with Aria, Acheron. Think of a delicate-looking flower, but one that holds enough power to take down an entire kingdom," Brander muttered, which had the others laughing.

"I heard she's quite the sight when she's using magic. But I had to get her out of a situation because they took her down and nullified her magic." Basilius had a point, but I would be employing a shield to protect us.

"That won't happen again for some time," Zyion stated, his eyes holding mine. Tipping my head, I silently thanked him.

"I will employ a shield, one created from magic. Once it's placed, they'll know we're there. I should have just enough time to put it up, then call up the dead army. Everyone else will spread out within them. They won't attack, nor will they fight during this battle. I have something else planned for them. The moment that they've finished with their purpose, I'll begin destroying her grids. There's one beneath the ground of the courtyard. That's her main source of power. A smaller one lies at the fork of the river. Soraya, you'll be disturbing it first. Then you'll reach for my magic. I will connect, you'll have less than five minutes to pass through a portal after connecting me with the grid. I'll then destroy it and move to the one Esmeralda will be disrupting."

"All we have to do is reach for you once it's been disabled, then leave?" Soraya asked carefully.

"Yes, because I'm not merely disrupting it this time. I'm destroying it so that she no longer has use of her intricate web of stored magic. I don't want to just hurt her. This time it's personal to me. She went after Lore, who was used against Knox, who she then sicced on me. She hit us hard and she hit us where it hurt."

Agreement went up around the table, which was sad. Considering she'd brought us down so low, and so effortlessly, was honestly terrifying. I wanted to make sure she didn't try it again anytime soon. Inhaling a soothing breath at what I was about to admit, I let it out slowly.

"I want to bring down the entire citadel."

All eyes swung to me, some with worry, some with wariness, but none with pride. Chances are, there were people inside who weren't filled with darkness. There could be some inside who weren't fully dark, as well. But if I intended to fight against a monster, then I had to become one.

"I know," I whispered. "I know what you're thinking, but if we do this, we have to be as cruelly savage as she is. We can continue fighting against her while holding the idea that we're the good guys. But Knox once asked if war made monsters, or if they were born. I now know the answer. War creates them because, in order to rise from the ashes, we have to die first. It wasn't about us at all, it was about what war creates out of pain. He also told me that this world needs a villain more than it does a hero. Do you want to throw a couple of soft hits, or do you want to fuck this bitch in her ass so hard that she can't sit without feeling us in her guts?"

"Dayum," Lore whispered and then smiled brightly. "I choose option two."

"Same," Killian concurred. The moment he did, the entire table slowly, begrudgingly agreed.

"What if there are children in there?" Esmeralda asked.

My eyes closed as I felt my stomach churning. "Then they die. I can't separate a few to take out the many. If they're in there, then she's either already used them or she intends to. In short, they're someone else's death. I don't want to murder children, but taking her down even for a little while saves many more. Their lives or the lives of the others. We can't be judge, jury and executioner. We have to pick one."

"Aria," she whispered, her eyes rounding. "This is fucked up."

"Life is fucked up, Esme. I wish I'd listened to him. To Knox, when he told me no matter how I tried, that I couldn't save them all. I can't be the girl who rushes in to save them, and the one who destroys the evil in this world. I learned that lesson already. But right now? If we don't hit the bitch right where it hurts, she's coming here to hit us. So, you pick. Pick which one we do. Who lives and who dies?"

"I can't choose who lives and dies," she gasped, horrified that I'd told her to do so.

"I know you can't. That's why I did. I am choosing to turn unimaginable pain into power. Right now, I'm choosing to hit her hard enough that she has to recover from what she's done. I told you that it isn't what we would do to win. We're going to do whatever it takes, and we're going to show her that she can no longer hide behind the innocence of others."

"May the gods have mercy on your enemies," she stated, shaking her head. "I get it, I do. But if you cross this bridge, where does it stop? What separates you from her?"

"I don't want them to suffer, she does. I want to free them from oppression. To have a chance at life without being amidst a never-ending war. One they didn't ask for. In order to do so, I may end up carrying their deaths with me. If I have to pay that price, I will. I'm not asking you— not any of you—to kill someone. I'm fine being the villain.

Right now, this world needs the monster, not the soft, caring girl I was."

"Okay. I just needed to hear you say it, Aria. I know you don't wish to kill them, which is the difference. But I needed to know if you realized the price."

"I'm always the price I pay when I unleash the magic inside of me onto a keep. Knox taught me that lesson as well. I unleashed my grief, but that isn't what this is. It's a hit to prevent Hecate from coming here to hit us when we're down. So, we'll turn our pain into power, strike her hard and fast. Everyone should rest. Tomorrow is going to be a long one."

CHAPTER 36
ARIA

I sat beside Knox, allowing myself a moment to imagine a world without him. There was no future I could see myself living, not without him there with me. It was a weakness. One I'd allowed to grip my heart harder than I'd ever imagined it could. Love was fucked up that way. I'd always preferred the antihero, knowing he'd burn the world down to be with me. But I'd never understood how divinely violent I'd become to protect him, either. That I'd willingly turn into the monster the world feared to keep him safe.

I'd walked through hell to save him, even if I'd pulled out his body. Would I kill innocent lives to protect him? No, not if it was only for him. That was a bridge he wouldn't want me to cross. But if I didn't get him back, Hecate would double down. The army of dark witches she'd gathered would come here, and it would kill many more innocent lives. Standing up, I walked over to where he was suspended in the glowing light of the land.

"If you're in there, I'm going to need you to let me in.

Either way, I'm coming inside that head of yours." Turning, I found Esme standing behind me.

"You know that's dangerous. I don't even need to say that, right?" she asked.

Exhaling, I nodded. "I know, but if he's in there, then I need to know. If Hecate is aware that he's gone, we need to know. I promised everyone I wouldn't take chances with them. If she knows, she's coming for him, and attacking her won't stop that. If she's got her claws into his mind, then I need to go in there and remove her."

"I know. That's why I'm here. That's why we're all here. Family doesn't let family do dumb shit alone, remember? You taught me that. Ours may be little, and it's a bit broken, but it's ours. So, lie down, we'll get the candles and herbs, and you'll do it with your sisters, and your best friend."

"Holy shit. You said it," I whispered, then hugged her tightly. "I love you, too, bitch."

"Whatever. You can stop hugging me before people think we're best lesbians," she whispered against my ear. Pulling back, I smiled, then winked. "Why are you winking?"

"It's our secret," I whispered back, winking twice.

"What secret?" Siobhan asked. Turning toward her, I smiled as Esme sputtered at a loss for how to deflect what she'd said.

"Nothing. Aria was just telling me that, if Knox didn't wake up, she's considering dating women," Esme replied, then waited for Siobhan to begin placing the candles around Knox before she stuck her tongue out.

"Real mature, Esme." I laughed, slowly lowering down beside Knox.

I hadn't heard Ember since whatever Knox had done to my forehead, which had silenced her. It was troublesome. He'd marked my forehead, which left me altered somehow. I felt it to my core, even though I hadn't told anyone. I didn't need Ember to fight every battle for me, which was why I'd planned this one around my magic, not including the things I'd gotten from her.

Soraya, Avyanna, Esme, and Siobhan began chanting, their voices echoing in my ears. The light of the candles erupted, sealing the circle around us. I felt the circle tightening, connecting. My lashes fluttered as the herbs eased the tension, lowering the walls of our minds to allow a merge into Knox's.

"Snuff" by Slipknot played inside his mind. Sitting up on the floor, I peered around, smiling as the sound of his laughter reached my ears. Lifting up, I slowly rounded the bookshelves, stopping dead in my tracks at the sight of a little boy.

"Sven, I'm going to find you." Knox's voice wrapped around me like warm silk after being cold for too long. "Are you hiding?" He'd called from just outside the doorway. My heartbeat slammed against my chest at an alarming speed, even as the air caught in my lungs.

Sven laughed, then darted for the couch he'd been standing in front of. I watched him duck, then heard the sound of footfalls coming. Stepping out of the shadows I took in the sight of Knox, with bright, azure eyes that sent me awash me on endless waves. A smile curved his full, kissable lips.

"I'm going to find you, Sven," he warned, slowly turning to look at the couch where the sound of laughter floated up from.

My heart squeezed as my mind pointed out what it didn't want to believe. If he was with Sven, then he was either with his ghost, or he was among them, barely clinging to life. A tiny baby laugh forced tears to sting my eyes. Another followed right behind it, forcing me farther into the room. Staring at two girls, one with silvery hair, and eyes the same stormy waters color as her father. Eleanora was beyond beautiful, with loose curls hanging down her back, in a fine white dress. Evelyn entered right on her heels, her dark blonde hair, with laughing turquoise eyes. Like Eleanora, she wore a white dress of the softest material.

"Daddy, Daddy! Find us," Eleanora cried, her eyes flooding with love as she rushed for him.

"Me too, Daddy! Find me," Evelyn echoed, her smile so wide and so beautiful it ached to look at it too long.

Knox picked up one and then the other. The girls laughed as Sven grumbled about stupid sisters. Tears rolled down my cheeks, forcing a soft sob to leave my throat. He was definitely playing with ghosts. Stepping closer, I pushed my fingers through Evelyn's curls, gasping at how real they felt. How real *she* felt.

"You can't stay here with them, Knox. I want to, too, but I need you. Our babies need you. Come home to me?" His head lifted, which caused my heart to flutter.

"Stay with me, Little Monster. It's better here. I've missed you."

"I missed you too," I whispered through the tears. "So

much," I agreed, only for something to step through me. My eyes narrowed on . . . me?

"They're winning, my love."

"They always do, Knox." I said, even though it wasn't me.

"Ember?" I asked, uncertain if that was even possible. She'd looked like me, which was the only explanation I had. Turning in a circle, I narrowed my eyes on the walls around the library. No, it wasn't the library. It was something like the library, but it was all wrong. Walking to the walls, I ran my fingers over the ink on the side.

"What are you doing?" Knox whispered against my ear. Heated breath drifted against my throat, forcing me to turn around. The way he looked at me caused my heart to still, then thud to life at the love shining within the ocean depths.

"This isn't real," I swallowed, uncertain how he could see me. The others were gone, which sent a trickle of unease through my mind. Why would he have sent them away? My eyes caressed every inch of him, feasting on the life breaming in him.

"It is," Knox argued before sliding his arm around my waist, then yanked me against the hard, warmth of his body. A devilish smile played over his lips, causing my mouth to dry with the need to kiss him. "Do I not feel real enough for you, gorgeous girl?" His lips brushed against mine, sending eddies of arousal slicing through my belly.

His palm touched my cheek, even as his head tilted, forcing a whispered breath from my lungs. The tenderness of his touch mixed with the lips drifting over mine in feather soft whispers of lustful promise. Arousal warmed my belly, sending heat coursing through my veins like an untended fire, burning out of control.

"God, I miss you so fucking much," I whimpered, unable to pull away from the tenderness he delivered.

"I'm right fucking here with you," he hissed against my mouth. "I have dreamt of you for months, craving to feel your soft edges against mine. You taste so fucking delicious. I love your noises, and the way you melt for me, wife." Knox devoured my lips, nipping the bottom one as he asked permission to plunder. He ravished. He destroyed. Knox devasted every sense within me, even as he tempted me, luring me into the sin his lips promised.

Knox went to war against my mouth. His tongue conquered, forcing me to submit with only his kiss. Heated lips provoked mine to part, allowing him to ravish my tongue as his slid against it, coaxing it to life. His growl sent arousal rushing toward my cunt, readying for him to plunder the treasure he'd earned.

"You feel real." His honeyed-whisky voice slipped all around me, warming me more than any drink could. "Touch me, Aria. I need to feel you." Lips whispered over mine, then danced their way to my temple, then the other side before slowly continuing down my jawline. "Fuck, woman. I've missed feeling you against me." Skillful lips drifted up one side of my face, then slid down my jawline, driving his fiery mouth to the other side to continue his wicked discovery. Then, he nipped my bottom lip between his teeth, forcing it to sting before sliding to my throat, sucking on the hollow of my throat. "I miss the taste of your skin against my lips. I could stay with you like this forever, touching, tasting, discovering every secret your body holds."

Tears burned my eyes as I slid my hands over his chest, leaning against him as he continued kissing my collarbone, and throat.

"So fucking tempting, Knox. I see the appeal." I did. To be trapped in a haven with our daughters? I wanted that, too. So fucking badly it ached. This man was my safety, my anchor. He kept me grounded with the world tried to break me. "I love you so fucking it hurts. I need you to come back with me. You can't stay here because I can't. And I can't do this without you."

"Stay with me," he begged against my shoulder, slowly trailing his scorching mouth over the skin of it, flicking his tongue over his mark, reminding me I was his. "I'll be your fantasy, your filthiest dream, whatever you want, My Queen. I will be it if it means I get to keep you with me. Our girls need you, too. Sven needs you, Aria." What he'd said had me battling against the sob seeking to escape.

His body against mine felt real, but I wasn't crazy enough not to realize something was crafting a dreamscape. He was living within his mind with our children. Knox brought his lips to my throat, dragging them over it to my shoulder, kissing the mark marring my smooth flesh. How could he feel so fucking real? And good. So fucking good.

"I dreamed of you. It was more of a nightmare. I couldn't escape, Aria. I woke up screaming for what I'd done to you. It fucking broke me, destroying me from within." That he'd probably dreamt of what had actually happened forced me back to reality.

"Knox, who made this world for you? Did Hecate create it?"

"You think I'd let her make anything for me? I'd rather light the bitch on fire so I could fuck you in the flames. I'd never let her around our children, ever. They're so fucking gorgeous. They look just like their mother, but fuck if they're not going to be a handful." Tears slowly trailed down my cheeks, even as I touched every fucking inch of him, I could reach. "I want to fuck you right now," he admitted, leaning over to brush his lips against my ear. "I want that pretty pussy to paint my lips with your pleasure. I already know it taste like heaven against my tongue." A shiver rushed through me, threatening to weaken my knees. "This is my heaven. My girl, our girls, and Sven. That's all I want. As long as you're here, I am home."

"This isn't real, Monster. You're not dead any more than this place is real. I know it feels like it, but you're in the library. The light is healing you, but you're not waking up. I need you. I need you to come back to me. You're going to be a father. I don't want to do this without you."

His hand collared my throat, walking me back to the wall. Hot, demanding lips collided with mine, devouring them. His tongue flicked against my lips, demanding I let him in. The moment I did, I moaned at the real feeling of his kiss.

Knox didn't merely kiss, he fucking dominated me with his fiery, passionate kiss. My mind melted to the pleasure he gave while consuming my thoughts, changing my mind with one wickedly skilled flick of his tongue, at a time. I felt him pulling my skirts up, and then his fingers were sliding through the wetness between my thighs. Pulling back from my lips, he pressed his forehead against mine.

"This feels real to me. So fucking real." Knox's fingers trailed through the wetness, tapping against my clit with each pass through the arousal. "You feel real to me, Aria. This pussy feels so fucking real. Such a messy girl for me. Fucking hell I love how you melt for me."

"It does feel real," I admitted, knowing that if it felt real, then it was some type of magic.

Knox lowered, his scorching breath touching my sex before his tongue flicked my clit, forcing a gasp of shock from my lungs. Pleasure shot through me as he continually licked between my lips, growling like a wild beast against them. The vibration alone almost sent me over the edge. Sensation moved through me like a never-ending wave of bliss.

Spreading my legs apart, he began sliding me up the wall, his mouth lavishing my cunt, mercilessly forcing more pleasure as he rose to his full height, feasting like a starved beast against my flesh. The way he lost control had my eyes rolling back in my head as my entire body shook, unable to stop the screams from tearing from my throat.

The sinful noises he made had even more arousal rushing to paint his lips. My fingers pushed the dark blond hair from his face, which revealed a symbol in the center of it. Turing my head, I noted it matched the one on the walls.

A warm ball formed in my belly, fueled from each pleasurable stroke of Knox's tongue. I whimpered as he allowed me to slide down the wall and right onto the rounded tip of his cock. There, he teased his thickness against my opening, purring as he held my eyes prisoner.

The man was a master at edging me to the brink of insanity.

"Do I feel real now?" he asked, then forced into my body with one, powerful thrust.

I cried out, but he captured my mouth with his, swallowing down every cry I released. Every moan. He devoured them, even as one hand gripped my hip, controlling the rhythm. The man was God of pleasure, even in his damn head. It was unfair. His tongue flicked against my lips, his other hand cradling my head, as he began picking up speed, thrusting wildly into my body.

"You feel so fucking good around my cock, Little One. Does this not feel real enough for you?" he whispered. Then his tongue was sliding against mine, devouring me as he penetrated me with similar thrust with each. My pussy fluttered, clenching as the orgasm rocked through me, sending me spiraling down a bottomless abyss. It was a soul-shattering orgasm that reverberated through every part of me, stealing control of every sense as he held me in his arms, caging my body protectively.

"Knox!" I screamed, even as I felt the familiar warmth of his release painting my clenching walls.

"I could do this forever. You're my heaven, Aria. You'll always be my sanctuary. The one place I know is home, is here, like this with you."

"Knox, I need you to come back with me," I whispered.

"Shh, you'll wake the girls and Sven. Then we won't be able to have more fun making more."

"I'm pregnant," I whispered into his kiss. Leaning my head back, I stared at the mark on his forehead. "And you're not with me. Not really. This is what you created to escape her, isn't it? You created a heaven with your ghosts. You can't stay here. This isn't your life. I'm waiting for you, Knox. I love you. Come with me."

"This isn't something I created, Aria. This is real. I am real."

"Yes, you are real. Our daughters died, Knox. Sven died. You didn't. I didn't. I'm real, and I'm pregnant with your babies. I need you more than our ghost do." I leaned to his mouth, kissing him hard, putting every emotion I had into it, showing him how real I was. "You're my haven, and my haven is missing from me. I'm in hell without you. Come back to me. Come back and be a father to our babies, who aren't inside your head. We need you to protect us, too."

"Then stay here with me. Nothing can hurt us here."

"That's because it's not real. It's your mind protecting you from the pain. It's understandable after what you've endured, but this? This isn't the library. Because right now, I'm lying in it beside you, but you're not with me. You're here, hiding from the agony you know is coming. Tell me about the nightmare."

"I don't want to talk about the nightmare. Fuck that nightmare. I wouldn't do that, Aria. If you're trying to tell me I did that? Then I don't want to come back. I don't deserve to come back." The pain in his tone told me he knew it was real, but he didn't want to believe it was.

"I didn't die, Knox. I'm right here with you. You're staying here because you don't want to leave."

"Lennox is gone. I can't feel him or sense him within me. He's here . . . somewhere, but I can't find him."

My eyes flicked to his forehead, and I chewed my lip. Evoking my magic, I leaned closer, kissing him as I brought my hands up, forcing my magic into the mark, which sent me tumbling out of his head, slamming me back into my body.

"Rude," I muttered.

"Were you fucking him?" Esme asked, her eyes worried but intrigued. "Because it smells like you were."

"There are runes on our foreheads. On the walls of the chamber that he was in. He's with ghosts. Our daughters were there. Sven was too." I sat up, finding a room filled with men who were all focused on me. "I think he created a realm inside his mind, but it's only the size of the library."

"Which would mean its endless," Brander stated, his eyes raking over my body with concern. "You should rethink your strategy. Besides, a queen doesn't leave her people when they're in need of leadership."

"Nice try there, Brander. But a queen's job is to protect her king. She protects him, but she isn't bound by the same rules. A queen without a true king, is nothing. So, I am going to that citadel in the morning, and I'm bringing Knox her fucking head for his throne. Because he's going to want it when he wakes up. I suggest everyone get some sleep. Greer, I need you to find me every book on ancient runes. We have to find the one Hecate used to suppress Lennox and Ember. You and Lore can help Avyanna find it while we're kicking Hecate's ass."

CHAPTER 37
ARIA

'd dressed for battle in sleek black breathable leather pants and a shirt. Greer had helped me into the lightweight cuirass. It was created from shimmering silver and crimson dragon scales, each one etched with the same detail of genuine scales. The pauldrons on the shoulder, neck and beneath my armpits were the color of freshly spilled ink, each carrying the outline of a raven in flight, its mouth open as if it roared the call to arms. The matching vambrace were the same ink-coloring of the pauldrons, yet there were veins of crimson and silver threaded through them, all extending upward toward the scales. My legs were left free of armor, but blades sat in sheaths upon my thighs.

"Wow," Esme whistled as she stood behind me.

"I look like I'm playing dress up," I returned, slowly moving my head to see the twin braids which created a crown atop my head.

"You look like you were born to wear that," she argued. "Listen, if shit goes south today? I need to know you'll come back from it, Aria. I don't want you going in there, then coming back here someone else. Doing this won't be as easy as you think it will be. You're going in there knowing and intending to take innocent lives. There will be a cost to your soul."

"I'm very aware of the cost to my soul. I've paid it already, or did you forget that?" I asked, my forehead creasing as I leaned closer to the glass, sliding my fingers through the black paint. Bringing it up to my face, I dragged it down in the center of one eyebrow, sliding it all the way to my forehead and then down to my jawline. Once I'd finished the right eye, I dragged the remaining paint over my lips and beneath the left eye to the ear. "We're naïve girls to think we could escape this war without spilling innocent blood. We can try to avoid it, but not at the cost of others. We're not gods, and only gods choose who lives and dies. We just send them to the veil, and let them sort the souls out."

"I just meant don't let her turn you into something you cannot live with after this war is won. If we cannot live with what is left of us once we've triumphed, then Hecate still wins. There's what we are willing, and then what we wouldn't do, which I get. But I'm worried about how we will survive if we let her turn us into something as wicked, and cruel as she herself is."

I caught her eye in the mirror, staring at the inky dark paint coloring her face. Slowly turning toward her, I nodded. Reaching back to dip my fingers into the ink, I brought them up as her face scrunched up.

"We're trying to look terrifying, Esmeralda. You look like you're about to walk out on stage for a high school musical." Mirroring what I'd done with my face, I smiled as she held my eyes. "This world is trying to change us, and if we don't change, then we never evolve. There's no escaping this unless we learn to be better than she is. We must become the monsters this world needs, but without losing sight of who we were. I don't intend to murder innocent lives, but I know I can't choose them over the children here. Knox knew the cost, which is why he never argued when I called him a murderer, or unjustly blamed him for being an unfeeling, sadistic monster. He took no joy in the deaths he caused. I was accused of slaughtering those who hadn't dipped their toes into the darkness."

"I don't envy any ruler forced to endure the agonizing choices they've made during this endless war. I just hope there's something after this, something worth everything we've endured. You know?" Lifting her chin with the fingers not covered in paint, I smiled.

"There is going to be so much fucking peace, and so much time to waste that we won't know how to handle it. We'll be bored more often than not, but our children will keep our idle hands busy. You are going to fall in love. You'll have children to play with mine. Our husbands will argue about swords, bickering about who's is larger. The thing is, Esme, we'll live. Because I won't accept anything less."

"Your entire purpose is to destroy her. You're not worried about dying in order to end her reign?" she asked, her lips quivering.

"What are you asking?" I countered, uncertain what she meant.

"What if the cost of fulfilling your destiny is your life,

Aria?" Fear trembled in her words, even as she tried to pretend she wasn't upset.

"Well, then I will pay it. One life to save the entirety of the Nine Realms? It seems like a deal too good to be true. If it sounds too good to be true, then chances are it is." Pulling her in, I hugged her tightly. "We're going to get through this. Don't waste time on things we cannot change. If you're going to waste energy, then waste it on something worthy of employing it on. Come, it's time. Let's go stomp this bitch's ass."

Pulling back, I smiled at the tears falling down her cheeks. "Basilius is my mate, Aria. I feel him so deep inside my soul that it aches. He won't listen when I tell him to back off, which is worrisome. You're going to need to help me kill him." My mouth opened, but a sob exploded from her chest.

"It isn't that bad," I whispered, uncertain how to make her see he wouldn't be a bad choice.

"I let him . . . you know?" When I shook my head, she frowned. "With his tongue down there. Literally, the bastard made me shake so hard it covered his lips like a pastry. I've never felt anything like that. It was like I was the earth, and it was *trembling*."

"Oh, you poor unfortunate soul."

"That wasn't the worst part. I sucked his . . . you know," she whispered, even though it was more like a whispered scream. "I swallowed it, like, I couldn't get it deep enough inside me. My creature? She was cheering me on, as if it was pleasurable to her."

"I fucked Brander last night," Soraya said as she swept into the room.

Great, I was the only one not having actual sex.

"He's . . . teaching me to take pleasure in sex again. Brander is on an entirely different level than what I've dealt with before. He didn't expect me to do anything other than what felt good to me. I'm not sure he's even normal. The moment he approached, I tried to suck his cock."

"I'm failing to see the problem, ladies. You both seem rather troubled about getting good dick. Meanwhile, my dick is sleeping beauty and I'm a fucking the vertically challenged one throwing rotten apples at the evil queen. Did he also use his tongue on, you know . . . down there?" I asked, frowning as I felt dream Knox between my thighs.

"No, he told me if I was his good girl, he'd teach me anything I wanted to learn. I said I wanted to learn what he liked."

"And the huge romantic guy that he is, had you suck his dick?" I asked with my face scrunching up at the strangeness of this entire conversation.

"It was a punishment. He'd asked me what I enjoyed done to me. My answer was sucking his cock, which, apparently, wasn't the right answer because he knew I only said it to make him happy." Soraya's brow creased as her lips tugged down into a deep frown. "I need to know what the answer is before tonight."

"Tell him that you've had pleasure before. That it is his job to try everything so that you can answer him correctly." At my reply, she nodded slowly. "Use him, he's one of the smoothest guys I know."

Siobhan rushed into the room, forcing my eyes to close. "Killian . . ." She exhaled with a little shiver. "I have never been so thoroughly fucked in my entire life." Eva entered with Avyanna, both smiling as if they'd spent the night along the lines of the others.

"This is my life now." Ember would've said something if she was within me. After seeing myself in Knox's mind, it worried me that he'd taken her from me somehow. She'd have been pissed to know *everyone* had gotten laid last night except us. "We have a battle to wage, so if you're intending to add to the sex happening last, save it."

"Someone is cranky she didn't get dick. Maybe try feeding Ember, she'll wake Knox up real quick," Siobhan muttered, then stared at me strangely. "Are you okay?"

"I'm fine. I'll be much better once I hand Hecate her ass," I muttered beneath my breath. Walking down the corridor, I paused as the men came into view, full armor covering every inch of them, except their heads. "Damn." I looked like I'd slipped on knee and elbow pads compared to the men. "Are you ready?"

"Are *you* ready?" Zyion asked, his armor the same he'd worn when he'd fought against Aden.

"I'm ready. If we stall any longer, she'll be outside the gates. Siobhan, did you set the wards around the castle?"

"I placed wards with Killian as my witness. No one will be able to come inside the gates, or leave them once we portal to the citadel." Her eyes slid to Killian, a smile played on her lips. He, on the other hand, looked unaffected by her. It was discerning that he'd fuck her, and then not even bother to acknowledge her.

"Basilius, you and the others are ready?" I asked, then felt relief as he nodded in reply. "I need you to tell the others that I need them to remain away from the citadel. I can't control my magic as well as I'd like. In order to ensure no harm befalls the dragons, you're going to need to wait until I bring down the walls."

"How the hell are you planning to bring down the walls of the citadel? They're impenetrable, and reinforced by magic," he asked, his lips jerking into a smirk, as if he thought I was lying. "If you think I'm walking in there with some girl who is bluffing about her abilities, you're fucking wrong."

"She has leveled an entire castle to the fucking ground. If you're scared, Basilius, just say so. I'm sure Aria can find something for you to do here. The cook probably needs help cleaning the kitchens," Esme shot back, forcing my eyebrows to shoot toward my hairline. Shots fired! "You're obviously not man enough to be comfortable taking orders from a woman, anyway."

"Careful, Little Bird. One might think you need another trip to the supply closet. Was I man enough in there for you?" Basilius stepped closer, his rattle registering in my ears before it even built within his chest.

It was dominant, but Knox would easily subdue him. Esme, on the other hand, slowly began pressing her thighs together, clenching against his demand to submit. Her spine curved, even as she glared murderously at him. The moment she began to lower, his rattle silenced. Tipping his dark head, he smirked. Her eyes slid to mine with a look of I-told-you-so simmering in them.

"Everyone knows the plan?" Waiting for the eyes to go up, I exhaled. "Here goes nothing. May the gods be merciful, because I won't be."

CHAPTER 38
ARIA

A dense fog drifted up from the riverbank of the Red River. It hovered within the ground inside the citadel, blanketing it in foreboding stillness. Footpaths high on the walls began flickering with flames, slowly revealing the soaring walls until they encircled the entire stronghold. As if they thought to ward off the moisture churning into a dark, foreboding obscuring cover. The more they fought to remove the mist, the thicker it laid on the ground, slowly rising to ensure no eyes fell upon us outside of the wrought iron gates, and stone bastion.

The denizens within loitered, unable to flee the moistness that soaking their cloaks, gowns, or tunics. It weighed against their lifeless flesh, adding dread to their sickly, lifeless minds. The foul, acrid scent of death clung to the wet air, forcing it beyond the fortified walls. Rotting corpses were pungent, revealing the level of the depravity within.

The rotting corpses weren't the worst of the acrid, putrid scents drifting from inside. The flesh of the creatures Hecate exhausted beyond their worth, were currently

503

being incinerated. The smoke was so thick I could taste it from where I stood, slowly and meticulously unweaving the multiple lines of magic drifting through the city around us, fueling the goddess within the towering protection of the citadel.

I moved my fingers, but not enough to even be perceptible to anyone around me. The entire army of the dead sat just beneath the surface of the ground beneath our feet. I felt the disturbance of the city at our back, the wrongness of those dwelling within the residences. Hecate had either taken control or she'd placed her own batteries close enough within range for to use at her convenience.

"The village is filled with dark witches. Hundreds of them," I whispered barely above a breath of air. "They'll need to handle them. There's also a convoy of witches' incoming from the farthest southern pass of the Valley of the Dead."

"We'll handle them easily," Basilius said, his hand touching the small of my back. "The right side, correct?" He turned, and looked down at me.

"Correct. Killian, until we reveal the others, aim the majority of the archers toward the village in case they join in, which I'm nearly positive they will. Instruct them not to hesitate no matter what they appear to be," I instructed continuing to find each slithering whisper of magic drifting throughout the land, straight to Hecate.

"They're adept in murdering witches," Killian said with a calmness I didn't share.

One wrong move and we would end up dead. Hecate may be weakened, but she'd taken precautionary measures. She'd brought in reinforcements, along with several lords she'd forced to accept her darkness. Rolling my shoulders past the chafing of the untried armor, I heard Killian chuckle.

"Normally, you'd wear a new set of armor to train in before wearing it to battle. Due to all leather, you should stretch it before wearing it," he divulged, and I narrowed my eyes at him. "Greer meant well. He's not a fighter, though. He'd take a book—or a dick—any day over a sword."

"He does like his books, and anyone willing to play willing victim."

The scent of sweat and apprehension from the army behind our back, still coming through the portal clung heavily in the air. It was probably a good thing the mindless witches within were burning the expired batteries.

"Remember, once she's seen you, you are to appear to 'protect' me aside from her intended hit, Basilius." At my air quotes, he'd frowned. "She will strike through the middle, aiming for me. You shove me, I protect you."

"How skilled are you at protecting people, Aria?"

"I don't want to jinx it, Basilius, but one of the two numbers is zero. In my favor, of course." His grunt was the only confirmation of acknowledgment to confirm he'd heard me at all. Turning to Brander, who'd forced Lore to stay behind in his stead, I called to him. "Brander, check on Siobhan in the back. Make sure the girls are almost finished. Hecate is right fucking there," I whispered, watching as she moved forward, inching toward the front gates, then stood in the tunnel leading outside, directly in front of me. Her dark head tilted as if she were listening for something.

The bitch was walking straight toward us. A sadistic smile played on my lips, even as the air caught in my lungs, my pulse quickening as I watched her pause halfway down the tunnel, which led to the iron-wrought gates. My heartbeat was hammering in my ears, part excitement, part fear. She just needed to remain inside long enough for the girls to finish their part. They were close. I could feel them reaching, as the weavers beneath me braided each tendril of magic. Carefully, precisely, I slipped one after another to them through the shared bond.

Esmeralda pulled on her end, even as Soraya tugged on hers. Exhaling the dread, I counted to thirty inside my head and then forcefully ripped the larger, thicker veins of magic to me. Hecate's head swung left and then right before the largest grid she'd crafted, the one that fed her the lion's share of her magic, imploded beneath the ground, shaking through the entire citadel.

Her eyes rounded, feeling each vein collapse. I'd cut off the blood supply that threaded throughout the body. The moment she darted toward the tunnels, I unleashed hell on the citadel. The first, largest, ball of fire slammed down in the back, thundering through the air, deafeningly.

Inside my head, freeing the music to the air around me, In This Moment's cover of "In the Air Tonight" by Phil Collins hummed to life, hummed to life. Her head whipped toward me as I moved from the thick, whispers of the fog. Several fiery meteors slammed into the walls, damaging them. Then I brought the entire thing down with precisely timed blasts of what remained of the meteors I'd constructed last night.

I waited until I could scent the grease burning on the

arrowheads of the archers behind me before I lifted my arm. When I dropped it, a volley of arrows lit up the air around me. As they hit their marks, I heard the grunts of them tearing flesh to bone, igniting the corpses afire. Wiggling my fingers, I brought up the army, slowly strolling forward. Once I could see past the fog, I turned, watching a helmetless Basilius strolling exactly like his brother, toward me.

The moment he was beside me, I turned and continued to move toward Hecate. I felt her rage as she surged, sucking power to her for the attack.

"Slowly," I whispered as I turned to Basilius. He paused beside me, grabbed my throat with his ungloved hand, brushing his lips against mine.

"I hope you're as good as everyone thinks you are, Aria."

"Me too," I whispered and then turned as her blast came through the barrier. "Now." Basilius shoved me to the ground, but my hands were already up, blocking the blast from hitting him. With a softer, less lethal hit, I sent him crashing to the ground before Hecate's magic could make contact.

Replacing my shield as Hecate's horrid laughter danced in my ears, I counted to thirty, allowing her a moment to think she'd hit him. Rising, I rushed to him, shaking him and putting on an award-winning performance.

"The king is down!" I shouted, turning toward the beautiful sight of the village aflame. From where I sat, I could see the witches scattering with the arrows peppering their bodies. "The king is dead!" I shouted, slowly bringing in more mist, allowing Basilius to crawl on his stomach to the line behind us. Bringing up one of the large corpses from my army, I continued screaming for help. It only took me imagining Knox not coming out of the catatonic state to sob heartrending cries. Men rushed forward to pull the lifeless corpse from me, leaving me sitting in the center of the misty field, pretending to be crying. Only, I was.

"It was nice of you to show up here. It saved me the trouble of hunting you down." The smugness in her tone had my smile returning. "Like I said, if I can't have him, then neither can you. Such a waste, he was such an amazing lover."

"That he was, grandmother," I agreed, slowly rising. "I warned you not to touch that which belongs to me, didn't I?" I questioned, my tone holding real rage, and I sent a pulse of my power slamming into her mind. Every emotion she'd fed me slammed back into her, tenfold.

"So you did. But, you see, he was mine long before he was yours, little slut." Her tone was breathy, which I wondered if she used when she wanted to conceal emotion. She'd used it in the library too, only through Luna's lips. I could see her gaze flicking to the village, needing them to survive long enough for her to siphon enough of their power to fight back.

"Something wrong, Hecate?" I asked, my tone bored but level.

"What's the matter, darling? You should be out celebrating your victory."

"I was just thinking how you're going to die screaming. It's how you should go down after what you've done to this world. You destroyed mystical creatures. All because you feared having to work for what you needed."

"I'm a goddess! I worked for everything I have ever had. You think it was easy forcing this world to mold to what I wanted it to be?" she snarled.

"I think you're a petty, pathetic, washed-up goddess who no one will remember once I am finished."

Power erupted around her, which forced me to collect and gather the remaining threads fueling her magic. "Little Girl Gone," by Chinchilla filled the entire air, echoing throughout the space around us. I sang along with the first song, ensuring it pissed her off. The more pissed off she got, the more access I gained to the waves of power drifting to her. I had come to take it from her. Her jaw clenched, which allowed me to see the mindboggling veins of ink-colored wispy lines that connected to her grids drifting throughout the land.

"I was all dressed up and thought why not come bash in your fucking after I've ripped your heart out. I mean, do you even have a heart inside that sadistic, empty chest?"

"I think you're suicidal or stupid. I'm not sure which yet, honestly. It has to be one or the other. You can't beat me, Aria. I am eternal. This world holds pieces of me within it that you'll never entirely eradicate," she hissed vehemently.

"Do you know what the problem is with an invasive species? Okay, let's be honest, in your case, it's more of a parasite issue." Her nostrils flared at my reference to her not belonging here, or maybe it was me calling her a parasite. Either way, she allowed emotions to lead her, which was my intention. "If you don't know the answer, it's okay to admit it, Hecate. Seriously, no one knows everything. Since you're too stupid to even make a guess, I'll explain."

"You little bitch."

"Name calling is the lowest form of argument on the Graham's Hierarchy of Disagreement chart, I can explain that too if you need. No? Still, I expected better." I tutted as I tilted my head. "The problem with parasites is that all one must do to rid the world of them is to give it a natural cleanse. In the sake of you needing small words, we'll call it a purge. Once you begin this purge, one by one the parasites begin to vanish. They're also easy enough to spot, since again, they don't belong here. So, to get this show started? I'm going to send every single victim you've ever created after your sources of power. We'll call it karma."

"You don't even know what my power is, Aria. I bet you think you're so fucking clever, don't you? But you're not. Just as you lost Knox, you'll lose this fight as well."

"It's in the witches you've created by infecting them with pieces of yourself. It's something you've been doing since you first got banished to the Nine Realms." Her composure slipped just enough to tell me I'd been right. "You never needed them. You merely wanted them to worship you to feed that over- inflated ego. But you realized that they held power *you* could use. If they held the power for you, then you never would weaken. That was something you'd already attempted with the humans, which was why they put you here, among creatures who weren't as feeble. They assumed you'd merely slip in without much of a fuss. But not you."

"Oh, don't stop now. I'm enjoying your little made-up fairy tale."

Snorting, I forced my nails to push through my fingertips. "You see, you *were* a powerful goddess before they sent you here. You *had* worshipers who'd idolized you—and rightly so. After all, you didn't start out so vicious or inhuman. You were a symbol of witchcraft, the night, the moon, and lastly, necromancy. Things that didn't bring you the adoration you desired." Slicing through my palms, I held my hands out with my palms down. Droplets rolled to the tips of my fingers before dropping to the ground, summoning the dead.

"I'm not the only one who can control the dead, darling." Her eyes sparkled with pride, which made my stomach churn. "I take it you intend to raise King Karnavious as well, yes? If not, I'd enjoy his corpse. After all, I enjoyed him while he lived."

"We'll see about Knox, since he's no longer among us. And no, I'm not like you, but where you murdered them for your sick enjoyment, or as batteries. Me? I'm about to unleash them as a form of cosmic karma, right back at you. They're going to hunt down *every* single dark witch housing your dark magic and release them. The moment they fall, I'll claim them and add them to the hunting party."

"You can't kill all of them or me. The only creatures who could are—" Dragon fire erupted behind me, bathing the city in molten flames. The heat of it scorched my back, and the flames reflected in Hecate's eyes. The pentagram on her forehead glowed, even as the rattles of the many dragons echoed through the night, lighting it up until it mirrored day.

"Didn't your mother ever tell you that it was rude to interrupt people?" Tapping my chin, I feigned ignorance. "Oh, yes. There's a balance in every world. So, of course, we'll be keeping your magic, but you? You'll go back into your tomb. It's not personal, but you see, you fucked with the wrong bitch. I warned you not to touch him, but you just couldn't help yourself. Are you listening? If I were you, I'd listen."

The fear in her eyes was thick in the air. Her eyes continually trailed the dragons, who were now throwing dark witches into the air, tearing them apart. They flew over the ruins of the citadel, gliding through the air, effortlessly. Dragons were a thing of true beauty. Savage, murderous beauty, but semantics.

"It's rude not to listen when someone speaks to you. Especially when that person is the Queen of Dragons, Hecate." Flicking my lethal claws open, I licked one, staring right at her. "Make me forget where I was again? Oh, into the tomb you'll go. In fact, I intend to shove you so fucking far deep inside that tomb, that'll you'll be ringing the devil's doorbell. To clarify that, I'm not talking about your fucking clit. But I'm not a complete bitch, granny saggy tits. Once a month, I'll bring Knox's corpse to your tomb."

"You'd let me have him after all the effort you endured in order to get him back?"

"Of course, I intend to bring him to you at least once a month. Aren't you listening to me? Of course, I'll have to make it worth his time. So, I'll fuck him on top of your coffin. You'll get the pleasure of hearing him moan my name while you lay there, unable to move or escape. You'll have to put up with my screams, but honestly? He's a fucking beast when he fucks. Oh, that's right. You don't know that because your darkness makes them, how shall I put this? Unfuckable? Impotent? How much of your power did you waste trying to get him to stand up? Because I saw the kiss he gave you, but you couldn't even get his lips to move. Damn, must really piss you off. After everything you did to take him from me, and you still didn't get that monster dick of his."

"I had him *many* times," she lied as her chest heaved with her anger intensifying. It was fine since she had no magic I'd allow her to use. I'd walked right in and had taken it from the bitch.

"You and I both know the truth of it. He never even kissed you. Not unless you call placing lifeless lips against yours. Let us not forget that, when he did, he dripped goo onto your old, saggy-ass tits? That's because you had to fill him to the bream with your oily magic even for a lifeless kiss from him. How fucking desperately pathetic it was to watch you forcing his lips against yours."

Her snarl of outrage caught the ear of a dragon, who dove for her. Hecate dove for the ground, escaping the flames by mere inches. Once they passed over her, she stood, slapping against the skirt of her gown. Wide, horrified eyes darted between the dragons flying above her. Lifting her hands, she aimed them toward the dragons, only for me to forcefully pull her magic away each time she sought to use it. I just smiled.

"I warned you, Hecate. He's mine, and even as he is, I am keeping him." Stepping closer, I smiled as my head canted to the side. "The best thing about Knox, Hecate? Is his soul. A soul you've spent eons attempting to destroy. It still shines from within that beast. If you stare into his eyes when those shields are down? You'll be able to see how truly exquisite they are. Of course, you fractured it as you sought to force the darkness into him, but you created fissures. All you did was create a way for the light to reach in, to heal him. How do I know? I've felt the heat from his actual soul when I'm with him. His flame calls to mine, which made little sense at first. My flames were red, as were his—"

"He's a murderer of witches, in case that's slipped your empty head." Hecate's inability to not be the center of every single thing happening was telling. She was the true definition of a narcissist.

"There was no such thing before you entered the Nine Realms. You created the history of witches. But it wasn't enough, you forced it down everyone's throats until they believed it to be true. You changed the history of the events. That's why no one remembers the wars before your entrance into this world. Well, other than those who actually fought them. That's why you attacked the royal families, killing the elders and every king and queen who refused to bow or bend a knee." She was panicking, but I remained unaffected. I didn't want to take joy from anyone's misery, but I allowed myself to taste the bitterness of hers.

Flaming arrows shot through the air, slamming into the witches she'd been calling to her. Her hair singed as one of the arrows barely missed giving her a haircut. A snort of amusement left my lips as another bevy of arrows crashed into the next wave. Then, dragons shot through the air to the right of us, opening their mouths to reveal the serrated teeth, which reflected the fire within their throats, seconds before it released, decimating the witches.

"Once you'd murdered the weaker ones, you then went

after the more powerful ones. Of course, you brought the weaker beings with you, in your army. But what to do about those ones that terrified you most? Wasn't it the races who'd been able to wield flames? Can't have fire around all the witches you'd crafted. No, because the light they wield is pure. It would have exposed you, and driven the darkness out. That would have exposed you, since the day you came here is the same as the first existence of witches or witchcraft. Then there was the pesky issue of a prince, one who'd pissed you off. You didn't want him gone, not with all the plans you had in mind for him. But, alas, when in their true forms, dragons and phoenixes could discern the truth behind your little secret infliction that created an entire race."

"I admit, you are much smarter than you look. It doesn't change the fact that I won, and I'll always win. This world is mine! You're not strong enough to stop me, little girl. You should've chosen your side more carefully." She folded her arms across her ample chest, and I snorted. "So, pray tell, what the fuck are you doing here? If you came to die, I won't hesitate to end you."

She was trying to pull on millions of lines at once, which allowed me to send one after another to the dead army. Merging minds with the weavers, I gave the signal as I handed off braided ropes of thin, wispy lines allowing them to diligently hand each one. The largest ones, which were here, I held in place with mana.

"No, I came for my fucking throne, and I'm intending to leave here with it as well as your fucking head."

A malicious smile spread over my lips as she caught the flicker of gold lines swirling over my forehead. The bright, startling shade of turquoise glowed as the radiance of the gold fleck floated within them, as well. Thin wispy tendrils slowly slid down my throat, then encircled it like the finest jewelry.

She ducked as a dragon turned, sending his leathery wing toward her. "Do you think your little symbol scares me?" she asked, darting her eyes to the skies as dragons, flaming arrows, and the din of swords meeting in battle echoed around us.

Spinning on my heel, I took in the melee forces she'd called in, who were even now being mowed down, easily. Without her controlling each one with her magic, they were worthless corpses. Unlike mine, who I'd enhanced with the ability to wield weapons from countless hours of watching Knox, and his men train before he'd returned, forcing me to the battlefield where he'd kept my sister in a cage.

"I don't care if it does or it doesn't. I'm not here for just you. No, that's the easiest part of this visit. I'm here to make good on exactly what I said I'd do to you. I'm an honorable bitch like that."

Lowering my head, I let the land fuel my magic. My hands lifted as "Popular Monster" by Falling in Reverse reverberated throughout the entire kingdom. Let them hear my wrath and feel my flames. As the song began, I turned to the dead and spoke in a dead language she couldn't understand and turned them into dust particles. Miniature cyclones shot throughout the land, following every line of her magic to the source.

"There, now that your battery tickets have been punched, we can get to it, grandmother. Are you ready to hear me sing? You had Knox ask me to do so if you recall."

My eyes opened up, showing her every fucking emotion I'd bottled up since the moment I'd returned. I sang along with the lyrics, letting it all come out as wrath, violence, and pain. Raising my hands, I sucked more mana as it collided with my magic and then prepared to be released when the song hit the second chorus.

The moment the song hit it, I shot the largest blast of energy I'd ever managed to aim at the statue I'd left standing in the center of the citadel, by some miracle. Hecate dodged the falling stones of her self-erected monument as they slammed down around her.

I sent more magic punching up through the air before it propelled the lifeless bodies up from the courtyard, then used wind to drive them high, into the air. The dragons shot toward them, catching them before throwing them here, then one by one, they consumed portions, allowing the others to rain down around her. A laugh bubbled in my chest as she dodged them, barely missing being hit.

Inside the library, I'd realized the large pentagram placement on the map. The moment I'd seen it, I'd realized it was hers. I'd then routed the path to each element, followed the river, pinning each one before the largest palaces, which all had rivers in front of them. I'd realized I could neutralize her for a while if I disturbed the largest structure, which was connected throughout each realm. The power from each one flowed throughout the pentagram-shaped grid and fed Hecate the realms' power. Now, all of the realms would have their power back. They'd need it to help us drive the bitch back to her tomb, for good.

Hundreds of grids placed beneath the soil detonated, forcing even more lifeless bodies to shoot through the air. When they dropped, they were impaled on branches or hit the ground like decaying water balloons.

Hecate gradually spun in a circle, eyes flooded with horror, and then light began slamming down into any witch left standing still. The citadel was rubble behind her, which only had me smiling with satisfaction. I'd harnessed every single emotion she'd forced me to feel, saving everything to release against her. The entire time, I'd heard Knox whispering for me to turn my pain into power, as he'd done so many times throughout his lifetime.

Hecate hummed, which called to her familiars. A desperate move to save herself. Dire wolves began tearing at the shield, and the smile on my face dropped, turning icy. Bringing them through the barrier, I forced balls of violent, violet-colored light inside every one of them. The moment they turned toward me, I grinned as I made a popping sound, watching as they exploded to ash.

"That was for Lore. No one fucks with Daddy on my watch, mutts." I turned back to Hecate. "Sorry, were those your dogs? It must have been something they ate."

She inched backward as I used the wind to blow the ashes back to her.

"This isn't happening!" she snarled, which caused a sick, twisted amount of enjoyment to rush through me.

My rattle grew within me, not needing Ember's help to get my words to come out layered so they echoed around her. "Where the fuck is your god now?"

She turned in a circle, seeking to escape the dragons that were landing, corralling her and preventing her from escaping. Using an unhuman rush of speed, I slammed into her, smiling as she went ass-over-head, rolling over the debris littering the ground. Slowly, I walked around her as the others watched from behind the shield. Her wide, horrified eyes fed my excitement, wanting to rip her apart, bathing in the putrid blood.

"I warned you when I got here, that I'd fucked your world up. Should've listened and learned the first time. Next time? You should take a moment to consider how you fuck around. Then calculate what happened, because I will do whatever is needed to ensure you find out how back you fucked up. You have no home because you messed with those inside of mine. Your network of magic, along with your grids are down, and won't be easy to repair. I've sent a call out to every realm, asking them to divert the river away from your kingdom. My undead army is even as I speak, killing your dark witches. One by one, they'll all fall down, Hecate."

When I held my hand out, Killian placed the stake from a white oak tree in it. This was the reason she'd insisted on having trade open to Norvalla. It was the one thing that weakened her, forcing her true form to work ten times harder to heal when harmed. Luckily, she was still fucking stuck inside it, regardless of the time mess up I'd had.

"Don't do this to me!"

"I warned you. I don't make idle threats any longer. If I tell you I will do it, believe me."

Stepping closer, I jerked on the medallion, snapping the chain free from her throat. "I need that!"

"I know you do," I said as her skin began to age. "I won't stop taking from you or hunting you until you die or are returned to your tomb. There's no hole dark enough for you to hide in anymore. You wanted this battle. I brought you with a war unlike any other the Nine Realms has ever seen before. A united Nine Realms, which shall stand as one against you, Hecate. You grossly miscalculated when you hid behind the walls." After digging the butt of the stake into the ground, I gripped her around the throat and shoved her back onto it. Killian and Zyion secured the rope around her chest and legs, and when they finished, we stepped back, watching her trying to escape.

"The rope is hemlock, grandmother. I brought it just for you. Know this, I am no savior, but I am a monster. Not like you—*never* like you. I'm the one they needed to fight to take you down. I won't rest until your reign ends, and mine begins. Oh, and the best part? My chaos hasn't even fully reached its full potential. And Knox? He's not dead. He's merely allowing his Queen of Chaos to sharpen her claws. So, shall we test them? Oh, wait. I also promised him a gift when I returned from killing you." Turning my head left and right, I smiled brightly and then clapped my palms together. "Perfect! Lovely, I've decided on my gift for my king. Since I can't allow him to outdo me, your head will do nicely. Plus, he made me a throne to match his, one created from your children's skulls. So, hold still, I'd hate to fuck it up." I sliced through her throat, smiling as her blood sprayed everywhere.

"Ashes to ashes," Killian said beside me.

"Dust to dust," Zyion growled.

"In no goddess, shall we trust." I laughed, biting my lip as the coppery tang of her blood lined my teeth. Flicking my fingers, I brought the vibrant blue flames up to my lips and blew on them until her head caught fire. Stepping back, I smiled as it charred the skin to black flakes, which drifted upward until the flames died out. What was left was nothing but the skull with a circle-less pentagram on the forehead. "You look much better without a head. It's a vast improvement, Hecate. If Knox were here, he'd thank you for the skull. We must never forget our manners, right?" I asked the men standing beside me, who were watching the bitch burn. "Anyone bring marshmallows? I've been craving some lately."

CHAPTER 39
ARIA

The battlefield was bathed in blood that ran in rivers. My heartbeat drummed in my ears, the entire group celebrated by throwing body parts, which caused my stomach to churn. I stood in the midst of it all, dragons swooping down to feed on the dead while the girls danced around barefooted. Tears rolled down my cheeks as I thought of what Knox would be doing if he'd been here.

Would he dance with me? It would be rather morbid, but Hecate was afire, her witches were being hunted down and rounded up for extermination. I'd allowed the dead a chance to deal with those who'd harmed them in life. It wasn't much, but even now, I could feel the souls singing with relief, knowing they'd survived long enough to help wash away the sickness within the land.

Hecate wouldn't remain dead, but in order to put her down, she had to be drained. There was also the issue of Aurora, who'd begun feeding on the magic of those without darkness. It meant she'd need to be handled before she became like her mother. The girls would need to be checked for darkness as well.

"Why aren't you celebrating?" Esme asked, clapping me on the back. Her violet eyes were aglow with adrenaline.

"I was thinking about how Knox would've loved to see this. This moment is one that will be remembered, he should be here with me. He helped me learn how to be this person. Now he's missing out on it. For so long, I've wanted to hurt her for what she's done to him and the realms. I should be celebrating, but really? All I want is for him to hold me and tell me I'm not a horrible person for enjoying the small things. Like murdering my grandmother."

"Yeah, how are those hormones working out?"

"He should be here with us."

"King Karnavious wouldn't care if he was here or not," Zyion stated, even as Eva smiled warmly at him. "He'd be glad you kicked her ass. It doesn't matter how you do it, or when it happens, as long as it happens. Tonight, she burns. The Nine Realms sleeps free of her wrath, and will for a while. You did that, Aria. You led his army today, and did what every king wishes of a queen. You protected him and his people, and you didn't flinch once."

"If he were here?" Killian muttered. "You wouldn't be allowed to celebrate. He'd have you back in that library celebrating alone. That's what you'd be doing. So, enjoy it while you can. Knox doesn't celebrate victories. He said the only one he'd ever celebrate was the end of this forsaken war."

"I think you have an ear on you," I stated, reaching over

to pick it off, examining it before tossing it over my shoulder.

"Did you see her, Basilius?" Esme asked, her smile fully reaching her expressive eyes. "Best fucking friend."

"Best lesbian, maybe," Ember snorted.

"Holy fuck. Where have you fucking been? You fucking left me. I needed you. Knox needed you! Ember, answer me now!"

"Maybe sleeping. I don't recall. Wow, who fucked shit up? Can we have him?" she asked, even as I snorted.

"You have her. Me, I'm the one who unleashed hell on Hecate and stomped her ass. Without you. Sleeping? Are you fucking kidding me? I thought fucking lost you, Ember. I've never been more terrified in my entire life."

"I love you too, Aria. I'm proud of you." Warmth washed through me, as if she was trying to show me how much she loved me. *"Dragons! Oh, can we ride them? One, two? Can we ski on dragons?"* Her excitement caused my lips to tremble.

"No, we cannot."

She made a disgruntled sound and then softly purred. *"Our babies are going to be dragons. I can feel it."*

"I guess that's a good thing since I'm the Queen of Dragons."

"Wait, you're the Queen of Dragons, and we still can't ride one?"

"No, in a moment, I need to go check on something."

"I found this over by where you removed Hecate's head," Siobhan stated, handing me a bloodied crown.

"Fantastic. Thanks." I took it from her and plopped it on my head. "Does this blood make my eyes pop, Esme?"

"Honestly, it brings out the evil in them. But if I may suggest something?" She frowned before moving her finger toward the blood dripping from my crown. "Might want to clean the brain matter off before putting it on next time. It ruins the whole pretty but evil vibe. Might I also suggest using Hecate's bones for your next crown, My Queen?"

"Shall we use her fingers or ribs? And can we add jewels? Or quartz maybe? Quartz would make the blood stand out more." I pondered, tapping my chin.

"I think either would stand out well," she said, giving me a cheeky smile, which I returned.

"Okay. I'm going to go check on Knox," I admitted, smiling at her as Basilius stepped up behind her, offering me a subtle nod.

"I am honestly impressed. Liliana would never have survived being on the battlefield, let alone fought beside us. She never did like being anywhere blood was let. But you? You wear it beautifully, My Queen," he confessed, bowing.

"Thank you, Basilius." I glanced at Killian, who winked before he threw a head toward Brander, who caught it. Within moments, the men were playing some twisted version of soccer. "That's so wrong," I muttered.

"Speak for yourself." Esme laughed, darting over to steal the ball from Basilius.

The others rushed forward, each one teaming up with one of the men. Exhaling, I turned to stare at the blue flames burning still. The white oak would burn for a thousand years, which was more than long enough for me to travel to the Kingdom of Fire and unearth the two final elements. It could wait until I had Knox back.

Opening a portal, I entered the silent library, spotting a sleeping Lore outside the chamber where Knox was. I stopped to cover him up and kiss his forehead, smiling at the peacefulness of Lore's face. If I had to guess, I'd say his feeding frenzy hadn't had anything to do with his other half being incubus. It had probably been the pain he'd endured. As quietly as I could, I let myself into the room where Knox slept and pulled the door closed behind me. Then I removed the crown and set it as well as the bloodied head on the table.

"We won, Knox. I led your brothers and your army onto the field today. I kept them safe, as I knew you'd have done if you'd been there." Wiping both my face, and hands off, I leaned over, kissing his lips. "I missed you out there beside me. I should've enjoyed it, but I couldn't without you. But I also couldn't wait for you to wake up. I became a monster today, and I don't feel anything. Numb, I guess? I just really miss you and need you to come back to me. You'd have some sage advice about holding on to who I was, wouldn't you?" I peered down, frowning. "If I'm being honest?" I glanced at our hands, ignoring the tear rolling down my cheek. "I liked hurting you. Of course, I didn't like that there could be innocent creatures within the citadel, or the city. But you were inside my head holding me steady." Rubbing my thumb over his palm, I smiled as tears slowly fell without stopping. "Save one, or save many. Your people —who I guess are our people now—would've been her target. I couldn't let that happen. A queen protects her king, that's what you told me." Chewing my lip, I released a shuddered breath. "I need my king back, Karnavious. I can't do this without you with me. I love you. Do you hear me? I'm in love with you, and I need you to come back to me. Your chaos stirs mine, and I can't be the queen if I

don't have my king beside me. You're my King of Chaos."
His hand tightened against mine, and my breath stalled as
I slowly dragged my eyes to his face. Black eyes with flickering crimson embers floating within them watched me
without blinking. My lips parted as a sob burst free from
my lungs. Knox's eyes slipped to the color of an angry sea,
sending me adrift as the world seemed to mute. Then a
loud, heartrending sob broke from my lips as a shattered
breath of sound. "Knox."

THE END, FOR NOW
THANK YOU

Thank you for understanding that I'm human, and that this year has been very turbulent and horrifying for my family. This year knocked me down, but I'm getting back up. I promise. I raised Miranda since she was fourteen, so for us, we lost a child, my daughter. I may not have given birth, but I taught her how to size a bar, how to cook, how to raise her child, drive, and to be a good, caring human being. She was one of my children, and I personally took care of her in my home, tending to her while she was on hospice. I was the one to call her time of death, which knocked me down so hard that I wasn't certain I'd get back up for a while. But here I am, rising from the ashes. I'm learning how to live without her here with me. I'm helping my son raise their son. Both of them needed me to be present for them as they said their final goodbye to his best friend, and his son goodbye to his momma, who was only 28 years old.

I promise not to leave you teetering on the cliff too long. Thank you for being supportive during this unimaginable heartbreaking time of loss. You are all truly amazing humans, and I couldn't ask for better fans. ~Amelia Hutchins, the crazy, exhausted author person.

Nine Realms' Compendium

Karnavious Bloodline

Knox Karnavious—King of Norvalla,
High King of the Nine Realms
Brander—Brother of Knox
Ronin—Brother of Knox
Basilius—Brother of Knox
Acheron—Brother of Knox
Kael—Brother of Knox
Loren (Lore)—Brother of Knox
Faderin (Fade)—Brother to Knox
Gideon—Brother of Knox
Mateo—Brother of Knox
Celia (Kalyria) Moreau—Sister of Killian
Killian Moreau—Knox's best friend
Liliana—Deceased wife of Knox, sister of Killian
Greer—Friend, teacher, and butler to Knox, vampire
King Lennox Karnavious—Former King of Norvalla,
and father of Knox

Queen Eira Karnavious—Former Queen of Norvalla,
and mother of Knox
Draghana Karnavious—Former Queen of Norvalla
Dracarius Karnavious—Former King of Norvalla
Sven—Son to Liliana, and Knox Karnavious
Evelyn Karnavious—Daughter of Knox, and Aria
Karnavious
Eleanora Karnavious—Daughter of Knox, and Aria
Karnavious

Prometheus Bloodline

Aria Primrose Karnavious—Queen of Sunfire,
Queen of Dragons & Phoenixes,
and Official Queen of Chaos.
Esmeralda Prometheus—Cousin to Aria
Aden—Cousin, to Aria.
Eva Prometheus—Cousin to Aria
Griffon Prometheus—Father to Aria Karnavious,
dethroned King of Phoenixes
Tirsynth Prometheus—Previous King of Phoenixes
Scylla Prometheus—Previous Queen of Phoenixes,
descended of Fafnir
Hagen Prometheus—Second born son of Tirsynth and
Scylla
Vane Prometheus—First born son of Griffon Prometheus
Zyion—Zyion the Vicious, Crowned Prince of the Aesir.
Head of the Queen's Guard
Baldrick—Tirsynth's Bastard born son

Hecate Bloodline Introduced So Far

Freya—Daughter of Hecate
Aurora—Daughter of Hecate
Hysteria—Daughter of Hecate
Kamara—Daughter of Hecate
Hecate—Goddess of Magic, and Queen of Witches
Amara—Daughter of Freya
Kinvara / Valeria—Daughters of Freya and succubi twins
Aine / Luna— Daughters of Freya and alpha werewolf twins
Sabine / Callista—Daughters of Freya and nymph twin
Reign / Rhaghana—Daughters of Freya
Tieghan / Tamryn—Daughters of Freya

Alpha Pack

Dimitri—King of the Wolves, pure-born alpha werewolf
Jasper—Pure-born werewolf, Fallon's son, and Prince of the Alpha wolves, deceased
Fallon—Pure-born alpha wolf, King of the Wolves, deceased

Minotaur

Gerald—Old King of the Kingdom of Unwanted Beasts
Garrett—King of the Kingdom of Unwanted Beasts
Other people worthy of mention
Neven—Queen of Nymphs
Karter—King of the Nymphs
Ilsa—Old Queen of Witches
Elias—Prince of Incubi
Isadora—Queen of Demons

Taren Oleander—King of Gargoyles
Soraya—Witch
Julia —Dark Witch
Siobhan—Witch
Bekkah—Witch
Avyanna—Witch, and part Cervitaur
Jasmine—Clairvoyant/Shape shifter Friend to Aria

Items and more

Grimoire—A book of ancient spells
Scrying—The ability to search a map with magic to find a location
White Oak Trees— Grown only in Norvalla in the Arcadian Forest of Knowledge
Frost fire—Ice from the Dark Mountains, appears as regular ice until it swallows up anything, or anyone it can touch. Unbreakable by anything other than witches fire, a spell that only rare witches can use. It was used to protect Norvalla from the Kingdom of Unwanted Beasts
Midnight Blooming black roses—Grown in the darkest passes in the Dark Mountains. A rare type of rose that blossom's in the icy snow caps of the mountain, holding a unique essence that witches covet
Tonics—Medicinal potions for healing
Gargoyles— Protectors of the Library of Knowledge

The visited lands within the Nine Realms to date

Dorcha—The Darkest Realm, realm in which Norvalla sits as capital

Norvalla—Knox's Homeland

Kingdom of Unwanted Beasts—Realm that borders Norvalla

Kingdom of Vākya—The witches' realm, and location of the Palace of Magic

Valley of the Dead—Land that borders between Vākya and Dorcha

House of Magic—Destroyed

The Dark Mountains—The Mountain range bordering The Kingdom of Unwanted Beast and Norvalla's high passes

Library of Knowledge—An ever-changing room that only reveals its treasures to those it finds worthy of the knowledge it holds

Beltane Circle—Temple of celebration for Beltane, where celebration of Rebirth occurs

Kingdom of Fire —The new Kingdom of Fire created by Griffon to hide, and protect the phoenixes and dragons from Hecate

Valley of the Red River—Aria's new palace

Swamplands—Filled with Orcs, and discarded creatures

Laveran—Capital City of the Nine Realms

ABOUT THE AUTHOR

Amelia Hutchins is a *WSJ* and *USA Today Bestselling* author of the Monsters, The Fae Chronicles, and Nine Realm series. She is an admitted coffee addict who drinks magical potions of caffeine and turns them into magical worlds. She writes alpha-hole males and the alpha women who knock them on their arses, hard. Amelia doesn't write romance. She writes fast-paced books that go hard against traditional standards. Sometimes a story isn't about the romance; it's about rising to a challenge, breaking through them like wrecking balls, and shaking up entire worlds to discover who they really are. If you'd like to check out more of her work, or just hang out in an amazing tribe of people who enjoy rough men, and sharp women, join her at Author Amelia Hutchins Group on Facebook.

STALKER LINKS

Facebook group:
    https://www.facebook.com/groups/
1240287822683404/

Facebook Author Page:
    https://www.facebook.com/authorameliahutchins/

Instagram:
    https://www.instagram.com/author.amelia.hutchins/

Made in the USA
Columbia, SC
14 October 2024

44277888R00304